DEVIL'S EMBRACE

Catherine Coulter

A SIGNET BOOK

SIGNET
Published by New American Library, a division of
Penguin Putnam Inc., 375 Hudson Street,
New York, New York 10014, U.S.A.
Penguin Books Ltd, 27 Wrights Lane,
London W8 5TZ, England
Penguin Books Australia Ltd, Ringwood,
Victoria, Australia
Penguin Books Canada Ltd, 10 Alcorn Avenue,
Toronto, Ontario, Canada M4V 3B2
Penguin Books (N.Z.) Ltd, 182–190 Wairau Road,
Auckland 10, New Zealand

Penguin Books Ltd, Registered Offices:
Harmondsworth, Middlesex, England

Published by Signet, an imprint of New American Library,
a division of Penguin Putnam Inc.

ISBN 0-7394-0945-X

PUBLISHER'S NOTE
This is a work of fiction. Names, characters, places, and incidents either are
the product of the author's imagination or are used fictitiously, and any
resemblance to actual persons, living or dead, business establishments, events
or locales is entirely coincidental.

To my husband, Anton

Chapter 1

Edward Forsythe Lyndhurst, fifth Viscount Delford, drew a deep breath of sea air and guided his bay mare closer to the rocky cliff. The day was unusually warm for the end of March, and the early afternoon sun reflected brightly from the blue water as it rippled gently toward the shoreline.

He tugged at his unfamiliar waistcoat and wished again he was still wearing his comfortable officer's crimson and white uniform. He suspected that his batman and valet, Grumman, felt the loss as much as did he. The fiery little Irishman had been full of voluble complaints about the hoity-toity fashions newly affected by English gentlemen. "Just like the ladies you'll look now, m'lord," he'd said, smoothing Edward's light blue coat over his shoulders, "all lace and bright colors, a strutting coxcomb."

Grumman, Edward thought, had a point.

Edward shifted in his saddle, shaded his eyes, and looked into the distance up the coastline toward Hemphill Hall, an ancient stone structure that stood at the very edge of the cliffs. He felt a powerful sense of anticipation at seeing the home of the Broughams, Cassie's home.

He drew a small miniature of Cassandra, painted on her fifteenth birthday, from his waistcoat pocket and gazed into the young girl's smiling face. Even at fifteen, her face had begun to take on a young woman's contours. Her high cheekbones, set above a well-formed stubborn chin, were delicate and finely etched, her large blue eyes vivid and questioning. He smiled at the thick wheat-colored hair braided about her head, and remembered how it rippled in deep, natural waves to her waist. He had thought her beautiful even when she was but eight years old and he a lad of fourteen, intolerant of other girls. He had painted outrageous adventures for her, with himself the brave military man, and she had listened to his every word, her eyes serious and intent.

Edward shook his head, bemused by memories that had not come to him in years. What an ass you were, he grunted to himself. But Cassie hadn't thought that. He still pictured her looking at him solemnly, her hair in scraggly ringlets about her small face, saying in her soft child's voice, "You must wait for me, Edward. I shall be a woman grown soon and then we shall wed. I shall follow the drum with you and share all your adventures."

He gazed once again at the miniature and wondered if Cassie was still the same long-legged, skinny girl. He thought about a letter she had written him some six months before, hinting at some rather perplexing changes in her appearance, and grinned at her oblique way of informing him that she was becoming a woman.

A frown passed over his brow and he snapped the miniature shut, replacing it gently in his waistcoat pocket. He turned his mare from the path that led to Hemphill Hall, down the rutted trail to the beach below. Cassie had been much on his mind since his Uncle Edgar's death some two months ago, when he had felt compelled to resign his commission and return to England to oversee his estates. But he had spent the months in London, with a simple note to Cassie that he would be delayed. Even now, he felt ambivalent. She was, after all, but eighteen years old, and undoubtedly looking forward to her first Season in London. He had felt he had no right to deprive her of an experience that every young lady of her station should enjoy. But he could not help feeling intensely jealous at the thought of her being courted by other gentlemen. What would he do if when he met her she gazed at him and felt nothing more for him than childhood friendship? He had cursed himself for a coward and ridden home to Essex. Now, but one day later, he was still dawdling, and not one mile from her home.

Edward dismounted when his mare gained the beach,

and tethered her to a sturdy bush that had thrust itself up in a small crevice between the rocks at the base of the cliff. He strolled slowly up the beach, blankly watching his boots crunch into the coarse sand, deep in thought. He was caught unaware when a large wave broke and sent water lapping up over his boots. He took several irritated steps back and gazed out over the water. To his surprise, he saw someone swimming through the breakers, bare arms moving in sure, graceful strokes. Although he was some distance away, it would have taken a blind man not to see that the figure emerging from the water was a woman. He watched silently as she rose to her feet and walked through the shallow water to the beach.

He could not make out her face, for her head was bowed. But it was not her face that held his attention. She was wearing only a thin white shift that reached to mid-thigh, but she might as well as have been naked, for the wet shift was molded against her like a second skin. His practiced masculine eye took in every line and curve of her. Her breasts were full and high, straining against the thin material. His eyes followed the slender lines of her waist and flat belly, to the small triangle of hair outlined by the clinging wet material. She turned slightly, revealing the curve of full buttocks and long, long legs. He felt a jolt of desire and forced himself to look away from her. He tried to calm himself, reasoning that he had been too long without a woman. He recalled the very giving young woman with whom he had spent two delightful nights but the week before and decided with a grin that he must find another excuse.

She must be a local village girl, he thought, and began to walk toward her without precisely deciding to. She leaned negligently over to wring the water from the lower part of her shift, and her hair, bounded in braids atop her head, was suddenly illuminated by bright shafts of sunlight. It was a light wheat color, glistening with golden streaks.

Edward pulled up short in his tracks and simply stared at her. As if aware that she was not alone, she grew still and raised her head toward him, shading her eyes with her hand. A name formed in Edward's throat, and he called it aloud.

Cassie froze for an instant when she heard his voice and gazed at the tall, slender gentleman who was loping quickly toward her.

"Edward!"

Cassie ran toward him and flung herself against his chest. Her voice was a jumble of sobs and laughter. "Edward, it's really you. I can't believe it. You have finally come back." She hugged him fiercely, then pushed him away to look into his face.

"Cass," he said, and gently cupped her face between his hands. How differently he had envisioned their first meeting, with the pained and awkward silences that he had thought inevitable. For the first time in their lives, he kissed her.

Cassie had often wondered how she would feel at her first kiss. She had even, upon occasion, pressed her palm against her lips to see if it would make her feel somehow different. She had felt nothing but foolish, and was totally unprepared for the sensations that coursed through her body. His mouth grew demanding, and his tongue moved over her lips. Tentatively, she parted her lips and let him possess her mouth.

Edward felt a shudder pass the length of her, and reveled in it. His hands moved urgently over her, kneading her hips and pressing her belly hard against him. It was the gentle moan of budding passion escaping her lips that brought forth the honorable English gentleman. Almost violently, he clasped her arms in his hands and pushed her away from him.

Cassie gazed up at him, her eyes full of wonder. She felt strangely breathless, somehow urgent.

Edward gave a low laugh that ended in a groan. "God, Cass."

She tried to wrap her arms about his neck again, and he forced himself to step back from her, holding her hands tightly in his.

"It's good to see you again, Cassie," he said, trying to force lightness into his voice.

She frowned at him, confused by his sudden formality. Her frown lightened as she looked closely at him for the first time, and took in every contour of his face. "You are much a man, Edward," she said finally. "But you have not much changed."

A smile touched his lips, and he was unable to prevent his eyes from sweeping over her. "And you, my love, have changed much."

She dimpled up at him innocently. "I trust you approve the changes, my lord." She gazed at the white ruffles at his throat and added shyly, "It was so very warm today. I was swimming."

"Yes, I know. I was watching you. I did not think that young ladies indulged in such manly pursuits."

"You, Edward, are far too used to the company of foreign ladies, who are, I daresay, quite indolent."

"Just because foreign ladies do not swim in the sea, Cassie, I would not say that they are precisely lazy."

"I hope, Captain Lord Delford, that your neck has not grown stiff in your collar." She shivered as the sun dipped behind a cloud.

Edward pulled off his riding coat and draped it over her shoulders. "You must dress, Cass, before you take a chill."

"Now that you are returned, my lord, that would never do. Oh, Edward, it's been such a long three years. I have missed you so." She slipped her hand through the crook of his arm and squeezed him to her. "You have much abused me, my lord. I have been waiting and waiting ever since I got your letter two months ago. I did not even know where you were staying in London. Your mother just sighed helplessly in that way of hers when I asked her where you were."

Edward paused a moment, and said only, "One never picks fruit from the tree until it is ripe."

She waved away his words. "I will thank you, my lord, not to liken me to an apple or a pear. And if you are not careful, you might find that I will fall into someone else's basket."

Though he felt a moment of uncertainty, he said lightly, "I found that I wished to conduct my business in London;

it was better done there in any case." He paused a moment and gazed about at the calm sea and up at the ageless cliffs. "Life is different here. It's as if time touches life here only insofar as the fashions in clothes change. It is not so elsewhere, you know."

"You so dislike the blissful existence in this Garden of Eden?"

He smiled crookedly. "You have always had the knack of boiling things down until there was no water left in the pot." He looked a moment at the soft tendrils of her hair that the sea breeze pressed across her cheek. "Where is your chaperone, Cass? Surely you would not come to a deserted beach alone."

"It would seem to me, my lord, that you would have been much embarrassed if Miss Petersham had been witness to your exuberant welcome."

"What? Becky is still with you?" The plump, brisk little woman had been with Cassie as far back as he could remember. Although she had always been polite to him, he had had the inescapable feeling that she somehow did not approve of him. "The mother lion is still guarding her cub," he said aloud.

Cassie laughed, and Edward watched her soft tongue dart over her even white teeth. "Becky the lioness. What a marvelous metaphor. She has become quite like a mother to me, you know, Edward, and a watchful one at that. She is quite fond of a nap after lunch and thus I was able to come here alone. I refuse to believe, my lord, that you would have preferred meeting me for the first time after three years across the expanse of the drawing room."

"It would have been better for both of us had I seen you fully dressed and not soaking wet like some half-naked sea nymph."

Cassie drew to a halt beside him and said softly, "But then I probably would not have been certain that you still cared for me. You would have been all stiff and full of trite, formal phrases."

"I would have been far more the discreet gentleman."

Cassie felt a stab of apprehension. "Edward, you have

not found another lady, have you? Is that why you stayed away from me in London?"

"Dammit, Cass, you're but eighteen years old."

"Yes," she said quietly, "and a woman grown."

"If you'll recall, you told me in great seriousness that you were nearly a woman grown when you were eight years old."

"Good heavens, I had forgotten all about that. It was, as I recall, the first time I ever proposed marriage to you, my lord. But you, if I do not disremember, were a stiff and starchy lad, full of ambition, and would not take me seriously."

Edward gave her a light shove toward a large rock where her clothing lay in a neat pile. "Get dressed," he said roughly. "I trust you have a dry shift."

"Yes, of course I do. Would you care to help me dress, Edward?" she asked, hoping to coax him out of a mood she did not understand.

"No. But I shall ensure that no other man comes along to see you naked."

"But, Edward," she said demurely, "we are on Brougham land. You are the only man who has ever come to the beach and seen me swimming. Which makes me wonder, my lord, do you often make it a habit to spy on young ladies? I will not believe you if you tell me that you recognized me immediately."

Edward flushed, despite himself. Had she been a village girl, and willing, he was not at all certain what he would have done.

"Ah, Edward, you have become a rake, I see. Is that why you seem to care so much for indolent foreign ladies?"

"Cassie, you are a baggage. How do you know about such things as rakes? Surely Eliott would not discuss such matters with you."

"You know that Eliott is twenty-two now, and no longer a boy. I have asked him again and again, but he will not tell me what he does when he goes to Colchester or to London. He always mumbles something about business, which I know is a lie."

Cassie stripped off his riding coat and Edward turned

away. "It would appear to me that you have been allowed to run wild since your father died."

"Alas, it is true, but all I had to warm me at night were your rather infrequent letters. And from the beatific grin on Eliott's face each time he returns from one of his jaunts, I would say that mere letters are hardly a fulfilling substitute."

He smiled, but refused to be drawn. "I was sorry, Cass, to hear of your father's death."

"It was probably for the best," she said matter-of-factly. "He had grown quite odd, you know, particularly during the past two years. I had the inescapable feeling that he tried to avoid me. It is Eliott's opinion that I am too much like mother and that looking at me brought him pain. I think he always disliked me, because I killed mother."

"Don't be a fool, Cassie," he said sharply, turning to face her.

"But she died birthing me, Edward, and she was but twenty-three. I become depressed every time I think about it."

Edward did not immediately reply as he stared at her. She was seated on a rock, dressed in a light blue muslin gown, sashed tightly at her waist, fastening the strap of her sandal. He glimpsed a long white-stockinged leg before she whisked her dress down over her ankle.

She rose and gave him her hand. "Are you now more approving of my appearance, Lord Edward?"

"You are almost as beautiful as the fifteen-year-old girl I left three years ago."

She gave him a dazzling smile. "And you, my lord, are still the most handsome gentleman of my acquaintance." She appeared to inspect him closely, from head to toe. "I cannot decide which I admire more about you, your size or—" She cocked her head to one side.

"My height or?"

"Or your beautiful eyes," she said promptly. She touched her fingertips gently to his cheek. "They are such a deep brown with golden flecks, just like your hair. I suppose that many ladies have told you that."

"Perhaps one or two, but it meant very little to me." His

eyes softened on her face. "What did mean a great deal to me was receiving your letters. Your spelling is atrocious, Cass. Many a time I felt as though I were deciphering a military code."

"Well, your letters, my lord, read for the most part like a campaign log. I have become quite adept at making salt and flour maps, so I knew where you were. Poor Becky could never figure out why I became such an avid student of geography." She paused a moment and dug the toe of her sandal into the sand. "I many times had the feeling that you were not being altogether honest with me, Edward. I could never grasp what your life was like."

Edward said with deliberate coolness, "Suffice it to say, Cass, that warfare and military life did not bear much resemblance to the exploits I dreamed of as a boy. There is never much satisfaction in dispatching another fellow human to his Maker. Now, Cass, what of you? Have you been a sad trial to Miss Petersham?"

She accepted his rebuff, though it hurt her to think that he would likely never tell her much of his military years. She replied easily, "Not really. For the most part, I have been as circumspect as even you would wish, Edward, though I still sail and swim as often as possible. I daresay that our parties and dinners hardly made fascinating reading for you."

"You are quite wrong. Your letters always reminded me of what was really important to me. What did Miss Petersham think of your writing to me?"

She had been frowning thoughtfully over his words, but at the mention of her companion, her eyes twinkled. "Poor Becky. We are quite close, you know, except in matters that concern you. Eliott and I discussed it most thoroughly and decided that in the case of our letters, it would be best to commit a sin of omission. She never found out."

"Then I daresay that she will not welcome me with open arms."

"True, but Eliott is my guardian and she can hardly turn you away. She will come about, you will see. I fear though that she will be excessively disappointed that we will not be going to London. I fancy she expected me to snare a royal duke."

"You and one of the fat German dukes. Good lord." He squeezed her hand. "Come, Cass, let us get my mare, and I shall escort you back to the hall."

He felt her fingers close over his and saw that she was looking up at him, a disturbing smile on her lips.

"Before we go, Edward, I would that you kiss me again. I have never been kissed before and I must own that I like it a lot."

He leaned down and kissed her lightly on her closed lips. She stared up at him doggedly. "That is not at all how you kissed me the first time." She added hesitantly, "I like the other things you did—with your hands."

He stood stiffly before her, trying to still the twisting desire in his loins. "Cass, it is not proper."

"But why, Edward? Did you not come back to be my husband?"

"No—yes. Dammit, I have not yet spoken to Eliott. And as much as you scoff at the idea, there is your Season in London."

One thick-arched brow flared upward. "Season in London? Come, Edward, I was but jesting. Now that you are returned, everything has changed. I shall have no duke, not even a royal one."

"It is important, Cassie," he said heavily. "You have been sheltered. It would not be fair of me to prevent you from meeting other gentlemen. Don't you understand? You may meet someone else whom you would prefer to wed."

Cassie raised her chin in a proud, stubborn gesture that he remembered well. "I admit that I am young and not much experienced. But I am not a fool, Edward, nor am I a silly, romantic girl whose mind is filled with maudlin drivel. I have long known that you are the man to suit me. I beg you not to question my motives or my feelings."

"You call this place a Garden of Eden, Cass. You know nothing of what lies beyond even Ipswich."

"Edward, you make it sound as though I have been raised in a convent. You know that Becky needled Eliott the moment I turned seventeen to let me put my hair up and entertain lavishly. I assure you, I have been most feted by many gentlemen, even some from your precious London. I have found them, for the most part, to have very little under their powdered hair save empty, vain heads. Now, I would that you cease this nonsense."

"Very well, Cass, we shall discuss the matter another time."

"Edward, if you do not believe me, I shall simply have to seduce you and force you to wed me."

"What do you know of seduction, Miss?"

"If you will kiss me again, I daresay that I shall come by it quite naturally."

There was a woman's smile on her face, and Edward's honorable intentions crumbled. He pulled her roughly against him and kissed her temples, the tip of her straight nose, the hollow of her throat. His lips touched hers, featherlight. "Part your lips, love."

She obeyed him willingly. His hands cupped her hips as he explored her mouth, lifting her off the ground to press her against him.

Through her gown and petticoats, Cassie felt the fierce hardness of him. She had seen animals mate and knew that when men and women coupled, men entered women's bodies. She felt an almost painful ache building between her thighs and realized that she wanted more than anything to feel Edward naked against her, caressing her, making himself a part of her. She dug her fingers into his back and pressed her body so tightly against him that she could feel his heartbeat against her breasts.

She gave a cry of frustrated disappointment when he abruptly pulled her away from him.

"Enough, Cass," he said harshly. "No, don't argue with me. I refuse to be seduced by a slip of a girl who supposedly knows nothing about it. Come, let me escort you to Hemphill Hall."

Chapter 2

Cassie drew Edward up the wide front steps of Hemphill Hall and thrust open the door, nearly toppling Menkle, the Brougham butler.

"Menkle, look who is home, finally. And to stay."

Menkle forgot his dignity and bestowed a toothful smile upon the viscount. "Welcome home, my lord."

"Thank you, Menkle."

"Where is Eliott, Menkle?"

"In the library, Miss Cassie, reviewing the account ledgers, I believe."

Cassie laughed. "Poor Eliott, I'll wager he is muttering to himself and tugging his hair. Guilder was here all morning—our agent, you know—and left Eliott frantically toting up columns of numbers. He will be pleased to be rescued, Edward."

Eliott Brougham, fourth Baron Tinnsdale, was in fact staring past his account books out over the east lawn, a young lady in his thoughts. He started guiltily every few minutes and forced his attention back to his task. He looked up, startled, as Cassie burst unceremoniously into the library.

"Close your books, my love, for I've a surprise for you."

"What, Cass, you've finally caught that large sea bass for my dinner?"

"It's not a fish, Eliott, but I trust that I have finally caught him."

"Edward. Good God, man, it's been ages." Eliott quickly rose to shake Edward Lyndhurst's outstretched hand.

"I trust we do not disturb you, Eliott. This madcap sister of yours dragged me in here without a by-your-leave." He has become a man, Edward thought, gazing at Cassie's brother. Though he had the same open, smiling face, three years had added firmness to his jaw, and his light blue eyes seemed to hold widened experience, if not wisdom.

"I am quite used to her bursting in upon me." Eliott laughed. "I am only safe when I am taking my bath."

"Edward is home to stay, Eliott," Cassie said, tugging at her brother's sleeve, "forever."

"Oh?" Eliott said carefully, his eyes upon Edward's face.

"As Cass said, Eliott, she's finally caught me," Edward said blandly.

"He kissed me, Eliott. Would you not say that he has compromised me irrevocably? He must now do the honorable thing."

"I think what he should do first, Cass, is join us in a glass of sherry. Despite all your letters, Captain Lord Delford, I vow we have a good deal of catching up to do."

"Your letters were so terribly military, Edward," Cassie said by way of explanation, "that I saw no reason for Eliott not to read them. There was only one that I did not show him, for he would have been obliged to call you out."

"To your safe return home, Edward," Eliott said as he clicked his sherry glass to Edward's, then to his sister's.

"To a new beginning," Cassie said.

"To a continuation of a long ago beginning," Edward said.

"Let us sit down," Eliott said. He had often wondered if Cassie's lifelong infatuation for Edward would endure into adulthood, but as he watched them, he could not doubt that it had. He saw their eyes meet, and although they made no move to touch each other, they might as well have been locked together.

Eliott cleared his throat. "Your mother is well, Edward?"

"She enjoys her ill health, as always. Uncle Edgar's death came as something of a shock to her."

"Your uncle was an honorable gentleman," Eliott said. "Your estate was in capable hands. Speaking of hands, Edward, did that shoulder wound you suffered a couple of years ago heal well?"

"Not even a twinge now. I was fortunate enough to fall into the care of a sober surgeon. In India, that commodity is hard to find."

"I insist upon seeing the scar," Cassie said.

Eliott frowned at his sister. "Really, Cass, Edward will think that you have not been properly raised. You should have seen her, Edward, when you finally wrote of your wound. She was like a raging virago, and if it had not been for my calm good sense, I think she would have sailed her sloop to India by herself."

"I was very worried, though speaking of Eliott and good sense together is far off the mark. But since he became Baron Tinnsdale, he is so full of self-consequence that he must needs continually make up all sorts of outrageous qualities for himself."

"At least his idea of good sense does not include swimming like some sea nymph in the ocean or taking his life in his hands in a rickety sailboat."

"My boat is not at all rickety, my lord. And as for my imitating a sea nymph, I will doubt your honesty if you say that you were displeased."

"Cass, I trust you were wearing *something* while you were swimming."

"She was like Venus coming from the sea. Quite a lovely prospect, I must admit."

"I was wearing a shift," Cassie said, gazing from her brother's raised brows to Edward. She rose gracefully and shook out her skirts. "Now that you know the extent of Lord Delford's brazen behavior, Eliott, I shall leave you to deal with him. Do not let him escape, brother, else I shall have to take my shredded virtue and hie myself to a convent."

After Cassie left the library, Eliott turned to Edward in some embarrassment. "She is ever forthright to a fault, but of course you know that." He tugged a moment at his collar. "You did not, that is, Cassie did not—"

Edward blinked in surprise, and said in an amused voice, "She was wearing a shift, Eliott, a very wet but quite modest shift. My intentions are honorable, you know, so there is no need to call me out. I want to marry her, but I must admit I am uncertain what to do about her London Season. She flatly refuses now even to consider it. As well as being forthright, she is headstrong."

"Stubborn as a mule once her mind is made up."

"True. Still, if you insist that she spend the Season in London, then between the two of us, we should be able to rein her in."

"She has never wavered in her affection for you, Edward, though I believed for some years that it was naught save hero worship for a brave—and absent—military man. If you wish to wed her now, I'll not cast a rub in your way."

"Such support will likely result in Cassie naming our first son after you."

"Cassie a mother." Eliott shook his head, bemused. "It seems but yesterday that she was a child herself, intent only upon learning how to bait her hook. Yet I remember the time I crammed my horse over a fence and broke my leg. She was motherly, bullying me and forcing all manner of vile potions down my throat."

"I am glad that I did not return to England when I was laid up with my shoulder wound." Edward smiled gently at the still-bemused Eliott. "What do you say, Eliott, can we arrange a wedding in, say, two months?"

"Captain Lord Delford moves quickly once he is on the attack, I see. I can see no problem. Becky will take charge and see that everything comes off aright. Speaking of Miss Petersham, it is better that I deal with her myself."

"As you will, Eliott. Now, my friend, there is much I wish to discuss with you. How has Eliott Brougham found life as the fourth Baron Tinnsdale?"

Chapter 3

E liott Brougham smiled down at the agitated Miss Petersham. "Come now, Becky, Edward Lyndhurst is one of my oldest friends and a man of honor. If Cassie wants him, I'll not kick up a ruckus."

"She just turned eighteen, Eliott. She's but a girl and can't know her own mind. Her dashing viscount comes galloping home, dripping with countless stories of his exploits, no doubt, and practically begs her to fall into his arms."

"You're off the mark there, Becky. If I know Cassie, it is she who very likely encouraged Edward to fall into her arms. It's certainly not as if Edward were a stranger—after all, they've written to each other for the past three years."

"They have what?" Miss Petersham drew in an appalled breath.

Eliott had the grace to look sheepish. "Now, Becky, Cassie and I decided not to tell you, for you'd have disapproved."

"You mean that Cassie decided not to tell me and you, you wretched boy, fell in with her. You are four years her senior, and her guardian since his lordship's death." Miss Petersham groaned and took several perturbed steps about the room. "Promise me, Eliott, that you will not let her wed him until after her Season in London."

Eliott shook his head. "I cannot understand why you are not content that Cass is making a love match. Lord knows that there are few enough of them nowadays. And you must admit, Becky, that she has shown nothing but indifference to all the young pups who have gathered about her like bees to a honeypot. All she would find in London, I daresay, is more of the same. I have given my approval and they want to marry in two months."

"Two months. Oh no, surely not."

Eliott set about soothing her. "It's not as if you're going to lose her to some gallant who lives God knows where. Delford Manor is but two miles away and I fancy that all of us will continue much as we always have."

Miss Petersham drew a deep breath to calm herself. "I suppose what's done is done. I only wish that I had known sooner."

Eliott patted her plump shoulder, not without affection. "You know when Cass gets the bit between her teeth there's no stopping her. I daresay with your genius for preparations, we shall be able to pull off the wedding as if we had had six months to plan it." Eliott beamed at her, thankful that the weight of all responsibility was to be on Miss Petersham's capable shoulders.

Miss Petersham gave him a thin smile. How many times she had thought that Eliott should have been the girl and Cassie the boy. While Cassie was strong, quick-witted, and an expert in getting what she wanted, Eliott was guileless and malleable, clay in his sister's hands.

"Spare the rod and spoil the child," she said obliquely. She tugged at her lacy cap and left the drawing room, her black skirts swishing with each brisk step.

Eliott drew a sigh of relief and looked up to see his sister peep her head around the door.

"Is it done? You have told her, Eliott?"

"Yes, minx, and I can tell you that she is none too happy about it."

"I know. I heard her rustling skirts and hid myself behind the urn until she flounced upstairs." Cassie walked to her brother and gave him a quick hug. "Thank you, my love, for bearding the lion. You do not really believe that she wanted me to marry some paunchy old German duke, do you?"

"Lord knows. Perhaps she wanted the London Season for herself." He looked down at his shapely white hands. "Unfortunately, I let slip that you and Edward have been corresponding for the past three years."

Cassie tugged at the long, thick curl that fell habitually over her shoulder. "Well, I shall just have to let her batter at me for a while. Then we shall send in Edward and let him charm her out of her sullens."

"She's convinced that Edward dazzled you with all of his military exploits."

"I shall have to tell her that rather than dazzle me, Edward refuses to tell me much of anything about his experiences. It is too bad of him."

Eliott thought of some of the more gruesome tales Edward had recounted, and held his tongue. He looked up to see Cassie chewing on her lower lip, a habit from childhood.

"I suppose," she said, "that I will have sufficient years to convince him that our sons belong in the Royal Navy and not in the army. It would seem to me to be a far more exciting career. Can you imagine anyone preferring the land to the sea?"

Eliott laughed and gave her a light buffet on her shoulder. "Take care, Cass, for Edward is a man of strong principles and even stronger notions of what is proper for young English ladies. He might well beach your sailboat and clip your mermaid's tail."

Cassie tossed her head. "That is nonsense, Eliott. Edward knows my love for the sea, and I cannot imagine that once we are married he will try to give me orders."

Eliott imagined that Edward would not only give her orders, he would also expect them to be obeyed, but, for now, he merely smiled and said, more to himself than to his sister, "I suppose that Becky will live with you at Delford Manor."

"If you would not miss her too much, Eliott. She has been much like a mother to both of us. I, for one, cannot imagine her not sitting across the breakfast table from me, tutoring me in darning sheets and ensuring that the pantry has enough haunches of ham."

Eliott gave her a rather sad, resigned smile. "I will lose both you and Becky. Hemphill Hall will hardly seem the same."

"I shall feel its loss sadly, my love, but do not think that just because I shall reside at Delford Manor, I shall never darken your door again." She gave him a quick hug. "Oh, Eliott, I am so happy. And not just because of Edward. We shall all be together—even our children will grow up together."

"Viscount Delford, my lord."

Brother and sister turned at Menkle's announcement.

Edward Lyndhurst stepped into the drawing room and stood for a moment, staring at Cassie. It was not her face and figure that held him, but the joyful expression that lit her eyes as she looked at him. She took a quick step toward him, as if impatient of any distance between them.

Eliott cleared his throat. "Lord, Edward, you'll have all your life to stare at her."

"Wretch. Don't mind Eliott—he has so little in his head that he must needs forever tease me."

"Do come in, Edward. Cass and I were just discussing the advantages of the Royal Navy over the army. I suppose the two of you want to be alone, so I'll take my leave."

"To see Miss Pennworthy, Eliott?"

"I don't know why the devil not. With you and Edward staring at each other with sheep's eyes, I have a fancy to try it myself."

"Miss Pennworthy has such great brown eyes, I think she will do it quite nicely. Eliza already hangs on his every word, Edward, as if he were some sort of Greek god, bestowing gems of wisdom on us mortals."

Eliott gave his sister a crooked grin and Edward a quick salute. "Beat her, my lord, that's my advice."

Once they were alone, Edward held out his hand to her. "Come here, love."

"Will you beat me, my lord?"

"There are too many other things to do with you that first require my attention."

She shyly took his hand. "I trust that we will always be in such perfect agreement. I do not believe, my lord, that I have told you how much I love you since last evening."

"Do you mean you love me today as well?" he asked, his fingers tracing over her parted lips.

"I suppose that I have no choice," she said, as she

rubbed her cheek lightly along his palm, "else you would think me a fallen woman, for just thinking about you brings all sorts of very physical thoughts to mind."

She kissed his palm, then stepped into the circle of his arms and pressed her cheek against his shoulder.

"There can be no more fortunate man than I," he said, and drew her tightly against him. He felt an awakening shudder pass through her body as he lightly kissed her mouth, and knew with certainty that her passion would rival his own. He kissed her small white ears and reluctantly pulled her away.

"Come, Cass, Old Winslow has put up a hunter for sale and I have promised to see her this afternoon. May I have the pleasure of your company?"

"Indeed you may, my lord. If we must spend the afternoon looking at a hunter, I would far rather do it now than after we are married."

Chapter 4

"Drat you, Miss Cassie. Hold still, else you'll have your buttons all askew."

"Oh, do hurry, Dolly, our guests will arrive at any moment."

Dolly Mintlow shook her head fondly at her fidgeting mistress and curled her arthritic fingers to fasten the tiny buttons on the back of Cassie's ivory satin gown. "There, Miss, all done now. But look at your hair, you've already shook loose a curl."

Cassie sighed and forced herself to sit quietly as Dolly put her hair to rights again. She frowned at herself in the mirror.

"I wish we didn't have to bother with all this nonsense. Why can't I just look like me? All that powder, it makes me feel like an old woman."

"You're no longer a girl, Miss Cassie, and young ladies powder their hair. If only you had more vanity. With the way you're always bouncing about, I wager you'll have white powder all over your gown."

"At least the gown is white."

"Dolly is right, Cassandra. A little more decorum on your part would not be at all amiss. There are many important guests coming tonight, and I don't want them to think you a hoyden."

Cassie assumed a docile expression, lowered her head, and began to twiddle her thumbs. "Now do I have your approval, Becky?"

Miss Petersham merely grunted, and patted several errant strands of pepper-colored hair primly into place beneath her lacy cap. "No need to play off your tricks with me, Cassie. Now stand up and let me see how the gown fits."

Cassie rose and obligingly performed a slow pirouette in front of Miss Petersham.

"You'll do. Come along now, you must needs greet the guests with Eliott and the viscount."

"Oh, Becky, why must you always refer to Edward as the viscount? It's so terribly impersonal, as though he is nothing more than a casual guest in this house."

Miss Petersham merely gave her an austere look, and said, "And you treat him with far too much familiarity."

"Very well, my beloved dragon, I shall be most circumspect—at least for the next week. But after Edward and I are married, I vow I shall become very sinful."

"You look like an angel, Miss Cassie," Dolly said, unaware that she had interrupted at an opportune moment.

"With all this white powder, I even feel like an angel. You will help me brush it all out later, Dolly?"

"Of course, Miss Cassandra. I'll be waiting up for you."

Cassie gave her maid a quick hug and followed Miss Petersham from the bedchamber. As she trailed after her companion down the wide, winding stairs, she felt a delicious shudder. Just one more week and she would be the Viscountess Delford. She smiled at Miss Petersham's straight back, knowing that her thoughts would bring a shocked squeal from that lady. Only that afternoon, Becky had called Cassie to her room and, after some roundabout conversation, had stiffly inquired if Cassie understood what would be demanded of her on her wedding night.

Cassie stifled a laugh and displayed what she hoped was maidenly shock. "I believe I do have a very general idea, Becky."

Miss Petersham breathed an audible sigh of relief. "A very general idea is all that is necessary. Your husband will see to the specifics."

"I daresay Edward does have sufficient experience to be able to carry everything off smoothly." She gazed up apprehensively at Miss Petersham after her unthinking comment, and saw that she was regarding her oddly, her expression serious and her hazel eyes narrowed in concern.

"I am sorry, Becky, to tease you so," Cassie said quickly, her hand on her companion's arm.

"No, child, you are not teasing me." She looked as if she would have said more. Quickly, she was behaving in much her old way, briskly reminding Cassie not to chew on her thumbnail like some peasant child.

"You look beautiful, Cassie."

Cassie looked up to see Edward standing at the foot of the stairway, dressed elegantly, without affectation, in black and silver, his chestnut hair powdered like hers and drawn back with a black ribbon at the nape of his neck.

"And very grown up."

"It's all this dratted white powder," she said, smiling up at him as she rested her hand in the crook of his arm.

"What? My lady doesn't want to be fashionable?"

"If that is what you wish, my lord," she said demurely. "Realize though that it all must be brushed out at night— before one can go to bed."

"An irrefutable point. Ah, Eliott and Miss Pennworthy." Eliott's fair curls were powdered and brushed in artful disarray. He took Miss Pennworthy's small hand in his, thinking that she made the perfect foil to Eliott's blond handsomeness, with her pert oval face framed with rich black curls.

"Well, one more week, old boy, and she's all yours." Eliott cast a critical eye over his sister and gave her a wink.

"Take care, Eliott, else Eliza will think that you don't care for your poor sister." Cass turned and smiled down at the diminutive Miss Pennworthy. "I am so abused, my dear. Eliott throws me at the first gentleman who offers marriage."

"Oh no, Cassandra, you disremember," Miss Pennworthy said in great seriousness. "Eliott told me that he'd been plagued for the past six months by your suitors. Why, there was Oliver Claybourne, somewhat of a slowtop, I admit, but still—"

Eliott groaned and firmly took Miss Pennworthy's hand in his. "She's teasing you, Eliza, don't heed a word she says."

"Well, I know, Eliott," Miss Pennworthy said. "But it

amuses you so to see me teased. Come, my dear, I must return to my mama."

"You mean that it is marriage that I offered?" Edward said in an appalled voice after Miss Pennworthy had removed Eliott.

"If you want my money, my lord, then you must first place a wedding ring on my finger."

"Since I am a fortune hunter—at least in Miss Petersham's eyes—I suppose I am doomed to take the chaff with the wheat."

Cassie suddenly felt the baleful eyes of Edward's mother turn in her direction. She held out her hands to the short, sparse little woman.

"I am delighted that you could come, ma'am. We shall see to it that you do not overtire yourself."

"Dear child." Lady Delford sighed. "Though I am unwell, I felt it my duty to stand together with you as one family this evening. How very *white* you look, Cassandra. I vow I would not have recognized you. And look at Miss Petersham. Such energy she has. She tells me that she has never been ill for a single day in her life." Lady Delford sighed again and gazed up at her son.

"You must be brave this evening, Mama, else people might think that your illness is not really illness at all, but rather that you are not delighted to welcome Cassie into the family."

"People who know me, dear Edward, are quite aware that my illness is never feigned. Now, my dears, I believe I shall speak to Lady Halfax. Such a wasting cold she has suffered, and all because she wouldn't heed my advice. Riding in the rain after the hounds with Lord Halfax. I trust that you, Cassandra, will be more alert to the dangers that can afflict a lady's fragile health."

"Yes, ma'am, of course," Cassie said.

Edward grinned at his mother's retreating back and said behind his gloved hand, "Don't worry, Cass. She is leaving for Bath, to live with her sister."

"Oh, that is terrible, Edward," Cassie said, truly distressed. "I am certain that we can deal well together under the same roof. I promise you that I am not the managing type of female."

"It has nothing to do with you, Cass. If you must know, I told her that Miss Petersham would be making her home with us. That information quite resolved her to leave."

"You are a wicked man, Edward Lyndhurst."

"That is probably very true. Come, love, let us greet our guests."

They stood with Eliott and Miss Petersham beneath the great stone arch that led into the ballroom, an addition to Hemphill Hall made by the third Baron Tinnsdale, their father, some twenty years before, and accepted congratulations from the colorfully attired local gentry. Sir John Winslow, Old Winslow as Edward called him, greeted them; he was bluff, good-natured, and suffering from gout.

"He always smells of the stables," Cassie whispered behind her hand. "I think I should take him swimming with me in the sea."

"Lord and Lady Dawes," Menkle said.

Poor Lady Dawes, Cassie thought, as she bade them welcome, she must needs tolerate a profligate husband who treats her like a stick of wood, deaf and dumb to his rakehell behavior.

Cassie was beginning to shift her weight uncomfortably on her high-heeled slippers when half an hour later, Anthony Welles, Earl of Clare, strolled negligently toward them, his powdered hair in startling contrast to his deeply tanned face.

"Lord Clare, how kind of you to come," Cassie said, smiling at the elegant man she had known most of her life.

The earl lightly kissed the palm of her hand, then bowed slightly to Edward and Eliott. "You have assembled an elegant group, I see," he said, gazing for a moment into the crowded ballroom. "Ah, the musicians from Colchester. They have a nice way with the minuet, I believe. I trust you will save a dance for me, Cassandra. Eliott, Lord Edward, Miss Petersham, your servant, ma'am."

"He is usually the last to arrive at any party," Eliott said.

"Poor Menkle will be quite hoarse in the morning if there are many more guests to arrive. I, for one, have very sore feet." Even as Cassie spoke, Mr. and Mrs. Webster appeared, ready to be greeted and to be pleased.

"I shall have to hide the brandy," Eliott said.

"Mr. Webster and your father were very close," Miss Petersham said severely. She saw a drooping Menkle signal to her. "You may now rest your tired feet, Cassie, but first, of course, you must dance with the viscount."

"Such sacrifices I already make for you, my lord." As she took Edward's arm, she heard Miss Petersham say sternly to Eliott, "Do not spend the evening in Miss Pennworthy's pocket, else her doting mama will have you to the altar before you catch your breath."

Chapter 5

Edward negligently wrapped a curl of golden hair about his finger as he looked past the tree branches overhead to the tranquil sea beyond the cliffs. During his five years of army life on the baked, miserably hot plains north of Calcutta and in the ruggedly beautiful Port of Pondicherry, he had almost forgotten the placid life of the English countryside, where foreign upheavals, the misery of war, even the growing political chaos surrounding King George III and his inept ministers, seemed as far away as England's colonies across the Atlantic.

He would never regret his years in the army, though he knew that to his dying day he would remain appalled at the devastation and the utter waste of human life he had seen. Still, he wondered if he would have so readily given up the disciplined life to which he had grown accustomed had it not been for Cassie. Now, he thought, he was embarking on the unexceptionable career of the English country gentleman. Though objectively it seemed like a rather boring prospect, he could not imagine it being so with Cassie beside him, Cassie and his sons and daughters.

He released her hair and watched the curl he had wound over his finger spring back over his hand.

Cassie awoke from a light sleep and raised her head from Edward's shoulder to gaze up at his face, a face whose expressions she had come to know quite as well as her own in the two months since his return.

"So pensive, my love?" she said, raising her fingertips to his lips. "I do hope that you are not regretting taking me to wife."

Edward lightly nibbled her fingers and shifted her in his

arms. "Actually, Cass, I was trying to decide if I prefer a boy or a girl as our first child."

"Good lord, Edward, can I not remain skinny for at least a while?"

She was looking at his mouth. "I will allow you to remain skinny, if you promise not to fall asleep in my company, at least until after we are married. If you find me so boring now, I fear to think how you will treat me a year from now."

"A year from now, my lord, you will not be constrained by ridiculous codes of propriety, and I trust we will have discovered more entertaining pastimes." For a moment Edward allowed her hand to move across his chest and down to his belly, in innocent exploration.

He pulled them both to their feet. He was straining against his breeches and he turned away from her to get control of himself. He doubted that in her innocence she realized the effect her touch had on him.

"And you, Edward," he heard her say from behind him, "if you cannot bear to look upon me before we are married, will you force me to wear a sack over my head after a year?"

"If you promise to wear nothing else, I suppose I would not quibble."

She laughed in delight, and he pictured the dimples deepening on either side of her mouth. He turned about, his desire for the moment calmed, to see her standing close to him, her eyes sparkling outrageously.

She was wearing a light muslin gown of pale green, whose bodice was, thankfully, fastened with small buttons to her throat.

"Look, Edward," she said suddenly, shading her eyes with her hand as she gazed out to sea, "in the distance, to your left. What a gorgeous yacht. Look how her sails are billowing in the wind. I believe I can even make out gun mounts on her port side."

It was a beautiful craft, Edward thought, his eyes following her pointing finger, of sufficient size for ocean travel.

"Drat," Cassie said, turning back to him. "She is moving

so swiftly that I cannot see whether she is English." She added, with a small sigh, "How I wish I could captain her."

"She is probably London-bound. In any case, my love, you are going to be far too occupied to concern yourself with yachts. There is our wedding trip to Scotland, you know. And then we will be married and you will have far more interesting things to do than concern yourself with such unfeminine pursuits."

She frowned at him, but just for an instant. "There are undoubtedly sailing craft in Scotland, my lord, and if you would but once come sailing with me, I know you would change your opinion."

"It is not that I doubt your prowess, Cass, it is merely that I have a very healthy respect for the sea and its power. Come, let us walk down to the beach. I can tell that you are fairly itching to remove your sandals and stockings and wade in the water."

"It is so warm, my lord," she said in a demure voice. "Perhaps I could convince you to come swimming with me."

"I suppose you have brought an extra shift for just that purpose."

"Oh no. I think it would be far more interesting to wear nothing at all."

At his threatening glance, she laughed aloud, picked up her skirts, and dashed away from him toward a path that led to the beach below them.

"Don't break your neck," she heard him shout after her.

Cassie gained the beach and turned, panting, to see him running down the rocky path toward her. The taut muscles in his thighs and belly flexed rhythmically as he neared her, and she wanted to touch him, to feel the lean hardness of him.

Edward clasped her shoulders in his hands and shook her lightly, his eyes alight with laughter. She did not respond in kind, but merely stared up at him, her lips slightly parted.

She realized dimly that they were standing motionless, in plain view; it was unlikely that she could even convince him to kiss her. She remembered a small cave, private and protected, some twenty yards up the beach, carved long

ago by the crashing of the sea into the rocks. She pulled
away from him and ran full speed up the beach, hoping
she could reach the cave before he caught her.

Startled, Edward stared after her a moment. "Cassie,
what the devil," he shouted, but she did not stop. He shook
his head and galloped after her. The beach curved sharply,
and when he rounded the cliff, she was nowhere to be seen.
"Cassie, if you don't come here this instant, I am going to
beat your bottom."

He saw a flash of green from the corner of his eye and
turned to see her standing in the mouth of a cave.

"You must catch me first, my lord," she cried, and disappeared into the cave.

Edward's eyes grew quickly accustomed to the dim interior, and he saw Cassie standing quietly some feet away
from him.

"Alas, my lord," she said in a breathless voice, "it appears that you have trapped me."

"You deserve a good beating, my girl."

"Yes, Edward," she said, and bowed her head.

In an instant, she felt his hands grasp her shoulders and
his breath warm upon her forehead. She raised her head
and parted her lips in mute invitation.

He realized vaguely that she had tricked him, but she
was standing on her tiptoes, her mouth close to his, and he
felt rational scruples slip willingly from his mind. They were
to be wed, after all, in but two days' time.

"I love you so, Edward." He felt her breasts pressing
against his chest, and wrapped his arms tightly about her
back.

"And I you, Cass." He brought his mouth down to hers
and kissed her, savoring the taste of her. He grew more
demanding, and wrapped his hands in her hair that hung
to her waist. He shuddered when she dug her fingers into
his back. She was filled with passion, innocent passion, and
it was driving him mad.

"Please, Edward, touch me the way you did on the
beach, when you first saw me."

He released her hair and his hands caressed her. He

cupped her buttocks and lifted her to press her belly tightly against him.

"Damn your ridiculous skirt and petticoats." He pulled away from her and shrugged quickly out of his coat. He spread it on the sand and eased himself down. "Come here, Cass," he said, and held his hand out to her.

Cassie fell to her knees beside him and let him pull her into his arms. She fell onto his chest and let her hair swirl about his face. Edward circled her chin with his fingers, tilting her face to him so he could look into her eyes. They were huge and dark in the pale light, full of tenderness and excitement.

"Lie on your back, Cass," he said softly.

He balanced himself on one elbow and smoothed her hair away from her face into a golden halo about her head. "God, you're beautiful," he whispered. His fingertips traced the straight line of her nose, and gently outlined her cheek.

"I feel so urgent, Edward," she said, as his fingertips lightly touched her mouth. "My heart is pounding so, I can scarce breathe."

He saw her eyes widen as he cupped her breast and pulled her to him, and felt a shudder pass the length of her body. "There is much, much more."

"Please teach me, Edward. Let me become a woman."

Although he had had much practice, Edward's fingers trembled as they probed at the small buttons on her bodice. He wanted her as he had never before desired a woman. She lay passively, staring up at him as the material parted, and he pulled free the blue ribbons that held her chemise close over her breasts. When cool air touched her skin, she stiffened, for no man had ever before seen her naked.

"Don't be afraid, Cass," he said. He parted the chemise, baring her breasts. They thrust up firm and full toward him, delicately white and smooth, her creamy nipples a dusky pink.

"Do I please you, Edward?"

He groaned deep in his throat, and closed his mouth over her. She sucked in her breath in surprise as he licked and tugged at her with growing possessiveness. He felt her quicken and arch her back instinctively to press more tightly against him.

Edward sat back on his knees and jerked open his white lawn shirt.

Cassie raised her hand and tangled her fingers in the light brown hair of his chest. She lightly traced the diagonal white scar that slashed down his shoulder. "Let me feel you against me," she whispered.

He lowered himself down upon her, his senses reeling at the giving of her, and he kissed her deeply, savagely, until she moaned breathlessly into his mouth. He drove his hands frantically beneath her, to the buttons on the skirt of her gown.

Cassie joined her fingers to his as he jerked free the bowed sash, and tugged at the strings of her petticoats.

Edward gave a shaking laugh as he clumsily helped her to rise to free her of her clothing. As her shift fell from her hips to land on her discarded skirt, Cassie hesitated and furtively crossed her hands over her thighs. She remembered starkly having overhead whispered words of two young maids when she was but twelve years old. Molly had said hoarsely, "He'll drive it into ye and ye'll scream with pain and bleed afore ye learn to like it."

She realized dimly that she was afraid to give herself over to him, to lose the mystery and innocence that bound her to herself, to a self that was known and safe. She stood stiff with uncertainty, lacing her fingers tightly together.

"You needn't fear me, Cassie. Come, look at me, love."

She forced her eyes to his face and saw understanding there. "I'm being quite silly," she said in a low, nervous voice.

"No, you are being you. Trust me, Cass. I'll not take anything from you, nor would I ever hurt you. I want to give you everything that I have and that includes my passion and my body." As he spoke, he traced her throat with his fingers, and then her breasts. He felt her quiver at his touch and drew her into his arms, closing his mouth over hers.

His fingers caressed her until she dropped her arms to her sides and leaned against him.

"Do you want me now, Cassie?"

"Yes." She closed her hand over his caressing fingers.

He fell to his knees in front of her and she felt his eyes upon her, looking at her. His fingers touched her, and her embarrassment at his intrusion slipped away from her as his gentle caressing sent intense sensation down to her belly. His other hand was kneading her buttocks, pressing her closer to him. His fingers caressed her until at last they parted her. Cassie panted, her breathing hoarse. Her legs trembled violently, and she felt she would collapse if Edward were not holding her.

"Oh, please, Edward." She moaned, and tugged at his shoulders.

He lifted her in his arms and laid her gently on his coat. He pulled at the buttons on his breeches, so caught up in his desire that he did not at first hear the nearing shouts.

But Cassie did. Her face paled in consternation and she scrambled to her feet, her passion turned to furious embarrassment.

Edward dropped his hands from his breeches and whirled about toward the mouth of the cave.

"Cassie! Edward! Where are you?"

"It's Becky," Cassie said between clenched teeth, feverishly pulling on her rumpled shift and petticoats.

"Damn that woman to the devil," Edward said under his breath, but he too reached down to retrieve his shirt.

"Cassie! Edward!" Miss Petersham's voice was growing closer.

"It is too bad of her. We are soon to be married, and we are not children."

Becky Petersham was on the point of calling out again when she saw a disheveled Cassie and Edward emerge not twenty paces away from a narrow rift in the side of the cliff. She sucked in an angry breath, angry with herself for trusting in the viscount's scruples.

The viscount appeared as pale as Cassie was flushed. She drew her lips in a tight line, her foot tapping the coarse sand.

"What a pleasure to see you, Miss Petersham," Edward

said in a tone of bland sarcasm. "You wish to explore the cave with Cassie and me?"

"I imagine that there has been sufficient exploration, my lord," Miss Petersham snapped, her eyes narrowing on an open button of Cassie's bodice.

"For heaven's sake, Becky," Cassie said, "Edward and I are to be married in two days. You are acting as if we were both ten years old. I'll thank you to mind to your own affairs in the future."

"You are my affair, Miss, until the day that you are married."

"I believe everyone's points have been clearly made," Edward said. "Cass, Miss Petersham, may I escort you ladies back to the Hall?"

Chapter 6

Eliott looked up from his late luncheon to see his sister tugging at an old muslin gown that had become an indeterminate gray from its many washings.

"Where are you off to, Cass?"

"I am going fishing, as if you didn't know. I promised Cook some fresh sea bass for dinner tonight."

Eliott laid down his fork and sat back in his chair. "And just what does your fiancé think about your fishing jaunt the day before your wedding?"

"Edward is spending the day in Little Wimmering with his agent, and will not be here until this evening."

"So the bride is having her last outing before the groom cracks the whip?"

Cassie frowned down her nose at him. "I'm sure there will be even more outings after Edward and I are married. Actually, it was Becky's suggestion that I get out today. She thinks some fresh air will do me good."

"Off with you then, Cass, and don't forget your hat. Don't want to have you sunburned on your wedding day."

Cassie gave her brother a quick hug and stepped outside into the bright afternoon sunlight. She crammed her wide-brimmed straw hat firmly over the braided coronet atop her head and walked briskly across the east lawn to the line of landward-bowed beech trees that sheltered Hemphill Hall from the sea winds. A narrow path snaked through the trees, down the rocky cliff to a small protected cove below. A long wooden-planked dock stretched from the beach some thirty feet into the inlet. She firmly grasped her bucket of bait, small minnows which she had learned from long experience brought her as many sea bass as her baskets would hold, and walked gingerly over the floating boards to the end of the dock where her twenty-foot sloop lay anchored.

It heeled sharply as she stepped aboard, and she clasped the thick-stalked mast to steady herself. She stepped to the helm, stowed her bait safely on the shelf below-deck, and pulled out the folded canvas mainsail. She smoothed out the wrinkles and attached the slides sewn into the foot of the sail to the boom, smiling happily as her eyes followed along the luff to ensure that there were no twists in the sail.

From long habit, she gazed out beyond the mouth of the cove to the sea, and saw that the wind was whipping the waves into stiff whitecaps. She put a double reef into the mainsail and tied the sheets loosely. She cast off the hemp lines, drew out her long-handled paddle, and rowed with deep, sure strokes toward the mouth of the cove, the familiar sounds of squawking birds and the loose flapping of the mainsail in her ears. She sniffed the tangy salt smell and enjoyed the wind slapping lightly at her cheeks until she reached the open sea and eased out the sail to catch the wind. She examined the wildly fluttering wool telltale tied to the shroud to gauge the strength and direction of the wind. She smiled ruefully, knowing that with the tide outgoing and the stiff northeasterly wind, she would be spending more of her afternoon with her hands tightly on the tiller and working the sheets than lazing back with her fishing pole dangling comfortably over the side.

She let her sailboat continue on its starboard tack, and the mainsail bellied out as it caught the full wind. She laughed aloud when the bow of her boat sliced through the trough of a wave and sent a fine mist of salt spray into her face. She steered away from the wind to slow her speed, and relaxed her grip on the tiller, content for the moment to let her boat glide smoothly in a course parallel to shore. She baited her hook with a small minnow, flung the thin hemp rope over the side and rested the fishing pole between her knees.

She sat back contentedly on a cushioned plank and allowed her thoughts to drift with the lulling motion of her boat to the afternoon before and the incredible moments she had spent with Edward before Becky's wretched interference. The image of Edward's lean chest and arms as he had stood over her and the vivid memory of his hands and mouth on her body made her tremble even now. She wished she had seen him naked. She had felt the swollen, demanding hardness of him as he had pressed her belly against him, but she had been too shy to touch him as he had her.

Cassie gazed up into the cloudless blue sky and decided that making love with Edward in the middle of the day would be a delicious experience. Her sail suddenly luffed wildly, and she pushed quickly at the tiller, chiding herself for her inattention, before she promptly fell back into pleasant fantasy.

She was disturbed again by waves slapping sharply against the bow, and looked up to see a large sailing vessel in the distance. She drew in her empty line, dropped the fishing pole into the boat, and shaded her eyes, trying to make out the lines of the ship.

She gave a crow of delight when she realized that it was the yacht she and Edward had seen the afternoon before. It rode high in the water, its many square-rigged sails tautly full as it held its northeasterly course close into the wind. She saw the gun mounts on the starboard side and several sailors perched high up the mast, unfurling the royals and topgallants.

Cassie wanted to see the yacht more closely before it passed her by, and she jerked on the tiller, bringing her boat high into the wind. She eased in the sheets, and the mainsail bulged tautly as it took more wind.

As she drew closer, she could make out sailors standing on the quarterdeck. She fancied she could see the captain of the yacht shouting commands to the sailors swarming over the rigging, and to the helmsman as he steered the ship past the dangerous shallow inlets. She was suddenly able to see the name of the yacht, painted in bright yellow letters on the starboard bow. She stared with growing confusion at *The Cassandra.*

The yacht was overtaking her, and she was perplexed to see that its course had shifted more northerly. In a few minutes, if she was not careful, it would cut in front of her small boat. Grim visions of the huge vessel ramming her, blind to her presence, sent her speeding into action. She jerked the tiller sharply, and tacked to starboard and landward. In her haste, she backwinded her sail, and for a few frantic seconds, her sloop lay dead in the water, bobbing up and down in the crest of waves from the approaching yacht. She let the sheets fly free, and ducked as the boom swung with a grating thud to starboard. She pulled at the tiller to put the wind to her back, and her small sail took the wind with agonizing slowness. Cassie fought off her growing panic, secured the tiller between her thighs, grabbed her paddle, and rowed furiously toward shore.

She heard a man's shout, and slewed her head about for a moment to see the yacht bearing down on her, its graceful, full bow slicing cleanly through the water.

The huge shadow of the yacht blotted out the sun, and Cassie moaned low in her throat as the specter of death rose before her.

A man's voice commanded sharply, "Veer off! Hook the ropes and haul her in!"

Cassie gazed dumbfounded at several sailors hanging precariously from rope ladders over the side, each of them holding in his free hand a thick looped rope. By God, they are pirates, white slavers, she thought. She saw herself tied in irons, bound for servitude on the Barbary Coast, and pulled frantically with her paddle.

She heard a whirling sound over her head and was suddenly thrown backward against the teller as looped ropes encircled the mast and the outjutting bow. She shook off the pain in her back from the sharp-edged tiller and scrambled forward. She tugged at the thick hemp rope about the mast, but it was pulled taut.

She looked up when one sailor shouted upward to a man who stood at the railing. "All secure, captain!"

"Pull her close in! Steady now!"

There was something oddly familiar about the commanding deep voice, but her mind was so clogged with fear that she did not heed it. She saw that fumbling with the thick rope about her mast would gain her naught, and quickly stumbled to the stern of her wildly lurching boat. She measured her distance to shore and groaned with frustration, for in her heavy skirt and petticoats she would drown long before she reached shallow water. She was thrown to her knees as her boat heeled sharply, drawn closer to the yacht by the ropes. She watched numbly as the captain gingerly stepped over the side and began his descent down a rope ladder. He was a powerfully built man, dressed in a full-sleeved white shirt, and tight-fitting knit breeches above his black boots.

He is a pirate, she thought, their leader. She grabbed the long wooden paddle and held her weapon tightly against her.

Her boat heeled as he stepped into the cockpit, and he closed his hand about the mast for support.

She took in his thick black hair and deeply tanned face and gasped in astonishment.

"Lord Clare! Oh, thank God it is you. I thought it was a pirate and that I was to be taken, or killed." She ceased her babble of words when Anthony Welles only gazed at her, unspeaking.

Cassie drew a shaking breath and lowered her wooden paddle. "You frightened me, my lord," she said more calmly. "I do not think I like your joke; you could easily have rammed my boat. Pray tell me, why have you done this?"

"My purpose was not to ram your boat, Cassandra, only to capture it," he said in his low, clipped voice. "You gave me quite a chase until you backwinded your sail."

Her fingers tightened about the wooden paddle. "What are you saying, my lord? You wished to capture my boat?"

"I commend your bravado, Cassandra. However, I must ask you to drop that deadly paddle and accompany me aboard your namesake."

"Lord Clare, what is the meaning of this? I asked you just why the devil you have secured my boat. I demand that you answer me." She took an angry step toward him.

"Come, Cassandra, enough of this foolishness. The time

grows short. You will come to understand everything, in time." He stretched out his hand toward her. "Drop the paddle and come here."

"You can go to the devil, my lord." She took a wobbly step backward and lost her footing. Her attention wavered from him as she struggled to regain her balance, and a strong hand clasped her arm and jerked her forward. She tried to raise her paddle to strike him, but he twisted it easily from her grasp and pulled her against him.

"Damn you, let me go. My brother will hear about this, my lord. As will Edward."

Even as she yelled at him, her arms were pinioned to her sides as he lifted her easily and hoisted her over his shoulder.

"Don't fight me, Cassandra," he said, and stepped from her boat to the ladder.

Cassie felt a numbing sense of disbelief sweep over her. She had known Anthony Welles for most of her life, as a gentleman, a sophisticated yet kind man. She realized through a haze of fear that he was really someone different, a man she did not know or understand.

She wailed aloud, reared up from his shoulder, and twisted about, smashing her fist against his cheek.

The quickness of her assault took him off his guard and he nearly lost his grip on the ladder. Cassie heard shouts from the sailors above and struggled against him, until she looked down and saw that if he lost his hold, they would be plunged into her boat, not into the water.

She went limp on his shoulder.

"Death is never preferable, is it, Cassandra?"

She gritted her teeth and said nothing.

He stepped over the side, onto the quarterdeck, gently eased her off his shoulder, and set her on her feet. She ran until she felt a palm flattened against the small of her back.

"Leave her be, Scargill, she is not a fool."

"Aye, my lord."

Cassie whirled about. "You are Lord Clare's valet. I recognize you. Will you not tell me the meaning of this?"

She heard the earl say crisply, from behind her, "All in good time, Cassandra. First I must see to your boat."

She turned slowly. "What do you mean?"

"You will soon understand," he said, striding toward her. Cassie forced herself not to move, and thrust her chin upward, unwilling to let him see how frightened she was.

He reached out and lifted off her wide-brimmed straw hat. She watched as it floated in the stiff breeze to the polished wooden deck.

"You will have no further need of your hat. I have never really liked them, you know. Your face should be tanned golden by the sun." She blinked, and before she could respond, he turned abruptly away from her.

"Dilson, is the bow firmly secured?"

"Aye, captain."

Scargill stepped from her side to stand beside the earl. Cassie gripped the bronze railing and watched as her small sailboat lurched clumsily through the waves, drawn forward by the yacht.

"Harden up a little, Angelo," she heard him order the helmsman. "No nearer, the rocks are treacherous. Keep her so." She saw him turn and nod to the sailor, Dilson, and the little man climbed like an agile monkey over the side and down the ladder to her boat. He drew a sword and with several powerful strokes hacked through the wooden mast. It teetered an instant and fell, shrouded in its white sail, into the water.

"No!" She rushed forward, without thought, to climb over the side of the yacht.

She felt a strong hand on her arm and turned in her fury to strike him. He efficiently clasped both her wrists in one large hand.

"I am truly sorry, Cassandra. I know that you love your sailboat, but it must be done."

He shaded his eyes with his free hand, took in their distance from the clumps of outjutting rocks near shore, and commanded suddenly, "Cut her loose, Dilson."

Dilson's sword sliced through the looped rope about the bow. In an instant, he scrambled back to the ladder and pushed off the sailboat with his booted foot.

"Please do not," she whispered, tears stinging her eyes. "The tide will smash her against the rocks."

"Yes, I know, but you will not witness it." He turned to the helmsman. "Lay the course, Angelo. Come, Cassandra."

Chapter 7

Cassie walked beside him down the deck to the companionway, vaguely mindful of low-pitched sailors' voices blending with the sounds of flapping sails overhead. He drew her to a halt below deck in front of a closed door.

"After you, Cassandra," he said as he opened the door, and stood back for her to enter.

Cassie stepped into a shadowy cabin, aware of the tangy scent of lemon polish and sandalwood. She dully noted the rich mahogany paneling and the elegant furnishings. It was a cabin fit for a captain and an earl. She whipped about at the sound of a key turning in the lock.

He turned to face her, a broad-shouldered man, who now seemed a dangerous stranger to her. His eyes appeared black in the soft afternoon light of the cabin, darker than she remembered, almost as black as his arched brows and his thick hair.

"Would you care for a cup of tea?" he asked.

She stared at him, and shook her head out of habit.

"Forgive my lapse of memory. You do not care for tea, do you? Most un-English of you, Cassandra."

She watched warily as he crossed the cabin, his steps noiseless on the deep pile of the blue carpet, and eased himself onto a high-backed leather chair, one of four that stood about an elegant circular table.

"Will you not sit down?"

Cassie forced her feet forward to stand behind one of the chairs, and clutched at its carved back.

"How stupid of me to have forgotten," she said finally, forcing her voice into momentary calm. "I saw your yacht once, long ago, at Clacton."

"Perhaps you did, but then her name was not *The Cassandra.* She is lovely, is she not? Even Farmer George wanted to purchase her, but of course, I refused."

She waved away his words. "If you would not mind, I should like to know the meaning of your senseless behavior."

"My behavior is never senseless, Cassandra. In this particular instance, perhaps, I was forced to employ some rather rough and ready methods to secure your presence."

"Damn you, my lord, tell me the meaning of this." She drew a deep breath and swallowed the growing lump in her throat. "You are an English peer, my lord, an earl. I did not believe that gentlemen of your rank and wealth indulged in white slavery. Are there other young English ladies aboard your yacht?"

Anthony Welles blinked at her, then threw back his head and laughed aloud, his white teeth contrasting with his tanned face. "White slavery. Good God, Cassandra, what an imagination you have. A slaver in the English Channel."

"In that case, my lord, there is much that requires my attention at Hemphill Hall, for I am to be married tomorrow, as you know since you are an invited guest. You will please set me ashore at once."

The humor fell from his face, and he sat forward in his chair. His rugged features softened as his eyes rested intently upon her face. "You are not going back to Hemphill Hall, Cassandra."

"I do not understand you," she said slowly. "I have been told that your wealth is great, thus I cannot credit that you wish to hold me for ransom. I ask you again, my lord, what is your purpose?"

"My purpose, Cassandra, is to make you my wife."

She jerked back at his softly spoken words and stared at him in shock. "I do not believe you, my lord. And I find your jest repellent. Set me ashore, I demand it."

He was silent for what seemed an eternity to Cassie, and she rushed on in furious speech. "My family will miss me. They will mount a search when I do not return and—" Her words died in her throat, and she felt herself go white.

"And, Cassandra," he finished for her, "they will find

your boat smashed upon the rocks. You know yourself that the tides in this area are vicious, unpredictable."

"They will believe me drowned, dead." She raised wide, uncomprehending eyes to his face. "But this makes no sense. Why are you doing this to me? I have always believed you to be my friend, that you liked me."

"Indeed, I am your friend, only now I will be much more to you."

Cassie stared into his face, a face that many ladies she knew admired, one that over the past few years even she had come to think harshly beautiful. Now, in his black knee boots and billowing white shirt, his black hair unpowdered and blown into disarray by the sea wind, he looked the swarthy pirate, not the English earl.

She said, still trying to cling to her image of him, "You seem different, changed. I have always thought of you as an indulgent uncle . . ."

He winced, but remained silent.

"A gentleman, a powerful lord, whose esteem gave me confidence. You were someone who never cared if I did something stupid or didn't behave like a simpering girl. You treated Eliott as a brother after my father's death, teaching him his responsibilities as baron, helping him. By God, he was even touting your praises at our ball last week."

"And I am fond of your brother. Though he will never have your strength of character, he is nonetheless an amiable boy. You will see him again."

She shook her head at him in disbelief, unable to grasp the enormity of his words. She said in a shaking voice, "Damn you, this is ludicrous, my lord. You cannot do this. I am to be married tomorrow."

"I suppose that my thirty-four years do seem ancient to one of eighteen. As for Edward Lyndhurst," he continued with calm detachment, "you were never meant to belong to him. Your turbulent girl's infatuation for him would not have lasted, you know. Although you have known him all your life, he is cut from a very different cloth than are you."

"You do not know what you are talking about, my lord. I have loved Edward all my life, and nothing you can do or say will change that."

"I daresay that I shall say and do many things, Cassandra, that will help you to change." He shook his head in mock reproof. "It came as quite a surprise to me that a well-bred English girl would correspond surreptitiously with a soldier. It was stupid of me, I suppose, to believe Lyndhurst out of your heart and mind when he left three years ago."

"He has never been out of either, my lord," she said coldly. "I would like to know how the devil you found out about our letters."

He waved an indifferent, dismissing hand. "It's not particularly important. Suffice it to say that his abrupt return and your immediate announcement to wed with him forced a dramatic shift in my plans."

"What do you mean—your plans?"

"Simply that I fully intended to court you during your Season in London in proper style and wed you at Hanover Square, with all the pomp due to the Countess and Earl of Clare."

She regarded him with cold contempt. "You lied to yourself, my lord, for never would I have wed you, nor will I. How very convenient for you that I came out in my boat today. Have you been skulking about long?"

"For the past two weeks, if you would know the truth. I did not expect Lyndhurst to have such control over your actions. Did he plan to burn your sailboat, Cassandra?"

"He will come to understand, I know it." She saw that he was regarding her with disbelief. "Damn you, it's none of your affair in any case."

"I have told you, my dear, that you are now completely my affair. I beg you not to forget that."

"When I look at the coward who speaks, of course I shall. And what would you have done, sir, had I not come sailing today?"

"Ah, a question that I posed to myself several times. You would have come to my yacht dressed in your nightgown,

Cassandra. Certainly a more harrowing solution and one that would have left untidy questions. I thank you for being so obliging."

She slowly shook her head back and forth, and rising panic filled her voice. "You cannot do this. Please, you must let me go home."

"You home is with me now, Cassandra. I have watched you grow into a lovely young woman, watched you let your skirts down and cease scraping your knees. I have much time and energy invested in you, my lady, and since your seventeenth birthday, I have been determined to marry you. Though I regret that you will feel grief for your lost viscount, I know that it will pass. Hearts do not break, you know, they merely bruise for a while."

She turned on him viciously. "I find you repellent, my lord, and quite mad. If you believe that I shall ever change my mind or forget Edward Lyndhurst, you are a fool. As to marrying you, I shall see you in hell first."

She dashed to the cabin door and twisted frantically at the knob. She raised her fists and pounded at the door, blind to anything save her escape from him. She dug her nails relentlessly into the small space where the door met its frame, and tore them on the wooden splinters. A defeated sob ripped from her throat, and she sank slowly to her knees, her cheek pressed against the door.

Anthony Welles rose quietly from his chair and walked to her crumpled figure. He frowned at the sight of her torn fingernails, several of them ripped so deeply that they bled. He dropped to one knee beside her and laid his hand upon her shoulder.

"Come, Cassandra, you have hurt yourself." As he slipped his arm about her waist to pull her upright, she twisted about, and with a cry of rage, smashed her fists against his chest. She caught him off balance and he toppled backward, pulling her with him. He grabbed her wildly flailing arms, rolled her over on her back, and pinned her hands above her head. He saw the blind fury in her eyes and slammed his leg down over hers to stop her from kicking him. She lay panting beneath him, her chest and belly moving in deep gulping breaths.

She grew suddenly still. "Let me go," she said in a voice of deadly calm.

He stared down at her pale, set face. "You were the attacker, Cassandra," he said finally. "I will release you if you promise to keep your knee away from my manhood."

Slowly, she nodded.

"Will you also promise to let me take care of your hands? You have torn your fingers quite badly."

She closed her eyes for a moment and said, "I promise."

The earl released her and helped her to her feet. "Come and sit down."

She stared at streaks of her blood on his white shirt and became aware of throbbing pain in her fingers. She sat down on the chair he held for her and splayed her fingers on the table top.

She lowered her head and did not look up even as she felt him lifting her fingers, one by one, sponging off the blood with warm water.

"Don't move, Cassandra. I must fetch some bandages, several fingers must be bound."

She kept her head bowed as he wrapped slender strips of white linen about her fingers.

He looked up from his task when she said in a low, tightly controlled voice, "The first time I remember seeing you was when I was a small child. You were very kind to me I recall, even brought me a pastry from a fair stall in Colchester."

"I remember."

"But then you left and it was some years before I saw you again. Miss Petersham said you were a great nobleman both in England and in Italy and that you did not spend all your time in England. I also remember now that I had nearly forgotten you when you suddenly returned when I was fourteen. You gave me an ivory chess set for my birthday. I asked Miss Petersham if you had a daughter of my age and whether that was why you were so attentive to me."

The earl gently cupped her chin in his hand and forced her to look at him. "You are the image of your mother and it was her face that was in my mind until yours replaced it."

"My mother?" she asked, knitting her brows.

"Yes. You see, I loved Constance, even though I was hardly more than a boy at the time, but unfortunately she had already wed your father. That she was my senior by six or so years was unimportant to me. The last time I saw her, her belly was stretched full with child—with you."

"Then you should hate me, for I killed her."

"Perhaps I did, for a time, just as I hated your father for planting his seed in her womb. I left England and did not return for some five years. When I came back, I met you, her daughter, and you were the image of her. You were such a lively child, full of wonder, your eyes bright with intelligence. It was in my mind to take an interest in Constance's daughter, to watch her grow up, to be a part of her life in some way. When I saw you at fourteen, it was only Constance's face that I beheld, not her character or personality. I was drawn to you as a young girl, Cassandra, and when you turned seventeen, I realized that I wanted you, loved you for yourself."

"You lie to yourself, my lord. It is my mother you love."

"You are quite wrong," he said.

"You do not really know me. You cannot love someone you do not know."

"But I know you quite well, Cassandra, believe me."

In her bewilderment, she tried to close her hands, and winced from the pain in her fingers. She felt his long fingers close about her wrists, and she knew it was to keep her from hurting herself. The small token of his caring made her sick with despair.

She raised bleak eyes to his face. "How can you want someone who does not love you?"

"There are few things in life that are unchangeable."

She reared back. "Damn you, I don't want your glib words, my lord. I shall never change."

"You are but eighteen years old, Cassandra," he said gently, and abruptly released her wrists. He sat back in his chair and regarded her silently. She saw tenderness in his dark eyes, and drew back instinctively. She hated herself, but could not prevent her pleading words. "Please, just take me home. I swear I shall tell no one about what you did. Just take me home, I beg you."

He said with cold finality, "No. And never again abase yourself, Cassandra, it ill befits your character."

"How dare you speak so arrogantly about my character? You can have no real notion whatsoever about me. If I choose to plead or abase myself, even to a knave like you, it is because it is in my character to do so."

Her torrent of words, spoken with such perverse defiance, made him smile. "I suppose that next you will tell me that a woman's tears come easily to you, that a woman's guile are also part of your character."

"Go to the devil."

"Ah, the lady finally speaks words I understand. I wager that other young ladies of your age would have demonstrated sufficient sensibility by this time to have swooned at least twice. I thank God for your character, Cassandra, for fainting ladies are a damned nuisance."

She turned stiffly away from him and felt cold despair once again pervade her mind like a familiar cloak. She could feel the swiftness of the yacht and knew that each minute took her farther away from her home and from Edward.

"Where is your yacht bound?" she asked, not looking at him. Perhaps he would dock somewhere in England and she could escape him.

He extinguished the small glimmer of hope with one word. "Italy. Genoa, to be exact. We have a long voyage ahead of us. You know, of course, that my father was an English peer, the third Earl of Clare. My mother was Italian. Over the past years I have spent roughly equal periods of time in both countries. Now, my mother's homeland will be mine—ours."

Cassie had wondered why she had been taught Italian, not French, like the other young ladies of her acquaintance. It was not possible, she thought with mounting confusion, that he could know that. She said, "The Union Jack is flying at the jackstaff."

"Of course. *The Cassandra* has flown England's colors for the past six months and she will continue to do so until we are in French waters."

"What do you do then, my lord earl, strut like a Frenchman and become the Comte de Clare? Have you a French flag to cloak your cowardice?"

"Such a masquerade might prove amusing, but not at all necessary. The Genoese are the bankers of the French. Even the bucolic Louis has the good sense to protect the funnel to his royal coffers."

"And if the French attack by error?"

As if he read her thoughts, he said, "Believe me, Cassandra, to be taken by French privateers or the French navy would not result in your return to England. In any case, it will not happen. Did you not notice the gun mounts? They are not toys, I assure you."

Cassie slumped forward in her chair, her thoughts upon Edward and Eliott and the grief they would feel when they found her wrecked sailboat. Even at this moment, Eliott was probably growing concerned that she had not returned. "You are an evil, ruthless man, my lord," she said, her voice as dead as her heart.

"Perhaps. Ruthless, at least, for I would have gone to any lengths to secure you as my wife." He saw the glazed look in her eyes, and said no more. He glanced at the clock atop his desk and rose.

"It grows late, Cassandra. I must go on deck for a while to see to our course. If you wish to bathe, you will find fresh water on the commode. Gowns, underthings, stockings, hairbrushes are in the dresser and armoire. We will dine when I return."

Cassie merely stared at him, mute. Vaguely, as if from a great distance, she heard a key turn in the lock.

"The wee lass, she is all right?"

"She will be," the earl said as he released the helm to Angelo and turned to Scargill, a plucky, straight-spoken Scotsman, his valet for some ten years.

"It was like ye killed a part of her when ye sent her boat toward the rocks."

"Yes, but she shall have another, once we are home again."

Anthony Welles gazed starboard for a long moment over the choppy water, toward the English shoreline. "She is very young, Scargill."

Scargill's coarse red hair flapped up and down on his forehead in the sea wind, and out of habit, he raised his forefinger to smooth it down. He studied his master's strong, proud profile, outlined in the orange glow of the setting sun, and shook his head. "It's a ruthless thing ye've done, my lord."

"Precisely Cassandra's words, Scargill, but there is little point in repining now. She is mine, and that is the end to the matter."

"As I've told ye afore, my lord, I've never known a man to raise his own wife. I thought ye'd forgotten her when that spitfire, Giovanna, got her hooks into ye."

"The Contessa accomplished part of her desire, my friend."

"She was hot for ye, I'll grant ye that, my lord. But besides warming yer bed, she has an eye to yer title and fortune. She'll not prove kind to yer English lass."

The earl turned slowly and an amused smile lit his dark eyes. "In the unlikely event that Giovanna shows her claws to Cassandra, rest assured that Cassandra will dish her up without any assistance from me. She is like quicksilver, I think, arrogant and proud. She has a core of strength that her mother never possessed. Be kind to her, Scargill, but I caution you to be watchful. She very nearly unmanned me with her knee."

Scargill guffawed. "She did, did she, my lord. So the wee madonna is not taking well to yer kidnaping her."

"Not at the moment. You call her madonna now, Scargill?"

"Yer Genoese sailors have called her nothing else, my lord. It's yer mixed blood, they say, that makes ye one minute the cold imperious lord, and the next, the unpredictable man bent on his own passions. They believe it's yer Italian blood that makes ye go to such lengths for a woman."

The earl stood rigidly straight, his features impassive. It was always so when his lordship was angered, Scargill thought, particularly when someone referred to his fiery Italian blood.

"Have I a rebellion brewing with my men?"

"Nay, ye know as well as I do that they'd follow ye to hell, if ye asked it of them."

"Never would I demand anything so final. See that they get an extra ration of grog, Scargill, but not more, mind you. I will be much occupied this evening and have no wish for *The Cassandra* to run aground."

Scargill grunted. "The men will come to accept her, my lord. Even Angelo, as superstitious as any man with a woman aboard, admitted that she had a fine way with her wee boat."

"That is quite an accolade, coming from my close-mouthed helmsman. Unfortunately, I do not believe that Cassandra would have the slightest inclination at the moment to value such a compliment."

"Do ye think she'll agree to wed with ye, my lord?"

"She will wed me," Anthony said calmly. "Now, my friend, I must use your cabin just this once to bathe and change for dinner. See that Arturo prepares the English fare that I ordered. You will play the English butler this evening."

"Aye, my lord." Scargill watched his master walk down the highly polished deck toward the companionway, his step jaunty, and the set of his broad shoulders assured.

It was dark when the earl straightened his black satin waistcoat and unlocked the cabin door. He could make out Cassandra's figure in the near darkness as he opened the door, seated in the same chair next to the table where he had left her. He frowned, for she had not bothered to light the lamps.

He performed this task, and when the cabin was flooded with light, he turned to face her. She was wearing the same old muslin gown, and tendrils of hair, unbrushed, curled haphazardly about her set face.

"Good evening, Cassandra," he said, and sat down opposite her.

"I see the pirate clothes himself like a gentleman," she said, her eyes flitting over him with open contempt.

"And I see that you are still clothed as a peasant girl. You do not find the wardrobe I have provided you to your liking?"

"I will never touch anything that belongs to you, my lord."

"In that case," he remarked imperturbably, "you will soon find yourself naked." He saw her expressive eyes narrow in disbelief, then widen in ill-disguised fear. Obviously, she had not considered that he would make sexual demands of her.

"Our dinner will arrive shortly. Would you care for a glass of wine?"

Cassie nodded dumbly, aware suddenly that her throat was parched from thirst.

He handed her a glass of French Burgundy and watched her clumsily take it between her bandaged fingers. She downed it in one long gulp and fell into a paroxysm of coughing.

"It is heady stuff, Cassandra. You must learn to sip wine, not gulp it down like water."

She frowned at him from watery eyes and thwacked the delicate glass on the table.

"Would you care for some more?"

He saw her hesitate perceptibly and guessed that she feared that he would make her drunk. He liberally watered down another glass and placed it in front of her.

There came a knock on the cabin door. "Ah, our dinner has arrived. Enter."

Scargill appeared in the doorway, dressed in an English butler's formal attire, his arms laden with covered silver trays. The earl bit back a bark of laughter at the look of pained resignation on his face.

Cassie moved away from the table and sat upon a blue velvet settee. She watched the earl silently as he lifted each cover and sniffed at the dishes. "You may tell Arturo that he has performed wonders," he said to Scargill, who was looking with worried eyes at Cassie.

Cassie said sharply, "Is it your wish to go to the gallows with your master? That is where brigands and pirates end their days."

Scargill turned to face the flushed girl. "If it is God's will, lassie, then so be it."

She rose unsteadily to her feet and shouted at him, "I will see that it is God's will. How can you obey a man who ruthlessly kidnaps a woman from her family and those she loves? He is a devil, without heart or honor."

Scargill shook his head slowly, his hazel eyes softening. "Ye're wrong, lassie," he said gently.

Cassie drew a shattered breath, and without thought to consequences, took two quick steps forward and hurled the remaining wine in the earl's face.

"Oh, my God," Scargill whispered behind her.

Anthony Welles silently drew a white lawn handkerchief from his waistcoat pocket and mopped the wine from his face.

Scargill could not help but admire her, for although her face was perfectly white, her chin was thrust forward and her shoulders were squared.

The earl lowered the handkerchief and said quietly, "You may leave now. Cassandra and I wish to dine."

"Aye, my lord," Scargill said slowly, his eyes searching his master's face.

The earl shut and locked the cabin door after his valet and walked to the filled basin atop the commode to dash water over his face and neck. He toweled himself dry and said calmly, "Sit down, Cassandra. Arturo went to great pains to prepare an English meal to your liking."

Cassie looked at him uncertainly, for after her unthinking act, she had expected him to retaliate. She sat down at the table, unwilling for the moment at least to provoke him further.

She soon found that she was as hungry as she had been thirsty, for she had not eaten since breakfast.

He watched her wolf down a rare slice of roast beef, and a goodly portion of the boiled potatoes and parsley. Her hunger eased, she slowed and sat back in her chair.

"I am delighted that you approve of at least one thing I've done for you."

She looked at him and he saw her fingers tighten about the stem of her newly filled wine glass.

"Do not do what you are thinking, Cassandra," he said. "I allowed you one childish act, but no more."

She gritted her teeth and raised the glass, but her hand shook.

"If you do what you are thinking, rest assured that I shall reciprocate." He saw the unspoken question in her eyes. "If you hurl the wine at me, I shall throw you over my knee, bare your bottom, and thrash you."

"You would not."

"Try me, Cassandra."

She slowly lowered the glass to the table and let her fingers fall away from it.

"Now, my dear, would you care to try some of my Italian coffee?"

"I am not your dear."

"Coffee?"

She nodded, hopeful that the coffee would counteract the dizzying effects of the wine.

She walked to the settee and sat down, silently sipping the thick black liquid. When Scargill returned to clear the table, she saw the earl speak quietly to him, but she could not make out his words.

When they were once again alone, she stared at the huge dark man and felt a knife of fear twist in her stomach. "I want more coffee."

The earl hesitated but an instant, then poured her half a cup.

To Cassie's consummate embarrassment, she discovered that all the wine and coffee she had consumed had created a distressing problem. She shifted uncomfortably on the settee for some moments, and finally she said, "I have to— that is, I must— please leave me alone."

The earl cocked his head to one side, then grinned. He rose and walked to the door. "The chamber pot is by the bed. You have five minutes, Cassandra, no more."

After seeing to her most immediate need, Cassie looked frantically at the clock and saw that she had only two minutes before he would return. Though she knew she would not be able to keep him away from her, she pulled the heavy settee over and braced it against the locked door. She grew red in the face trying to push the table before she saw that it was fastened securely to the floor. She gave a cry of frustration and dashed to the far corner of the cabin when she heard the key turn in the lock.

She heard a low, deep chuckle and saw the settee move easily aside as he pushed open the door. The smile was still wide on his face when he came through the door.

"It appears that I gave you too much time. Perhaps next time I will not leave you." His tone turned suddenly serious. "Come here, Cassandra, I would speak to you."

She shook her head, fear clogging her throat.

"If you do not do as I tell you," he continued patiently, "I shall simply carry you over here and sit you down."

Her feet dragged forward, but she refused to sit in the chair, and stood facing him from across the small expanse of table.

He straddled a chair and regarded her in silence. He saw the stark fear on her face and regretted what he had to do. Better to get it over with quickly, he thought. He cleared his throat and said levelly, "As I said this afternoon, Cassandra, I intend that you become my wife."

"And I think you dim-witted, my lord, for I told you this afternoon that your intention is mad. I would sooner wed the devil himself."

"And to assist you to accept me more quickly as your husband, we will begin tonight in married intimacy."

"No, damn you, no."

"Yes, we shall."

"I will not let you. Damn you, you will not touch me."

"Cassandra, heed me. To allow you to continue in your virgin state would be the height of foolishness, for it would encourage you to nourish unfounded hopes and keep you all the longer away from me."

"I am not a virgin," she said baldly. She saw the flicker of surprise in his dark eyes, and hurried on. "Not only am I not a virgin, my lord earl, I am also pregnant. Nearly two months pregnant, my lord, with Edward Lyndhurst's child. You waited too long to kidnap me, for I carry proof of my love for Edward."

"That is not possible," Anthony said slowly, his eyes flitting to her waist.

"Do not lie to yourself, my lord. Of a certainty it's possible." Her voice rose. "Let me tell you of it, my lord. Shortly after Edward's return, he saw me swimming. It's a lonely isolated stretch of beach, far away even from your prying eyes. As I was very nearly naked, he could not help himself. I much enjoyed the touch of his hands, the feel of his body against mine." She saw that she had shaken him. "I am damaged goods, my lord, not the virgin wife you thought to have. You have another man's woman and another man's child on your hands."

She gazed steadily at his face and crossed her arms over her belly.

When he finally spoke, his voice was curiously flat. "I am sorry, Cassandra, for now it will take you longer to forget your viscount. I shall not harm your child. Indeed, I shall raise it as my own."

She jerked back, unable to believe his words. "You cannot mean it. Have you not understood me? I have freely given my body to another man. Damn you, you cannot still want me."

He slowly unstraddled the chair and rose. "Come, my love, I will help you to undress."

He stretched his hand to her.

"No," she yelled and backed away from him. "You will not do this to me, do you hear?"

"Since you are not a virgin, Cassandra, and know a man's body well, you must also know that I will not hurt you. You will learn my touch and the feel of my body against yours." As he spoke, he moved slowly around the table. She saw the purpose in his eyes and ran to the corner of the cabin, her shoulders pressing against the windows astern. He loomed huge and dark, towering over her. She struggled wildly when he clasped her shoulders, trying to twist free of him. She jerked up her knee, but it connected with his thigh. He pinioned her arms easily against her sides and lifted her to his shoulder, one hand cupping her hips and the other holding her legs tightly against his chest.

He dropped her onto the bed and sat down beside her, holding her hands above her head. "Don't fight me, Cassandra, it will change naught." His mouth closed over hers.

"No," she yelled, and twisted her face away from him. She arched her back and brought up her legs to kick at his back.

In a swift movement, he uncoiled his body and lay beside her, throwing his leg over hers to hold her still. He felt the giving softness of her, and instinctively moved atop her, and pressed himself against her.

He saw that her eyes were filled with fear and forced himself for the moment to calm his desire. He gently stroked the firm line of her jaw, the whiteness of her throat, his touch light and undemanding.

"Do not do this to me," she whispered.

"I must, Cassandra."

She felt his hand upon her breast, and his touch, hated and alien, unleashed her fear. She writhed and twisted until one of her hands slipped loose from his grasp, and she raked her bandaged fingernails down his face.

He rolled suddenly off her and rose to stand beside the bed. She watched him in frozen silence as he shrugged off his waistcoat and his white shirt, baring his chest. He was not lean and slender like Edward. His chest was covered with black curling hair. Her eyes fell to his muscled flat belly above the line of his breeches, and in a spasm of terror, she tried to fling herself past him. He picked her up easily with one arm and tossed her lightly back onto the bed.

"Cassandra, listen to me," he said sharply. "If I must rape you, then so be it, but I will not allow you to fight me like some wild thing. You will only hurt yourself, and

I do not wish it. Either you accept me, or I shall tie you down."

"I will never stop fighting you. Never, do you hear me?"

"Very well," he said flatly, and strode away from the bed, out of her view.

She scurried to the far side of the bed and came up on her knees, her back flattened against the rich mahogany paneling and crossed her shaking arms over her body.

He appeared suddenly, two silk handkerchiefs in his hand. She shrank back.

"Stay away from me."

But he climbed swiftly over to her and dragged her back toward him. He straddled her, holding one arm down beneath him while he grabbed her wrist and swiftly knotted a handkerchief about it. He jerked her arm up and secured the other end to a wooden lattice in the headboard. She heaved wildly beneath him, but if he felt pain from her legs striking his back, he gave no notice. He pulled her other arm above her head and secured it. She felt the silk tighten about her wrists as she struggled to free herself. He moved off her and she lay panting, staring up at him, her eyes dark with fear.

She tried to stop the deep upward and downward heaving of her breasts as his hands moved over them, unbuttoning her bodice. He appeared unhurried in his undressing of her.

"You have set me a problem," he remarked. "How am I to get that dress off you with your wrists secured?"

"Go to the devil."

"I must sacrifice your gown, I fear," he continued, as if she had not spoken. He unfastened the small buttons at her wrists, and in a powerful motion, ripped the sleeves up to her shoulders and jerked open the fine stitching about her throat. His hands were curiously gentle as he pulled her free of her bodice. He untied the ribbons of her chemise and eased her out of the material, leaving her naked to the waist.

He gave a sharp intake of breath and gazed down at her.

"I had imagined that you would be all pink and white, Cassandra. You are quite exquisite."

"I cannot be so different from your women in Italy, my lord."

"But you are, my love, quite different," he said. She felt his hands move lightly over her. She swallowed an impotent cry and concentrated on her hatred of him. She lay rigid even as his mouth closed over her and she felt his tongue.

"Stop it," she yelled, arching and twisting her back to escape him.

The earl circled her waist with his hands to hold her still and let his mouth rove over her breasts, loving the feel of her. He felt her shudder, not with desire, but with fear, and for an instant, he hesitated. He had envisioned many times possessing her body, bringing her to a woman's pleasure, and felt a shaft of anger at Edward Lyndhurst for being the first to awaken her. He thought about the viscount's child lying small in her womb and cursed himself for not having taken her a year ago, when she was seventeen. He raised his head from her breasts and saw her eyes were tightly closed, her lips drawn in a thin line.

He drew a resolute breath and quickly removed the remainder of her clothes. When she was naked, he rose slowly and stared down at her. She lay motionless, her face turned away, her thighs locked together. His eyes followed the curved, soft lines of her, from her slender waist to her flat white belly. His gaze lingered upon the curling blond triangle of hair that covered her, and he was startled at the delicate yet provocative sensuousness of her. He felt a surge of lust for her, and pictured her long legs wrapped about him, drawing him deep inside her. He wanted to part her, caress her, taste her. He was hard, straining against his breeches, and with a low moan, he shucked off the rest of his clothes.

Cassie heard his boots fall to the floor, and, despite herself, turned her face on the pillow toward him. He stood before her, indifferent in his nakedness. Her eyes fell inevitably to the mass of black hair at his groin, and she gasped aloud at the sight of him.

She struggled at the bonds about her wrists and jerked her hips away from him.

"I won't hurt you, Cassandra, you know that." He sat down beside her and stroked her belly, caressing her, until he was touching her. She tried vainly to jerk away from him, her legs flailing wildly, but he held her down with his body. He eased his fingers between her thighs and stroked her gently.

"You are beautiful." She felt his fingertips stroking her thighs, probing at her, and she felt a shuddering sensation that made her draw in her breath.

"Please stop," she said breathlessly, pressing her thighs together, away from his fingers.

"No, my love. Relax, give in to me, Cassandra." He pulled her thighs apart and held her open to him with his body. He lowered his head and she felt his mouth touch her. She frantically tried to jerk away.

"No. Damn you, no."

Reluctantly, he released her. He straddled her quickly and lifted her hips up on a pillow. She felt his fingers part her and arched upward to see him guiding himself into her.

Her cries died in her throat when he suddenly went rigid over her, straining against her. Her eyes flew open and she saw him staring at her in bemused surprise.

"You little liar," he said softly, incredulously. "By God, you missed your calling, Cassandra. It's an actress you should have been. So you are pregnant, my love? Quite an accomplishment I should say, given that your maidenhead is very much intact. No wonder your shock at seeing a naked man." He pulled away from her and rose.

"What are you going to do?"

"What I would have done had I known you were a virgin."

She drew her legs together and pulled impotently at the handkerchiefs. When she felt his weight upon the bed, she looked to see him holding a small jar in his hand.

"What is that?" she said, lifting her head from the pillow to see him better.

He did not answer her, but wedged his hand between her thighs, forcing them apart. Cassie felt his finger ease inside her, and her muscles tightened at the feel of something cool and soothing inside her.

The earl saw her eyes, wide and pleading, upon his face, and though he wanted to reassure her, he knew that anything he said would only prolong her fear.

Cassie felt herself stretch to hold him when he entered her, but she felt no pain. She felt him pushing against her maidenhead, and she stiffened.

"Cassandra," he said, his voice bringing her eyes to his face, "I must hurt you, but just for a moment."

She cried out once at a sharp pain, and felt him move deep within her. She felt a numbing shock that brought hopeless tears to her eyes. His large hands were clasping her hips, drawing her upward to meet him. She heard him moan above her, curiously tense, and felt his seed deep inside her.

She heard herself sobbing aloud, and tears streaked down her cheeks, their salty heat upon her lips.

Cassie felt a warm wet cloth touching her face, soothing away her tears, and slowly opened her eyes. She felt defiled, awash with helpless anger at her weakness, at her womanness.

"I hate you," she whispered to the dark face above her.

"Yes, I know," he said gently. "I am sorry that I had to hurt you, Cassandra." He paused a moment and pulled damp tendrils of hair away from her eyes. "If you would know the truth, I wanted only to get the damned business over with. Next time, I promise you that there will be no pain, indeed, I want to give you pleasure, for that is the object of lovemaking, you know."

The thought that he would force her again made her hollow with despair. She felt the cloth moving over her thighs, pressing lightly against her. She drew her stiff legs slowly together.

He continued calmly, as if in polite conversation in a drawing room. "In Genoa, and indeed in many parts of

Italy, it is a tradition among the peasants for the bride-groom to hang the bedsheet out the window after the wedding night. There must be spots of blood on the sheet, you see, so that all will know that his wife came to him as a virgin."

She said, her voice trembling with fury, "So you will fly the damned sheet from the mast?"

He looked up and smiled, delighted at her spirit. "I just might," he said coolly, "if for no other reason than to celebrate your remarkable lie."

She felt his fingers brush over her belly. "You will be a bit sore, but it will pass quickly."

"So that is how you dismiss brutal rape, my lord. Your victim will only be a bit sore—nothing of any importance."

"Not my victim, Cassandra, my wife."

"You may take your insane notion and go to hell."

"Then you will meet the devil with me. Now, if you promise not to lash out at me—physically, that is—I'll release your wrists."

She felt beyond caring, though she was aware of a growing numbness in her hands. She turned her face away from him.

She felt him unfasten the silk knots and bring her arms down to her sides.

Anthony frowned at the welts about her wrists as he gently rubbed feeling into them again.

"Do you feel better now?"

"I would feel better if I could stick a knife between your ribs."

"Ah, yes, much better, I see. Poor Eliott has never been a match for your acerbic tongue. And if he marries Miss Eliza Pennworthy, I fear that his God-given wit will rust with disuse within a year. As for what Edward Lyndhurst would say about your spirit, I daresay it would not be loving."

She did not answer him, and he continued lightly, "Nor do I believe that you would have managed to subvert your opinions and ideas for very long with Edward Lyndhurst. He has very set notions about the wifely behavior of English ladies, you know."

Cassie felt a raw surge of grief. "Edward must believe me dead by now."

"Probably not yet. I'll wager that he will scour the coast for you for some days to come before he finally accepts the fact."

"You must listen to me," Cassie said, easing herself up on her elbows. "Now that you have used me, will you not cease this cruel charade and take me home? Since I am no longer a virgin, there can be no sport left for you." She was aware that his eyes wavered from her face, and she grasped the corner of a sheet and pulled it over her.

"My lady shows such modesty." He grinned as he rose. "I am naked too, and yours for the asking."

"Answer me." she yelled at him.

"If you speak nonsense, you leave me nothing to say," he said easily. He stretched, and Cassie's eyes dropped to the thick bush of black hair at his groin. His man's sex lay flaccid and soft.

"I cannot be erect for you all of the time, my lady. Even your faithful servant must rest upon occasion."

She felt tears sting her eyes, and gulped down a sob, turning away from him. She felt his hand touch her loosened braids.

"You must brush out your hair, else it will be a mess on the morrow." She made no move and he sighed. "Very well, then I shall do it for you. Will you hold still, or must I tie you up again?"

She turned back to him wearily. "Give me the bloody brush."

Though her arms ached, she ruthlessly jerked the brush through the masses of hair, smoothing down the deep ripples from the braids with her fingers.

"Your hair, like the rest of you, is exquisite."

She stared stonily ahead of her.

From the corner of her eye, she saw him turn and look toward the clock atop the ornate oak desk. "It is time to sleep, Cassandra. It has indeed been a long, quite fatiguing day."

"Where will you sleep?"

His dark eyes twinkled. "Wrapped around your lovely body, of course."

"I wish a nightgown."

"I am sorry, my lady, but a nightgown is the only item of apparel that you will not find in your wardrobe."

"I never sleep without a nightgown."

"Then it is time to break such prudish habits."

She choked down an angry curse and gave in to her exhaustion. The earl moved about the cabin and extinguished the lamps. He again stretched his muscles in the darkness and allowed his nerves their first respite in two months. With a smile of contentment, he climbed into bed beside her.

He lay on his back, his arms above his head, listening to her angry breathing. "Come here, Cassandra," he said finally, bringing his arms down. "I will not take you again, I promise." He could picture her drawn into a small ball, pressed against the starboard wall. "If you do not do as I bid you, I shall go back on my promise."

She cursed and moved reluctantly against him.

He gathered her stiff body in his arms and pulled her tightly against his chest. "Good night, love," he whispered, and pressed her cheek against his shoulder.

He felt her lashes brushing against his flesh, as she lay wide-eyed in the darkness. He sought for words to comfort her, but as he was her nemesis, he could think of nothing that would not upset her more.

He thought about the vagaries of fate that had led him to commit what he himself considered an outrageous act, an act that would keep him from English shores for many years to come, and for an unwonted moment, he felt doubt in himself that he would eventually succeed.

He felt the wet of her tears touch his shoulder and brought his hand up to brush them away. She tried to pull away from him, but he held her tight. "Go to sleep, Cassandra. All will be well, you will see."

"Damn you to hell, you bastard. If I were a man, I would stick a sword through your gullet."

"If you were a man, I would be cast in the role of pederast, a thought I find truly appalling. You will have countless hours to upbraid me. I suggest that you sleep now. Your wits will be all the sharper in the morning."

Countless hours—his words rang like a death knell in her mind. Damn you to hell, she swore silently, pulling herself from despair. I will escape you.

Chapter 8

For an instant, Cassie was at home at Hemphill Hall, in her sunlit bedchamber, waiting to hear Dolly Mintlow's shuffling steps at her door with her morning cup of chocolate.

Her bed seemed to lurch wildly, and she awoke with a start.

She grabbed at the lattice headboard as the yacht gave a loud creak and heeled sharply to port. She sat up and gazed dumbly about the cabin, eerily gray in the dull morning light cast through the square bow windows. Heavy rain battered the yacht, and thunder sounded like muted gunshots overhead. Would be that it were, she thought, her throat constricting. She prayed that the earl and his precious yacht would be plummeted by the storm to the bottom of the Channel. At least her nightmare would be over and she would truly be an eternity away from Edward and her family. The yacht creaked and floundered, but the wild lurching lessened, and it held, she imagined, to its course.

"Thank God for the storm," she whispered. It was in all likelihood the only reason he was not with her. At the thought of the earl returning, she swung her legs over the side of the bed and stared down at herself. She was quite naked. She rose slowly, aware of a dull twinge of tenderness between her thighs. She drew a deep breath to steady herself and made her way carefully to the commode. She poured water from the fat-bellied pitcher into the basin and began methodically to bathe herself. This was to have been my wedding day, she thought blankly, oblivious to the water sloshing over the sides of the basin onto the carpeted

floor. She splashed water over her face furiously, for she
felt tears welling in her eyes.

She cursed at the sight of her tattered gown tossed in a
heap where the earl had left it the night before. As she
had no intention of facing him naked, she opened the oak
armoire and eyed the row of brightly colored gowns. She
thought belatedly of undergarments and jerked open the
drawers of the dresser. She ground her teeth at his thor-
oughness, and quickly shrugged on a set of exquisite lace
and silk underclothes. She selected the least colorful gown,
a soft dove-gray muslin, but discovered that its neckline
wasn't as high as she'd hoped. The gown fit her perfectly,
just as did the undergarments. She pulled an ivory-handled
brush through her tangled hair, tied it at the nape of her
neck with a black ribbon, and smoothed the muslin skirt.

Once fully clothed, she felt more confident. She walked
to the closed cabin door and gingerly turned the knob. It
was locked, of course. Her anger rose with her confidence,
and she found herself fairly daring him to enter.

She paced in impotent frustration, her steps growing
more certain as she discovered the rhythm of the yacht.
Her stomach growled for her breakfast, and she cursed him.
Was he trying to starve her into submission?

The wild pitching of the yacht became gradually more
predictable, and the pounding rain, too, slowly lightened.
She turned at the sound of footsteps outside the cabin door
and squared her shoulders.

A key grated in the lock and the door swung open. The
earl strode in, filling the doorway. He was like a vital,
threatening force, and she drew back from him. She saw a
black canvas cape, glistening with drops of rain, lying in the
companionway outside the door before he shoved it closed.

"Good morning, Cassandra," he said, his voice obnox-
iously cheerful, as he wiped his full-sleeved shirt over his
wet brow. "Or rather I should say good afternoon."

She gazed at him, not speaking.

"The gown becomes you," he continued easily, his gaze
sweeping over her stiff figure. "I trust everything else that
I purchased for you fits as well."

She thought of the silk underclothes that caressed her

and took a step backward, her hand moving unconsciously to cover the expanse of her white bosom.

The earl, seemingly blind to her discomfort, walked to the table, poured himself a glass of water, and tossed it down. "Scargill will be here momentarily with our lunch. Forgive him for not bringing you breakfast, but he has been mightily occupied. Channel storms can be dangerous, you know, else I would have never left the warmth of our bed." He pictured her as she looked in sleep, her face peaceful and her golden hair fanned over her shoulders and breasts. When he had reluctantly eased away from her early in the morning, she had sighed softly and curled into a small ball, her sleep unbroken.

"My lady is remarkably silent today," he remarked casually, as he sank down into a chair. "No venomous words? I shall begin to believe you afraid of me, Cassandra, if you continue to cower so in the corner."

She said, "I was hungry, my lord, but enduring your presence has made me quite lose my appetite."

"I do hope you regain it for I should not like your splendid charms to waste away."

There was a light knock on the cabin door, and at the earl's command, Scargill entered, his arms laden with covered plates.

The valet glanced furtively at Cassie as he moved silently about the table, setting the places. Although she tried valiantly to ignore him, she felt her cheeks grow red. She wanted to dash to the mirror above the dresser to see if she somehow looked different, if her expression, her eyes perhaps, betrayed her lost innocence. She became aware that the earl was speaking to her and raised her eyes warily to his face.

"The idea was mine," he was saying modestly. "There may be a veritable tempest above deck, but your plate will remain just where you place it."

She looked blankly at the heavy pewter dishes.

"Loadstones," Scargill said, lifting a dish for her inspection. "Ye see these strips here? Ye set the dish along this line and it will take a man's heavy hand to pry it up. If ye will be seated, madonna, I've a tasty lamb stew for yer lunch."

The talk of loadstones flitted from her mind, for the smell of the lamb stew made her mouth water. She did as she was bid, wondering while she sat down at the table why he had called her "madonna." She ate her fill, all the while keeping her eyes upon her plate.

The earl regarded her from time to time, but remained silent, guessing that any attempt at conversation from him would make her forget her hunger. He regretted the storm that had kept him away from her throughout the morning. He knew she was in turmoil and he wanted to be with her, if only to give her the chance to lash out at him. He cursed the fickleness of the weather.

At the close of the silent meal, the earl tossed his napkin on the table and rose. "I am sorry to leave you again so soon, my dear, but Mr. Donnetti is laid up with influenza and Angelo is uncomfortable at the helm in such weather. My strong hand is much needed, elsewhere."

Cassie thoughtfully sipped her wine. "I will pray that you fall overboard, my lord, though I doubt that even the fishes would be interested in your carcass."

"Excellent. And I had feared your wits had grown dull in my absence."

He gave her a bow, and left the cabin.

Cassie's shoulders sagged within minutes of his leaving. The lamb stew did not settle well in her stomach and she stared resentfully around the cabin, knowing her nausea would only increase if she remained confined. She walked to the window and pressed her cheek against the glass, trying to ease her discomfort by watching the tossing sea outside. Her disgruntled stomach slowly righted itself, and she resumed her ferocious pacing. She considered how she could escape him, but nothing occurred to her that was in any way reasonable, and she turned her thoughts to other things, out of frustration. She thought about the earl and wondered if he were not very likely mad to have done what he did. She did not care about him or his motives, only that he had turned her life into a shambles. He had had the effrontery to tell her that he loved her, that he wished to wed her, and had then proceeded to force her. Although he had not overly hurt her, she felt humiliated that a man could do such a thing to her. She remembered him holding her down, caressing her body and thrusting himself into her. Her nausea returned, and she walked with slumped shoulders back to the window. *This cannot be happening to me,* she thought. Although she did not wish to, she thought of Edward and of their wedding. In her mind's eye, she lovingly fingered the fine Brussels lace that layered the bodice of her wedding gown. She pictured his face, his brown eyes heavy with desire for her, and wondered what her wedding night would have been like with him. His eyes were not filled with desire now; they would be dimmed with grief. A lone tear squeezed from the corner of her eye, and, angrily, she dashed it away. She raised her fisted hand toward the quarterdeck.

"Damn you to hell!"

She drew up in her tracks, and turned a confused face toward the cabin door. Was that a chuckle she heard?

The door swung open, and she saw the earl's laughing face. "My poor Cassandra, just tell me which of my belongings has so angered you and I shall stick my sword through it."

"Then you may stick it through your black heart."

He grinned at her and tossed her a bundle of clothing. "Here, my love, change into these and you can come up on deck with me. The breeches are a donation from the smallest of my men."

She wanted to yell at him to take the clothes and himself to perdition, but she realized that she had to get out of this wretched cabin and settle her stomach. She thought of the salt spray on her face and the feel of the wind against her, and nodded. She bent down, picked up the breeches and the shirt, and held them against her chest.

"You will find boots in the armoire. I will come back for you in five minutes."

When the earl returned, Cassie was seated on the settee tugging on her boots.

"May I assist you, Cassandra?"

She ignored him. When she rose, the soft leather riding boots hugging her calves, she saw that his eyes were sweeping over her.

"You cannot be so unfamiliar with men's breeches," she said, and walked toward the door, holding herself stiffly so that her hips would not sway.

"It is good of you to remind me," he said.

Bundled in a large canvas cape, a woolen cap pulled over her head, Cassie walked onto the deck. The earl held her arm tightly, as if he thought her a child who would hurt herself if not kept on a short leash. She ignored him and raised her face to the spattering rain, closing her eyes for a moment as she drew a deep breath of fresh salt air.

She had hoped to make out land, but the yacht was shrouded by low billowing dark clouds that stretched impenetrably as far as she could see. The sails were tightly furled against the ripping cross-winds, and the huge masts, like winter-stripped trees, reached starkly upward. The Union Jack still fluttered at the jackstaff, and she wondered idly why the earl had not secured it. The yacht suddenly slammed at an odd angle through a deep trough of a wave, and she was thrown against the earl. He gripped her arm more tightly, and smiled.

"An awesome and beautiful sight, is it not? I have always fancied the notion of men daring to combat the power of the sea, with naught but their will and the strength of their arms. We have again won, for the winds have slackened. Perhaps we shall even see a glimmer of sunlight before nightfall."

Cassie was not heeding him; her attention was upon the canvas-cloaked sailors, crouching forward into the force of the wind as they worked the rigging.

"We are sailing too high in the wind," she said, steadying herself on the rigging.

The earl gazed down at her a moment, an arrested expression in his eyes. "I do believe you are right."

There seemed to be pride as well as amusement in his voice, and Cassie looked away, wondering why she had even said anything.

"Would you care to take the helm, Cassandra?" he asked as they gained the quarterdeck.

"I?" She brushed the rain from her face and looked at him.

"Certainly." He continued casually. "If you do not mind though, I do not think it wise to let my men know. They would be aghast if they found out an eighteen-year-old girl was holding their lives in her hands. Come, we shall relieve Angelo."

He clasped her hand firmly in his and guided her carefully over the slippery deck down into the cockpit. He tapped the small, black-cloaked sailor on the shoulder and ordered him in flawless Italian to take himself below-deck. She saw Angelo's dark gimlet eyes dart over her as he released the helm to the earl. With a salute to his sodden woolen cap, he turned and walked jauntily away on the lurching deck, as surefooted as if it were a drawing room floor.

"Come here, Cassandra."

The earl pulled her in front of him before the wide, spike-handled wheel and raised his arms in a circle about her, his billowing cloak hiding her from view.

"The helm is yours."

She wanted to yell at him that she wanted nothing to do with either him or his miserable yacht, but the temptation to take the helm of such a magnificent vessel kept her quiet. Without looking at him again, she grasped the smooth wooden spikes of the wheel and felt the strength of the sea. She felt a surge of sheer joy sweep through her at the challenge she was facing. A towering wave slammed against the bow, and the yacht yawed, jerking the wheel to starboard. She felt sharp pain in her arms as she tried to pull the massive wheel back to port.

The earl knew he had placed her in unfair disadvantage, but fought the impulse to help her. He rested his hands lightly on her shoulders and felt her muscles tighten as she struggled to control the wheel.

"I believe you said we were too high in the wind?" he said coolly, as the yacht glided smoothly, for the moment, in the trough of a wave.

"Aye," she said. She clutched at the handles and threw her weight to port, pulling with all her strength. She overshot and knew an instant of panic as the yacht heeled sharply. Her feet slipped out from under her, but she did not release the wheel. She felt the earl's hands about her waist, hauling her upright, but he made no move to pull her out of the way. With her arms stretched wide to encircle the wheel, she did not have the strength to steady it. She chewed furiously on her lower lip, smiled suddenly into the battering wind, and placed both hands on one side of the wheel. Slowly, panting with effort, she bent her knees to gain the needed leverage, and pulled upward. She gave a shout as the yacht righted.

"Bravo, Cassandra. An ingenious solution. With practice and of course my instruction, you'll make a fine helmsman."

"I have no need and no desire for any instruction from you, my lord."

He merely smiled at her. "You think not, Cassandra? Well, we shall just have to see."

Although she did not like his tone, she held her peace and concentrated her attention on the demands of the yacht. When he took the wheel from her after some fifteen minutes, she was not loath to give it up, for her arms were trembling with fatigue. The ease with which he brought the yacht to obey his slightest command did nothing to improve her temper.

"Look to starboard, Cassandra."

Cassie followed the earl's direction and saw a blurred rainbow across the horizon, illuminated like a brilliant stained window by a sliver of late afternoon sun that sliced through the dark clouds. She breathed in the beauty of it, but said nothing. There was nothing she would share with this man.

"Angelo is back to relieve us. You are soaked through, Cassandra. It's time for a hot bath."

She shook her head vigorously, wet strands of hair slapping her cheek. He released the wheel to Angelo and turned to her. His hands closed about her shoulders and she shivered, not from cold, but from the threat of him.

His voice grew hard. "Do not forget, Cassandra, that I am the captain. You will do as I tell you, just as everyone else does on this yacht."

"And just what will you do if I do not obey your orders, captain? Toss me to the fishes? Keep me prisoner in that wretched cabin all of the time?"

The earl gazed down at her upturned face, flushed and rain-streaked, framed by the woolen cap pulled nearly to her eyebrows. He felt her fear of him and imagined that if he allowed it she would remain above deck until she collapsed from cold and fatigue.

A smile touched his lips. "I could beat you, I suppose. Your arms are likely so tired, though, that you would scarce give me a good fight. Do not make me carry you below-deck, Cassandra, in front of my men."

Cassie eyed the small Angelo and hoped that he did not understand English. She felt humiliated and helpless, without choices.

The earl arched a black eyebrow at her and said to the helmsman, "The helm is yours, Angelo. The weather is clearing and your evening should not be too unpleasant.

"Come, Cassandra."

The short command brooked no refusal. Cassie bit her lower lip and reluctantly placed her arm into his.

As they left the quarterdeck, she was thinking of Angelo and whether she would be able to enlist his support. It seemed unlikely. There was another man, though, the earl's first mate. Perhaps he would not be so loyal to the earl as Angelo was likely to be. She asked casually, "Who is Mr. Donnetti, your first mate who is ill?"

If the earl wondered about her reasons for asking about his first mate, he gave no sign of it. "A man to whom I would entrust my life, and yours. He is of mixed parentage, as am I. His mother was French. Donnetti became a mercenary in the French army. When it was demanded of him to become a French spy in Genoa, he refused. It was my gain to save him from assassins. However, I was unable to save his wife or child."

Cassie shivered. Violence in almost any form was alien to her. It was also borne forcibly upon her that Mr. Donnetti, if the earl's story was true, was very unlikely to help her.

"He will be fit soon, Scargill tells me. Once we reach Genoa, and remove to my villa, he will be captain of *The Cassandra* in my stead."

Cassie could not imagine being in Genoa, a place that was as foreign to her as faraway China. And one did not live in a villa; one lived in a manor or a hall, or perhaps an abbey. She felt tears sting her eyes, and she stumbled. The earl's arms were about her in an instant, steadying her. She hated herself at that moment; it was her physical weakness that ensured his mastery over her. She pulled away from him and hurried down the companionway toward the cabin.

She heard him say easily behind her, "It is my experience that the day following a storm is glorious. If I am proven right, you will be able to see the coast of France."

Her hand was on the doorknob when he said, "Please remove your cloak, Cassandra, I do not wish the carpet to become soaked."

She shrugged out of the heavy canvas and pulled off the woolen cap. Her hair cascaded down her back in salty wet ringlets. His hand touched her arm, and she turned unwillingly to face him.

"Take off your wet clothes. I will be along presently after I order up hot water for our bath and our dinner."

He opened the cabin door and gently pushed her inside. "Please do not shove the furniture against the door. It might put me out of temper."

Cassie slammed the door closed on his smiling face. She stripped off her wet clothing as quickly as her cold fingers would allow. Fearful that he would return at any moment, she pulled on a dark blue velvet dressing gown from the armoire and sashed it tightly about her waist. She wrapped her hair in a thick towel and fastened it turban style about her head.

She walked to the center of the cabin and stood waiting. Someone had attended to the cabin. Scargill, most likely. The lamps were lit against the dim late afternoon light, the bed was neatly spread, its bright blue cover smoothed. Her tattered gown was gone. She glanced at the clock atop the earl's desk and saw that it was nearly five o'clock. Without wishing to, she pictured the dining room at Hemphill Hall, festively decorated for the wedding dinner. There would be no garlands and white streamers; there would be only the black somberness of tragedy. *Edward, I don't know if I can bear it.* And there would be much more to bear, she knew. She had no doubt that he would rape her again, and she sagged where she stood.

The cabin door opened, and the earl entered, followed by two hefty sailors, each carrying buckets of steaming water. Cassie moved away, watching silently as the copper tub was filled. She heard the earl order the sailors to bring more water and leave it outside the door. He turned his eyes upon her, studying her.

"Your bath awaits. Because I am a gentleman, I shall let you go first. There is lavender-scented soap for your hair, your favorite."

It did not occur to her to question his knowledge of her soap, for she was frantically searching for a screen to keep her hidden from his view. Always, at home, Dolly had placed a screen in front of her tub.

"Come, Cassandra, before the water cools. Since I am to follow you, I have no wish for a cold bath." He saw her strained embarrassment at the thought of stripping naked in front of him and cursed the violent storm that had taken him from her side early in the morning. She had had a day to steel herself against him.

"I would like a screen."

"There is none," he said crisply. "I shall keep my back to you." At least for the moment, Cassandra, he amended silently to himself.

Cassie walked slowly to the tub and unwound the towel from her head. She made no move to pull off her dressing gown until he turned away and poured himself a glass of wine.

The earl heard the gentle splash of water and turned to see her, chin high in the water, her wet hair fanning about her like a golden cloud.

He downed the remainder of his wine, stretched loudly,

and stripped off his own damp clothing. She lowered her head as he strode, naked, to the armoire, and shrugged into his own black velvet dressing gown. The wine relaxed him, and he eased into the large leather chair at his desk. It had been a damnably long and fatiguing day, a wasted day. He watched her from beneath closed lids as she clumsily tried to lather her hair. It was likely, he thought, a smile upon his lips, that this was one task she rarely performed by herself. Likely too that her arms ached from her exertion at the helm. Perhaps tonight, he thought, he could make her respond to him. He felt his loins tighten, picturing her naked in his arms. He rose and walked to her.

"Since I have deprived you of your maid, the least I can do is offer my services." He picked up a hank of wet hair.

She jerked away and winced, for he did not release her hair. She felt her body tense with fear. "Can you not even keep a simple promise, my lord? You did say you would keep your back turned."

"For God's sake, Cassandra, I merely wish to help you. You need not fear me, you know. I assure you that when I wish to make love with you, you will know it."

"I do not wish your help and I am not afraid of you."

He grinned down at her. "Such a liar you are, my dear. What a mane of hair—you've more than my stallion, Cicero."

"I don't give a damn about your wretched horse."

"I don't propose to argue with you further. Hush, and accept my help."

She ground her teeth and bowed her head. As he vigorously lathered her hair, she dropped her hands and furtively covered her breasts.

"Would you like me to scrub the rest of you?"

"No. And you may remove yourself, my lord, so I can rinse my hair."

He returned to his chair, sat down, and closed his eyes, allowing himself to be lulled by the gentle rocking of the yacht. When he opened them, she was sitting on the edge of the bed in her dressing gown, toweling her hair. He rose and stretched.

"Prudish modesty really doesn't become you, Cassandra," he said as he stripped off the dressing gown. He was amused when her eyes, despite herself, fell to his belly, and he felt himself respond to her gaze.

"There is nothing like a hot bath or a lady's eyes to revive one," he said as he eased himself into the tub.

Cassie did her best to ignore him, but his booming baritone voice soon filled the cabin. He sang a lusty sea chanty, and she felt her cheeks flush red at the vivid image of the serving maid lifting her skirt for the amorous captain.

"I would that you be quiet."

He laughed and stepped from the tub, huge and dark and dripping wet. "Would you care to hand me a towel?"

"Fetch it yourself, my lord."

"Would you care for some more wine, Cassandra?"

Her hair swirled softly against her cheek as she shook her head.

"Shall I peel an orange for you?"

"No, I am quite full, my lord."

"Excellent. I am delighted that my chef has again pleased you." He paused a moment, and added softly, "And now it is time for me to show you that I, too, can please you."

"You will not, you must not." She pressed herself flat against her chair.

"Ah, yes, my love," he said, and rose to pull at the bell cord.

Her weariness fled, and she slipped nimbly out of her chair. Instead of fear, she felt numb with anger.

"Damn you, you cannot be such a villain."

There came a knock on the cabin door, and Scargill entered.

"All was as you wished it, my lord?" he asked carefully. He was acutely aware of the shrinking girl cowering in the corner and did his best to ignore her.

"Most admirable, given the storm and its constraints in the galley. You are much in need of your rest, Scargill. Remove the dishes and take yourself to bed."

"Aye, my lord. Is there aught else that you wish?" A foolish question, he thought, as he followed his master's eyes toward Cassandra. She looked like a skittish filly, ready to bolt if but given the chance. He prayed that his lordship knew well what he was doing. He filled his arms with the heavy pewter dishes and bowed himself out of the cabin, straining under their weight.

The earl leaned back in his chair and tapped his finger-tips thoughtfully together. "At least you are not wearing that damnable gown."

"You will not touch me, my lord."

"I fear you are growing repetitious, Cassandra, in your conversation. How else will you learn a woman's pleasure if I do not touch you?"

"I will never feel anything but hatred for you, I swear it. Damn you, take me home."

He waved away her words and rose.

"No." She thrust her hands in front of her, but he pulled her to him, crushing her arms to her sides. She jerked her head away from him, but his mouth found hers, the heat of his breath upon her as he forced her lips to part. She struggled as she felt his hand upon her buttocks, his fingers caressing and exploring her through the velvet.

"No!" she yelled again as his mouth left hers. But his mouth was on her throat, his tongue tracing over her wildly beating pulse.

Even as she twisted against his arm, she felt his fingers pulling free the sash from her waist and easing her out of the dressing gown. She was oddly aware of the soft brief touch of velvet at her ankles. She shuddered at the cold air upon her back, and the fierce heat of him against her. She had scarce time to draw her breath before he had shrugged off his own dressing gown. To her horror, he lifted her off her feet and pressed her belly against him.

"No. You will not rape me again." Her final words were muted as he closed his mouth again over hers. She felt his tongue probing her mouth and the incredible power of his surging body, searing her, engulfing her in his passion. Her mind froze and her body went slack against him. An intense shudder coursed through her belly. She whimpered softly, aghast at herself.

"I don't believe that I will, Cassandra," he said. He looked into her eyes, glazed with confusion and with burgeoning passion. He wanted her to moan her desire into his mouth, to welcome him into her body.

"Please do not," she whispered, but he paid no heed and carried her to the bed. She felt the smooth, cool cover beneath her back, and his hard body against her as he pressed himself down upon her. She felt the hair on his chest against her breasts, and his swelled sex, frightening and urgent, between her thighs. She thought wildly of Edward, of his love for her, of his passion, and an anguished moan broke from her mouth. Whether it was from the pain of her loss or from the scalding sensation building within her, she did not know. She realized dimly what was happening to her and she fought with all her will to deny herself and him.

His mouth caressed her breast, and she felt both her body and her will to resist him begin to slip away from her. She cursed herself, willing herself to fight him, but her hands lay limply above her head, clasped lightly in his.

He reared back and her body cried out at the loss of his touch. She drew a ragged breath, and curled her hands, now free, into fists to strike him. She felt his tongue caressing her breasts and then her belly.

"No," she said, forcing her body to tense. But his mouth closed over her, and she knew that she could not bear it if he were to stop. She felt her body opening to him, felt her hips moving upward against his mouth. Her hands closed over his shoulders, kneading the taut muscles, pressing at him to bring him closer to her.

Suddenly, with a force that left her gasping, a shock of burning pleasure exploded within her. His mouth left her, but the burning need remained, and she was trapped within herself, within her own passion. She moaned aloud, not really understanding, a helpless cry of frustration.

When he drove into her, her body surged to meet him. She felt his belly against her, felt him driving into the depths of her. Her hands moved down his back, urging him, drawing him closer. She was aware of his ragged breathing above her cries. A jagged moan broke from her throat and she cried breathlessly, "Please, oh please." Her hips thrust up against him and her legs, without instruction, wrapped themselves about his sides.

Suddenly, her legs stiffened as incredible spasms of pleasure crashed through her, holding her a willing prisoner for an endless moment. She cried aloud, unable to help herself. She felt his hot breath against her cheek, and then his mouth closed over hers and a tremendous shudder passed the length of him. He moaned his release into her mouth.

Cassie lay quietly beneath him, thinking nothing, wanting nothing. She was breathing heavily, between parted lips, and felt her heart finally slow its furious pounding.

"I don't want to crush you, Cassandra," the earl said, and slid his arms beneath her back. He rolled onto his side, bringing her with him, and clasped her tightly against him. He gently stroked her tumbled hair as she lay slack, soothing her, comforting her. He lightly kissed her temple and stroked her. He drew a deep, relieved breath, a slight smile touching his lips. She was capable of passion that rivaled his own. He wanted to tell her that she had brought him to consummate pleasure. He held his tongue, unwilling to risk her struggling away from him. The smile on his lips became rueful. She would likely yell at him like a fishmonger's wife on the morrow; her intense pride would force her to. She would see passion at his hands as submission to him. He did not mind that, for now; he was confident now that he would make her forget her viscount. His fingers curled around her buttocks, lightly caressing, and he heard her sob softly, deep in her throat. He drew back so that he could see her face.

Tears were welling in her eyes and rolling down her cheeks. "I have betrayed him. God, I have betrayed him."

He drew her closer and stroked his cheek against hers, wiping away her tears.

"No, Cassandra," he said, his mouth next to hers, "it is not for you to cry. You have betrayed no one. You must believe that."

She drew another sob and he kissed her ear, her smooth cheek, and gently nudged back her head until his mouth found hers. He tasted the salt of her tears upon her lips.

To his delight, she made no move to pull away from him. Though she kept her lips tightly locked, he felt her quicken. He grew hard again and he felt himself filling her once more. His fingers moved over her, lightly teasing, and her soft belly trembled against him. He pressed his mouth more firmly against hers.

"Please, no," Cassie whispered, only to feel his tongue smooth over her mouth. He was moving slowly, deep within her, his hand cupping her hips to press her against him. She drew a deep breath, and slowly, inevitably, she let herself move against his thrusts.

He withdrew from her and his fingers caressed her. She thrust her hips toward him and pounded at his chest until she felt him enter her again.

The earl clasped her to him and rolled over onto his back, bringing her with him.

"I would look at you, Cassandra." He smiled at the dazed bewilderment on her face.

She tried to pull away from him, but he encircled her waist with his hands and drew her upright. She felt him deep inside her and quivered, not looking at him.

His hands moved from her waist, upward, to cup her breasts.

She moaned softly and spread her hands on his chest to support herself.

The earl went slowly with her. He lifted her, kneading her as he moved her over him and pressed his fingers against her belly, splaying them downward to caress her. She writhed at his touch, and her thighs tightened about his sides. She arched her back to draw him deeper. The intensity of her response broke his control.

Engulfed in her own desire, Cassie felt his shuddering climax deep within her, and gave herself to him and to her pleasure.

She had not the strength to support herself, and fell, her hair cascading over his face and shoulders, her cheek against the hollow in his throat. Gently, he straightened her legs and felt the length of her soft body against him.

"I love you, Cassandra."

His words floated vaguely through her mind, but they did not touch her. She fell into an exhausted sleep, lulled by the gentle rocking of the yacht and enveloped by his warm, hard body.

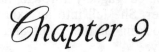

Chapter 9

Cassie awoke feeling cramped and hot. There was something tickling her lips. She opened her eyes and tensed. She was locked tightly in the earl's arms, her cheek against his shoulder. She drew back her head, scarcely able to weave her thoughts together. *I have given myself to this man.* She gave a shake of her head, recalling the intense, rampant sensations that had driven all thought from her mind, remembering vividly moaning her lust to him, holding him against her as if she would have dissolved into jagged pieces if he had released her. She was a woman now. But she had given herself to a ruthless man she did not love, the man who had abducted her. She wanted to scream her fury at herself and her hatred of him for making her respond to him. How could she have felt what she did but one night after he raped her? Her unspoken reply made her shrink within herself. *But I am a lady, an English lady.* No, she was not a lady, she was a slut, with no more moral fiber than the cheapest harlot, and she had betrayed Edward. She remembered her words, wrenched from her last evening. He had been gentle and comforting, had spoken words to her that had stilled her guilt. *I let him seduce me again and I did not want it to stop.*

Stop it, Cassie. She held her breath, for he stirred. How could she face him when she could hardly face herself? She felt his arm slip down to her hips. She tried to ease herself away from him, but realized that if she moved he would surely awaken. She looked down at him. He appeared strangely vulnerable in sleep, a lock of raven hair falling over his wide forehead. Vulnerable indeed, she thought. His black eyelashes were long and thick, lush as a girl's, but there was nothing else about him that was remotely feminine. She looked at his straight nose, a Roman nose, his finely etched cheekbones, his wide sensual mouth, his square jaw. She remembered other ladies of her acquaintance talking of him as devastatingly handsome, wickedly handsome. She decided that wicked was the more apt term. She felt his belly beneath her thigh, tautly muscled, his hair caressing her skin.

He sighed deeply in his sleep and rolled onto his back. Slowly, Cassie slipped out of his hold and wriggled off the bed. She breathed a sigh of relief that he still slept. The water in the basin was cold, but she paid it no mind. She wanted to be bathed and dressed before he awoke. She was leaning over, scrubbing herself, when she heard his voice from behind her, lazy and teasing.

"I would be delighted to perform that duty for you, Cassandra."

She whipped around, the washcloth dangling from her fingers. She looked wildly about for something with which to cover herself, but there was nothing. Her dressing gown was on the far side of the cabin, on the floor, where he had stripped it off of her the night before.

"You are awake," she said, holding the washcloth in front of her belly.

"Yes. I missed you. Come back to bed, Cassandra, it is so early the seagulls are still at roost."

"I am not tired."

"Then we will talk. You do not mind that I am unshaven, do you?"

"You are very dark."

"I really do not wish to come and fetch you." He patted the bed beside him.

She wanted to tell him to take himself to the devil, but she found herself gazing at his body. A light, tingling sensation pulsed through her belly, and she shivered. "We will talk?" she whispered. "You promise?"

"Of course. We shall do whatever you wish."

She placed the damp washcloth atop the commode and walked slowly to the bed, not looking at him. He held the cover back and she slipped in, pulling it down over her and clutching it to her throat.

She lay on her back, her eyes fastened on the cabin ceiling.

He was on his side facing her, his head propped up on his hand. "You slept well?"

Her wayward breathing calmed, for he had made no move to touch her. She replied honestly, without thinking, "Yes, very well."

"Excellent. I will not remind you of the reason." The teasing went out of his voice as he continued easily, "Don't be afraid of me, Cassandra. I will keep my word."

"I am not afraid of you."

"I know. Now you have only to be afraid of yourself."

She choked, hating him for so easily guessing her thoughts. She compressed her lips into a tight line and turned her face away.

"I told you last night that you had betrayed no one. It is true, you know."

"That is a lie." She turned back to face him, surprised at the desolate calmness of her thoughts and voice. She drew a deep, steadying breath. "But it will not happen again. I will not allow myself to feel such things again."

"One cannot control passion, Cassandra. It is a mighty force, one that cannot be denied. It simply happens between some people."

But I felt passion for Edward. But even as she thought it, she could not be certain. She had felt curiosity, to be sure; she had never doubted that the strength of her love for him would allow them to share physical pleasure.

He saw her confusion, and her pain, and sought for soothing words to help her. He was taken aback when she said suddenly, her voice deadly calm, "My mother. Did you feel such passion for her?"

"I never made love to your mother. As I told you yesterday, I was but a lad at the time, though as you can imagine, I dwelt with a boys's fervent imagination on what the experience would be like."

"Did she desire you?"

Constance. It had been such a long time since he had

thought of her in that way. So many years. If Cassandra did not so closely resemble her, her face would have become but a blurred image in his mind long ago.

"I cannot be certain. The years blunt the edges of every memory." He paused a moment and gazed closely at Constance's daughter. The physical similarities to his mind were all that they shared. He saw that she was waiting for him to reply, her eyes almost accusing on his face. He said deliberately, "Even though I was quite young at the time, I can remember thinking that your mother feared anything that she did not understand. That is why, I believe, she married your father, a man who cared little for people, a man who was most content contemplating his possessions. She was but another possession, one to be prized and cherished, to be sure, but nonetheless a possession."

She interrupted him, her teeth clenching. "You speak with such certainty about my family. Could you possibly know more of my father's character than did I?"

"You regarded him through a child's eyes, Cassandra. I know that you suffered because you sensed his indifference to you, but so did Eliott. At least he treated you no differently because you were a female."

She was silent. What he said was true, but it pained her too much to admit it. "We were speaking of my mother and your love for her."

"No," he corrected gently, "you asked me if she felt passion for me. You are unearthing old memories. In all honesty, no, I do not believe that she did. She was always afraid, not of herself, but of society and what her friends would think if they believed her to be indulging in such a liaison."

"If she had been your . . . lover, and if she had been afraid of herself, felt that she was betraying my father, had told you that she hated you, would you have released her?"

He smiled at her ruefully. "You are like an agile spider, weaving her web. I was younger than you at the time, Cassandra. For many years I believed that all women, all women with incredible beauty that is, were like Constance: vain, without character, save when it achieved their desires, and spineless. And, because she did as she was bid, and wed your father, she sealed her own fate. She used me, a boy who adored her, worshiped her, to bolster her image of herself as a desirable woman. Your father, she admitted to me once, was not a sensual man." He stopped abruptly, sensing her bewilderment.

"I will always hate you."

"And I, my dear, have enough love for the both of us."

She turned on him, rising up on her elbows, unaware that the cover dropped below her breasts. "It is ridiculous, my lord. You cannot love me. If I have my mother's face, I cannot help it. To love someone simply because she looks like someone else—it makes no sense."

He kept his eyes resolutely upon her face. "I suppose that I cannot expect you to have given me your full attention our first afternoon together. I told you then and I will repeat it—the fact that you resemble your mother merely pleases me, for she was a beautiful woman. All else about you is unique. It is you I love, Cassandra, no one else. When I saw you at seventeen I was more sure about my feelings for you than anything in my life." A sudden, rueful smile lit his eyes. "If you would know the truth, I had thought that I was beyond the age of romantic attachment, and it came as quite a shock to me, I assure you. I remember—it was not above a year ago—a dinner and ball at Belford House. At seventeen, it was your first excursion into society. You were so unlike the other girls of your age. Do you not remember dancing with me and in the most candid manner imaginable telling me that you were having a marvelous time but that your slippers were pinching your feet?"

She nodded slowly. "Yes, and you offered to lift me in your arms so I would not have to walk."

"And I recall that you laughed delightedly and told me it was a fine idea. You also told me that you were not a featherweight and trusted that I would be strong enough to oblige you. It required a great deal of resolution, Cassandra, not to oblige you."

A reluctant smile appeared, deepening the dimples on either side of her mouth. "I do not remember how it happened, but you escorted me to dinner. You filled my plate and I choked on my lobster patty because I was laughing at one of your stories. You called me graceless while you thumped me on the back. I thought you very nice, and terribly amusing."

"Do you not remember what else I said to you?"

She dropped her eyes from his face, and said in a voice dulled with insight, "You told me that you would be delighted to provide me instruction, since one day I would doubtless be called upon to fill a position of importance."

"Not precisely, but your memory is accurate enough. And the day I offered to mount you on an Arabian mare that I doubted you could handle. You coldly informed me, your eyes twinkling all the while, that you were quite up to snuff and could manage any piece of horseflesh from my stable. I recall that you would have taken a nasty spill had I not, at the last moment, lifted you off the mare's back."

"Have you forgotten nothing?"

"Anything that concerns you, I trust not. I think you much liked being held in my arms, though you did not guess what it was that I was feeling for you. You quite artlessly confided in me that it appeared that I was certainly strong enough to oblige you."

Myriad other memories flashed through her mind, memories that now held new significance. What pained her most was that all the memories were pleasant, all filled with his wit and kindness. Oddly enough, she recalled now how some ladies had regarded her with suspicion, had treated her coldly; she had thought it was her youth, her inexperience. She saw now that it was jealousy, jealousy of her attachment to the earl.

"What are you thinking, Cassandra?"

"Nothing. I don't wish to speak any more about the past."

"Doubt it not, Cassandra, I will not change in my feelings for you."

"Nor will I, my lord." She saw that his eyes had fallen to her naked breasts, and she clutched wildly at the cover. His hand stayed hers.

"Leave me be. I don't want you."

He cocked a disbelieving eyebrow at her and lowered his mouth to hers.

Please, I don't want to feel anything. I don't want your passion.

She shoved at his shoulders and bucked her hips upward to push him away from her. Her mind fought him even as his body smothered hers, pressing her into the soft feather-down. His mouth closed over her breast, and his tongue caressed her. She felt her body urging her to surrender to him, to give in to her own senses, and her struggle dimmed, her mind releasing her, more quickly, more easily this time. She tangled her fingers into his thick hair, and tugged at him eagerly to bring his mouth back down to hers. She parted her lips to him and returned his kisses, frantically, urgently.

When he reared over her, she wanted to feel the power of him. He surged deep within her, possessing her, and she sobbed aloud, clutching his back. Shuddering waves of pleasure coursed through her and she could do naught but cling to him, moaning her climax into the hollow of his throat.

"Ah, Cassandra," he whispered, his breath warm against her lips. He pulled her onto her side, and took his own pleasure.

It was nearly ten o'clock at night. The earl rose from his desk, closed the ledger book, and stretched. He gazed at Cassandra, who was curled up on the settee, seemingly absorbed by the novel she was reading.

A smile turned up the corners of his mouth. Two fingers wrapped and unwrapped a long curl that fell over her shoulder. It was a habit of long standing, one that he remembered from over a year ago. The blue silk gown she wore was cut low over her breasts, with no adorning lace to hide the expanse of rounded white bosom. He pictured her freed from her chemise, and the feel of her breasts in his hands.

He smiled again to himself. During the last several days her struggle against him had become but a nominal reluctance. Actually, he amended to himself, that was not true of the days, only the nights. During the day, she lashed out at him, her temper, it seemed, made more acid because she gave herself to him willingly at night.

He walked over to her and held out his hand. "It's time to go to bed, Cassandra."

She shrank back against the brocade cushions and did not reply.

"Cassandra," he repeated softly, closing his fingers over her bare arm.

She pulled away. "I am not the least tired, my lord, and have no wish to go to bed."

There was something in her eyes, now resting fleetingly upon his face, that held him silent for a moment.

"You like the novel so very much, my dear?"

"Oh, yes," she said quickly, too quickly, pulling the slender volume close to her chest. "It is so very interesting, my lord, that I have no wish to put it down until I have finished it."

"Perhaps I should provide you with a tutor."

She stared at him, at sea.

"You have been reading the entire evening, and have managed to get only to the third page. Really, *cara,* with your obvious intelligence, I would expect a more believable lie than that."

She closed the volume with a snap. "Very well, my lord, you will have the wood without a coat of paint. I have no wish to be ravished by you tonight. I will sleep here, on the settee."

"Ravished? Good God, my girl, you know there has been no question of ravishment since our second night together. Indeed, I have sometimes felt that I am the one succumbing to you. Perhaps you fear that I will not wed you now that I have repeatedly plucked the fruit from the tree, so to speak?"

"You officious bore. I tell you again that I will never wed you. If you have a shred of honor, you will leave me be."

"I am sorry, Cassandra, but I do not believe honor has anything to do with our pleasure. Come, my love, I would like to hear your cries of passion again tonight."

Furious color stained her cheeks, and she blurted out,

"It's you who make me like that. I do not want to be abandoned, indeed, I never wish you to touch me again. Leave me now, I order you."

"That is a lovely gown," he said. "If you fight me, it will become shredded. You are a passionate, exciting woman, Cassandra, and I have yet to discover the depths of your feeling. No more nonsense. I want you in my bed and in my arms."

She squirmed from the settee and scrambled to stand behind it. The earl cocked an inquiring eyebrow, then shrugged. He turned and began to remove his clothing. He heard a relieved sigh, and said over his shoulder, "Although it was I who set the rules, you will abide by them. We will live as man and wife, and that, my love, means the intimacy of the marriage bed. Now, take off that gown."

"No."

Behind the furious defiance of that short word, his ears detected a pathetic plea, and he turned to face her, now dressed only in his breeches. He gentled his voice. "Why, Cassandra?"

Her fingers fretted mercilessly at the pleats in her skirt. "Please," she began, her voice barely above a whisper.

He strode to her and clasped her shoulders in his large hands. She stood rigid, even as his fingers caressed the slender column of her neck. He slowly traced the softness of her cheeks, and the firm line of her jaw.

"Why, my love? You know you will want me, you know that you forget your viscount in my arms. Let us not wrangle."

She raised her wide eyes slowly to his face, and he saw no fear in them.

He leaned down and closed his mouth over hers. She tried to pull free of him, but he held her fast, winding his fingers in the thick masses of hair that lay unbound down her back. She cried out softly, but not with desire.

He released her mouth, and she pleaded softly, "Please, you must not, I cannot—"

"What do you mean you cannot?" He raised her chin up with his thumbs, so she could not look away from him.

She flushed scarlet and closed her eyes tightly. "Please,"

she whispered, "cannot you simply leave well enough alone?"

Sudden understanding dawned upon him and, unwisely, he threw back his head and laughed.

"You beast. You braying ass."

He grinned down at her. "However could I forget that you must needs be a woman in all ways? I could show you, Cassandra, that your womanliness is but a minor obstacle to lovemaking." He stopped, for her face was pale with embarrassment.

"Perhaps some day soon," he said, and walked away from her.

He retrieved a full-cut white nightgown from the bottom drawer of the dresser and silently handed it to her. "You need not say it. I do think of everything. Never would I wish to wound your maiden's sensibilities. You may wear this garment a given number of nights each month."

He patted her cheek, dowsed the lamps, and climbed out of his breeches. As he climbed into bed, he heard her breathe a sigh of relief. Some minutes later, she slipped into bed beside him, and as was his habit, he pulled her into his arms and gently stroked her hair.

Chapter 10

"The stop knot is too loose, madonna," Angelo said in his soft Italian. He dropped to one knee and with light, sure tugs, adjusted the tension. He grinned as he handed it back to Cassie, shaking his dark head. "A lady as a sailor, I never would have believed the day. You'll do, madonna, you'll do."

"*Grazie,* Angelo." She flushed slightly at his rare words of praise.

He nodded and turned away from her at the shouted command of Mr. Donnetti. In the next moment, he was agilely climbing the rigging of the mainmast.

Cassie watched his graceful ascent. Squawking seabirds soared in wide circles above, hoping, she supposed, for some stale crusts of bread. She rose slowly and dusted her knees, an unnecessary gesture, since the deck always sparkled from the continual efforts of the Genoese sailors. She gazed to port. In the hazy afternoon sun, she could barely make out the coastline of Spain, some twenty miles distant.

"Ye can't see much from here."

She turned to Scargill, who was shading his eyes with his hands, looking toward land.

"Ye'll turn dark as a blackamoor, if ye don't have a care." He indulgently eyed the light sprinkle of freckles across the bridge of her nose.

She raised her golden-tanned face toward the sun, disregarding him. "We will put into port, Scargill?"

"Nay, madonna, it's hardly likely."

At the tightening of her lips, he added lightly, "If ye know yer politics, ye'll realize that the Spanish are no friends to the English."

"His lordship does not have a Spanish flag?"

Scargill shook his head at her ill-disguised sarcasm.

She doubted that the earl would put into port in any case, unless, of course, she thought bitterly, he were to lock her in the cabin for the duration. At least this wasn't the case as long as they were at sea. The earl had given her free run of the yacht, though he forbade her the wearing of breeches. "I think it would be unwise," he had said one evening, grinning at her crookedly, "to tempt my men more than they already are. The sight of you in breeches would doubtless encourage them to mutiny."

She looked midway up the mainmast at Angelo's perched figure and sighed enviously. Her skirts billowed in the sea breeze, and she slapped them down, her ill-humor mounting.

As though he had read her thoughts, Scargill said gently, "Ye know that his lordship is in the right, madonna. To see such a figure as yers climbing the rigging would surely cause the men to forget their duties. Ye wouldn't wish to be the cause of a man having the skin flailed off his back. It would be the lightest punishment his lordship would mete out, ye know."

"I daresay that such a display of viciousness would well fit his character."

Cassie bit her lip as the earl's voice boomed out behind her. "Perhaps, Cassandra, but then I have never informed you what your punishment for such disobedience would be."

She whirled about. "Is it also your habit to eavesdrop on other people's conversations, my lord?"

"There's no need to get yerself all a-twitter, madonna," Scargill said easily, raising a placating hand. "Ye know his lordship is the captain and thus must keep himself apprised of all that goes on."

"And just what would my punishment be, my lord?" Cassie demanded coldly, ignoring Scargill.

"What do you think would be just?"

"I would say, my lord, that the punishment I have received already at your hands is sufficient for anyone's lifetime."

The earl waved Scargill away, a signal that the valet obeyed with alacrity. He took a step nearer to Cassie, and she held her ground, her expression forbidding. His voice dropped to a caressing murmur. "It is no way my fault, Cassandra, that you have felt punished for our four days of abstinence."

"How dare you?" Angry and embarrassed color mounted her cheeks.

"How dare I what? Remind you that you are a woman and not a sailor to be climbing over the rigging dressed in breeches?" As the gleam of fury did not abate, he added placidly, "If we have another storm, I will approve the breeches for its duration."

"How very kind you are."

"Remind me to hide your dinner knife, *cara,* since you are in such a foul temper." She turned away from him, and he stood quietly for several moments watching her walk quickly to the forecastle deck where several of his men were working.

" 'Twould appear to me that ye make little headway, my lord," Scargill said pensively, walking into the earl's view. Out of habit, he smoothed down the coarse lock of red hair that fell over his forehead.

"It has been but two weeks," the earl said coolly, shifting his gaze toward the distant Spanish coastline. "If I do not despair of the outcome, why should you?"

Emboldened by the earl's direct question, Scargill said quickly, "Ye have the habit of twitting the girl mercilessly, my lord, and though the madonna is sharper in her wits than most ladies I've known, she has no chance with ye, what with ye being so much older and experienced. Hardly loverlike ye be, my lord."

The earl laughed. "The madonna, as you and the men persist in calling her, despite her tender years, is quite able to cross swords with me. Verbally that is. And as to my not being loverlike, I doubt that you or anyone else is qualified to judge. Now, if you have done with dissecting my character, I suggest you speak with Arturo. I require a special dinner this evening for my lady, something very English

for her waning appetite. It will be in the nature of a celebration. You might even call it a monthly celebration."
Grinning to himself, he turned away, his destination the
helm and Mr. Donnetti.

As he strode along the highly polished deck, his eyes
strayed toward Cassandra, who was sitting cross-legged, her
skirts modestly tucked over her ankles, listening with avid
attention to undoubtedly outrageous tales spun by Joseph,
a rotund little Corsican once in the employ of the Barbary
pirates. Hie men had taken to her, no doubt about that. A
lady to her fingertips who did not lord it over any of them,
and a lady whose sailing skills bettered those of many a
man. When it became common knowledge that she spoke
Italian, he had noticed with a rueful smile that the habitual
foul language his men used all but disappeared.

The earl paused a moment and gazed up at the wind-
bloated sails, estimating their speed. Since the storm in the
Channel, the weather had turned glorious and warm.
Though it was the end of June, the Atlantic was not famed
for such a continued spate of good weather. If it held, they
would reach Genoa a good week beforetimes.

Cassandra was standing now, and the wind flattened her
skirt, outlining her hips and thighs. It was just as well that
the weather was so mild, he thought, for she held all his
attention. He felt a growing ache in his loins and turned
away. Tonight he would possess her body, just as she would
possess his. He did not believe that she would fight him,
for he had unleashed the woman in her, and their four
nights of abstinence had likely made her physical need as
great as his. He suspected that she desired him, despite her
monthly cycle, but he had not pushed her. He wanted her
to accept him as her companion as well as her lover. They
had passed hours on deck in the evenings, gazing at the
brilliant constellations, and he had spoken softly of the past
that he had known with her.

"Captain."

The earl wiped the placid smile from his mouth and
brought his attention to his first mate. "Yes, Mr. Donnetti?"

"There is a ship closing off port. She's likely Spanish."

He handed the earl a spyglass.

"It's a Spanish frigate, two gun decks. Keep us windward, Mr. Donnetti. The Spanish captain is a fool if he thinks to engage us."

"Aye, captain. The frigate is riding low in the water, heavily loaded, and cannot elevate her guns."

The earl lowered the spyglass. "Command the men to battle stations. If the Spanish captain is unwise enough to engage us, we will fire broadside as a lasting lesson and outrun her. Needless to say, our cargo is far too precious to risk full battle."

Cassie raised her head, startled at the sound of a beating drum.

"Beat to quarters!"

"Get below-deck to the captain's cabin, madonna," Joseph said sharply, and wheeled away from her, toward the gun deck.

"What is happening, Joseph?" she cried over the beating drum.

She whipped about at the sound of the earl's voice. "It's a Spanish frigate, Cassandra, and as yet, we do not know her intentions. Do as Joseph said and go to the cabin." She hesitated, and he roared at her, "Now! I will come to you when there is no more danger."

"But I would like to see—"

The earl grabbed her shoulders in an iron grip. "Dammit, do as I tell you. I do not want to have to worry about your safety when the ship must be my first concern."

"You needn't shout at me."

"Then obey me. That is an order." He pushed her away and strode toward the quarterdeck without a backward glance.

Cassie felt a surge of excitement, and her step lagged as she neared the companionway. Crisp orders boomed about her and purposeful sailors ran past her, oblivious of her presence. A Spanish frigate. She had never seen such a ship. Stealthily she made her way to the mainmast and crossed quickly, crouched over, to the railing. She saw the three-masted vessel bearing toward them, its hull massive even in the distance. She heard the earl's booming voice and felt the deck beneath her shift slightly as the port guns were hauled into the gunports, and the sailors shifted their iron mouths toward the approaching frigate. She felt goose-flesh rise on her arms. She guessed that the frigate was now only a mile distant.

"Damn," the earl cursed under his breath. "It appears that the fools want to test our strength. Order the first ranging shot, Mr. Donnetti. Perhaps that will be enough for them."

Cassie was thrown back on her heels as the four guns, in unison, belched forth their iron balls. She saw great explosions of white smoke, then veils of spewing water. In an instant, it cleared, and to her disappointment, the frigate emerged unscathed. She watched, her heart pounding in her chest, as it veered off.

Mr. Donnetti chuckled. "Cowards, the whole mess of them. One round from our guns and they scurry away, like rabbits."

"Don't underestimate them," the earl said softly. "My guess is that they are bound for bigger game and do not wish to risk any damage. Full into the wind, Mr. Donnetti, I have no desire to tempt fate if the Spanish captain happens to change his mind."

"Aye, captain," Mr. Donnetti said. The earl remained on deck until the frigate became but a distant white speck. Satisfied that there would be no more danger from that quarter, he made his way quickly toward the cabin. His eyes caught a flash of blue muslin at the base of the main-mast. He whirled about to see Cassandra gesticulating with great excitement to Joseph.

His stomach knotted in sudden fear for her, and then in anger. She had disobeyed him. If the frigate had engaged them, she could have been hurt, even killed.

"Cassandra."

She continued speaking to Joseph some moments more before turning reluctantly to face him.

"Come here."

Joseph's head jerked up at the deadly tone in the captain's voice, and he whispered urgently to Cassie, "Go quickly, madonna."

Because she had never seen the earl in a rage, Cassie shrugged her shoulders indifferently and took her time reaching him.

"What a paltry encounter, my lord," she said, clearly disappointed. "At least I have seen a Spanish frigate. Are they always so cowardly?"

The earl grabbed her arm, and, without a word, dragged her along the deck, down the companionway, and pushed her inside the cabin, slamming the door closed.

Cassie rubbed her arm when he released her and frowned at him. "You needn't be such a ruffian, my lord. Is it that you too are disappointed that there was no battle?"

"You disobeyed me, madam."

She blinked at the cold fury in his voice. "I believe, my lord," she said steadily, "that you are making a fuss out of nothing. There was no danger."

The earl held himself stiffly, his arms rigid at his sides. Her ridicule of the situation made him all the angrier.

"I will say it again, madam. You disobeyed me. You will now tell me why."

She stood her ground and raised her chin. "I did not think your order reasonable, my lord. The frigate was a good mile distant from us when we fired. Given that she was heavily loaded and thus unable to elevate her guns easily, we would have been able to outrange her, handily, even if she had chosen to engage us. The yacht is much faster and if there had been the need, we could have outrun her."

He was taken aback. "Just how the devil do you know that?" She had analyzed the situation with impeccable accuracy, and it did nothing to improve his temper.

"I do not know why men persist in believing that women are stupid, useless creatures who have nothing in their heads but spun cotton. You know that I have sailed all my life. Do you believe me so buffleheaded as to be ignorant of the subject?"

"Very well, Cassandra, I commend your education. But

the fact remains, madam, that you did not do as I bid you. Given all your experience and reading, you must know that without obedience and strict discipline, a captain cannot effectively command. Just what do you think would have happened if all of my men had decided to do whatever pleased them, rather than obey my orders? That, Cassandra, is insubordination, and subject to exacting punishment."

Her forehead knitted into a thoughtful frown, and her eyes wavered from his set face. She drew a deep breath. "Though I am not one of your crew, what you have said is just. A captain's orders cannot be ignored. I will submit to whatever punishment you deem fitting for what I have done."

"The punishment, madam, is at the very least a flogging that would take the flesh off a man's back."

She paled visibly.

He pressed his point, wanting to assure himself that she would never again do something so foolish and dangerous. "If a man were not to obey my order in the face of impending battle, I would seriously consider hanging."

There was silence between them for some moments. Finally, she said, "I think it would be wasteful of you to hang me."

A slight smile hovered at the corners of his mouth, and he sternly repressed it. "I doubt not that you are right. I have never cared for wasteful hangings. The offense, however, remains the same."

The earl found that his anger was rapidly dissipating. He had made his point well, and she had clearly accepted his reasoning. He thought to remove her obvious fear when she squared her shoulders and said in a calm voice, "I would ask only that you not demean me by flogging me in front of the men. Nor do you have to tie me up, for I will submit to your flogging."

He stared at her, at a loss. Although he greatly admired her courage, he wanted to enfold her in his arms and reassure her, to see the fear disappear from her eyes. But she would see that as an insult to her courage, condescension to her as naught but a weak woman. He would well imagine that she would be enraged, and justifiably so, for everything that he had said to her would have a hollow ring. He was struggling to find an answer to this ridiculous situation when she asked in the same calm voice, "What kind of whip will you use, my lord?" She added, poised still, "Do I take it from your silence that I must be flogged in front of the men? And tied to the mast?"

"No," he said finally, "I shall not beat you in front of my men, nor will I tie you down."

"Thank you," she said, her mouth now quite dry with fear. She closed her eyes a moment, praying that she would neither cry out nor faint. It was on the tip of her tongue to apologize to him, to beg him not to whip her, but she could not bring herself to do it.

"Will you do it now, my lord?"

"No, I think not," he said. "I will leave you, Cassandra, to think about what you have done. It will be settled when I return." Since he had no idea of what the devil he should do, he knew he had to have some time alone, to try and untangle this mess. He gazed a moment longer at her pale, set face, and left the cabin.

He paced the deck, deaf to the shouts of taunting laughter from his men as they waved toward the now-distant Spanish frigate.

"Ye do not seem justly pleased, my lord," Scargill said, as he walked into his master's preoccupied line of vision. "The men performed well, as if they had all been trained in the English navy."

The earl breathed deeply and turned rueful eyes to his valet. "It's not that, to be sure, Scargill. I have got myself in a rare mess and am wondering how the devil to get out of it."

"Ye speak in riddles, my lord."

The earl drew a deep breath and ran his fingers through his rumpled hair. "Cassandra disobeyed me, Scargill, and I was a forceful fool." As Scargill still gazed at him, at sea, he told him briefly what had passed between them. "She is at this moment," he concluded, "waiting for me to return to flog her. Her only request is that I not flog her in front of the men."

Scargill sucked in an appalled breath. "Jesus Christ," he said succinctly.

The earl slammed a fist against his open palm. "Hellfire and damnation, this entire situation is ridiculous. And you, Scargill, you have done naught but add needless expletives."

"I beg yer pardon, my lord, but it was a reference to the Almighty above, though I have gained no assistance from its use." He suddenly flung back his head. "I will take her place, my lord. Ye will have her watch and the lesson will never be forgotten."

"She called me a braying ass not long ago. Now I must bequeath that charming title to you. Under no circumstances would I do anything so reprehensible."

"Ye abducted a lady, my lord, and against her will."

"If you do not keep your tongue between your teeth, I shall have you flogged for insolence. If you have not the wit to see that the circumstances are utterly disparate, I wash my hands of you."

"Methinks it is the fiery Ligurian gentleman speaking and not the English lord."

The earl shot him a look so filled with frustrated anger that Scargill quickly mumbled an apology and fell silent.

The earl said finally, a black brow arched, "If you, Scargill, had disobeyed a direct order, even if it imperiled only yourself and not the yacht, you may rest assured that I would have had you flogged without hesitation."

"Aye, my lord, but I am a man."

"Ah."

"What will ye do?"

"Go to the devil," he said, and turned away.

Cassie heard the sound of his boots outside the cabin door, and quickly squared her shoulders. She pinched color into her cheeks and rose to stand by the table, one hand laid carefully on a chair arm to support her trembling legs.

He filled the cabin with his presence, as he always did, and her hand tightened about the chair. He looked like a pirate, she thought, with his black tousled hair above his thick-arched black brows, and his full-sleeved white shirt, open at the neck and topped with a loose black vest.

He closed the door behind him and leaned against it, his thumbs hooked in the wide leather belt around his waist. His expression was unreadable, but to her eyes, his mouth was set in a pitiless line.

"Is it to be now, my lord?"

The calmness of her voice was belied by the flash of fear in her eyes.

He said slowly, still hopeful of inspiration, "I am not certain if a flogging is what is most needful. Perhaps a flogging, like a hanging, would be wasteful."

Her fear made her blind. "Wasteful. It is your needless cruelty that is wasteful. Damn you, why must you torture me? Do it and be done."

He realized that there was no hope for it. Hellfire, he muttered under his breath. Aloud, he said, "Very well."

His voice sounded remote, and it required all her courage not to back away as he slowly unfastened the wide belt from about his waist. He dropped his hands and walked quickly to the dresser. From the bottom drawer, he drew out a soft, narrow leather belt.

"Strip to the waist, Cassandra."

His jaw tightened as he watched her trembling fingers prod at the tiny buttons on her bodice. She was as white as her chemise when she slowly slipped the lace straps from her shoulders and let the soft satin slip to her waist. Absurdly, she covered her breasts with her hands.

"Pin up your hair, it is covering your back."

As she jabbed pins haphazardly into the masses of hair, she remembered, foolishly, their verbal battle earlier in the day about what her punishment would be if she wore breeches without his permission. It had been so ridiculous; they had done naught but spar with words. She tried to think objectively about pain, but she could recall nothing but the broken arm she had sustained at ten years old after being thrown from her mare. She must have felt pain, she thought, but there was nothing real for her to grasp. She remembered the possets forced down her throat by Becky

Petersham, and the cast that made her skin itch, but no pain. She drew a deep, resolute breath and turned to face the earl, her hands still covering her breasts. She blanched at the sight of the belt, its buckle and clasp wrapped tightly about his hand.

"You may support yourself against the bookshelf."

She walked numbly to the inset mahogany bookshelves that lined the cabin wall beside his desk, her eyes resting foolishly for an instant on the novel she had been reading. She stretched her arms above her head and firmly clasped her fingers about the edge of a shelf. She rested her forehead against the edge of a lower shelf and clenched her teeth tightly together. Help me not to make a fool of myself, she pleaded, more to herself than to any deity. She tensed her muscles and waited. She knew he was standing behind her, his hand in all likelihood poised in midair, ready to lash the belt across her back.

You are a fool, my girl, she said to herself, her muscles straining in taut fear. You fight him with all your strength, yet the result is unbelievable pleasure. Yet now you stand of your own free will for him to flog you.

The earl lifted the belt only to lower it again. He looked at her slender white back. An errant strand of golden hair had escaped its pin and fell in a long lazy curl down to her waist. His fingers lifted the hair from her back. She quivered. His hand shook and again, he lowered the belt.

"Damn you," she said suddenly, her voice shrill in her fear. "Are you so cruel that you delight in making me wait, knowing what must come?"

The earl raised the belt and brought it down as lightly as he dared across her shoulders.

She tensed and tightened her fingers more tightly about the shelf edge, more from surprise than from pain. But when the belt slammed against her back again, she felt a tingling of pain that made her start.

Six lashes, the earl counted, knowing that he could give her no less. He rigidly controlled the strength of his arm, but still, it was not enough.

Cassie's eyes burned as the pain increased, but she made no sound. Her fingers dug into the shelf as she swore over and over that she would not disgrace herself and collapse. Suddenly, the burning pain ceased. She held herself rigid for several moments, waiting. She turned slowly and felt a raw throbbing as the shelf touched her back. She gazed up, unseeing, into his pale face.

"Is it over?"

"Yes."

"I am so glad. I feared that I would make a fool of myself."

She blinked her eyes upon his face and said, her voice breathless and high, "May I lie down now?"

"Yes. Let me help you."

He clasped his hands beneath her hips and raised her, careful not to touch her back. He laid her on her stomach, and she felt the softness of the cover beneath her breasts.

The earl stared down at her quiet figure. How many times he had read guilt and hatred in her eyes before he had brought her to pleasure. Yet now, he had inflicted pain and she had willingly accepted it. There had been no hatred in her fine eyes, only her fierce pride.

He shook his head and made haste to mix some laudanum with wine.

"I never faint, you know," she said as he handed her a filled glass.

"No, I wouldn't imagine that you would. It is wise that you lie still, Cassandra. This will make you feel better."

"What is it?" she asked after she had downed the wine.

"Laudanum and French burgundy. In a few minutes you will feel drowsy."

He fetched a soothing cream to rub into her back, but did not touch her until her head lolled on the pillow and her breathing evened into sleep. Six welts stood out against her white skin, red and ugly, but none so deep as to cause him worry. He gently rubbed in the ointment.

He eased her out of her clothes and pulled a cover to her waist, then drew up a chair beside her. He found himself studying her closely. Her beauty was startling, but he knew that his feeling for her was drawn strong by her own strength of character, and he reveled in the knowledge that he possessed her. Had she ranted at him, or even resorted to tears to save herself from punishment, he would not have loved her less. Perhaps, he thought ruefully, if she had guessed that her fierce sense of honor would result in his wanting her all the more, she would have behaved differently. But she would not know, for the time being; he would not tell her.

He had caused her many kinds of pain, he knew, and his jaw tightened in stubborn resolve. Someday, in the aftermath of their lovemaking, she would smile at him with love. Dammit, it would be so, he would make it be so.

Cassie stirred. Before she could plant her mind firmly in reality, she moaned dully from the effect of the laudanum. She opened her eyes and saw the earl gazing intently at her.

"What day is it?" she asked, and saw him blink.

"You have been sleeping for but an hour."

"How odd," she mumbled, and tried to raise herself on her elbows. She realized that she was naked and let herself fall again.

"There is no sign of the Spanish frigate?"

"No."

"Will my back be scarred?"

He grinned at her belated display of vanity. "I do not believe so. You will be sore for several days."

"You will not tell the men, will you, my lord?"

"I do not think that will be necessary," he said. Actually, he imagined that he would have a mutiny on his hands if his men were to discover what he had done.

He started forward in his chair at a tear that fell from the corner of her eye and trickled down her cheek.

"Cassandra," he said, uncertain.

She raised her hand and dashed it away. "I am sorry," she choked out. "The laudanum is making me a fool. I cannot seem to help it. I wish you would but leave."

"No. I will not leave."

She flinched at the anger she saw in his eyes. "Do not be angry. I am sorry to shame you."

He scraped back his chair and rose abruptly. He guessed that she felt pain but was too proud to admit to it. "Be quiet. It is not a question of shaming *me*. Do not move, I will get you more laudanum."

With shaking hands, he poured a few more drops into a large goblet of wine. It was much more than she needed, but he needed it to relieve his guilt as much as her discomfort.

He thrust the glass to her lips. "Here."

It took her some minutes to down the entire contents, and a trickle of wine fell down her chin. He wiped it away with his fingertip.

He realized that her wits were indeed addled when she clumsily pushed herself onto her side, facing him, heedless of her bare breasts. Her eyelids appeared heavy, her cheeks flushed.

"It is dreadfully uncomfortable to lie on one's stomach," she mumbled.

"I daresay that you are right."

"I feel rather strange, as if I were floating outside of myself. And my words don't seem to speak themselves easily."

The earl sat back in his chair and crossed his arms over his chest. "It is because you are drunk, Cassandra," he said.

"I have never been drunk before, you know," she said aloud, trying to focus her eyes upon his face. "Nor," she added thoughtfully, "have I ever been beaten before."

"I did not want to thrash you, but you gave me no choice."

Her hazy thoughts wove themselves together as his gently spoken words penetrated her mind. "No, there was no choice. You did what was just." She sighed and whispered, her words so slurred that he could barely make them out, "But there have been other things you have done to me, things you have made me feel that I did not wish. There was choice there, I think."

Before he could decide how to respond to her, she said, "Your laudanum and French burgundy have worked. I do not hurt now."

"I'm glad."

She closed her eyes and rested her cheek against the pillow.

He leaned forward and smoothed a strand of hair from her forehead. Her breathing was even. She slept.

He rose and pulled the cover again to her waist, and returned to his chair.

Chapter 11

The cabin door burst open, and Cassie quickly stepped back and clutched the satin chemise to her breast. The earl filled the doorway, looking, as ever, powerful and confident. "Can you not at least knock!"

"*E una bellissima giornata, cara.*"

"I do not care if it is foul or beautiful weather, my lord. You have no right to burst in unannounced."

He disregarded her outburst and studied her carefully. He could detect no remnants of pain, no discomfort, save, of course, her usual unease in his presence. He smiled, pleased with her temper. She had been too restrained the last day and a half. Of course, his dosing her wine with laudanum because he could not trust her to admit to any pain she felt had dulled her mind and rendered her more tractable.

"It would appear," he said easily, closing the door behind him, "that your temper at least is back to normal. I have come to help you dress. We are in the Straits of Gibraltar and have the good fortune of a westerly wind—very uncommon for the summer months."

For an instant, Cassie forgot her ire and the fact that she was clothed only in her petticoats. "The Pillars of Hercules," she said, her eyes sparkling with excitement.

"So you have learned your history, I see. Such knowledge you possess, Cassandra."

"I have enough knowledge to realize that you are an overbearing ass, my lord. Now, if you would cease your nonsense and leave, I will dress."

"How is your back?"

His abrupt inquiry took her off guard. Though she rarely

felt any pain, she had been on the point of fetching another chemise, for this one was embroidered with stiff lace that would bind tightly across her back. She didn't want his concern.

"I am quite all right now, my lord."

He frowned at the frothy satin and lace garment she still held protectively against her breasts. "Surely a muslin chemise would be more comfortable for you." Without a by-your-leave, he strode to the dresser and tossed undergarments aside until he found a soft, lightweight muslin chemise that was cut high in the back.

"Ah, here it is," he said, grinning at her. "It is fortunate that I thought to add this dowdy garment to your wardrobe, is it not?"

"It is obvious that you had in mind all along to beat me."

"Oh no," he said cheerfully. "Indeed, I can think of fewer things less pleasurable than beating you. But it is a question of control, is it not, Cassandra? I think we have both learned a lesson."

"You will never control me, my lord," she said in a voice of deadly calm. "And you are a fool if ever you begin to believe your own braying. I accepted my punishment from the captain of this ship. There is nothing that I will willingly accept from the man."

"How well you have trimmed my sails, *cara,*" he said, his calm undisturbed. "Before you lash out at me again, I wish to rub more ointment into your back. And you needn't argue with me, because if you do, it is likely that we will be through the straits and you will have missed your Pillars of Hercules."

She gnawed her lower lip in uncertainty, but she knew him well enough by now to realize that he would have his way. "Very well," she said, and turned her back to him.

The earl lifted her mane of hair, tousled from her night's sleep, and looked at her back, still lightly crisscrossed with fading welts.

"Bend over a bit and keep your hair out of the way."

His fingers made light circular movements over her skin, their motion gentle and caressing, turning her back white with the cream.

"Am I hurting you?"

Cassie jumped at his voice. "No. Please, my lord, just be done with it." He finally dropped his hands, and she drew a thankful sigh, allowing herself to relax.

He silently handed her the muslin chemise. She did not turn to face him until she had laced the bodice together over her breasts. Her expression was one of dogged wariness, and he smiled.

"I will await you on deck."

Ten minutes later, the earl turned to see her walking crisply toward him with the firm stride of someone well used to the gentle rolling of the deck. He smiled at her choice of gowns—a pale green muslin, chosen undoubtedly because it fastened in the front and not the back.

"That is Gibraltar?" There was wonder in her voice as she gazed to port at the huge outjutting rock, stark and awesomely harsh under the brilliant morning sun.

"Yes. Impressive, is it not? Look to starboard, Cassandra. That is Jebel Musa, in Morocco." He enjoyed her excitement, and her naturalness. Her eyes readily followed his pointing finger.

Cassie shaded her eyes against a sun so bright that it bathed the land in shimmering shades of white. She looked again to port, and then to starboard. It was as if someone had carved the straits directly through a range of jagged hills.

"I had no idea that the straits were so narrow," she said at last. "Why the Moslems are at our very door."

"A mere nine miles at the narrowest point. As to the Moslems, they have throughout the ages many times crossed through our door and made themselves quite at home in our drawing room."

Cassie nodded, scanning the Spanish coastline, and then again the rough-hewn African terrain. "I never believed that I would see any more of the world than England. This is very unlike England, you know."

He smiled and pointed starboard. "On the point there, touching the Mediterranean, is the Spanish town of Ceuta; and there, northward, is the little hill town of San Roque. Unfortunately, it is too hazy for you to see Tangier. Look at the color of the water. It is difficult to describe, is it not? Like a sapphire, perhaps."

She nodded enthusiastically, and the earl was both amused and pleased by her eagerness. The yacht sailed swiftly through the straits, the westerly wind holding the billowing sails taut overhead. He closed his eyes a moment, listening to the squawking of the sea birds, the sound of lines slapping against the wooden masts, and the voices of his men as they went about their morning work. He opened his eyes to see Cassandra gazing open-mouthed at the sheer-faced, awesome rock. "The name *Gibraltar* comes from Gebel Tarik, which means the rock of Tarik, or the hill of Tarik."

Cassie turned to him, frowning. "But Gibraltar is such an *English* name. Surely you are mistaken."

He shook his head. "Tarik was a Moslem who captured Gibraltar long ago, in the eighth century, I believe. He built a castle, which is still very much in use. The English are relative newcomers."

"Yes, it was the Treaty of Utrecht in 1713 that forced the Spanish to give it up." She looked pleased with herself for remembering such a useless fact.

"The Spanish have not given it up yet. Indeed, the situation grows more tense by the year. Charles III is not a man to accept English control of such a strategic site. It is a constant thorn in his imperial side."

Cassie shrugged her shoulders contemptuously. "Oh, the Spanish, they are nothing compared to us."

The earl smiled wryly. "Unfortunately, most Englishmen share your opinion. Only time will tell."

"Are there still pirates about? We are near the Barbary Coast, are we not?" She eagerly scanned the jagged African coastline, but saw nothing save craggy black rocks and barren rolling hills. There was no sign of activity anywhere.

"Yes, that is the Barbary Coast. There are pirates, unfortunately, but not so many as a hundred years ago. You see those inlets cutting into the coast? They look deserted enough, but looks are many times deceiving. The pirates move swiftly, for their livelihood depends upon surprise. Now, if it were the sixteenth century, we would not be standing here by the railing enjoying the scenery. That was the time of Barbarossa and his Turkish pirates."

"Barbarossa," Cassie repeated slowly. "How dashing his name sounds." She sighed. "I wager you are not being honest with me, my lord. There are probably no pirates left at all now. Today is terribly modern and unexciting."

"I will let you read some accounts of Barbarossa," the earl said, his tone dry. "No man, woman, or child was safe from his raids. He much enjoyed pillaging, taking the men for slaves in his galleys and ravishing the women, a pastime I find hardly romantic."

Cassie slowly turned at his words. "And just how would you describe the ravishing of women, my lord?"

She thought he flushed, but his tan was so deep that it was difficult to be certain.

He regarded her steadily, and when he finally spoke, his voice was curiously gentle. "It is said that Barbarossa once deflowered twenty-four virgins in one day. The girls were of various ages, the youngest supposedly but twelve years old. As this exploit was the result of a wager with a neighboring prince, Barbarossa filled the long hall of his palace with many men to witness his prowess. None of the girls resisted him, for to have refused Barbarossa would have meant a painful, lingering death. They were all naked, of course, with no veils over their faces, for Barbarossa wanted all the men to see their faces when he thrust through their maidenheads. He did not concern himself with what became of them after he won his wager. It is written that many of the girls were stoned to death, for what man would want a girl who was no longer a virgin, who had no longer any claim to honor?" He paused a moment, and looked at her whitened cheeks.

"I believe, Cassandra, that there are differences, if you wish to find them."

She shivered, even though the sun burned hot and white overhead. She looked at the man beside her and thought inconsequentially that if she were standing closer to him, she would not be able to see the sun. She felt oddly bereft. Her voice was cold and crackling dry. "I believe, my lord, that men have changed little since the time of your cruel story. Women are still to be possessed as a man's chattel. They are to be protected or cast aside, according to a man's whim. I see little difference, my lord. Regardless of what you make me feel in your bed, I shall always hate you for what you have done to me."

"You are wrong, *cara,* and I shall prove it to you."

She turned on her heel and hurried away from him.

"Cassandra."

She felt fear at the cold fury in his voice, but continued her headlong flight, nearly tripping over a coiled rope that lay close to the mainmast.

His fingers closed about her upper arm, and he jerked her none too gently about to face him.

"You are worse than Barbarossa. At least he did not cloak his villainy—"

"You will be silent."

She drew a shattered breath and saw from the corner of her eye that members of the crew were watching them.

He drew her close to his chest, and she winced, for her back was still tender.

"What is it you intend, my lord? Another beating so that I will learn to cower before your wrath? I will see you in hell first."

"Come, Cassandra. Don't make me carry you."

She thrust her chin up defiantly, but fell into stiff step beside him.

Her step lagged at the cabin door, but he shoved her inside, and ground the key in the lock. His fingers closed over the silver buckle on his belt.

"I will not submit to this beating, my lord. You will have to tie me down."

He stared at her. "By God, you witless little fool. You honestly believe that I—"

He got no further, for at that instant a heavy book struck his shoulder.

"Witless, am I, my lord?" she yelled at him. "You will see that I am not helpless." She grasped two more weighty books from the library shelves and flung them at him with all her strength. He raised his arm and knocked them aside.

He strode toward her and Cassie, with a sob of anger,

abandoned the books, clutched the huge ivory candle holder from atop his desk, and flung it at him. He ducked it, vaguely wondering as he heard one of his prized possessions crash heavily to the floor if the ivory had cracked.

He reached her behind the large mahogany desk and she lashed out at him. Her fist connected with his belly.

"That is quite enough, Cassandra," he said, and pinned her arms to her sides. She tried to kick at him, but he pulled her so tightly against his body that she could not move.

Her heart beat wildly and her breasts heaved against his chest. She had believed—still believed—that he was going to beat her.

"Cassandra, look at me."

He shook her slightly. Reluctantly, she raised her head. Her face was drained of color, yet there was defiant anger in her eyes.

"Why would you think that I would beat you?"

Although his tone was gentle, Cassie felt her stomach churn, for she knew she was impotent against him, impotent in all things.

"You are cruel."

"Like Barbarossa?"

His expression was impassive and she felt uncertainty about herself, and about him. "Why do you mock me?"

"I do not mock you, *cara,* nor was it ever my intention to beat you."

"Don't lie to me. You were furious at me and you were taking off your belt."

"Yes, I was angry at your vicious tongue. But understand me, Cassandra, I would never thrash you because you behave like a stupid child or a raging termagant. As to my belt, it must be removed if I am to strip off my clothes. It is my body you need, *cara,* not a beating."

"No." She twisted frantically against him to break his hold. She felt the hardness of him against her belly and color surged to her cheeks.

"You are worse than Barbarossa."

He merely smiled at her and leaned against the desk. He spread his thighs and pulled her between them. He held her hands behind her with one hand, and let the other move casually over her hips.

"Why hold yourself so rigid, my love?" he whispered, his warm breath against her temple. "Think about how you will feel very soon now. We have been apart for much too long a time." His fingers continued their gentle probing, and she felt his hard member through her gown and petticoats, throbbing and hungry for her.

His voice, deep and sensual, sounded again in her ear. "Think about my mouth moving over you. You are so pink and soft, *cara*. You taste so sweet."

Cassie reared her head back. "Damn you, I will not let you seduce me with words. I will not listen to you."

She felt his mouth close over her, and the now familiar gentle probing of his tongue against her lips. His fingers caressed the back of her neck, then moved slowly to the bodice of her gown. She felt him pulling away the velvet ribbon that bound her hair. He released her mouth, and his lips trailed over her throat, and up to nibble at her ear. She felt a sudden bolt of heat burn through her. She was scarce aware that he no longer held her hands behind her, that her arms of their own volition tugged at his shoulders to bring him closer to her.

"Please," she whispered brokenly, "don't make me feel like this." But even as she spoke, she pressed against him, consumed by her own desire.

As his fingers parted the buttons of her gown and drew open the ribbons of her chemise, he murmured, "I want to touch you, be close to you, be drawn deep inside of you."

His mouth closed over her breast, and she arched her back against him. He weaved his passion about her patiently, tauntingly, until at last she cried out brokenly, her voice slurred with desire, "Please, I cannot bear it . . ."

"Do you want me, Cassandra? Do you want me inside you?"

Her eyes took on a vague, smoky sheen as his fingers glided lightly over her breasts.

"Do you, Cassandra?"

"Yes."

The small word seemed wrenched from her. He let his

mouth close once again over hers. He felt her hands fumble with the buckle of his infamous belt and was delighted that for the first time she was showing initiative. But she could not free the silver hook and with a moan of frustration, she pounded her fists against his chest.

"Savor your passion, my love," he said softly, his eyes never leaving her face. "Let it build inside you until you feel you will die if you do not find release."

As he spoke, his hands, with the smooth skill of long practice, pulled her free of her gown and petticoats. She wanted to help him, to tear off the offending garments, but he would not allow it. Soon, her undergarments and silk stockings bunched softly about her ankles.

He let his fingers slowly trail over her belly until they touched her. Her eyes widened upon his face in mute surprise as his fingers caressed her. He smiled.

"Do you know how soft you are, *cara?*" His lips touched her cheek, the tip of her nose, her chin.

She felt his finger gently ease inside her and she gasped aloud, clutching her hands about his neck to support herself. He felt her tense.

"Not yet, my love."

He took her hand and led her to the bed. He slipped out of his clothing as smoothly as he had removed hers.

She drank in his body without fear or embarrassment, her fingers clenching at the sight of his muscled chest and his taut belly. Her eyes fell to his sex and she felt a warm, insistent heat between her thighs that made her legs go slack.

"You are so different from me, so exquisite," she whispered, scarcely aware that she spoke her thoughts aloud.

He laughed, a rich sound from deep in his throat. "All of me or just part of me, *cara?*"

"All of you."

"Ah, we make progress." He sat down beside her and laid one large hand lightly on her thigh. If only, he thought, gazing at her soft, parted lips, he could make her tell him that she loved him. But it was too soon, much too soon, and he knew that it was the passion he awakened in her that drugged her mind. She turned suddenly toward him, pressed her breasts against his chest, and tentatively placed her hands on his shoulders. He moved his hand slowly from her thigh, and stroked her belly.

He felt his control near to breaking. He eased her down upon her back and gently parted her thighs.

"Remember I told you how you tasted, Cassandra?" He pressed his mouth over her belly and she felt him nuzzling at her, until his lips closed over her.

She whimpered softly, and arched her back, raising her hips to let his mouth burn into the depths of her. He felt her body shudder, quicken, and rose to enter her. Her thighs closed about his sides and her hips lurched upward, drawing him deeper within her. He felt her hands pressing against his back, and he knew that he was lost. He drove into her, and she cried out. As she stiffened in her climax, he let himself go.

He sprawled on top of her, his head beside hers on the pillow. He knew that he must be crushing her, but when he made to move, her hands tightened about his back. A deep ripple of pleasure shot through him, and he smiled, contented. He remembered her still tender back and turned onto his side, drawing her close in the circle of his arms. Her breasts stilled their rapid heaving, and he felt her go slack. Within minutes, she slept.

Cassie shivered and reached out her arms to draw his warm body to her. Her hands closed about a soft feather-down pillow and she opened her eyes. She drew herself upright and gazed about the cabin. He was gone. She looked at the clock atop his desk and started in surprise. She had slept only briefly, for it was but a few minutes after eleven o'clock.

She pushed her hair back from her forehead and swung her legs over the side of the bed. For a long moment, she simply stared down at her body, unable to weave her thoughts together.

She looked at the rumpled bed and saw herself writhing beneath him, her hips surging upward, her hands urgently kneading the hard muscles of his back. The memory sent a sudden tingling down her back. She pictured herself as he must have seen her. Her virulent anger had turned quickly to passion. She had become a quivering woman begging for his man's body. How very pleased he must have been to see her fall asleep like a sated young animal, replete with the pleasure he had given her.

Cassie rose shakily and rushed to the commode. She scrubbed herself viciously until she felt raw. She dropped the damp cloth and shook herself. "Oh, God," she whispered into the stillness of the cabin, "what is happening to me?"

Unbidden, the memory of the afternoon she had been with Edward in the cave, but two days before their wedding, rose in her mind to taunt her. Had it not been for Becky's interference, Edward would have taken her virginity. She had felt passion then, to be sure innocent, tentative desire, but nonetheless it had been she who had encouraged him.

She sobbed aloud and buried her face in her hands. Could any man touch her and set her body on fire? Was she a willing, loose little slut who would part her thighs at a man's touch, at a man's mouth closing over hers?

She gazed listlessly toward the port windows and a word formed on her lips.

"Gibraltar." An English military outpost. There were Englishmen there who would help her, soldiers who could send a message to Eliott and to Edward.

Cassie sped to the portholes and pressed her cheek to the glass. The huge rock was now well behind the yacht, but she could make out a sandy expanse of beach. She moved swiftly, and within minutes, she was dressed in the breeches and white shirt the earl had allowed her to wear during the storm in the Channel. She pulled on her boots, jerked her hair back from her face and knotted a ribbon about it.

She rushed to the earl's desk and pulled open one drawer after another. Papers, charts, ledgers; there appeared to be everything but the money she needed. She jerked at the bottom drawer and found to her surprise that it was locked.

She grabbed a hairpin from atop the dresser and thrust it into the small lock. She muttered a frustrated oath, for she could feel the yacht moving swiftly eastward, before the lock sprang loose and the drawer slid open. Her fingers curled about a leather pouch; she pulled it open and saw to her delight that it was filled with *louis d'or*. She quickly fastened the pouch to her waist. She was on the point of rising when she saw an elegant English dueling pistol, half covered with a velvet cloth. Uncertainly, she touched its shining silver handle and drew it out. Her jaw tightened. If someone tried to stop her, she would use it.

Cassie was not much familiar with guns, but from the little she knew, she could tell that it was primed. She laid it on top of the desk and shoved the desk drawers back into place.

She felt a light draft touch her face and looked up to see the earl standing in the open doorway, the remnants of the smile on his face turning into a cold question.

"Just what the devil are you doing?"

Cassie straightened to face him, her fingers curling about the pistol. She said curtly, "I am leaving, my lord."

"I hardly think so, Cassandra." He leaned against the door frame, his arms crossed over his chest. "Indeed, I believe it more likely that you will take off those ridiculous breeches and put on one of your gowns. We will have lunch shortly." He added, "How fortunate that I opened the door so quietly. I had thought you still asleep, you know."

She stared at the intimate, caressing tone of his voice.

"Damn you, my lord earl. I will no longer be your whore. Now move aside for I am done with you."

"My whore, *cara?* You have not sufficient experience to fill that position."

Her body shook at the amusement in his voice. Slowly, deliberately, she raised the pistol and aimed it at him.

"I have no desire to swim more than a mile, my lord. You will now stand aside or I will shoot you."

The lazy animal grace left him. She was not fooled by the conversational tone of his voice, for she saw the tensing of his body. "How enterprising you are, Cassandra. But foolish, very foolish. Put the pistol down."

"Go to the devil, my lord."

"Put it down, Cassandra."

He walked toward her, his stride confident, his dark eyes resting intently upon her face.

"Damn you," she cried, and pulled the trigger.

A deafening roar filled the cabin. A trail of gray smoke billowed from the pistol as it dropped with a sickening thud to the floor. The earl grabbed his shoulder, the impact of the ball hurling him backward.

She rushed past him, through the cabin door and along the companionway. She heard him shout her name, but she did not slow. When she reached the deck, she forced herself to a walk. Sailors were looking about with surprised faces at the sound of the pistol shot. She paused for but a moment at the railing, gauging the distance to shore. The deep blue water was calm, as smooth as the surface of glass. In a fluid movement, Cassie climbed over the railing, stood poised an instant with her arms raised over her head, and kicked off.

"Madonna!"

She heard the shout just as her body knifed through the surface. The impact jarred her, and the shock of the cold water momentarily numbed her senses. Belatedly, she arched her back and fought her way to the surface. She gulped precious air into her lungs and slewed her head about toward the yacht. She heard sailors shouting and saw them lining up along the deck, gesticulating wildly toward her. She looked back toward the beach and felt a lump grow in her throat. It was far distant, more than a mile. She drew a resolute breath, kicked her booted feet and swam with sure, firm strokes away from the yacht.

"Cassandra!"

She turned her head and saw the earl at the railing. The next instant, he stiffened and dove into the water. His head cleared the surface much too close to her.

"Fiends seize you!" she yelled at him, and inadvertently gulped in a mouthful of water. She sputtered and coughed, aware that she was wasting valuable time. She ignored the burning in her constricted throat and stroked with all her strength away from him, toward shore.

A powerful arm closed about her hips, pulling her inexorably back and downward. Water closed over her head, and for an endless moment, she was locked against him in silent combat. She tried to kick free of his hold, but he drew her against his chest and bore her to the surface.

"You are insane, my lord. Let me go." She struggled wildly against him, striking his chest, kicking her booted feet against his thighs. Suddenly his arms loosened and she wriggled free.

"Cassandra."

Her name sounded barely above a low whisper and she flipped about to face him. To her horror, she saw that the water between them was red with blood. She gasped aloud. His head disappeared beneath the surface of the calm water. She saw him struggling, his arms thrashing weakly. He did not have the strength to bring his face above water.

She turned frantic eyes to the yacht. She saw Scargill, Mr. Donnetti, and half a dozen other sailors lowering a longboat. They would never reach him in time. He would drown.

"You fool," she yelled at him. He floated near the surface, face down, in a widening pool of his own blood.

She swam back to him and clutched him under his arms, but she did not have the strength to raise his face above the water. She locked her arm beneath his chin and pulled him back against her chest, forcing his head back and up.

She looked frantically toward the approaching longboat. Her legs felt leaden, but she forced them to keep pumping. She feared she would drown with him if they did not hurry.

"Row harder," Mr. Donnetti shouted as he flung off his cloak and boots. He was on the point of diving overboard when Scargill stopped him.

"Nay, Francesco, she may lose her hold." A slight smile broke his grim expression. He could hear Cassie cursing the earl as they approached, berating him in broken sobs for his stupidity, his ridiculous stubbornness.

Mr. Donnetti muttered under his breath, "It makes no sense. She shoots him, then saves his life."

"It would not be in her character to do otherwise," Scargill said, but Mr. Donnetti paid him no attention.

The earl stirred.

"Hold still, damn you, else we'll both drown."

Mr. Donnetti and several other men slipped over the side of the longboat and freed Cassie of her burden. It took them some moments to pull him into the boat. She heard the earl's voice, weak, but fiercely commanding. "Save her, Francesco, quickly, before she loses her strength."

Mr. Donnetti grunted and grabbed Cassie none too gently around her waist. He lifted her toward the boat and several hands closed about her arms, hauling her upward.

Cassie crouched down at the stern of the boat and wrapped her shivering arms about her knees. A sailor threw a cloak over her shoulders, but it did not warm her.

The men huddled around the earl, and no one seemed to pay her the slightest attention. If she had had the strength, she might have slipped over the side of the boat before any of them noticed. She tried to see the earl, but Scargill and Mr. Donnetti were crouched in front of him, blocking her view. She heard Scargill tell him not to move.

Four sailors, two on each side of the narrow longboat, rowed furiously back toward the yacht. Cassie gazed toward *The Cassandra* and marveled at how quickly the sails had been lowered. As they drew nearer she could hear the grating sound of the iron-linked anchor line being dropped. She strained forward at the sound of the earl's voice.

"Dammit, Scargill, none of you is strong enough to carry me up the ladder. I'll climb it myself. Francesco, stay close to me."

She could not believe that he would try to climb the ladder himself. She wanted to yell at him not to be such a fool, but his foot was already on the bottom rung, his face forbidding in his determination. She watched with held breath as the earl slowly and painfully pulled himself upward. A cry tore from her throat when he nearly lost his grip halfway up the ladder.

Joseph drew a relieved breath once the earl was finally hauled over the railing onto the deck. He turned to her and said crisply, "Now it is your turn, madonna."

She shook her head mutely, for her arms felt like useless sticks of wood hanging at her sides. He misunderstood her. "I'll not let you escape, madonna, and you haven't now a pistol to shoot me."

She licked her lips. "I cannot, Joseph."

He studied her exhausted face and, without another word, hauled her over his shoulder and climbed the rope ladder. He set her down upon the deck. When she did not move, he said sharply, "Go to the captain, madonna. He'll not be easy until he knows you are safe."

Cassie entered the cabin quietly. The earl was stretched his full length on the bed, gritting his teeth against the pain as Scargill and Mr. Donnetti stripped off his wet clothing.

"Where is she, Scargill?"

There was an undercurrent of panic in his voice. She walked quickly forward into his line of vision. "I am here, my lord."

He stared at her for a long moment, and closed his eyes.

Scargill straightened over the earl, his face grim. "Ye've lost a lot of blood, my lord, and the bullet must be drawn out."

"Very well," the earl said, without opening his eyes. "Get it over with." Blood trickled through the black mat of hair on his chest. She felt an unwonted surge of guilt.

Dilson suddenly burst through the door.

"Captain, it's the pirate, Khar El-Din. We spotted him before we brought you on board. Now he's demanding to come aboard!"

"That bloody bastard," Mr. Donnetti exclaimed, turning sharply.

The earl turned his head on the pillow and said calmly to Dilson, "If our friend wishes to pay us a visit, we'll not say nay. Francesco, go welcome him and bring him here. He'll not accept less, you know."

"But, my lord—" Scargill began.

"Enough, Scargill. Cover me, I cannot greet my friend naked. And bind my wound. Let him smell blood, but not see it."

Cassie took a shaking step back, her eyes flying to the earl's face. A pirate. The earl had told her that such men still existed, but she had not believed him.

"Cassandra."

"Yes," she whispered.

His eyes swept over her wet clothes, the breeches that

clung tightly to her thighs and hips. He could make out her nipples pressing against the thin white shirt. Although her hair hung in tangled wet masses about her pale face, it seemed to make her all the more alluring. He felt a shaft of fear.

"Listen to me, *cara*, we haven't much time. Wrap yourself from throat to toe in a cloak. You will sit very quietly, your eyes down. You will keep your mouth shut. Do you understand me?"

She nodded mutely, though she did not understand.

"Quickly, Scargill, cover her. Cassandra, we are not in England. Trust me in this." He felt the pain drawing at his senses, and drew a deep, steadying breath.

"Do as his lordship has told you, madonna."

Cassie pulled the satin cloak he offered her about her and sat down.

Her eyes flew from Scargill's set face at the sound of heavy boots overhead. They drew nearer, sounding in her ears like the staccato beat of marching men.

A deep booming voice came through the open doorway, and a man entered whom Cassie would never forget. For an instant, her eyes locked to his, eyes so dazzling blue and piercing that they seemed hardly human. He was like a bull, she thought, short, but mammoth in girth. His blond hair was thick and long, bleached with streaks of white. His bare arms were thick with bulging muscle. He wore a loose red leather vest and baggy breeches that were held at his waist by a wide scarlet sash.

She dropped her eyes quickly to the floor.

"*Buon Giorno, Antonio! Godo di verderla!*" His voice held the swaggering tone of a man who knew himself to be in command.

The earl answered easily, in Italian. "And I am glad to see you, my friend. To what do I owe the honor of your visit?"

Khar El-Din waved a negligent hand, pulled up a chair and straddled it. His fierce eyes slewed in Cassie's direction and she felt as though he could see through her cloak, even through her wet clothing.

"Surely there need be no special reason, among friends,

Antonio. I see that you are not well. You have suffered an accident?"

"I still live, as you see. Scargill, fetch our guest a glass of wine."

"Ever gracious, Antonio, ever gracious. I see that you have another guest."

Cassie forced herself to keep her head down, to pretend that she did not understand.

"Not a guest, but my wife. She is English and of course does not comprehend our language."

Khar El-Din took the proffered glass from Scargill, tipped back his lion's head, and downed the entire contents. He wiped the back of his hand across his mouth and grinned hugely. "So my lord earl finally ties himself to one woman. She is lovely, my friend, though she looks quite wet and uncomfortable. My girls will be bereft at their loss. Zabetta, in particular, will miss her English stallion."

"I trust you will convey my regrets."

"Trust me to console them, Antonio, though it will take me many nights. But my friend, you really do not look at all well. My men told me the strangest story, so bizarre that I must needs see for myself. A young girl diving most proficiently from your yacht to be followed by you, Antonio, your chest stained bright with your own blood. How, my friend, can I avoid drawing the most distasteful of conclusions? The mighty earl felled by a mere girl. Assist me to understand, my friend, why a wife would shoot her husband and dive into the sea to escape him." He paused a moment, his eyes again upon Cassie. "If you had but left her in the sea, I would have been most delighted to save her and teach her the error of her ways."

Cassie thought that the pirate must hear the furious pounding of her heart. What a fool she had been. There would have been no escape for her. The earl had saved her, not she the earl.

"Your generosity, as always, my friend, moves me greatly. But a wife must always be her husband's responsibility. Surely you have enough wives to occupy your attention without concerning yourself with my stupid affairs."

"Ah, Antonio, you have the smooth tongue of the diplomat. You say everything so fluently, yet there is no meaning to be drawn. Could it be that you do not please your English wife in the marriage bed? I have heard it said that your English ladies are as cold as the northern winters. You carry the blood of your Ligurian ancestors, passionate blood, demanding blood. Can it be that you have terrified your lady wife with that huge shaft of yours?"

"I cannot believe that my prowess in the marriage bed can be of such interest to you, my friend, you who nightly may choose from so many beautiful women."

Khar El-Din threw back his head, his mane of thick hair swirling down his back, and laughed deeply. He pointed a gnarled finger at the earl and wagged it. "I grow old and exhausted in their service. Yet, Antonio, I have not in my fifty years been shot by one of them. Let me inquire of your lady wife why she holds you in such dislike."

Cassie felt his pale blue eyes resting intently upon her, and kept her head down. She was startled into looking up into his leathered face when he said in slow, precise English, "Give me your attention, girl. Your husband is a gentleman and thus skirts my every question. You had the courage to shoot him, and I must ask myself why. If it is your wish to leave him, my pretty one, you have but to tell me. I will willingly help you. You really do not have to render your lord husband dead, you know."

Cassie licked her dry lips. She did not look at the earl, for she knew that he could not help her. She was aware that in her fear she was rocking slightly back and forth in her chair. An idea came to her. She said in a vague, soft voice, "My husband but tries to protect me, sir."

Khar El-Din leaned toward her, his eyes glittering. "Protect you, my beautiful child?"

"Not from you, sir, but from myself."

Her voice held a peculiar singsong quality that made the pirate start.

Cassie felt a wet strand of hair fall over her cheek. In a slow, deliberate motion, she licked at the strand until it fell into her mouth.

"Yes," she said, her eyes going wide and vacant. "He does not wish others to know of my madness. He promised many years ago that he would wed me. He saved me from Bedlam, sir, by taking me from England."

Khar El-Din shifted angrily in his chair and spat at the earl, "What inane jest is this? Do you take me for a fool?"

The earl only nodded, wearily.

Cassie wrapped her arms about her waist and began to rock in huge dips in her chair. She mumbled an old nursery rhyme from her childhood.

Khar El-Din swiveled back in his chair toward her and she saw doubt narrow his eyes.

"I am not always so, sir," she said in a high child's voice. "They called me a witch, a witch with evil powers, for I made a man die because he dared to touch me. I cannot be certain that it was I who was responsible, but he died so quickly afterward, choking to death over his wine."

Khar El-Din thrust his empty wine glass into Scargill's hand. He drew back from her, and Cassie saw in his eyes that he believed her to be evil, mad. He rose quickly and stared down at the earl's drawn face. "You are a fool, Antonio, with your English honor. Let me drown her for you, 'twill most likely save your life. I knew a woman like her once, afflicted with the same madness. I had her stoned before she could devour men's souls."

The earl's growing pain kept the tempted smile from his face. "Nay, my friend, as I told you, she is my responsibility. I will take her to Genoa and hide her away. No one need ever know."

The pirate looked at her once more, and she forced a wide smile to her lips. How could such a beautiful, innocent face cloak madness? He shook his head and strode to the door.

"May Allah protect you. I hope to hear of your speedy recovery, my friend. *Addio.*"

"*A rivederci.*"

None of them moved or spoke until Mr. Donnetti appeared in the doorway. "He's gone, captain. And by the look on his face, I'd say he had seen the devil himself."

"He has just made the acquaintance of a witch, Francesco," the earl said. The smile on his lips turned to a grimace.

"Well done, madonna," Scargill said, beaming at her with approval. He turned briskly back to the earl. "Ye can explain to Francesco later, my lord. Now, I must draw out the ball."

"I cannot eat more, Scargill," Cassie said with a sigh, and pushed her plate away. The little food she had eaten lay heavy in her stomach. She glanced toward the earl, stretched on his back, a light cover drawn to his waist. The white bandages over his shoulder were stark against his deeply tanned body and the black hair on his chest.

"How long will he sleep?"

"If we are lucky, until morning. Thank the lord that the ball wasn't deep. If there is no infection, he should be quickly on the mend." No thanks to you, his eyes told her, and she looked away from him. She rose, shook out her skirts, and walked slowly toward the door.

Scargill's sharp voice forestalled her. "Nay, madonna. I promised his lordship that I'd not let ye out of the cabin. It's here ye'll stay until he tells me otherwise."

"You think I would jump overboard in my skirts?"

"I wouldn't have thought that ye'd have shot him, madonna. Nor would I have believed that wounded like he was, he'd still have gone in after ye."

She felt drained, both emotionally and physically. "Was I so very wrong, Scargill? What would you do, pray, if you were held against your will and saw an opportunity to escape? I did not want to shoot him, but he tried to stop me."

"Aye, he would. But do not try to draw me into an argument with ye, madonna, for it will gain ye naught." He began to clear away the plates from the table.

Cassie walked slowly to the settee and sat down. She closed her eyes and leaned her head back. The events of the day, jostled and fragmented, whirled through her mind. She heard the deafening report of the pistol, felt her arm beneath his chin as his weight and her fatigue threatened to pull them both into the depths of the sea. She saw the pirate, Khar El-Din, his fierce blue eyes boring into her.

"Can I trust ye alone with him?"

She shook away her lie of madness and saw Scargill standing uncertainly at the door.

"You believe that I would smother him with a pillow?" Scargill ignored the irony in her voice and allowed a faint smile to crease the corners of his mouth. "No, it was a foolish question. After all, ye could have left him to drown, but ye didn't. We will hope that that is what the men will remember and not yer shooting their captain. Go to sleep now, madonna, it has been a long day. I'll be in during the night to check on his lordship." He turned away from her, and she heard him turn the key in the lock.

Yes, she thought, her eyes again on the earl's motionless body, a long day and one that I am ending just as I began it—your prisoner. She wearily tugged off her clothes and curled up on the settee.

Cassie awoke with a start at the sound of a low moan. She shook the sleep from her mind, pulled her dressing gown about her, and sped to the earl's bed. Dull shafts of early morning light shone through the narrow windows, bathing the cabin in soft gray.

She laid her hand on his forehead, and gave a sigh of relief. There was as yet no fever. She gasped in surprise when his fingers closed over her wrist.

"Cassandra." His voice was low and slurred from the effect of laudanum.

"I am here, my lord."

For a long moment, his dark eyes searched her face. A ghost of a smile flitted across his mouth. "You must wash the salt from your hair."

"Is it so important that your whore be to your liking at all times?"

"Whore is your term, *cara*. I thought we had established you are a madwoman, and yet I will still take you to wife. It is my English honor, I suppose."

He closed his eyes, and his forehead furrowed in pain.

"You are in no condition to bandy words, my lord. Do you wish more laudanum?"

"How strange you are, Cassandra," he said, his eyes still closed over his pain. "Young English ladies are not bred to have such a fondness for pistols. Nor, I suppose, are they likely to be such strong swimmers. Although your skill with a pistol hasn't done me much good, I am relieved that you are a good swimmer. A good swimmer and a good actress. After your performance with Khar El-Din, I am almost tempted to forgive your other quite believable lie."

"Your wits are obviously addled, my lord," she snapped. "I have no notion what you are talking about."

"Do you not, my love? 'Twas our first night together. If I consider Khar El-Din a gullible fool for believing you mad, then I must say that I was no better. You really shook me, you know, when you told me you were pregnant with Edward Lyndhurst's child."

He heard her draw in a sharp breath. "I did not want to force you, Cassandra, but I knew of no other way."

"As you have said, my lord, it has not been a question of anything at all after that first night. Even if I still do not possess the skill of a whore, I seem to have the soul of one."

He chuckled, and if he had not been lying helpless, she would have struck him. "I marvel at your recriminations. I should not leave you alone, *cara,* your mind is too fanciful, and the conclusions you draw about your own character really quite unfounded. The truth of the matter is that I am a very desirable man and an excellent lover, most skilled at bringing a woman to pleasure. Curse me, Cassandra, for your awakened woman's passions, not yourself."

"Just as you have given Zabetta pleasure?" She drew back, aghast at the venom in her voice, but his fingers tightened about her wrist.

"Just so," he said softly. "But with such a fiercely loyal and jealous wife, you need never fear that I will again fall into old habits."

"I am not jealous and I shall never wed you. If you fancy otherwise, my lord, I fear you will know disappointment until the end of your miserable life."

The door suddenly opened, and Scargill entered. The earl released her wrist, and she backed away from the bed.

Scargill took in her flushed and angry face and said sharply, "I hope ye have had the good sense not to arouse his lordship, madonna."

"She has tried, Scargill, but alas, I fear I am not up to it. I hope you have brought me some breakfast. If left to her own devices, I fear that my nurse would starve me."

"I think ye'll do, my lord." Scargill nodded his approval as he studied his master's face. He saw pain darken the earl's eyes but knew enough not to say so. "Afore ye eat, my lord, I must see to the wound. Madonna, ye'll help me, if ye please."

As Scargill pulled the earl forward, Cassie unwrapped the thick bandages. She felt herself go white at the sight of his shoulder. The wound was sewn with black thread. It looked obscene. She felt him tense as Scargill gently probed the area.

"Ye'll be at the helm in a day or two, my lord," Scargill announced as he straightened. "But I'll not allow ye any wine, for it's said to bring on a fever. I'll bind ye tighter this time, my lord, so yer flesh will grow together more quickly."

"Just be done with it," the earl said in a low voice.

Cassie felt her forehead damp with perspiration by the time the earl fell into a drugged sleep. He had made no sound, and she wondered if she could have been as stoic.

She spent the rest of the morning in the copper bathtub, letting the hot water relax her. She washed the salty grit from her hair. She pulled up a chair near the bed and quietly brushed her damp hair. Every few minutes, she found that she looked at him, her eyes alert to any signs of fever. But he lay quietly, his breathing even, his chest rising and falling gently in sleep.

"I do not know why I should care," she said. But she did care, and the admission surprised her. "Please do not die, Anthony."

She sighed deeply, shaking her head. Tendrils of hair touched her cheeks. She thought again of her attempt to escape him and felt a shaft of fear slice through her. Even if she had succeeded, she would never have reached the English settlement. She would have become Khar El-Din's captive, to do with as he pleased.

The earl moaned softly, and Cassie laid her palm gently on his forehead. He was cool to the touch. She studied him, the sculptured contours of his face, the proud straight nose, the thick black-arched eyebrows, and the hard line of his jaw. He suddenly lurched toward his side, then fell again onto his back.

She pressed her hands gently against his shoulders. "No, my lord," she said quietly, "you must not move."

He grew quiet once again, and Cassie resumed her vigil. Her eyes passed from his face to his massive chest. In his restlessness, the cover had slipped below his waist to his belly.

She looked at him, at the curling black hair that covered his chest narrowed at his waist, thickening out again below. Even in sleep, he looked magnificent. She reached out her hand and lightly touched his belly, her fingers curling about the thick black hair. His warm flesh was smooth and taut. Her fingers explored him innocently. The cover fell away, and she saw his sex lying softly against him. She felt an intense curiosity and let her fingers close tentatively over him. She lightly caressed him, not used to his softness, and ran her other hand over his thighs. She gasped in surprise as his member began to grow in her hand. Her eyes flew to his face. He was watching her. She flushed scarlet, but she continued to hold him.

"I am sorry to awaken you, my lord," she said, her voice oddly high and breathless. "It is just that I have never, that is, I wanted to—"

"Do I please you, Cassandra?"

"No. That is, you moved and the cover slipped. I was curious. I've never really looked at a naked man before." Her eyes went inadvertently to him, straining against her fingers.

"You see the effect you have on me. No, do not move your hand, your touch gives me great pleasure." He smiled at her, his dark eyes devoid of arrogance or amusement. "Indeed, I am sorry that I have interrupted your explorations. You have me at your mercy, my lady, for I have not the strength to show you how very much you please me."

"I don't wish to please you, my lord. I only wanted to to see you."

She released him and he moaned. "Are you in pain, my lord?"

"Yes, *cara,* but it is not from my shoulder."

"I have caused you pain?" she asked, bewildered.

"To give me such pleasure and then to cease it causes me great discomfort."

"Oh." Lightly, she laid the palm of her hand flat against his belly and felt the muscles tighten convulsively.

"Touch me again, Cassandra." His hand closed over hers and gently guided it downward. As her fingers closed about him, he drew a deep breath.

She blurted out, "I wanted to touch you to try and understand why you make me feel as you do."

"And do you understand?"

She was silent for a moment, and her eyes roved back to his belly. "I can scarce hold you." As if suddenly aware of what she was doing, Cassie drew back her hand and clasped it in her lap. She shook her head, and he heard confusion in her voice. "No, not really. I only know that I much enjoy your body."

He wanted to grin, but the pain in his shoulder curved his mouth into a grimace.

She sat forward and touched her fingertips to his forehead. "I am truly sorry that you are in pain." She drew a deep breath. "And I am sorry that I shot you. I really did not want to, but you gave me no choice."

To her surprise, he nodded. "Yes, you are right. I did force you to pull the trigger. I only ask, *cara,* that you not become a better shot."

"Why did you not tell me that those wretched pirates were about? It is possible that I might have believed you. Instead, you acted the arrogant bastard."

"Damnation," he growled. At her start of surprise, he added quickly, "we will continue this conversation, Cassandra."

A moment later, the door opened and Scargill walked into the cabin.

The earl was very much aware of the bulge under the light cover and concentrated his wits on turning his desire to ashes.

"What be it that ye're doing, madonna?" Scargill looked at her questioningly.

"I was but seeing that his lordship is all right."

"She tells the truth, Scargill. She is an excellent nurse, and in truth, your presence is not at all necessary."

Scargill frowned. He peered down at his master's smiling face and shook his head. "Ye need sleep, my lord, not conversation with the madonna. Besides, the two of ye canna be together without cutting at each other. I do not want ye angered or excited."

The smile on the earl's face widened into a grin. He saw Cassie flinch, her face turning red. "Very well, you old preacher, I'll do as you bid."

"Do ye wish more laudanum?"

"No, just peace and quiet."

Aware that Cassie was moving restlessly behind him, Scargill said softly, "Would ye mind if I took the madonna on deck? The fresh sea air cannot but do her good."

"Yes, please, my lord, I would like it much."

At the earl's continued silence, Scargill said, "Ye need not worry that she'll escape ye, my lord. 'Tis a close watch I'll keep on her."

"You are a coward, *cara*," the earl said, and closed his eyes.

Chapter 12

"There she is, Cassandra, Genoa—*La Superba*—the queen of the Mediterranean. Is she not beautiful?"

Cassie had the impression that she was shrouded in white; even the air was white. As the yacht drew into the harbor, she leaned over the railing just behind the bow and shaded her eyes to better see the city, bathed in dazzling afternoon sunlight.

"Yes, but so very different from any city I have ever seen or imagined." It seemed to her that the tall, narrow buildings, many of them as white as the stark sunlight, were pressed so closely together that it was difficult to tell where one began and another left off.

The earl smiled down at her, guessing her thoughts. He had himself experienced the same feeling many times before. "As you can see, the city has had no choice but to press itself together. The hills behind the city are the Apennines. And farther back are the Maritime Alps. Genoa is compressed like a lady in her corset, the mountains at her back and the sea pressing at her—" He grinned. "I grow fanciful and see from your lips that you do not approve my simile."

He pointed westward. "You see the lighthouse on the point of land? That is *La Lanterna*. My home lies slightly northward, in the hills. You will find the view of Genoa and the sea most striking, particularly from the gardens. They are deeply terraced and so laden with trees and flowers that you will think that you have wandered into some impossible, exotic novel. Beyond the Parese vineyards, to the east, is a small lake, also called Parese. I trust you will find enjoyment sailing there."

Cassie thought of her small sailboat, crushed at his order against the rocks. "I don't think I shall," she said.

"We shall see," he said. He turned and flexed his shoulder. She saw a frown of pain briefly narrow his eyes.

It had been but four days since she shot him. Yet, if it were not for the white sling under his left arm that crossed his chest to tie behind his neck, she doubted that anyone would guess that he experienced any discomfort at all, for he made no reference to it. She recalled touching him, curiously exploring his man's body. A flush tinted her cheeks and she quickly looked away from him. She wondered in confusion if she were not his prisoner in her own mind and by her own volition. She drew back when he gently brushed tendrils of hair from her cheek.

The earl said, "You see the dock starboard? That is where *The Cassandra* will berth."

Cassie wrinkled her nose at the overwhelming smell of fish and sweat. Shoremen dressed in little more than heavy homespun trousers formed a human chain from the gangplanks of the ships to the dock, heaving huge crates and bales of foodstuffs. She saw men upon the decks of the ships, dressed in various uniforms, shouting orders that sent other men scurrying about to obey them. The din of men's voices was almost overwhelming, and she wondered how anyone could be understood, particularly since so many languages were being spoken.

The earl made a sweeping gesture with his arm. "Every country, I believe, is represented here. Normally, as I told you, either a ship pays tribute to the pirates or she travels with a sister ship to protect her cargo."

Cassie did not reply, for her attention was caught by a British cargo ship. "A Union Jack."

"Ah yes, the English are great traders and their ships dot the harbor. They sail from Genoa to the American colonies, even to such exotic places as the West Indies and Mexico." A hint of distaste entered his voice. "Unfortunately, their cargo is many times human."

She looked at him, cocking her head inquiringly.

"Human beings, Cassandra, black men and women captured on the coast of Africa to be sold as slaves."

"How fortunate for you, my lord," she said in a voice deep with sarcasm, "that you had to pay nothing for me."

He grinned at her. "You are really quite mistaken, *cara,* my payments will be endless."

"I will see that they are."

He laughed and said in an amused drawl, "Don't look so hopefully at the British ships, Cassandra. For the most part, the men who captain them are scoundrels. Traders in general have few scruples. If you offered your striking person aboard one of those ships, you would likely find yourself in a harem in Constantinople."

"We are, however, back to civilization, my lord." Her voice was clipped, inviting no response.

He gazed at her and shrugged, wincing as the untoward movement brought pain to his shoulder. He said easily, "We will ride in an open carriage through the city. I trust it will give you enjoyment to see Genoa. Scargill will follow with our luggage to my home—the Villa Parese."

She nodded, her attention drawn to the filth that floated in the harbor, refuse, she supposed, from the many ships. She saw a dead sea bird, and swallowed convulsively.

"Excuse me, Cassandra, but I must see Mr. Donnetti."

She watched him make his way to the quarterdeck to where Mr. Donnetti stood, legs apart, like a hovering lean eagle, shouting orders to the men.

Those sailors who were not securing the rigging and pulling the lines tight stood at the railing waving to people on the dock. True to the earl's word, *The Cassandra* moved sleekly into her berth, her masts, like those on other ships surrounding her, standing tall and bright in the sunlight.

Men climbed nimbly down the port ladders to the long wooden dock and moved easily to catch the lines tossed down from the deck. She heard the heavy anchor drop overboard and made a note to herself to ask the earl the depth of the water in the harbor. The runged gangplank was lowered and Cassie walked quickly to port. She looked up to see the earl striding toward her, a knit shawl in his hand.

"My lady," he said in a lazy voice, "I see that I must take care of you."

He handed her the shawl and with a great show of ceremony escorted her down the wooden gangplank. All she heard now was Italian, and she imagined, from some of the curious looks darted at her from assorted men at work along the harbor, that she was the subject. She frowned, for there were many phrases she did not understand.

The earl guided her past scores of bare-chested fishermen, yelling at each other amiably as they mended their nets, to an old barouche harnessed to a slope-shouldered bay mare who looked as ancient as the open carriage.

"Yours, my lord?" she asked, an eyebrow arched as she ran her hand over the cracked black leather seats.

"Do not be uppity, Cassandra. I am guaranteed that the wheels will not fall off."

As the barouche moved ponderously from dockside to the Via Gramsci, the earl said, "This street is one to be avoided unless one is accompanied by several hardy protectors. It is every bit as notorious for its villains and cutthroats as the wharf areas in London." They turned onto the Via San Lorenzo, and Cassie sucked in her breath. The cobblestone street was narrow, dangerously so. Pressing against the street and against each other were tall, narrow houses and enormous mansions, sumptuously appointed, and to Cassie's eyes, outlandishly out of place. The barouche climbed steadily, avoiding streets that were so narrow that three people could scarce walk side by side. When they turned onto the Via Balbi, the earl said, "The famous Genoese architect Bartolomeo Bianco designed this street. The palaces are renowned throughout Europe, particularly Number 10, the Palazzo Reale. The Balbi family commissioned this palace as well as the street in the last century." He would have continued, but he saw that Cassie, enthralled by the exotic sights, was not heeding him. He smiled and leaned back in the carriage, content to watch her and to see Genoa through her eyes.

The air had cooled perceptibly when the barouche finally rolled off the narrow cobblestone street just outside the western gate of the city. *La Lanterna*, the earl had called it. The road veered sharply northward and quickly became a rutted path, with wheel tracks so deep in the hardened dirt that the barouche lurched constantly from one side to the other. Cassie's attention was drawn to the wild profusion of colorful flowers that grew among the bushes along the roadside. She drew a deep breath, savoring the fragrance.

She had always thought of the English countryside as being as neat as a well-made bed, with its lovingly tended verdant fields surrounded by well-trimmed hedges. It seemed to her that nature was allowed to express itself more freely here, without man's interfering hand. There were so many odd trees and flowers the like of which she had not seen even in books. If her companion had been anyone but the earl, she would have been full of questions.

They were high into the hills when Scargill pulled the bay mare to a halt in front of a weathered wrought-iron gate. Carved at the top of the arch were the words, *Villa Parese*. A young black-haired boy, his face a deep swarthy hue, suddenly appeared at the side of the barouche. His dark eyes assessed the occupants but an instant before he pulled off his leather hat and bowed deeply.

"*Buon giorno*, Sordello," the earl said, leaning toward the boy. "You have grown. It's nearly a man you've become."

"*Si, signore*," the boy said proudly, his lips parting into a wide smile. "Welcome home." He turned quickly to Cassie and bowed again. "Welcome, *signora*."

It was on the tip of Cassie's tongue to correct him. *Signora* indeed. But he had moved away to open the huge gates.

"Sordello is the son of my head gardener. He is a bright lad who has already the lust for the sea. In a year or so, I will turn him over to Mr. Donnetti, who will teach him the skills of a cabin boy. How very polite he is, too. Did he not greet my wife with all due deference?"

"I hope your tongue may rot off," Cassie said through her teeth.

"Ah, but my tongue gives you such pleasure, *cara*."

The carriage moved through the gates and onto a graveled drive. A lush green lawn stretched beyond either side of the bordering trees and hedges, more in the English style, Cassie thought, unconsciously nodding her approval. Set toward the middle of the lawn to her left stood a fountain carved of the purest white marble. About its circular basin were carved statues of sea gods, Neptune and his minions, Cassie supposed. The drive curved slightly, and when the barouche emerged from the thick foliage of tree branches, Cassie saw before her the Villa Parese, a great white stone edifice, built in a square and rising two stories. For an instant, she was aware only of the severity of the white in contrast to the incredible array of surrounding color. Blood-red roses climbed trellises to the second-floor balconies, where they wrapped about black iron railings. Full-blossomed hibiscus, geraniums, and other flowers she couldn't identify, colored bright yellow, purple, and pink, lined the top of the railings in low wooden window boxes. On the front of the façade was a heavy cornice supported by solid corbels, giving the whole, to Cassie's reluctant eyes, a dignified simplicity. Two huge columns rose from the marble front steps, and the brilliance of the sun made the myriad windows appear as sparkling prisms. It was so very different from the weathered gray stone of Hemphill Hall, where few but the hardiest flowers survived the battering wind from the Channel, and the heavy salt air was so pervasive that one had to lean close to a blossom to smell its fragrance.

"Does the villa please you, Cassandra?" As she remained silent, he added with a smile, "No, you needn't say it. I know that it is very different from England. As you can see, the villa is set into the side of the hill, and the gardens are terraced into many levels, both up the hill and down." He drew a deep breath. "The smell is so sweet, unlike any place I have visited."

Cassie nodded silently, and allowed Scargill to assist her from the carriage.

A man and a woman, both dressed in rather somber black, emerged through the large gothic-arched portal. The man was quite short, and nearly as wide as he was tall. The woman was tall and gaunt, her complexion swarthy. Her full lips were drawn into a thin line. She had the look of a Puritan woman whose portrait Cassie had seen in a neighboring house in Essex. Even as the earl greeted them in his soft, musical Italian, Cassie was aware that she was being scrutinized to the tips of her sandals. She shifted her weight to her other foot and tried to avoid the woman's darting gaze.

"My dear," the earl continued in Italian, drawing her forward, "I would like you to meet Marrina and Paolo, who keep the Villa Parese running smoothly with or without my presence. Signorina Brougham," he added smoothly, acknowledging her maiden state.

Cassie mumbled her heavily accented *buon giorno,* aware that a flush rose to her cheeks at the widening of the woman's dark eyes. She wondered crazily if Marrina's scalp did not hurt, so tightly was her hair pulled back into a severe black knot at the nape of her neck.

"Welcome, *signorina,*" Marrina said stiffly, lowering her eyes from Cassie's face.

Cassie wanted to yell at her that her being unmarried was of her own choosing, that their master had forced her here against her will. She thought bitterly that she would likely have to suffer the condemnation even of his servants.

The earl led her into an imposing entrance hall, rectangular in shape, whose floor was made of black and white marble set in a triangular design. At the rear of the entrance hall a monumental staircase of intricately carved oak rose gracefully, bending sharply at the landing on the second floor. The heavy sweet fragrance of flowers hung in the cool air from ornate vases, filled with fresh-cut blossom, set at intervals upon delicate gilded tables along the walls. She turned her attention to the earl.

"These are my prized Brussels tapestries of the history of Alexander the Great," he said, pointing to the colorful thick hangings that stretched from floor to ceiling along an entire side of the entrance hall.

"And these are your Italian ancestors?" she asked, nodding at the dozens of paintings, some life-size, that covered the other wall.

"Yes. The Pareses trace their history back many hundreds of years. You will find their likenesses all over the villa. That gentleman, however, is not Italian. That is my father, the third Earl of Clare, painted when I was very young."

She heard a softening in his voice and studied the heavy-set man whose dark brown eyes seemed to mirror some secret amusement. He appeared a confident man, radiating masculine vitality, just as did his son. How many times she had seen the same arrogant tilt of the head, the same autocratic set of the jaw.

"There are many similarities between the two of you," she said. "And your mother?"

"She is there," he said, pointing a dismissing finger toward a portrait whose subject was a woman in her late twenties. Creamy white shoulders rose above a gown of severe black. She was beautiful, yet she seemed to Cassie rather cold and haughty.

"You have her eyes," Cassie said, wondering at the curtness in his voice.

"I trust that the eyes are the only trait I inherited from her."

She cocked her head at him questioningly.

He shrugged and said only, "She was far from a loving woman. She did not care much for my father, or for me, his son. She wasted no time remarrying after his death. Indeed, she had not the taste to last out her widow's year. Her son, my half-brother, will doubtless come to visit us soon. He is a likable enough fellow, charming and gallant with the ladies, and with an incurable penchant for extravagant finery."

Cassie started, for he had not told her of a half-brother. Before she could ask him more about this hitherto unknown relation, he said, "Come, let us go upstairs, and I will show you our room."

She flinched at this reminder of their intimacy. She walked stiffly beside him up the wide staircase, while he told her the classical themes of the colorful frescoes upon the white stucco walls and pointed out more Parese ancestors, who were displayed in what seemed an endless procession from the earliest century. The brightly polished oak stairs made not a sound as they ascended. She smiled, re-membering the groaning of the stairs at Hemphill Hall when the slightest weight was on them.

The earl turned at the top of the stairs and addressed Scargill, who stood in quiet conversation with Marrina and Paolo in the entrance hall. "Bring up the luggage when it arrives, Scargill."

"Aye, my lord." Scargill nodded and turned again to the woman. Cassie heard a sudden sharp tone in his voice but could not make out his words.

The earl chuckled. "If I am not mistaken, Scargill is likely upbraiding Marrina for her overt disapproval of you. No doubt he is telling her that you are to be treated as a valued guest in the villa and not as a mistress brought here for my dissolute pleasures." He patted her stiff shoulder. "I daresay, *cara,* if you consented to wed me, she would unbend toward you immediately."

"I don't want her to unbend." Cassie turned away from the carved oak railing to walk quickly down an imposing corridor. There was carpeting under her feet now, of thick, dark blue wool, touched as if with an artist's brush with small circles of white.

They passed many closed doors, bedchambers undoubt-edly, and Cassie would have preferred any one of them to sharing a room with the earl. He paused before a wide double door, turned the ivory knobs, and said grandly, "Our bedchamber, *cara,* and my favorite room in the villa."

She stepped past him into an awesomely large room, more nearly the size of a ballroom than a bedchamber. The white stucco walls were only rarely broken by portraits, giving the room an even greater feeling of airiness and space. Gold brocade curtains lined the opposite wall. At either end of the room were white marble fireplaces, adorned with swags of fruit and winged cherubs. The oak floor was strewn with several brightly woven carpets, each individual in color and design. There was an open arch at the southern end of the room, and as she neared it, she realized the room was even larger than she imagined and in the shape of an L.

She turned to the earl, who stood watching her intently. "It is impressive, my lord," she allowed. She looked a question toward the heavy brocade curtains.

"Now you will see why this is my favorite of all the villa's chambers."

She watched silently as he walked to the end of the curtains and tugged on a velvet cord. The gold brocade material slowly opened upon floor-to-ceiling windows that extended the length of the room. She stared out to a terraced garden filled with exotic flowers, thick ivy, and many kinds of trees. To the north, beyond the highest terrace, were rolling green hills that rose to meet the sky. She tightly clamped her tongue over an exclamation of delight and walked through the arched portal. Genoa spread out before her to the south, its distance only adding to its startling grandeur. The Mediterranean glistened in the afternoon sun, and she could see the tall masts of ships bobbing up and down in the harbor.

The earl suddenly turned a latch on a window and it became a door that led to a long, narrow balcony. Its white stone railing was covered with a profusion of flower boxes that made the air redolent with their scent. There were pink and white carnations, dazzling white camellias, jasmine, and even orange and oleander trees standing upright in pots at either end of the balcony. She leaned over the railing to look down into the terraced gardens and saw white marble statues of men and women in classical poses surrounded by bowers of orange and myrtle blossoms. She heard the cool, tinkling sound of water and saw on a lower terrace a graceful fountain, shaped like a huge cup, covered with ivy. A statue of a small boy, a water jug over his shoulder, stood upon it, pouring a steady stream of water into the fountain.

Cassie drew a deep breath. "It is lovely. Indeed, I have never seen so beautiful a scene in my life. It all seems to fit together perfectly."

"Yes," he agreed, leaning his elbows on an open stretch of railing next to her. "If it were not for the more restrained customs that prevail here, I would never miss England." At her questioning look, he continued, "The

Genoese are a very thrifty people. Indeed, many of the gowns I bought for you would be seen as ostentatious here. If you see me dressed frequently in somber black, it is because I wish my Genoese brothers and colleagues to see me as one of them and not some foreign nobleman." He paused a moment and shook his head ruefully. "There is one item that the Genoese do not consider extravagant, and that is the wig."

"But you never wear a wig," she said, smiling up at him despite herself.

"True, and I never shall. But the Genoese as a rule adore them—and the most outlandish concoctions. At the beginning of this century the Doge even passed a law against them, but you'll notice there is a wig on every head in all the portraits from that period. I believe the law is still entered in the books, but it is not heeded any more now than it was then. You will discover that there are more wig makers in Genoa than there are cafes."

"My father always wore one," Cassie said. "White with little sausage rolls over his ears."

"Yes, I remember," he said with a smile. He turned and Cassie followed him back into the bedchamber. "There are dressing rooms through that door." Even as he pointed toward the far end of the bedchamber, he was aware that Cassie was not looking at the dressing room door but at his giant bed, which was set upon a dais, its four thick posts carved with fat, naked cherubs.

He grinned. "It is rather impressive, is it not? My father was quite fond of it. When one becomes used to that expanse of bed, the one aboard *The Cassandra* seems like a niggardly bunk."

Indeed, Cassie thought, five people could stretch out, side by side, and not be overly crowded. She raised strained eyes to his face. "Surely there are many bedchambers in the villa, my lord. I would prefer to have my own room, if you please."

"No," he said easily, still smiling, but with finality. "Did I not make it clear to you that we would live as man and wife?"

"But your servants, visitors . . ." Her voice trailed off in embarrassment.

"Perhaps their disapproval will speed your change from *La Signorina* to *La Signora* and *La Contessa*."

"Never."

Scargill came in then, valises and portmanteaux under his arms. He was breathing heavily from exertion, and Cassie turned on the earl. "Where are your other servants, O most noble lord? Must poor Scargill do everything?"

"Paolo is seeing to the return of the barouche, I doubt not. As I told you, *cara,* the Genoese nobility are a thrifty lot. Paolo and Marrina see to the house and stables. Scargill looks after me, and I will have Marrina bring in one of her many female relations to be your maid. The gardens, though, require more attention than we mere mortals. You will meet Sordello's father, Marco, and his three minions in due time."

"It's fagged ye look, my lord," Scargill said, his eyes narrowed on the earl's face. "Ye need rest if yer shoulder is to heal quickly."

The earl could not disagree. His shoulder pained him. He turned to Cassie, whose attention was again upon the massive bed.

"Would you care to rest with me, Cassandra, before dinner? The bed would certainly accommodate any distance you wish to keep from me."

"Perhaps the madonna would like to see the rest of the villa, my lord." He added severely, "As to yer dinner, I'll instruct Marrina to serve both of ye here. The last thing ye need, my lord, is to force yer poor shoulder into evening raiment. Madonna, take yerself to the balcony and I'll assist his lordship into his dressing gown."

As the earl hesitated, Cassie said, "He is quite right, my lord. Someone of your age must needs avail himself of more sleep as the years pass."

The earl threw back his head and gave a loud laugh. "You can see, Scargill, you were right, she cannot match wits with me. Now, *cara,* do as Scargill has instructed, unless, that is, you wish to see me naked."

"I would prefer to see the gardens," she said finally, and at the earl's nod, she left the bedchamber.

Cassie found another glass door at the back of the villa and walked into the garden. She breathed a sigh of relief, for she had not seen Marrina and her narrowed sloe eyes. She wandered aimlessly through the lush gardens, stopping to sniff at a particularly lovely flower or touch the velvety petals. She came upon Marco, a slight man of medium stature, so tanned by the sun that he looked almost like a Moor. He was, he informed her in his low musical Italian, his lordship's head gardener. She remembered that Marco was the boy Sordello's father. He gave her a disinterested salute with a trowel and proceeded by and large to ignore her. She stood for a moment, frowning after him. But she decided that such treatment suited her mood, for she wished to be alone. She found that she repeatedly drew up with a start at the realization that she was in Italy, firmly installed in the earl's villa. She kept asking herself what she was going to do, but sensible answers eluded her. Each time she swore that she would not remain here, she felt a niggling sense of uncertainty. Even though she ranted at herself for her lack of determination, she could not dismiss the confusion that pervaded her thoughts. She shook her head, trying to clear the image of him from her mind. But she could not. She felt the earl's powerful body against hers, felt his mouth caressing her, and knew that she could not deny the passion he brought to her.

When the evening air became too chilly, she wandered back into the villa, only to be informed by Scargill that the earl was busy with business matters and would join her after dinner. She ate alone in the bedchamber, a meal of flaky fish broiled to perfection and topped with a thick wine sauce, and toyed with a single glass of wine until, finally, the earl entered. He looked tired and she felt a stab of guilt, thinking that his shoulder pained him.

"Forgive me, *cara,* for leaving you our first evening."

He sat down at the small table and poured himself a glass of wine. "You enjoyed your afternoon?"

"I met Marco, your head gardener. He does not seem to talk much."

He grinned, but she saw it was with an effort. "You should not have conducted business when you are not yet well." The grin deepened at her sharp tone.

"I shall take your advice on the morrow, my dear." He rose and stretched. "Lord, I think I could sleep the clock around."

Cassie felt sleepy herself, but did not admit to it. She excused herself and walked quickly toward the dressing room to undress.

"Do not forget the rules, *cara,*" he called after her.

She bit her lip and left him for a sufficient period of time, she hoped, to ensure that he would be asleep when she returned.

Only a single candle burned, low in its silver holder, when she quietly walked back into the bedchamber, clutching her dressing gown closely about her chemise. The earl lay on his back in the mammoth bed, the covers pulled but to his waist, his eyes closed.

"Don't force me to take off your dressing gown, Cassandra," he said softly. She jumped, nearly knocking the candle to the floor.

"You are a beast," she said, and reluctantly slipped out of her dressing gown.

"And the chemise."

She looked at him closely and saw that he was looking at her through his dark lashes.

"It is cold."

"Then come here and I will warm you."

"I would rather freeze to death." She snuffed out the candle, plunging the room into darkness. With angry, silent movements, she slipped the lace straps from her shoulders and let the chemise fall to the floor.

She heard him sigh, a mocking sigh, she thought, as she crept between the covers on the far side of the bed.

"Tomorrow, perhaps, you will wish me to reacquaint myself with that very provocative birthmark on your left thigh. Good night, *cara,* and sleep well. I am always here, you know, if you become cold during the night."

She locked her thighs together, pressing the tiny pink birthmark firmly between them, and drew into a small ball, her back to him.

The downstairs clock chimed one short stroke before Cassie, still uncomfortably cold, fell finally into a light, restless sleep.

Chapter 13

The earl stretched, carefully flexed his shoulder, and grimaced. He cursed softly and gingerly shifted his left arm into its sling.

"Ye'll need more time, my lord, perhaps another week, afore ye've got yer full strength back."

"I believe your telling me that, Scargill, was quite unnecessary."

Scargill chuckled, shaking his head in a bemused fashion as he gathered up his master's discarded dressing gown.

"May I ask the reason for your display of humor?" the earl asked as he sat down to have his boots pulled on. It wasn't the pain that galled him, but rather being so damned helpless. It did not sit well with him to have Scargill help him bathe, all the while clucking and scolding him not to get the bandages wet, as if he were some errant schoolboy.

"Aye, ye may, my lord." He pulled on a gleaming black boot before replying. "I was just thinking that if a man had shot ye, ye'd have likely stuck a knife in his gullet. Lord, what a man will forgive a woman."

The earl shot him a frown beneath his arched black brows. He could still picture Cassandra's white, strained face, her shock at what she had done etched in her eyes the instant after she fired the pistol.

"And yet, ye beat her for an offense that harmed ye or anyone else not one whit."

"Much must be forgiven since she did save me from drowning, my friend. And her quickness of wit with Khar El-Din surely must impress even a literal, dour Scotsman. Remember, Scargill, her only motive for shooting me was to escape. I cannot fault her for trying. Incidentally, she was not out of your sight yesterday afternoon, was she?"

"Nay, not for a moment. She spent most of her time wandering about the gardens or simply sitting staring at those immoral naked statues ye have scattered about. I had the feeling she knew someone was watching her."

The earl nodded and rose. "Joseph will be coming to the villa the day after tomorrow. Cassandra has a certain fondness for him, I believe. When I am not able to be with her, it will be his task to watch over her. I am fairly certain that she will fling her fury at me when she discovers his purpose, not him."

"Ye will rest the next couple of days, my lord, will ye not?"

"Yes. If my shipping and banking interests have suffered in my absence the past five months, a few more days will make little difference. I have been thinking also that we should hold a dinner party in, say, a week. I will be able to conduct any pressing business matters with the gentlemen present, and Cassandra can meet the cream of Genoese society."

"Will the wee lass meet them as a *signora* or a *signorina?*"

"I daresay that Cassandra Brougham will remain Cassandra Brougham. I can ensure her obedience in some areas, Scargill, but I cannot put a gag in her mouth."

"There will be some who will not be pleasant to her, my lord. Ye've already seen that prude Marrina's reaction to her. Rest assured that I told her the truth of the matter, but she did not believe me. I could tell by her unappealing snort of disdain. 'Tis ever the woman that suffers, ye know, regardless of the circumstances. And I ask myself, my lord, why ye want the madonna to mix with Genoese society. Do ye not fear that she'll denounce ye in front of yer guests?"

The earl gave him an engaging smile. "Do you take me for a fool, Scargill? I have, as a matter of fact, given the matter much thought. I am fairly confident that by the time of the dinner party, she will have no wish to complain to our guests about my fiendish behavior."

Scargill wanted very much to ask his master the source

of his confidence, but he realized that such an inquiry would be impertinent.

"I hope that ye may be right, my lord," was all that he said.

"Trust me, my friend," the earl said. "Now, if you will ask Marrina to fetch up breakfast, I will awaken Cassandra."

The earl walked quietly across the long expanse of his bedchamber and drew up to the side of the bed. Cassandra lay on her side so close to the edge of the bed that he imagined any sudden movement on her part would send her toppling to the floor. Her thick hair fanned about her face on the pillow. She had drawn herself into a tight ball, her knees close to her chest. His expression softened.

He was on the point of waking her when she moaned softly in her sleep and turned on her back, flinging one arm above her head on the pillow. He grinned to himself and gently eased the covers from her shoulders down to her waist. He stared down at her, gazing at the gentle hollows and curves of her body. She was almost too slender, he thought, pulling his eyes away from her breasts, to the outline of her ribs and her waist.

He pulled the covers lower. Her thighs were slightly parted, but he could not see the small spot of pink skin he had teased her about the night before. He lightly laid his flattened hand over the smooth hollow of belly. His hand didn't span the width of her, a good thing.

She shivered and brought her legs up, momentarily trapping his hand. He slowly moved his hand and pressed his fingers downward to touch her. He heard a soft moan, followed shortly by an outraged gasp.

"How dare you." She struggled frantically away from his hand, rolling away from him to the center of the bed, and pulling the covers about her.

He grinned engagingly at her and gingerly sat down beside her. "I was just returning your favor, *cara*. You were enjoying my touch, I believe, before you decided it wasn't ladylike to do so."

The final webs of sleep fled Cassie's mind and she sat up, drawing the covers about her like a shield.

"I was asleep."

"I know," he said. "That altogether encouraging moan was woven from an erotic dream, no doubt."

For a moment, Cassie's tongue lay leaden in her mouth. He always seemed to be able to twist her words and their intent. "You were looking at me."

"True, and a most pleasing sight you are, *cara*. Now, as much as I regret it, our breakfast will be arriving shortly and I fear that Marrina would be shocked to the soles of her rather flat feet were she to see you tousled and quite naked in my bed." He rose leisurely and fetched her dressing gown.

"Here, Cassandra." He tossed her the dressing gown, turned, and walked to the other end of the room to sit himself in front of the small table.

And not a moment too soon, he thought, gazing at Cassandra from the corner of his eye as she struggled into the dressing gown.

"*Entri!*" he called.

Marrina walked slowly into the bedchamber, her arms laden with covered dishes, and her full lips drawn into their now familiar tight scowl. Although Marrina did not wish to, her eyes slewed in the direction of the bed. The young foreign lady—lady, ha!, she thought—did not in Marrina's eyes appear to be undergoing any cruel treatment from her master. She did look rather flushed, and rightly so, in Marrina's opinion. Perhaps the girl did have some shame.

"*Buon giorno, signore,*" she said stiffly, forcing her attention back to her master's face. "I have brought your breakfast."

"*Mille grazie,* Marrina. *Ho appetito.*"

Il signore said something in English to the girl and she moved reluctantly toward the table. He turned to Marrina.

"*Grazie,*" he said shortly, and waved his hand in dismissal.

She curtsied stiffly and walked from the bedchamber.

The earl said between mouthfuls of warm toast, "I am at your disposal for the next couple of days, Cassandra.

There are many places for you to see and, I trust, enjoy. You can begin to accustom yourself to Italian sights, people, and living before you meet Genoese society."

Cassie said coldly, still smarting from the earl's provoking hand and Marrina's pursed lips, "You mean that after a couple of days I am to be spared your presence, my lord?"

"Oh, never that, *cara*," he said cheerfully. "Surely you would not believe me so ungallant. But I will need to spend some time in Genoa, though I do conduct most of my business from here." He paused a moment, then said meaningfully, "Joseph will be arriving shortly. He will watch over you when I am not here."

"What you mean to say is that poor Joseph is to be my guard."

"Perhaps, if you wish to view his presence in that light. I trust you will not try to shoot him." He softened his tone. "Your life is with me now, Cassandra. I pray that you will soon accustom yourself."

"I think not," she replied, quite softly, and rose from the table. "If you will excuse me, my lord, I wish to bathe and dress now."

"As you will, my love," he said easily, and moved to pull the bell cord. "I will have Paolo fetch your bath water."

The day passed pleasantly enough for Cassie, though she did not admit it to the earl. She became acquainted with the palm trees, whose bizarre layered trunks and wide serrated leaves lined the perimeter of the terraced gardens, and the odd gray weathered olive trees that seemed content in the most arid soil and climbed up the steeper slopes of the hills in neat layered rows. All the marble statues had titles, and each a fascinating story. When the earl showed her a colossal statue of Jupiter, framed by a rose-covered marble bower in a lower garden terrace, he said with a grin, "Each time I see old Jupiter, I think about another statue of this esteemed god, built over the tomb of a dog given by Charles V to Andrea Doria, who was, incidentally, one of my illustrious ancestors. The story goes that for his maintenance of the tomb, he received the principality of

Melfi. To thank the Emperor, Andrea Doria entertained him and a hundred others to a banquet, where the astonished guests saw three services of silver plates from which they had eaten flung into the harbor after being removed from the table. Andrea Doria, in the true Genoese spirit of thriftiness, achieved this magnificent gesture without being a penny the poorer—he stationed fishermen with nets below the terrace to catch the plates as they fell."

She laughed heartily and plied him with an endless stream of questions. It struck her forcibly that the earl was an amusing companion, and she frowned at her lapse.

"You are troubled, *cara?*"

"Must you even read my thoughts?" She sat down on a marble bench that faced another fountain.

"But, dear one, have I not told you that we are to be as one in all things?" As she stared stiffly ahead of her, he added softly, "I do thank you for sitting down. As you have said, my advanced years compel me to rest."

"Is your shoulder paining you?" she asked, unaware that her eyes narrowed in sudden concern.

"A bit, perhaps, but I shall survive. After luncheon, *cara,* I will introduce you to a sacred Italian custom."

"Pray what is that?" she asked warily.

"In English one would call it a nap. Here it is called a *siesta.* When the sun is at its zenith, Italians retreat indoors, close their shutters, and sleep. It is, of course, a marvelous opportunity for other pursuits as well."

He closed his hand over hers and caressed her fingers.

"When will you believe that I have no such demands of you, my lord?" She tried to jerk her hand away, but he held it fast.

"I will believe that, *cara,* when you cease to find pleasure in my arms." He rose and drew her up with him. "Let us have lunch, little one."

Perversely, Cassie was a trifle peeved when the earl made no sexual demands on her when they returned to the bedchamber after a light luncheon. Yet she found that she quite enjoyed the *siesta.* Clothed only in her chemise, the curtains drawn against the hot afternoon sun, she stretched out on the large bed and was soon asleep.

She was awakened by the gentle touch of a hand on her bare arm. An angry rebuke rose to her lips as she opened her eyes. To her surprise, she peered up into the fresh round face of a young girl who was staring curiously down at her.

"*Voglia scusarmi, signorina,*" the girl said in a soft musical voice.

Cassie shook English words from her mind. "Who are you?" she asked in Italian, struggling up on her elbows.

The girl grinned at the heavily accented Italian. "I am Rosina, *signorina,* niece to Marrina. I am to be your maid. *Il signore* asked that I help you to dress. He wishes to see you in the library."

"Very well," Cassie said, and swung her feet over the side of the bed. Rosina, she saw, was dressed in somber black, her glossy black hair pulled tightly back from her round face in as severe a knot as that worn by her aunt, Marrina. She looked quite young, perhaps sixteen. Cassie became aware that the girl was staring at her. "Well, what is it?" she asked, thinking the girl would be as sour-minded as her aunt.

"It is your hair, *signorina.* It is like spun gold, and so thick. I have occasionally seen hair of a fair color, but not like yours. I am said to have an ability with hair. If you would allow me, *signorina,* I would be most honored to dress yours."

Cassie felt instantly guilty at her rudeness and said in a friendlier voice, "Thank you for your compliment, Rosina. I would be most pleased if you would help me."

Rosina nodded her head and smiled. Two deep dimples appeared in her plump cheeks. "I will fetch you a gown, *signorina.*"

Cassie rose and walked to the commode in the dressing room to splash cool water on her face. When she returned to the bedchamber, she stood for a moment watching her new maid. She looked to Cassie to be a gentle creature, her dark brown eyes guileless. Cassie wondered whether she would ever see Rosina's placid expression replaced by tight-lipped disapproval.

"You are very young, Rosina," Cassie said as her new maid helped her into a light muslin gown of pale blue.

"*Si, signorina,*" she answered brightly, motioning Cassie to be seated before her dressing table. "The nuns told my mother that I was too efficient a servant to waste myself getting married just yet." She shrugged philosophically. "Perhaps when I am seventeen I will want a husband and babies."

As she brushed and arranged Cassie's hair, she continued in her soft voice, "It is honored I am, *signorina,* to be allowed to come to the Villa Parese. *Il signore* is an honored and much admired nobleman despite the fact that he is—"

A flush rose to Rosina's plump cheeks.

"Despite the fact that he is half-English," Cassie finished, smiling.

"*Si, signorina,* though most do not think of that now. It is only that he has just returned from England that makes one remember." She paused for a moment, concentrating on the thick plait she was braiding. Cassie, who had little liking for braids, frowned, but held her tongue waiting to see the result. In a very few moments, she stared at herself in the mirror, startled and quite pleased with the style Rosina had created. The maid had fashioned her hair in what Cassie thought of as a Roman style, with a coronet of braids atop her head, and the remainder of her long hair falling from the circle down her back.

"It is lovely, Rosina," she said, and shook her head to feel the mass of hair swinging free. "I could never achieve such a result."

Cassie saw a gleam of pleasure light the girl's dark eyes, and added, "I must thank your aunt for bringing you here."

Actually, the last person Cassie wanted to see was Rosina's aunt. But Marrina stood at the bottom of the staircase, her eyes narrowed at nothing in particular, a dust cloth in her hand.

"*Che cosa Le abbisogna, signorina?*"

Cassie pursed her lips at the rude tone. What did she

want, indeed. It was time, she decided, squaring her shoulders, to put this thorny woman in her place. Cassie stopped on the bottom step purposefully, so that she towered over the housekeeper, and said coolly, "I would like you to fetch me a glass of lemonade, Marrina. It is to be cold, mind you, and not too sweet. I shall be in the library with *il signore.*"

Marrina had very small, crowded front teeth, Cassie observed dispassionately, teeth unsuited for snarling.

"I am really quite thirsty, Marrina. Now, if you please." She walked around the rigidly silent housekeeper. "*Mille grazie.*" She drew up after several steps, a bit of devilment burgeoning, and asked in the blandest of voices, "*Voglia scusarmi,* Marrina, but are you a *signora* or a *signorina?*"

"*Signora,*" Marrina snapped. She turned on her heel and disappeared through a door on the far side of the entrance hall.

Cassie was still smiling at her minor triumph when she reached the great oak doors of the library. She held the griffen-shaped knob and cocked her ears. Either the earl was talking to himself or there was someone with him. She stood quietly for a few more moments before chiding herself not to be a timorous fool. Whoever was with the earl could not be more disapproving than Marrina.

She opened the doors.

She had had only a cursory glimpse of the library that morning, for she had been anxious to continue exploring the gardens. She had initially disliked the dark-paneled room. Its heavy leather chairs and prepossessing mahogany desk were too stark and masculine for her taste.

The earl stood against the desk, dressed as he had been earlier in black breeches, loose white shirt, and black boots, his right hand cupped beneath his slinged elbow. He looked up, a welcoming smile softening his features. Cassie looked upon a young gentleman who was lounging negligently against the mantlepiece of a black and white marble fireplace, his hands plunged into his waistcoat pockets. His black hair was powdered, and tied at the back of his neck with a dark blue velvet ribbon. He was slight of build, but finely proportioned, not much taller than was she. His black brows were arched above his olive complexion, flaring upward toward his temples, and his dark eyes seemed somehow familiar to Cassie. He looked every inch an elegant Italian gentleman. He parted his full lips slowly and smiled at her, bending slightly in a bow of recognition at the waist. He was also very graceful, she thought to herself, smiling back at him.

"Cassandra, my dear," the earl said to her. "I have a surprise for you. This is my half-brother, Caesare Bellini."

He moved forward to stand at the earl's side, and she recognized him as the earl's half-brother. He had the same high cheekbones and the same straight Roman nose. She saw that the young man's dark eyes were twinkling attractively and at the same time taking in every aspect of her appearance. He said slowly, as if fearing that she would not understand him, "I am honored, *signorina.* The Villa Parese has never housed such beauty."

Housed, she thought. He makes it sound as if I were a horse or a painting. Still, she nodded her head and made him a slight curtsy.

"I only discovered recently that the earl was blessed with any relatives, *signore.*"

"You must ask him if he believes me a blessing, *signorina.* My brother tells me that you are English."

She wondered silently what else the earl had told his half-brother. "*Si, signore,* I am English." She shot the earl a challenging look. "Although I find your country very interesting, I must confess that I miss my homeland immensely." She would have said more, but Marrina entered, a silver tray in her hands. Without even looking at Cassie, she walked to the earl.

"The *signorina's* lemonade, *il signore.*"

So you have engaged my housekeeper in battle, have you, *cara,* he thought. "Most kind of you, Marrina. You may set the tray on the table. *La signorina* is most fond of lemonade."

The housekeeper curtsied deeply and walked stiffly from the room, her lips so pursed that she looked as if she had been sucking a lemon.

After Marrina left the library, the earl said lightly to

Caesare, "As you see, brother, Marrina has not yet taken to the idea that she now has a mistress to obey."

"That is not exactly true, *signore,*" Cassie said sweetly. "If it were the contessa and not the mistress, I am certain that she would be all compliance."

"You have but to name the day, *cara,*" the earl said, his dark eyes gleaming.

Cassie opened her mouth, then closed it. She saw that the earl's half-brother was eyeing the two of them with considerable confusion.

She turned away and sat down in a deeply stuffed leather chair. She ignored her lemonade. "The earl has told me very little of you, *signore.*"

Caesare spread his hands before him. "It would obviously not be to his advantage to tell you all about me, *signorina.* He is such an ungainly giant and even wears a sling on his arm. So graceless, it seems, that he returns from England a battered man."

Cassie's smile at his gay banter disappeared. "It was not he who was graceless, *signore.*"

The earl gave a little chuckle. "Let us just say that I was careless, Caesare."

"It appears that I have hit upon a mystery," Caesare said gaily, looking from Cassie's flushed face to the earl's grinning one. As if he sensed further inquiry would add to Cassie's discomfiture, he adroitly changed the topic. "Genoa has been bereft without your dashing presence, Antonio, but your business concerns, as usual, continue to prosper. You'll not believe it, but old Montalto has been in hot pursuit of the charming Giovanna."

The earl appeared only mildly interested, but Cassie found that she was all attention awaiting his response.

"I fear Giovanna would topple poor Montalto into an early grave." He grinned ruefully and shook his head. "For a man so astute in worldly matters, it is a surprise that he would succumb to the charms of a woman half his age."

"Caesare, will you share a glass of wine with us? We can toast Montalto's success with the fair Giovanna."

Cassie experienced a twinge of disappointment when Caesare, regretfully, took his leave.

He gallantly raised her hand to his lips and lightly kissed her palm. "You must insist that Antonio invite me more often to the Villa Parese, *signorina.*"

"You know that you are always welcome, fop," the earl said, and gave his brother a light buffet on his immaculate shoulder.

Caesare shot him a mischievous smile. "But Antonio, with but your company to sustain me in the past, I really had no enduring interest. All is different now."

"I will look forward to seeing you again soon, *signore,*" Cassie said, and meant it.

"May we always be in such agreement, *signorina.*" He proffered his half-brother a mock bow and gave Cassie a droll smile when Marrina came into the library to see him out.

In the evening, as the earl and Cassie ate their dinner in a small protected veranda that overlooked the gardens, she lowered her fork to her plate and said in a silky voice, "I find myself wondering, my lord, what your very kind half-brother would do if I told him of your infamy. Surely he would not approve your ruthlessness."

The earl cocked a sleek black brow and sipped his wine before replying, "Actually, *cara,* I was pleased that you held your tongue. If you had not, I fear you would have been much mortified. Although Caesare much enjoys playing the gallant to a beautiful woman, his loyalty to me cannot be questioned."

Cassie looked away, angered by his amused drawl. "So you told him nothing."

The earl sat back in his chair and crossed his long legs. "I told him that you were English and my honored guest."

"Honored guest. You know very well that he now believes me your mistress."

"Doubtless you are right, Cassandra, but let us not argue about it. If you have wish to throw yourself at my poor half-brother and beg for his protection—" He shrugged eloquently. "He will likely admire my audaciousness."

Her shoulders slumped forward. His dark eyes softened upon her face, and he gentled his voice. "I told you, did I not, that Caesare is my only living relation? It is from our mother, and her dowry to my father, that I inherited the Villa Parese."

Cassie looked up. "Parese—that was her family name?"

"Yes. It is a very old, revered family in Genoese history, dating back many hundreds of years to Andrea Doria, when Genoa still ruled the seas."

"Andrea Doria—he is the one who tossed away all the silver plates." The earl paused a moment, his long fingers deftly peeling the skin off an orange.

He gave her an engaging smile. "Yes, he is the one. He was a brilliant man, an admiral, who saved Genoa early in the sixteenth century, primarily from the French, but of course there were others, like the Spanish and the Milanese. It was he who gave Genoa an oligarchic constitution and reestablished peace on the Riviera."

The earl leaned forward and handed Cassie a succulent orange slice. "It tastes quite sweet. I hope you will like it." His long fingers lightly touched the palm of her hand.

He watched her nibble at the orange slice between her even white teeth and smile as a drop of juice trickled down her chin. He sat back in his chair and continued, his tone somewhat pensive. "Unfortunately, since Andrea Doria, Genoa has been sadly bereft of heroes. But we survive, as Europe's bankers, primarily. And that, Cassandra, is what occupies my time when I am not being a nobleman of leisure, or traveling."

She looked up, startled. "You—a banker? An English earl is not involved in trade," she said succinctly.

"It is only the Genoese half that is so involved." He uncrossed his long legs and stretched them out in front of him. Her eyes were drawn momentarily to his thighs, encased in the black tightly knit breeches. "It is a long tradition," he said, handing her another orange section. "Back in the early fifteenth century, during one of the darker moments in Genoa's history, a group of local merchants pooled their talents and their resources and created the Banco di San Giorgio. Over the years, these men from Genoa's patrician families perfected the art of credit. If Philip II of Spain needed money for foreign conquest, it was to the bankers of Genoa that he applied. But, of course, things change. Genoa cannot protect herself from foreign intervention. In our century, we have known cruel conquest by the French, and the Austrians in league with the Spanish. Only eight years ago we had to sell that accursed island of Corsica to France." He leaned forward and gently wiped Cassie's mouth and chin with a white napkin. "It is sticky, but I hope you liked it."

"I very much liked it, my lord. It tasted very sweet." His gentleness confused her, and she did not draw away from his lightly caressing fingers.

"Enough of Italian history, *cara*." He tossed down the napkin and gently wrapped his fingers around a thick tress of hair on her shoulder. "I do not think I told you how much I admire your new style. It is very elegant."

"I wish you would stop being so nice," she said and pulled away from his hand. His lips were slightly parted, revealing his strong white teeth.

He grinned at her, a boyish grin so engaging that she smiled in response.

"But, *cara*, it comes quite naturally to me. I am really not such a bad sort of fellow, you know, if you will give me a chance. And it is my wish always to please you."

His eyes fell to the white expanse of bosom that swelled above her pale yellow silk bodice. She laced her fingers over her breasts, aware of a delicious tingling sensation spreading through her body.

She pushed back her chair and rose abruptly. "I am cold, my lord."

"I trust, my love, that I have a pleasurable remedy." He rose leisurely and walked to her. She licked her lower lip, but did not try to move away from him. For several moments, he did not attempt to touch her, but merely stood before her. When he finally reached out his hand to her, Cassie stepped into the circle of his arm and arched her back against his chest. She raised her face to his, mutely. He teased her mouth with his tongue, until with a deep sigh, she parted her lips and let his tongue mingle with hers. He felt the deep heaving of her breasts against his chest and tightened his arm about her back to press her closer.

"I cannot carry you, *cara*," he whispered, his mouth so close to hers that she could feel the warmth of his breath. She thought crazily that he tasted of sweet oranges.

"I know," she sighed softly, nuzzling her cheek against his chin.

He kissed the tip of her nose, and the base of her white throat. She parted her lips and moaned softly as he took her mouth.

"Will you make love with me, Cassandra?"

"Yes." The ache in her body was almost painful.

There were no more words between them. He smiled when Cassie, once in their bedchamber, walked hurriedly into the dressing room to undress. He did not tease her for her show of modesty.

Once he was naked, his clothing tossed in a pile upon the floor, the earl lit a single candle and climbed into bed. He had not long to wait. Cassie walked from the dressing room clothed only in a gossamer chemise, her hair brushed loose down her back.

He smiled at her, pulled back the covers, and lightly patted the space beside him. "That is a lovely chemise, Cassandra, but I would much prefer seeing it next to my clothes— on the floor."

She hesitated for a long moment before slipping the straps from her shoulders. She looked faintly flushed. "I really should not want—"

"Want what, my love?"

She shook her head uncertainly, slithered out of the chemise, and slipped into bed. She curled on her side, away from him.

He lay quietly, listening a moment to her breathing. "*Cara*, what should you not want?" He extended his arm until his hand touched her smooth flesh. He lightly stroked her spine, his fingers resting a moment at the small of her back, and splayed them outward over her hips. Slowly, under the exquisite teasing of his fingers, he felt her relax her muscles.

"I should not want you so very much," she whispered,

her voice breaking. She rolled across to him and pressed her shaking body against his side. She clasped her hands about his face and captured his mouth. He was undone at her innocent passion. He moaned into her open mouth and felt her tongue touch his.

He slipped his left arm out of the sling, grasped her hips, and lifted her on top of him. Her eyes were on his face, wide and dazed.

"Help me come into you, *cara.*" He lifted her slightly and felt her small hand close around him.

He groaned as he felt himself engulfed in the warmth of her body. He pulled her upright so that she straddled him and thrust deep into her.

Cassie splayed her hands on his belly, tangling her fingers in his thick black hair. She felt the surging power of him as he moved against her.

Suddenly, he groaned, deep in his throat, and his fingers dug into her sides. It was as if her own rising passion was held abruptly suspended. She felt him shudder beneath her and her eyes flew to his face. For an instant, she did not understand. She held herself stiff, uncertain, as if suddenly apart from him. His body tensed, and the hard muscles of his belly rippled under her fingers.

"Anthony," she whispered, her voice a confused question.

His response was a jagged moan, and he suddenly exploded deep within her.

The earl slowly opened his eyes at the touch of Cassie's hand over his chest.

"What are you doing, *cara?*"

Startled, she pulled back her hand. "I was but feeling your heart. The pounding is lessening."

"I hope so, else I should be in a sorry state." He blinked his eyes, taking in the thick golden hair that fell lazily over her shoulders, and onto her breasts. He raised his hand and stroked her. She quivered at his touch, her pupils nearly black in the soft candlelight.

"My poor love," he said softly, and lifted her off him onto her back.

"I don't understand," she began.

He knew that she needed only release, and when his

mouth closed over her, she gasped in delight. Just as she had listened to his moans of pleasure, he reveled in the soft, breathless cries that came from her mouth. He felt her slender body stiffen and writhe in her climax. She clutched his head between her hands, and pressed her hips convulsively against his mouth.

"Please, Anthony," she moaned, "come inside me now."

He grinned ruefully, kissed her quivering flesh once more lightly, and drew himself up to lie beside her on his side.

"My heart is still beating woefully fast. Will you not—" Her voice broke off as he kissed her parted lips.

"I am sorry, my love, but for the moment at least, I fear I cannot oblige you. You see, that is why a gentleman must give his lady her pleasure first."

"You mean that you should not have left me?"

"No, most assuredly I should not have." He stroked her breast with gentle tenderness. "You gave me great pleasure, Cassandra. No woman has ever before—" He stopped abruptly, for a tiny pucker had appeared between her brows.

She said, her tone strangely unreadable, "You mean that you have, that is to say, there have been many other ladies?"

He stretched onto his back and pulled her languid body against his side. Her directness and candor amused him. Surely, even in her innocence, she must realize that he had not spent his adult years as a celibate. He grinned at her, pushing back a cloud of hair from her face. "It is not at all important," he said, and surprisingly, she sighed and nestled her cheek against his shoulder.

He felt her fingers lightly stroke his chest and down his belly. Her lips touched his shoulder and her tongue gently caressed his skin. He felt himself respond to her, delighted that she wanted him and was not embarrassed to show him.

"You are an enchantress, Cassandra," he said. He entered her slowly, easily, for she was moist and ready for him. He pressed his hand against her hips, pushing himself more deeply into her. He watched her eyes slowly grow dark and smoky, and controlled himself, until finally she moaned into his mouth and pounded his back with her fists.

They lay quietly together, so close that each could feel the other's heartbeat. He gently kissed her closed eyelids.

"I love you, *cara*," he said softly, "and I want you and need you. I know that it is difficult for you to trust me and give yourself over to me. Believe me, I did not want to hurt you, but I could not let you wed another man. I had to take you away, give you the chance to come to care for me as I do you. I would that you cease thinking of me as a cruel, ruthless villain. I want your happiness, *cara*, and I want you to be my wife, my partner, my lover."

His gentle words, spoken without arrogance or demanding, touched her deeply. She sensed for the first time his vulnerability. For a brief instant, she wanted to respond to him. She struggled to understand herself. Was her passion so powerful a force that she was willing to forgive him all that he had done to her? Slowly, regretfully, she shook her head against his cheek.

"If you truly want my happiness, my lord, then you must grant me a very simple request."

His dark eyes narrowed on her face, but his voice remained soft. "Yes, my love?"

"Allow me to write to Eliott and to Becky."

"And to Edward Lyndhurst?"

She felt his pain through the sudden harshness in his voice.

"Yes."

"The answer is no, Cassandra."

She pulled away from him. "I do not understand. Why, my lord? Are you afraid that Edward will come here and take me away from you?"

"I must admit that it would be awkward for him to arrive unannounced in Genoa," he said calmly, his voice now devoid of gentleness.

"At least let me tell them that I am alive. If you insist upon it, my whereabouts will remain unknown."

He sighed deeply. "The answer is still no. You will write your letter only after you are safely wedded to me and are the Countess of Clare. I will not have Edward Lyndhurst searching Europe for his lost love when she will never be his. It would be needlessly cruel."

"Cruel? You think it less cruel that he believes me dead?"

"Yes, for he must forget you. When he finally hears that you have wed me, the result will be the same. You will no longer be a part of his life."

Cassie sat up, pulling the covers over her breasts. "How can you profess caring for me when you will allow me no freedom? If you want me to be happy, then give me choices. Let me go. I cannot and I will not surrender to you." She shook her fist at him. "You think it your God-given right to possess me, to add me to your worldly possessions as you would a house or a carriage! I will tell you, my lord, I belong to myself and never, do you hear, never will I let myself become a chattel."

"I said nothing of chattel, Cassandra," the earl said, growing anger breaking the calm impassiveness of his voice.

"Then let me go. To the world, I am naught but your current mistress, worthy only to be slighted. Your precious half-brother doubtless believes me the loosest of women, a harlot, a slut. Perhaps Italian ladies cower at your masculine arrogance and are seduced when you coat your words with honey. But I am not."

"You are tangling yourself in an argument that makes no sense. I do not want to own you. I want to cherish you, to love you."

"Ha."

"You are being unreasonable, Cassandra."

She sucked in her breath, so furious that she wanted to strike him. But she held in her anger and said in a cold, taunting voice, "You have told me, my lord, that I do not have a harlot's instincts. Therefore I must assume that your only claim to me is your talent in the bedroom. If I have wish to please myself with your body, I shall so inform you."

"Ah," he said, his voice so smooth that she was momentarily taken off her guard, "I believe that I shall have to write a letter to Edward Lyndhurst, congratulating him on his good fortune. To have leg-shackled himself to a shrew like you would likely have sent him back into the army, that is if you would have allowed him the breeches to wear to make good his escape."

"You are despicable."

He said quite calmly, knowing that he once again held the reins of command, "I am many things, *cara*. It is only you who must needs focus on my more undistinguished traits of character."

"I order you to cease calling me *cara*."

"Order away, little witch. Your conversation is very wearying, Cassandra."

He turned on his back away from her, snuffed out the candle, and pulled the covers to his chest. He fell asleep thinking that it would simply have to be his lot, for the time being at least, to enjoy the rose by night and the thorns by day.

Chapter 14

Il Conte Caesare Bellini stood at a marbled white fireplace, his thumbs hooked in the pockets of his pale yellow waistcoat, his expression questioning.

"My servant told me you wished to see me, Giovanna. I am delighted, for I believed you otherwise engaged this afternoon."

La Contessa Giovanna Giusti smiled slightly, revealing small white teeth, and waved her slender hand impatiently.

"You know, my dearest Caesare, that I would much rather be with you than that doddering old man, Montalto. He told me in that self-important way of his that the Earl of Clare has returned and he must needs attend him at the villa."

She strolled gracefully to him and laid a shapely white hand on his sleeve. "Would you care for a glass of wine, Caesare?"

"If I cannot have your lips, Giovanna," he said. She gave a tinkling laugh and wrapped her arms about his neck.

"You, *caro,* can have whatever you wish." She nuzzled his neck, and lifted her mouth to his. He drew her quickly into his arms and possessed her soft lips until she pushed him away, gasping for breath.

She waved an admonishing finger at him. "You have been without me for but a day, Caesare, and already you behave like a man long marooned on an island." She paused a moment and gazed up at him through thick black lashes. "The servants are to be gone all afternoon. Only I am left, a poor, lonely widow."

Caesare felt her small hand lightly touch his swollen

member, and shuddered. He looked at her slightly parted lips, and imagined them caressing his body. It surprised him that after nearly five months as his lover, she still held such fascination for him.

"It would be my pleasure to serve a lonely widow," he said as his fingers closed over the clasps on the back of her blue velvet gown.

Once in Giovanna's bedchamber, he found himself staring at her as she gracefully removed her clothing. He wondered, a slight frown puckering his forehead, if his half-brother had been as dazzled by Giovanna's white body, if he had also delighted in the touch of her mouth and hands upon him.

He lay on his back, naked, on her smallish bed, watching her brush out her thick raven hair.

"So Montalto told you that the earl had returned."

She turned her face away. After a moment, she said lightly, "Yes. It would seem, too, that your esteemed half-brother did not return from England alone."

Caesare propped himself on his elbows. He wished he could see her face. "I had hoped, Giovanna, that you would not care if my brother returned to Genoa with an entire harem."

Giovanna lowered her hairbrush and turned slowly to face him, a beguiling, teasing expression on her face. "Of course I do not care, *caro.* I merely find it amusing that his lordship must go to such lengths to find himself a woman. It is a woman that he has brought back with him?"

"Your sources of information are, as usual, quite accurate. She is just only a woman, though." At Giovanna's raised eyebrows, he added, "She is hardly more than a girl, eighteen years old at most."

"You have met her then." Her voice was light with indifference, but her brown eyes were watchful.

"Yes." He shook his head. Cassandra had not acted like any man's mistress that he had ever before met, and his brother had never before brought one of his women to his precious villa. "I found her odd," he said finally.

"In what way?" she asked softly, sitting on the bed beside him.

Caesare shrugged his shoulders and reached for her. "I do not wish to talk anymore."

His climax came quickly, explosively. He looked at her through glazed eyes, watching her gracefully wipe her mouth.

Giovanna offered him wine, quickly drinking her own to remove the taste of him.

Caesare laughed softly. "You know, I told my brother about Montalto pursuing you. God, you would topple the old man into his grave were you to give him such pleasure."

"And what was the earl's reaction to that news?" Her voice was light and unconcerned.

Caesare shrugged negligently. "It is hard to know. I remember that he grinned."

Giovanna restrained her impatience. "You agree with me, do you not, Caesare, that the earl should not discover that we are lovers? I am certain that his fierce pride would drive him to withhold even more of your birthright from you."

Caesare stiffened. "My brilliant half-brother must soon learn that I can be trusted with his precious business dealings."

For the moment, she sought to soothe him. "Of a certainty he will. You are young yet, only twenty-five." Young for a man, she thought, grimacing, but not for a woman. "And what of this English girl? How did the earl treat her?"

"I found her behavior curious, if you would know the truth. She is beautiful, if one happens to admire the pink-and-white English fairness."

"Pink and white tells me precisely nothing, Caesare."

Piqued at her insistence, he stripped Cassandra naked in his mind. "She is taller than most Italian ladies and slender as a reed, except, of course, in those places where it is to a woman's advantage not to be. Her eyes are dark blue, the color of the Mediterranean after a storm. And her hair, ah—like spun gold, Giovanna, thick and long; hair that entices a man to bury his face in its softness." He paused a moment and studied Giovanna's perfect oval face, pale now in the dim afternoon light of the salon. "You will of course meet her. My brother mentioned a dinner party. Undoubtedly you will be invited."

She said nothing for a long moment. "I find it odd that the earl, a most fastidious gentleman as you well know, would install this slut at the villa. Does he wish to mock Genoese society?"

"As I told you, Giovanna, I found her behavior unusual. She did not treat the earl with the deference one would expect from a mistress, dependent upon her protector for the clothes on her back. Indeed, she sometimes reverted to English, and her voice was sharp. A slut? I think not. No, she appears to be an English lady of high birth."

"But she is naught but his mistress. No lady of high birth as you describe her would leave her country only to be a nobleman's whore. What you say makes no sense, Caesare."

"I suppose you must be correct, but—"

She whirled about to face him, her raven hair swirling over her shoulders. "But what?"

Caesare shook his head, perplexed lines pulling down the corners of his mouth.

"Perhaps her display of ill-humor was prompted by a simple disagreement. Perhaps she was punishing the earl in front of you, his brother, because he had refused her jewels or gowns or marriage." She paused a moment, her thoughts weaving toward a conclusion that pleased her. "The earl would not long suffer such tantrums. He is proud, quite autocratic, and not used to having his word gainsaid, particularly by a woman. If this English girl is too stupid to realize that, and does not mind her tongue, then the earl will—nay must—soon grow tired of her. Then, all will be as it was."

Caesare merely nodded, his dark eyes straying down Giovanna's body. "Enough of the earl," he said thickly, and reached for her.

Cassie walked quickly around the east side of the villa from under the thick shade of magnolia and acacia trees toward the large iron gates of the entranceway. The young boy, Sordello, who usually attended the entrance to the Villa Parese, had but moments before been in the gardens in conversation with his father, Marco. Although she did not expect simply to walk away from the villa and from the earl, she wanted to test the bounds of her confinement, to discover if she was being watched and by whom. Her sandals were soundless in the grass alongside the narrow graveled drive, and her senses revealed nothing to her but the disconcerting sweet fragrance of the blooming roses.

She quickened her pace when she sighted the gates, and turned her head briefly to look back at the villa. There was still no sign of pursuit. Perhaps, she thought sourly, the earl in his sublime arrogance no longer concerned himself that she would try to escape him. He had not an hour before closeted himself in his library, leaving her to herself.

Her hand closed about the iron latch and she gave it a mighty tug. For a moment, the gate hinges only groaned. She pulled again and her heart beat faster as the gate inched open. Why had she not had the sense to take money and pack a small bandbox? She looked up and down the dry rutted road, parched and dusted by the relentless sun. She was on the point of slipping through the gate when she heard a familiar voice behind her. She froze in her tracks and whipped about, the look on her face ludicrous in its dismay.

"You should have told me, Cassandra, that you wished to explore."

"Oh, hellfire. I had thought you well occupied, my lord, in the library."

He walked toward her, a self-assured smile on his lips. She swallowed a curse, turned, and slithered through the opening in the gate.

Even as her sandals whipped up the dust about her skirts, his hand closed over her arm.

"Really, Cassandra, those shoes are hardly suitable for a stroll down the road. Come along to the villa with me, I have a surprise for you."

"It is simply a matter of time, my lord," she said in a low voice. "And you are a fool if you believe otherwise."

The earl smiled down at her flushed face, and his hand

moved down her arm until his fingers laced themselves through hers. "I am many things, *cara,* but I do not think that 'fool' numbers among them."

She fell into stiff step beside him. "Since you are a merchant, my lord," she sneered with a fine display of the English aristocrat's scorn of trade, "and must attend to your shopkeeping, I will have many opportunities to escape you. That is, unless you intend to keep me locked up."

Her words appeared to have no effect on him, indeed, she wished she could see his face, rather than his profile, for she suspected there was a twinkle in his eyes. She found it galling that he did not even have the grace to respond to her insults.

"Since I lock you in my arms each night, Cassandra, it would appear that my problem is what to do with you during the day. Thus, my dear, the surprise I promised you. I beg you not to be overbearing and rude to him, for poor Joseph really has no choice in the matter. He is fond of you, you know, and I am certain that you would not wish to make him feel uncomfortable."

"Joseph." She remained silent for several moments, but when he gazed down at her, his expression serene, she could not help herself. "He is to be my keeper. My guard."

She fell silent again, contemplating the blackness of his character.

"No insults, *cara?* I would that you hurl all your venom at me and save only your winsome charm for Joseph. Yes, he will be responsible for you and your safety when I am not available to be."

A gentle breeze whipped a strand of golden hair across her cheek, and without thought, the earl raised his hand to smooth it away. She frowned at him and walked quickly toward the villa.

The Corsican stood in the entrance hall where the earl had so abruptly left him, his woolen cap in his hands. He looked, Cassie thought, strangely out of place with a marble floor beneath his feet.

"It is good to see you again, Joseph," she said in her starchily accented Italian, which brought a smile to the earl's face. "I fear though that you will be bored, since, I presume," she directed this to the earl, "when you are not my companion, you will have little else to do."

The earl interposed smoothly, "If Joseph yearns to return to the sea, my love, we will simply have a changing of the guard, so to speak."

"Madonna, it is my pleasure to be with you again," Joseph said finally, his voice uncertain.

Cassie smiled at him despite herself. It would be churlish of her to treat him badly, since he was here at the earl's order. "I hope your stay will be pleasant," she said at last.

"Excellent," the earl said, rubbing his hands together. "Your first outing with Joseph will be to the lake, Cassandra. I trust you will not mind my accompanying you, for I have another surprise for you."

Joseph saw the young mistress stiffen and regard the earl warily. She said something, sharply, in English, which he did not understand.

"Another surprise, my lord? Have you built a wall around the far side of the lake so that I will not swim away?"

"I am sorry to disappoint you, *cara,* but I have not had the time to construct so formidable a structure. Are you ready, my dear?"

Cassie's curiosity got the better of her, and she nodded through her frown.

The Parese lake, a narrow, serpentine body of water, lay nestled in a small valley between the rolling hills, surrounded by long-branched trees whose thick leaves cast oddly shaped shadows over its calm blue surface. Cassie had visited the small lake but once and had foregone the pleasure of wading into its inviting water, for the earl had been with her. When they broke through the thick line of trees that bordered its perimeter, Cassie had an almost overpowering urge to strip off her clothes, now sticking uncomfortably to her back from the bright afternoon sun, and swim in its cool depths.

As if he guessed her thoughts, the earl smiled. "Not now, Cassandra. Just think of how embarrassed Joseph would be to see you as naked as a sea nymph."

She made no reply, for moored to the end of a narrow

dock was a sloop, its graceful lines and rigging so like her sailboat in England that she stood, open-mouthed, staring at it in dumb surprise. Painted on its stern in small black letters was the name *Fearless.*

"Joseph brought her from the harbor this morning."

"*Si,* madonna," Joseph continued, waving proudly toward the small vessel, "the men have worked day and night to complete her for you."

His voice contained a hopeful question, and Cassie, reeling in surprise, turned to Joseph, not the earl, and gasped, "Oh, Joseph, she is beautiful. You have worked wonders. How very kind of you."

Cassie picked up her skirts and sped down the dock to her new sloop.

Joseph called after her in an embarrassed voice, "No, madonna, 'twas not I. The captain drew her plans, I but supervised the building."

"It matters not, Joseph," the earl said quietly, taking pleasure at the joy in her eyes. The two men stood watching her as she explored every inch of the sailboat, from the curved hull to the thick wooden mast.

"She will breathe life into it," Joseph said.

"Yes," the earl said with a thoughtful smile. "And it is also likely that I will have to restock the lake every year. She loves to fish, you know."

Joseph was silent a moment, his eyes still on Cassie. "Have you met other English ladies like the madonna?"

"No, my friend, I have not."

Joseph chewed thoughtfully on his lower lip. He had known the answer to his question before the earl had replied. He studied his master's profile, remembering how he and the other men had believed that he had gone mad, kidnapping a young girl off the coast of mighty England and forcibly bringing her to Genoa. As a Barbary pirate, he had seen women captured on raids and ravished until their captors' appetites were sated, and it had not surprised him, for as a young man, his sexual lust had equaled his blood lust. But that the captain, an English nobleman despite his Ligurian blood, would capture his own wife made him shake his grizzled head. So young she was, spirited, like an untamed colt. He thought of his own young wife, Maria, dead before her twentieth year at the hands of mountain bandits. He felt no pain now, for too many years had passed. Cassie's crow of delighted laughter rang in his ears.

"Watch your footing, Cassandra." The earl suddenly ran forward.

Cassie, who had been perched precariously, examining the clew on the canvas sail, straightened suddenly at the sound of his voice and lost her footing. She clutched frantically at empty air and fell backward into the water with a resounding splash.

The earl was on the point of diving in after her when her head cleared the blue surface and he saw that she was laughing.

He frowned down at her, hands on his hips.

"Dammit, woman, you must be more careful. That you could be so graceless leads me to believe that it is a nursemaid you need."

The earl did not see the twinkle in her eyes when she asked him in a subdued voice, "Will you not help me, my lord?" She swam close to the dock and held out her hand to him. He closed his fingers about her wrist, unaware that she had positioned her feet against the pilings.

Little minx, Joseph thought, knowing full well what she intended. He could not prevent his shout of laughter when Cassie's limp muscles suddenly tensed and she pulled the earl, face forward, into the water.

Joseph saw a tangle of arms and legs and heard her crow of triumph. When the earl's dark head rose to the surface, she pressed her hands down on his shoulders, using all her weight, and pushed him under again.

Cassie was still laughing when the earl grasped her legs and dragged her down. When he finally released her, she broke to the surface, gasping for breath. Her golden hair streamed about her and a slimy water reed hung limply over her forehead.

"And you accuse *me* of being clumsy, my lord."

He swam to her and pulled the water reed off her face. "No, my girl, I am only guilty of trusting you." Her eyes were alight with mischief, and he grinned. "Are you ready to return to land?"

"Ah yes, my lord, now that I have given you your comeuppance."

Joseph hauled both of them, dripping wet, onto the dock. Cassie was still smiling as she pulled her thick mantle of wet hair over her shoulder and wrung it out. Joseph eyed her curiously. She certainly did not appear to hold his master in dislike now, indeed, she appeared carefree.

"Why did you name her *Fearless*?" Cassie asked as they walked back toward the villa.

"It seemed appropriate." He paused a moment and continued lightly, "I have finally done something for you that you approve?"

"Indeed you have, my lord," she said, pushing a heavy mass of wet hair from her forehead. "She is beautiful, so sleek."

"Would you subscribe, my dear, to the notion that one good turn deserves another?"

She drew up a moment and gazed up at him warily. "You mean, my lord, if you scratch my back, I'm to scratch yours?"

"I desire a promise from you, Cassandra." As her eyes gleamed suspiciously, he added with a smile, "Nothing in any way *final*, I assure you. Merely a stated agreement from you, of one evening's duration."

She pursed her lips, arguing with herself, and to his relief, she finally nodded.

"Very well," she said slowly. "I suppose that I must take your word at some things. What is it you wish me to promise?"

"I am planning a dinner party this Thursday evening and have invited the cream of Genoese society. Since you are here with me, in Genoa, I ask that you attend the party, meet my friends, and conduct yourself with propriety."

She looked up at him, her lips tightened. "So I am to pay the piper for my boat. You have planned this quite nicely, my lord. I hope you do not expect me to thank you for your deviousness."

"Surely it is not so much to ask, Cassandra."

"You are a villain, my lord." She hunched her shoulder at him, gathered up her sodden skirt, and walked toward the gardens.

During the next few days, Joseph wondered if he would spend the remainder of his days guarding his master's English lady, so sharp was her tongue around the earl. He knew it was only a matter of time before she approached him to help her escape. She did so on a lazy afternoon when they were fishing aboard her sloop in the middle of the lake.

"The fall months in England are beautiful," she began, her voice soft with sadness.

"The fall months are beautiful most everywhere, madonna, save of course in northern Africa." Joseph maintained a stoic countenance, knowing what was to come.

"But I am English," she said, her voice sharp now, "and to me, there is nothing to compare to the crisp, cool air and the changing color of the leaves." Her hands tightened around her fishing pole, and he sighed.

She laid a hand on his woolen sleeve. "Joseph, you know that I do not wish to be here, that I am naught but the earl's prisoner. Will you not help me?" Cassie mistook his brooding silence for uncertainty. "There are ships, English ships, in the harbor. I saw them when we went to the city. I can get money, I know that I can. We could even arrange it so that the earl would believe that I struck you and escaped. You will see, he cannot blame you. Please help me— you must."

Joseph raised a gnarled hand to her. "Madonna, why is it that you do not wish to wed the master?" She was not a fool, he knew, and the earl was of noble birth, titled and wealthy. Certainly, all the ladies he had observed appeared to find the earl most desirable, all the ladies save one.

"I have no wish to see my name inscribed in their precious *Golden Book,* and certainly not next to his. I will never wed him."

"But why, madonna?"

"Your master, Joseph, kidnapped me the day before I

was to be wed. He feigned friendship not only with my brother, but also with my fiancé."

So there was another man who held her heart, he thought. Of a certainty there had not been sufficient time for her to forget. "I suppose that many would see the captain's actions as ruthless. But I think, madonna, that his going to such lengths is proof of his feeling for you."

"You will not help me?"

"No, madonna."

Cassie nodded dully, and the subject was closed between them. It came as something of a shock to her to realize she had come to hold Joseph in great affection. He was unflaggingly patient, and never judged her even when her temper broke its bounds, merely regarding her in gentle silence, his brown eyes clear and untroubled beneath his bushy gray brows. Her temper had flared at him just the day before, because he had not allowed her to visit the harbor. She knew that he had acted on orders from the earl, but she could not contain herself. She wished now that she had not visited the city, though she had enjoyed seeing the shops, watching the flower girls weave bouquets of startling beauty, and drinking a cup of the thick Italian coffee underneath a sidewalk umbrella on the Via Balbi. Joseph had pointed out the Palazzo Reale, a magnificent structure, only one of many handsome palaces that lined the street, and had described its sumptuous rooms, the glowing colors of the tapestries and the pastel delicacy of the frescos.

There was a sudden tug on her fishing pole, and she turned from him abruptly. "Ah, a nibble," She hauled in the line. She stole a glance at his profile from the corner of her eye as she thrust the still-wriggling trout into her basket. She had been unfair to him. "Joseph, please forgive me. I have acted like a beast to you."

"Only at times," he said calmly, turning to help her paddle back to shore. "But we will say no more about it, madonna."

They worked the sail for some minutes in silence. Cassie said finally, "I know, Joseph, that you are Corsican. The earl has told me of the strife between Corsica and Genoa until the Genoese ceded your island to the French. How is it that you consort with an enemy of your people?"

His leathery features took on a thoughtful expression.

"My loyalty is to his lordship, madonna, not to the wretched Genoese merchants who have tried for years to break the pride of my people."

"Why does he merit such loyalty?"

"Ah, 'tis a long story and one that is not, I think, suitable for your innocent ears."

"If you will not tell me, Joseph, then I shall simply have to ask the earl."

The petulance in her voice amused him. "That is your prerogative, madonna. As for his lordship"—he shrugged—"it will also be his prerogative to choose to tell you about it."

She frowned at him, but said no more. They secured the sloop at the dock and walked back to the villa.

She left Joseph at the front gates with the boy, Sordello, who openly worshiped the older man, and made her way to the gardens.

Chapter 15

Cassie sat before her dressing table, clad in her petticoats and wrapper. Rosina stood behind her, powder box in hand, on the point of sprinkling her golden hair when the earl's voice stopped her.

"No, Rosina," he said, walking with negligent grace to stand behind Cassie. "I do not wish for you to powder your mistress's hair. A classical style, I think, but no white powder to hide her natural color."

Cassie, who had herself been looking balefully at the powder box, turned in her chair and said sharply, in English, "Do you wish to direct everything that I do, my lord? Must you even interrupt me with orders whilst I am dressing?"

He allowed a black brow to wing upward in surprise. "I happen to know, *cara,* that you have no liking for the powder box. I thought you instructed Rosina to apply it simply because you believed it would please me."

Cassie did not bother to respond, for she had turned around in her chair, and was distracted by the sight of him. He looked resplendent in his rich black velvet evening clothes. Layers of frothy white lace fell from his throat and wrists, and his black hair was powdered white as his lace and pulled back at the nape of his neck, held with a black velvet ribbon. Even to her jaundiced eye, he looked like a king.

"I am delighted that you approve my appearance, Cassandra."

"You are passable, I suppose," she said, and turned back to her mirror.

He seated himself near her, crossing one elegant leg over

the other, and watched Rosina deftly style her hair into a braided coronet atop her head, through which she drew out a long thick tress. When at last Cassie was dressed in a low, square-necked lavender silk gown, he rose gracefully and drew a long, flat box from his waistcoat pocket.

"You may leave now, Rosina," he said to the maid. "I shall complete your mistress's toilette."

"What do you mean, my lord?" Cassie asked warily after her maid had left the bedchamber. He answered her by withdrawing a long rope of pearls, lustrous and exquisitely matched. Before she could respond, he doubled the string of pearls and fastened the clasp at the back of her neck.

She stared at her image in the mirror for a long moment, and drew a resolute breath, her fingers touching the clasp. "They are lovely, my lord, but I must refuse them. I will not be bought."

He said lightly, his hand closing over her fingers, "Nay, *cara,* they are not for you to refuse, for I have not offered them to you. I do not seek to buy you, simply to enhance your beauty. You will, of course, return them to me at the close of the evening."

"I would rather wear nothing."

"The gentlemen present this evening would be much pleased, I doubt not. However, I would prefer to have them only guess at what lies beneath your gown."

"You wretched man, that is not what I meant, and well you know it."

"Guilty," he said with a quick smile. "I do apologize for teasing you, Cassandra. Would you do me the great honor of wearing the pearls, just for this evening?"

She regarded him suspiciously for several moments, but as the expression on his face remained serious, and indeed, he appeared to be contrite, she slowly nodded. "Very well, but only for tonight." She added with ill-concealed bitterness, "I suppose that if I must be put on display, it is only fitting that I look the part of the expensive harlot."

His thick black brows drew together. "I have told you, Cassandra, that it is not you on display this evening. My friends are here for your inspection. I would not hold this dinner party if I thought you would be slighted."

"No, I do not suppose that you would." She sighed. "It would make no sense. However, you will admit that my perceived position at the Villa Parese is not enviable."

"And you will keep your promise?"

"You mean that I am not to stand upon the dinner table and shout to your guests that I am your prisoner?"

"Precisely."

"Is it time to go downstairs, my lord?" As he made no reply, she added lightly, "You have more promises to wring out of me? Take care, my lord, it was but one sailboat that you gave me."

He smiled and shook his head. "No, little one, no more promises. There is, however, something I should tell you. One of our guests this evening will be the Contessa Giovanna Giusti. I did not particularly wish to invite her, but Signore Montalto, a close friend and business associate, is much enamored of her and very much wanted her company."

"Are you concerned that I will be rude to the contessa?"

"It is not your propriety that concerns me. If you would know the truth, the contessa was once my mistress. I of course broke off our affair before I left for England."

"Your mistress?"

The earl smiled, clasped her arms in his hands, and dropped a light kiss upon her closed lips. "Yes, but she needn't concern you. I only tell you to give you fair warning that Giovanna might not be all that is pleasant."

"Thank you, my lord, for the warning." Her voice was clipped and flat, and he wondered what the devil she was thinking. He drew her hand through his arm and escorted her from the bedchamber. To lighten her mood, he said, "Caesare will of course be here. You will, I trust, enjoy his company."

"Of a certainty I shall, my lord," she said, but her voice was cold.

He continued in a gently teasing voice, "To keep you at ease and help you to remember your promise, I will contrive to stay at your side throughout the evening."

"That, I daresay, is wise of you."

There was laughter in her voice, and he relaxed. As he

walked beside her down the wide stairway, he looked down at the creamy pearls about her throat. The pearls had belonged first to his grandmother, then to his mother. They were bride's pearls, the only jewelry allowed to a young lady before and during her first year of marriage.

Once downstairs, the earl nodded in satisfaction to Scargill, who was dressed in butler's wear, and surrounded by three young male servants hired for the evening.

"Don't look so pained, Scargill," the earl said. "All of us must occasionally make sacrifices." At Scargill's grunt, he added with a wide smile, "Just ensure that your men keep the wine flowing, and your success is assured."

Cassie gazed about her with pleasure. Fresh flowers overflowed from vases that lined the walls of the wide entrance hall, and branches of candles had been added, making the villa as dazzling bright as if it were day.

The knocker sounded loudly, and Scargill motioned one of the footmen to the door.

"It would appear, my lord, that you have approached this evening with quite a flair," Cassie said behind her hand as the wide front doors swung open to admit Caesare.

"I hoped that you would approve, *cara*. Ah, my dear brother, you are a vision to behold." He pumped Caesare's outstretched hand.

"As ever, Antonio, it must be I to carry on the Parese tradition of elegance. Ah, but you are the vision, Cassandra, not I," he said, his eyes resting a moment on the pearls. "Antonio, expect all the gentlemen tonight to yearn for your imminent demise."

The earl laughed. "I trust that you will protect me, Caesare."

"Nay, dear brother," Caesare said, "I shall be the one to head the list." He turned to Cassie. "You know, of course, that any party given by the earl is a topic of conversation days in advance."

Cassie raised her eyes from his bright plum velvet evening wear to the frothy silver lace at his throat, and cocked her head to one side questioningly.

"What Caesare refers to, my dear," the earl interposed,

"is my English predilection for providing an abundance of food."

"But what has that to say to anything, my lord? Of course one would provide a splendid meal for one's guests."

Caesare grinned, and shook his head. "Surely the earl has told you of the famous Genoese thriftiness? It extends, alas, to providing the most niggardly of refreshments to guests. Genoese society, I am persuaded, forgives my brother his half-English blood for this vagary."

Cassie was grinning reluctantly when the earl turned to greet the newly arrived Signore Montalto, a paunchy, heavy-jowled gentleman of middle years.

"Marcello," the earl said smoothly, "this is Signorina Brougham, the young lady I mentioned to you."

"Enchanted, *signorina,*" Signore Montalto said, bowing with some difficulty.

Cassie inclined her head and bid him welcome. His almond eyes flitted an unasked question toward the earl. As Cassie's attention was drawn by Caesare to Signore and Signora Accorambonis, she did not see it.

"How delightful to meet you, *signorina,*" Signora Accorambonis said in a pleasant voice. "We so rarely have new faces in Genoa. I do hope that you enjoy our city."

"The pleasure is mine," Cassie said ambiguously, knowing the earl was listening. She was aware that Signora Accorambonis was scrutinizing her from beneath her heavy eyelids, and stiffened for an instant. But she could not fault the lady, for she could well imagine how a foreign lady, living unmarried with an English gentleman, would be treated by the English aristocracy.

The wizened Signore Accorambonis was all complaisance. By the time all the guests had arrived and the earl and Cassie had made their welcomes, Cassie firmly on his arm, she was forced to admit that the earl seemed to have chosen his guests well.

She grinned crookedly at the earl when Scargill entered the brightly lit drawing room and announced dinner in the most formal voice she had ever heard from him.

The earl guided her firmly to the foot of the long table

in the dining room and seated her himself. He gave her arm a slight squeeze before walking to the master's place at the head of the table. She gazed down the expanse of table at him, but he merely smiled at her reassuringly. She stole a look at their guests, fourteen in all, and found to her amusement that the heavily laden table was the focus of their attention. Seated at her left was Caesare and to her right, a Signora Bianca Piasi, a young woman as vivacious as she was lovely.

"I see that you have decided to stay with us, *signorina*," Signora Piasi said, her fork already in her hand, hovering over an abundant portion of braised pheasant.

Cassie could not understand how Signora Piasi saw anything of the sort, but she merely smiled and said lightly, "Everyone is very kind, *signora*."

When Signora Piasi gave her attention to her plate, Cassie turned to Caesare, who was regarding her, a strange expression in his eyes.

"Whatever is the matter?" she asked him. "Have I gravy on my chin or wine spots on my gown?"

His expression changed instantly. He cocked his head at her and said in an amused voice, "You have nothing untoward on your person, Cassandra. I have observed that you are quite the success this evening."

Cassie said, "I think it is all because of my ghastly accent. People find me an amusing oddity."

"I think not," he said.

Caesare's conversation floated over Cassie's head some minutes later as she gazed around the table. Save for the fact that everyone spoke Italian, she could see little differences between the manners of Genoese aristocracy and the English. Perhaps laughter was freer, she quickly amended to herself, and certainly their guests very much needed their hands to emphasize their conversation. Her eyes stopped at the Contessa Giovanna Giusti, seated toward the middle of the table, Signore Montalto at her side. She was undeniably alluring, and a center of gaiety. Cassie had only spoken a few words to the beautiful contessa, for she was the last guest to arrive. The contessa had looked at her closely, and turned abruptly away.

"Cassandra, you have not heard a word I've said."

"Do forgive me, Caesare. Much here is new to me."

He gave her a look of mock reproof. "And here I was telling you about Genoese velvet, and how some Genoese ladies adore its quality to such a degree that their undergarments are also of velvet."

"But I have never heard of such a thing."

Some minutes later, at a signal from the earl, Cassie rose with him and led their guests back to the drawing room to enjoy more wine and cakes. After some moments, the earl drew her aside. "I hope you do not mind sharing a short business meeting with me, *cara*. Signore Montalto is awaiting me in the library."

Cassie looked up at him, puzzled. "I hardly think that appropriate, my lord. Surely Signore Montalto would not expect you to bring me to your meeting."

"I see you are too hidebound by societal rules, *cara*. Did I not promise not to leave you alone this evening?"

"I suppose so, my lord," she said doubtfully.

"A bit more enthusiasm, if you please," he said, and opened the thick double doors to the library. He stepped back to allow Cassie to precede him.

Signore Montalto looked up from his chair, clearly startled. He looked to the earl, expecting him to peremptorily dismiss the girl. But the earl appeared unperturbed at Signore Montalto's stiff countenance, and planted a guileless smile on his face.

"You are enjoying the party, I trust, Marcello," he said easily. "You, of course, have made the acquaintance of Signorina Brougham."

Signore Montalto rose ponderously from his chair and offered Cassie a stiff bow.

"You will share a glass of sherry with us, *signore?*" The earl added smoothly, an imp of mischief compelling him, "Marcello is here, Cassandra, to discuss a rather thorny problem with me. Perhaps you would not mind giving us your opinion." Much to his delight, a slight smile indented the corners of her mouth, and she inclined her head in graceful assent.

"I would be delighted, my lord, to provide you whatever assistance I can."

She graciously accepted a chair held for her by the flustered Marcello, settled her heavy skirts about her, and sipped the sherry the earl offered her.

The earl said, "It involves a Dutch shipping group trading with the southern colonies in America, which has recently suffered rather large financial losses. The losses are, unfortunately, much my concern, since I provided much of the capital. A Dutch representative has brought Marcello a proposal that he believes will pay us handsomely. You may tell *la signorina,* Marcello."

Cassie turned her eyes from the earl's sardonic expression and fastened them on Signore Montalto's heavy jowled face. He seemed to struggle with himself to speak, and Cassie barely managed to suppress a grin of amusement.

"As you know, *signorina,*" Signore Montalto began ponderously, imagining full well that she knew nothing at all, "England's southern colonies are exporting more cotton and tobacco by the year. Even their timber is gaining in importance as the English denude their own forests."

Cassie tried to curb her impatience at his condescending tone. "Your point, *signore?*"

Signore Montalto tugged uncomfortably at his black waistcoat. "The Dutch trade has been primarily with the West Indies. Pirates and Caribbean storms have brought them—and his lordship—substantial losses, and thus, their recent shift to trade with the colonies."

"A logical course, it would seem to me, *signore.*"

"Ah, but there is more, Cassandra." The earl waved Marcello to continue. Cassie was aware that the earl was regarding her intently, and she grew more alert.

"For every cause, there is an effect," Marcello said grandly. "The southern colonists have constant need of labor for their cotton and tobacco plantations. The Dutch proposal, a proposal, I might add, that meets with my approval, is simply to capture African savages, transport them to the colonies and sell them to the plantation owners. Immediately, there is a sizable profit. Cotton, tobacco, and timber could be brought back to England and Europe, and thus the profit is doubled."

"I am not certain that I understand, *signore,*" Cassie said. "You believe that we should encourage, through our financial backing, the capture of people to be sold as slaves in a foreign country?"

"People," Marcello scoffed. "They are naught but savages, dear lady. Their only value is that they breed at an appalling rate and work well in the fields."

"And how does one go about capturing these savages, *signore?* Are they trapped?"

"Oh no," Marcello hastened to correct her, "trapping would mutilate them and lessen their value at auction. They are like children, *signorina,* and can be herded together quite readily with but one musket shot over their heads."

"How odd it is that you now liken them to children. If it is true that they live in a state of primitive innocence, like children, then they should be protected from predators."

"Perhaps calling them 'children' was unfortunate," Marcello ground out. He shot a silent plea toward the earl, but received only an ironic smile.

"Everyone buys and sells these black beggars. Even the Church is not certain that they have souls."

"And, of course, they do not speak the civilized Italian tongue, do they, *signore?*"

"No, 'tis gibberish they utter. One can make no sense of them at all."

Cassie slowly rose from her chair. As Signore Montalto was not a tall man, she was very nearly at his eye level. "So it is your proposal, *signore,* that we should agree to the capture and sale of innocent men and women to fatten our coffers."

"I have told you, *signorina,* that they are animals, uncivilized savages."

"It is very curious, you know," Cassie said. "I was very near to believing that the Italians held no claim to civilization, since they do not speak the English tongue and do such barbaric things as locking their female children away in convents. But look how very wrong I was."

Signore Montalto turned a mottled red, and the earl intervened. "So, Cassandra, we will agree to leave the Africans to other, less scrupulous, men. However, my dear, our financial problem still remains."

The earl knew he was placing her in a situation that called for experience she did not possess, and he was on the point of rescuing her when she asked abruptly, "Is it not true that there are vast, unpopulated lands in the colonies?"

Signore Montalto had learned painfully not to patronize her, and thus responded cautiously. "Yes, *signorina.* It is so vast that all of Europe—and England—would fit on the eastern seacoast."

Cassie chewed furiously on her lower lip and turned to the earl, a hint of apology in her voice. "I ask that you forgive my ignorance, my lord, but since there is so much unused land, would not free men and women do just as well as slaves?"

"What do you mean, *cara?*"

"Could not the Dutchmen transport Englishmen and Europeans to the colonies? Men and women who want to begin a new life on their own land. Would not such men and women swell the colonies' population and increase the valuable exports Signore Montalto speaks of? Perhaps I am being naive, my lord, but would there not be profit to be made from such a venture?"

Silence fell, and Cassie shuffled her feet nervously.

Signore Montalto wiped the look of surprise from his face, and waved a dismissing hand. "A possibility, *signorina,* certainly, and one that I have considered. However, there is little profit in such a notion."

The earl said thoughtfully, his long fingers stroking the line of his jaw, "The profits would not, of course, be as great, for such men as Cassandra describes have little money. And the Dutch would of necessity have to refit their ships, since their cargo would not be slaves, but free men. But it can be done, Marcello. You will present the idea to the Dutch representative."

"It would serve, perhaps, if you insist," Marcello said.

"Excellent. Now that we have come to an amicable decision, I suggest that we return to our guests."

As they left the library, arm in arm, the earl turned to her, raised her hand to his lips, and kissed her fingers. "I thank you, *cara.*"

She looked up at him wonderingly and shook her head. "I do not understand you, my lord. What am I to make of a man who abducts me, brings me to a foreign country, and then proceeds to let me meddle with his fortune?"

His eyes rested a moment on the strand of pearls. He said smoothly, "You need make nothing of me, Cassandra. You need only to become my wife."

Cassie frowned him down, turned on her heel, and walked quickly back to the drawing room.

"You are enjoying yourself, Cassandra?" he asked, when he caught up with her.

"Let us say," she said deliberately, "that I am pleasantly surprised. Have you bribed your guests to be kind to me?"

"If you consider good food and drink a bribe, then the answer is yes."

"How interesting it would be to know the question."

Cassie whirled about at the sound of the Contessa Giovanna Giusti's bright voice.

"My dear Antonio," Giovanna said softly, her slender white hand touching his sleeve, "I have had the opportunity to speak only a few words to your charming guest. Things English, you know, I find most fascinating. Would you not leave the *signorina* and me alone so that we may learn more of each other?"

The earl hesitated, for the smile on Giovanna's lips was dangerous. He was on the point of including himself when Cassie said easily, "Yes, my lord, do leave us for a while. I have heard so much about the contessa that I am most desirous of learning more about her."

He looked at her searchingly for a moment. "Very well, my dear. But do not be too long, for there are other of my friends who wish to enjoy your company."

The earl stared after the two women, scarcely heeding the words of his friend, Jacopo Sandro, an aging aristocrat whose only pleasure appeared to be the purchase of outlandish wigs from Paris.

"So, *signorina,*" the contessa began, "you are enjoying your stay in Genoa?"

"I daresay it is always interesting to visit a foreign country, contessa." Although Cassie had not had much experience with ladies who were bitches, she knew enough to be on her guard.

Giovanna's eyes roved to the pearls about Cassie's neck. "The pearls are lovely and quite distinctive."

"*Grazie, signora,*" Cassie said simply, wondering what the contessa was about. It occurred to her that perhaps she had misread the lady's intentions toward her, and she unbent a trifle. "And your jewels are quite elegant."

The contessa inclined her graceful neck, her smile still firmly affixed to her full lips. "Did the earl teach you Italian?"

"No, it was my governess. I fear that my accent is quite fearful."

So Caesare was right, Giovanna thought, if the little slut had a governess, she is likely of acceptable birth. She looked again at the pearls and felt anger knot in her throat. "So you intend to wed with the earl, I see."

Cassie looked at her, puzzled. "What makes you believe that, contessa?"

"The pearls, of course. They have served as bride's pearls in the earl's family for several generations."

Cassie looked at her stupidly, until understanding of what the earl had done made her tremble with chagrin. *Bride's pearls!* Perfidious wretch that he was, the earl had convinced her to wear them. Was that why all the guests had treated her so kindly? Had they accepted her because the pearls announced his intention to wed her? She said stiffly to Giovanna, "It is merely a necklace, contessa. It has no particular meaning, I assure you."

Giovanna looked at her, perplexed, and then felt a surge of relief. Could it be true that the earl had no intention of wedding her? What a fool the little harlot was to so openly admit it.

"But my dear *signorina,*" Giovanna said sweetly, "you have so many persuasive charms." Her eyes fell to Cassie's rounded breasts, rising above the row of lace at her bodice.

"I fear, contessa, that charms have little to do with anything, though they admittedly lead some people to outrageous deeds."

As Cassie's Italian did not allow Giovanna to glean the nuances her words intended, she decided that the English girl was rather stupid, and not at all to the point. The earl couldn't abide stupid women, Giovanna thought, and with a pleased smile, she patted Cassie's sleeve and left her.

Cassie watched the contessa approach Bianca Piasi and heard her say in a low, laughing voice, "I think the earl must feel Genoese society lacking in diversity. But look at what he has done for our amusement—thrown an English whore in our midst. The little slut told me that the bride's pearls, dear Bianca, have no meaning at all."

Cassie's face flushed with anger and humiliation. How could she have been so stupid? Her fingers went to the wretched pearls. If only the earl had left well enough alone.

Cassie turned in feverishly bright conversation to Caesare. She found that she could not continue and stopped abruptly, bidding him dismissal over her shoulder. She walked quickly upstairs to the bedchamber and pulled the glass door open. The evening breeze from the Mediterranean cooled her burning cheeks. She closed the door behind her and leaned disconsolately over the railing. Her fingers closed over the necklace, and with a sudden, furious jerk, she sent them careening to the balcony floor. She heard some of them hit the marble statue in the garden below.

She stood momentarily frozen, aghast at what she had done. She sank to her knees, unmindful of her gown, and began to gather the pearls. But snatches of Giovanna's conversation sounded in her mind, and she flung the handful of pearls she had gathered away from her. She smoothed down her gown, forced her chin up, and walked back downstairs.

The earl was at her side in an instant, his eyes questioning. She resolutely ignored him as she mouthed polite good-byes to the guests. The absence of the pearls was noted by all, she knew.

"How very appropriate you look now, my dear *signorina*," Giovanna murmured, as she took her leave.

"Bitch," Cassie said under her breath. Still, she found herself smiling in genuine pleasure as other guests bid her good night.

When Scargill had closed the great front doors upon the last of them, the earl turned to her, his dark eyes glittering.

"I believe you owe me an explanation, *cara*."

She thrust her chin up stubbornly, and regarded him in dogged silence.

"Why, Cassandra?"

Words clogged in her throat, and to her disgust, she started crying.

He pulled her into the circle of his arms and stroked her silky hair. He said gently, "Forgive me, *cara*. I had hoped that you had enjoyed a pleasant evening."

"I did," she gulped, pulling away from him. "It is just that the contessa—your *amata*—" she paused a moment, her eyes flashing.

"My former mistress," he said.

She gave a watery sniff and hunched her shoulders. "She did me in. I was such a fool!"

The earl arched a sleek brow. "What is this? I would have laid a fortune on your ability to shut her down."

"Well, you must lose, my lord. She asked me about the pearls and I told her they had no meaning whatsoever." Cassie added, "She used it against me. I heard her whispering to several ladies about your English whore."

"Ah. And what, may I ask, did you do with the pearls?"

She smiled up at him, reluctantly. "They must be restrung, my lord, that is, after we find them all."

Cassie dismissed Rosina for the night and sat at her dressing table, trying not to look at the earl as he shrugged out of his dressing gown. But she always looked. He lazily stretched his large body. He was not a particularly vain man, but he knew well enough that his body was well made. Her furtive, embarrassed scrutiny always delighted him. He strolled up behind her and laid his hands lightly upon her shoulders.

"Have you no modesty?" she said, terribly aware that her body, as usual, was responding to him.

He leaned over and kissed her temple. "Very shortly, *cara*, I shall have the opportunity of accusing you of an equal lack of modesty." He took the hairbrush from her limp fingers and stroked it through her thick hair.

"Your shoulder has healed," she said, her eyes upon his reflection in the mirror.

He flexed it unconsciously. "Yes. I'm pleased that you have done no permanent damage to my body." He added with a wolfish grin, "I continue to enjoy, however, the temporary disability you force upon me."

"No more of a disability, my lord, than your infamous party forced upon me."

"Come, my love, you have admitted that you did enjoy yourself, at least for the most part."

"Joseph," she said suddenly, her voice heavy with accusation.

"Joseph, *cara?*" He laid the hairbrush on the table top and let his hands slip beneath her dressing gown to caress her shoulders.

She closed her eyes a moment, her body aching for his fingers to continue their movement, and leaned her head back against his belly. Long strands of golden hair weaved themselves into the thick black hair at his groin.

"Joseph?"

"Yes," she said, and with great effort pulled herself away from him to rise.

"You are exquisite."

She looked down and saw that her dressing gown had parted and her breasts were bare. She clutched the material together and turned her back to him, for her wretched eyes would not stay upon his face.

He laughed, walked to the huge bed, and stretched his full length upon his back. He patted a spot beside him. "Come here, Cassandra. I am not against a little conversation. Anticipation cannot but heighten pleasure."

She sat down beside him for the simple reason that her traitorous eyes would be shielded from his body. She frowned a moment, remembering. "Joseph acted quite strangely the other day. I asked him why a Corsican would serve the Genoese, whom he hates. He told me that his loyalty was only to you. When I asked him why, he informed me that such a story was not for my innocent ears. As you know, my ears are not so innocent, my lord. I am now asking you."

Her eyes were wide with sudden curiosity. The earl was silent for some moments as his fingers wrapped themselves around a thick tress of hair that fell upon his chest.

"Actually, Cassandra," he said finally, "you are much too innocent. Joseph was right in not telling you."

"I am not innocent. Do you not make love with me?"

"The fact that I have made you a woman, my dear, does not diminish your childlike innocence."

She was on the point of hurling insults at him when it occurred to her that guile would serve her better. "Have you ever asked a child to assist you in your business dealings?"

He looked up at her through half-closed eyelids and shook his head.

"Ah. And would you have expected an innocent to suggest a solution that served so well?"

He held in a bubble of laughter. Since she was handling the reins so lightly, he did not want to discourage her. "Certainly not," he agreed.

"Then, my lord, you yourself must conclude that I am no innocent, for you have agreed with my every point."

"Very well, *cara,* you have convinced me. I will tell you." He saw her gazing at him with suspicion, and hastened to say, having already censored the story in his mind, "Actually, I saved Joseph from being castrated at the hands of the pirate, Khar El-Din."

"What does castrated mean?"

"Castration, my dear, is the act of unmanning a man, the result being either death from bleeding or life as a eunuch."

Cassie gazed at him open-mouthed, and swallowed convulsively. She was beginning to wonder if she indeed wanted to know the tale.

"Joseph made the incredibly stupid mistake of fancying himself in love with one of Khar El-Din's harem girls. How he even got near enough to see her, I do not know. Although Joseph was high in the pirate's favor, Khar El-Din was so furious when he discovered a note written by Joseph to the girl that he had him staked out on the palace floor, his intent to castrate Joseph himself. It just so happened that I myself was a guest at the time and had gotten to know Joseph somewhat. Although his offense was grave, I did not want him to meet such a gruesome fate, and interceded with Khar El-Din." The earl paused a moment, at a loss as to how he would tell the rest of the story.

"Well?"

He saw no hope for it and continued in the most expressionless of voices, "Khar El-Din had purchased a young virgin from the Caucasus, captured by the Turks and sold at auction for an incredible sum. The pirate had such lust for her that he did not allow her time to forget her humiliation and accept him as her master, and as a result, she fought him like a tigress. He became obsessed with her, though each night he had to struggle with her to possess her. At the time I was visiting, she had been with him for some three months, and he confided to me that he was at his wits' end. To Khar El-Din, a woman's capitulation and pleasure at his hands was a point of honor, and he was so vexed he was considering having her throat slit. When I had the temerity to intercede for Joseph, Khar El-Din came up with a most ingenious wager."

"Yes?"

"I would spend one night with the girl with Khar El-Din watching. If I could bring her to pleasure, Joseph would be freed. If I did not succeed, then it would be I who would wield the knife."

He eyed Cassie closely at this disclosure and saw to his delight that her lips had tightened into a thin line. "I take it," she said, "that you succeeded, my lord."

"Yes, I succeeded, much to Joseph's relief, I might add."

"I don't suppose," Cassie said, amazed at the cold anger she felt, "that the girl's name was Zabetta."

He grinned at her, and Cassie's hand itched to slap him.

"What a memory you have, *cara*."

"And she named you the English stallion."

"Yes," he said, modestly.

"Well, I do not think you a stallion, my lord. An ass, perhaps. I am glad that you saved Joseph, though." She frowned, remembering their confrontation with the pirate. "Khar El-Din did not seem to be such a good friend when he boarded the yacht."

"Our relationship has deteriorated by the year."

"Why?"

"Because, Cassandra, Khar El-Din regretted his wager. It would have given him great pleasure to take you from me. If it had not been for your quick wit in taking advantage of his Moslem aversion to madness, he would have exacted a very sweet revenge indeed."

Cassie was beginning to believe that perhaps she was mad, for a quite inexplicable anger was washing over her. "How much you must have gloated after forcing that girl to pleasure."

"Actually," he said with disarming candor, "there have been few times in my life when I was more wishful that I had kept my mouth shut and minded my own affairs. And the point of the wager, *cara,* was that I was to force her to do nothing."

"Miserable wretch." She attacked him, smacking her fists against his chest.

"So my lady wishes to play, does she?"

His laughter rang in her ears. In a very short time, or so it seemed to Cassie, he had stripped off her dressing gown and flung her on her back.

"Our party lasted far too long," he said, still laughing, and before she knew what he was about, he grasped her legs and pulled them over his shoulders.

"What are you—" The rest of her question remained unspoken as he buried his face in her woman's softness, holding her hips so firmly in his large hands that she could not move. She felt his tongue, and went limp, a deep groan of pleasure tearing from her throat. His mouth closed over her, lightly caressing her, teasing her, and she gave herself over to him. He straightened, her legs still upon his shoulders, and slowly thrust his full length into her. She cried out, and he quickly eased back, cursing himself. She was too small to hold him thus.

"Oh, please do not."

"I have no wish to hurt you, *cara*."

"You do not hurt me. I will tell you if it is otherwise."

"By your leave then, my lady."

When he was again deep within her, he watched her face carefully. While her eyes darkened in pain, he felt her thighs tensing in pleasure.

"I love you, Cassandra," he said. Her eyes widened, and he thought that her lips moved, but he could not be certain. In the next instant, she was writhing beneath him, pulling them both to release.

The earl lay on his back, Cassie tightly locked against him, her body relaxed, her breathing already deepening into sleep. He found himself grinning ruefully into the darkness. Making love to her appeared to be more effective than a dose of laudanum, for always, she curled up against him, languid and trusting, and almost instantly fell comfortably asleep.

Chapter 16

Cassie pulled her cloak more closely about her shoulders as she strolled through the gardens. She breathed in the cool, clean air, hoping to calm her stomach, upset from breakfast. She stopped by one of the circular marble fountains and ran her fingers through the rippling cold water. When the water calmed, she saw not only her reflection but also the earl's.

"Would you like to catch some trout for our dinner?"

The thought of fish turned her stomach. "No, I think not, my lord."

As he gazed at her overlong, she said quickly, "If you would know the truth, I think I am becoming ill, perhaps the influenza. It must be the change in the weather."

"No, *cara,* I do not believe that the weather has anything to do with how you are feeling."

"Then perhaps," she said sharply, "it has to do with being forced to spend too much time in your company."

"Now that, my dear, is a distinct possibility." His dark eyes gleamed. She cocked her head at him, warily.

"I do not feel like arguing with you this morning, my lord. Now, if you will excuse me—"

"What an admission, *cara.* I begin to think you quite unwell indeed if you do not wish to fight with me."

"I would that you cease being a bore, my lord, and leave me in peace." She turned on her heel and would have left him, but his hand closed about her arm. She thought for once that if he wanted to make love to her, she would not be tempted. She felt too miserable.

"How long has it been since you have worn a night-gown, Cassandra?"

"A nightgown?" She was bewildered by the odd question and the gentle tone of his voice.

"A nightgown," he said again.

She shrugged. "Whatever does my wearing a nightgown have to do with anything?"

"My dear Cassandra, must you always forget that you are a woman?"

Suddenly, she felt herself go pale. She had not worn her nightgown for at least six weeks, since they had been aboard the yacht.

"That's right," he said, his eyes glistening with pleasure. "You are not the victim of an illness, Cassandra. Do you not realize what it means that you have not worn your nightgown since we have arrived in Genoa?"

Her mouth went suddenly dry and she shook her head wildly back and forth. "No," she said, "it cannot be true. No." But deep inside her, she knew it was.

"You carry my child, *cara*, our child."

She stared at him dumbly, so overcome that she could find no words. She was to have borne Edward's children, in England, not the earl's. She was to have been his wife. She heard herself say quite calmly, "You have known long that I am pregnant?"

"For a little more than a week."

"And why did you not tell me?"

"I had hoped you would discover it for yourself and tell me."

"You have planned this to happen, haven't you?"

"I have not the power of nature, Cassandra. Of course I could not plan such a thing."

"Bastard." She turned blindly and stumbled down the path away from him.

Her foot caught on a knobby growth at the base of a tree trunk, and she went sprawling to her knees. Nauseating bile rose in her throat. She felt the earl's hands on her shoulders, holding her firmly, his fingers pulling her hair from her face. Her body heaved in dry convulsions, leaving her so weak that she did not struggle when the earl lifted her into his arms. He set her down by the fountain.

"Wash out your mouth, Cassandra, it will make you feel better."

Numbly, she did as she was told. But no sooner had she spit out the water than the wretched nausea returned. She moaned and wrapped her arms about her stomach.

"I think you need some time in bed, little one, and perhaps a touch of brandy to calm you. In a few weeks' time, you will feel much better."

"You seem to be quite the expert, my lord."

"I am," he said calmly, and once again lifted her into his arms.

"What do you mean?" she said, her voice muffled against his shoulder.

"I have not been protected from either birth or death, Cassandra. I delivered the babe of a serving maid when I was but twenty years of age."

"Was it yours, my lord, or aren't you certain?"

He grinned at her, refusing to be drawn.

When he had laid her gently upon their bed, he pulled a light cover over her and straightened. "Lie still, my lady. I will fetch you some medicinal brandy."

She watched wordlessly as he strode from the bedchamber. Even if she had not felt so wretched, she would have been silent, for her thoughts were in jagged confusion. Her hand moved tentatively to her belly, and she moved her fingers over its flat surface. It seemed incredible to her that a child could actually be lying snug within her womb, and that she could have been unaware of its existence. Her becoming pregnant had been what he had hoped for all along, she thought, and her own unbridled passion had most assuredly assisted him toward his goal. Unwanted tears welled up and streaked silently down her cheeks. How very pleased he must be, and so puffed up in his male accomplishment. She cursed him, and railed at fate, until she lurched to her feet to dash to the basin in the dressing room.

The earl found her leaning limply over the basin, her face pale and wan. "Come, sweetheart, let me help you."

"I think, my lord," she managed to say, "that you have

helped me quite enough. If only I were a man, I would surely make you pay for this."

She seemed to realize the incongruity of her words, for she held her tongue even though she saw dancing laughter in his eyes.

"I know," he said only, and helped her back into bed.

He had put several drops of laudanum in the brandy, and within minutes her head lolled on the pillow. He quietly pulled a chair up beside the bed and eased his large frame into it. His long fingers formed a steeple and he tapped them thoughtfully together, his eyes resting intently on her face.

He smiled slightly, remembering her hurling the charge at him that he had planned her pregnancy. He supposed that if it were indeed possible to plan such an event, he might have given it some consideration. With such a change coming in her body and in her life, he was hopeful that after she had finished ranting at him, she would come to realize that she did wish to be with him.

There was a distinct gleam of pride in his eyes, and if Cassie had been awake, she would doubtless have yelled at him. He sat back in his chair and allowed himself a grin.

Some time later, he rose from his chair, lightly stroked his fingers over her face, and left the bedchamber.

He met Scargill downstairs in the entranceway, and proceeded with a wide grin on his face to tell him the news.

"So, ye've won, my lord," the Scotsman said slowly, pulling on the shock of red hair that fell over his forehead.

"Don't, I pray, accuse me of having planned it."

"I'll wager that is what the madonna thinks—wee innocent that she is. She has just told you, my lord?"

"Nay, old man, it was I who informed her of the happy event. She is, at present, asleep, for she became ill."

"Ah."

"Ah, what?"

"That starchy bitch, Marrina, was filling my ears with yer immoral behavior. She was yelping about that ye were carrying the madonna up to yer bedchamber, in the middle of the morning, mind ye, for more debauchery.''

The earl frowned. "I had thought, my friend, that you had managed to put a muzzle on that woman. If she does not mend her manners after Cassandra and I are wed, I shall have her bound and gagged and taken to a convent.''

Scargill shrugged philosophically. "At least ye have naught to concern yerself about with the girl, Rosina, or, for that matter, the rest of the servants. It's fond of her they are.''

"Now, Scargill, I'm off to tell Joseph. It's to be hoped that he can curb some of her more devil-may-care activities.'' He said over his shoulder as he strode down the staircase, "If she lashes out at you when you see her, consider yourself warned.''

"My congratulations, my lord,'' Joseph said when the earl had tracked him down in the stable. But there was a hint of disappointment in his voice. He laid down the haying fork and turned to stroke the earl's stallion, Cicero. "I suppose you'll not be needing me anymore.''

"On the contrary. She'll certainly need you more than my horse does. I trust you, you know, to keep her in line and prevent her from from doing anything foolish.''

Joseph nodded, his calm gray eyes clear again. Suddenly, he laughed and shook his head. "Do you know, she told me that you had recounted the story of my near-disastrous end with Khar El-Din. She called me a fool, but assured me that she was pleased that I had remained a man. She was certain that I would not have been happy as a eunuch.''

"I hope you do not mind, Joseph. As I recall, I really had no choice in the matter other than to tell her. She can be quite insistent, you know.''

"And she took no offense at the part you played, my lord?'' He whistled, clearly amazed that the earl had told her.

"You may be sure that she did, much to my delight. She will be a fiercely loyal wife. If ever in the future I am tempted to stray, I would fear as grave a punishment as Khar El-Din planned for you.''

During the next several days, the earl left Cassie to herself, sensing that she needed to be alone. She was often silent, her brows drawn together in thought. He was able, at least, to plan her meals carefully, and she was ill only once.

One evening after they had finished their dinner, a silent meal in which Cassie had spent most of her time pushing her food back and forth on her plate, she suddenly laid down her fork and raised her eyes to his face.

"You have eaten practically nothing," he said, frowning at her near-full plate.

She waved away his words. "I would speak with you, my lord."

She pulled her shawl more closely about her shoulders, and he saw her fingers nervously twisting around the stem of her wine glass.

"What is it you have to say to me, *cara?*"

"I am pregnant."

She sounded very positive and he allowed himself a slight grin. "Indeed, I believe that you are right."

"I have given it much thought and have decided that I can no longer return to England, or to Edward, in my current condition."

He drew a sharp breath, aware that his heart was racing, and waited.

"I suppose that you could not have *really* planned for me to become pregnant. However, the result is the same. I cannot allow my child to be born a bastard."

He nodded, and waited for her to continue.

His dark eyes widened in amazement when she said in a calm voice, "I have observed, my lord, that you have been avoiding me, both during the day and at night. Is it that you now find me distasteful?"

"Distasteful? Good lord, woman, I have merely done what I thought you wanted of me—left you time to yourself to sort through your feelings. Now, *cara,* I will show you how distasteful I find you."

He rose from his chair, scooped her into his arms, turning a deaf ear to her protests, and carried her upstairs.

"Tell me, my love," he whispered, as they made love, "do I seem like a man who holds you in distaste?"

He allowed himself to move deep within her, and she moaned softly, her golden hair swirling about her face.

"Do I?"

"No."

He was moving with her, his hard body covering her, consuming her in its heat, and she clutched him to her, burying her face against his shoulder. For the endless moments her body exploded into climax, she felt bound to him, possessed by him, body and soul. When her body calmed, her mind reeled from that incredible feeling, and she burst into frightened sobs.

The earl, who was blissfully recovering from his own pleasure, gazed down at her, astonished. She was clinging to him like a limpet, and he could feel the wet of her tears against his chest.

"Good God, woman, whatever is the meaning of this?"

"I hate you," she sobbed, but her hands tightened about his back.

"Ah, a natural enough feeling, I suppose." He became concerned that his weight was too great for her and rolled over on his side, bringing her with him. He imagined that her pregnancy was making her unpredictable and allowed himself to tease her. "At least you haven't taken your pleasure with me and rolled over to sleep and to snore."

He felt her breasts move against his chest as she reared up to frown at him. "How dare you, you wretched man? I don't snore."

"No, of course you do not." He stroked her tousled hair back from her flushed face.

He said, "Will you do me the honor of becoming my wife?"

For a fleeting moment, he saw naked pain in her eyes and wished that Edward Lyndhurst had never been born.

But he was only partially correct. Edward had been but a vague, shadowy thought. Her pain was born of her fear, fear of herself and fear of a future that she could not as yet fathom. She lowered her eyes from his face and whispered, "Yes, if it is what you want."

"It is what I have always wanted," he said firmly, and

lightly kissed the tip of her nose. He eased her down
against his side. "Sleep now, my love, and don't be concerned that you will keep me awake with your snoring. It
is soft and ladylike."

Chapter 17

L a Contessa Giovanna Giusti was in a rage. She hurled a priceless, exquisitely designed Ming vase, a prized possession of her late husband's, against the mantlepiece and watched it shatter into myriad broken slivers.

"Don't just stand there, you fool," she screamed at a cowering servant, "clean up the pieces!"

She found the violent act calmed her enough to prepare to meet Caesare.

She lay beneath him that afternoon, grimacing at her body's discomfort. He had taken her violently, with no thought to her pleasure. A smile curved her lips upward. She had heard it rumored that Caesare was not always the polished and gallant gentleman, that he had forced more than one woman. She gently eased herself away from him.

"My dearest Caesare," she said gently, "you have sorely used me. Have I said or done anything to make you angry?"

"Damn him," Caesare said in a low voice. He seemed to recall himself and turned slowly to face Giovanna. "Forgive me," he said, almost as an afterthought.

"You have heard the news, I see," she said, her voice soft, commiserating.

"Yes," he said, not questioning how she knew of Cassandra's pregnancy. "The earl joyfully informed me last evening at dinner. Later, he told me of the need for haste." He paused a moment and pulled himself up on his elbows. "Damn, the English wench has done me in. I will become as nothing to his great lordship, now that this girl holds all his attention, not even his heir."

Giovanna's mind raced ahead. "Perhaps," she said thoughtfully, "the wench can be bought off."

"You talk like a fool, Giovanna. Do you forget how very wealthy my half-brother is? Buy her off with what?"

Giovanna lowered her head. "I am sorry, Caesare. It is just that I so dislike seeing you upset by all of this. Surely you always knew that the earl would wed and sire legitimate children—sons to carry on his name and title."

"I am still his heir now, Giovanna."

"Not for many more months, it would seem."

He wanted to hit her, until reason asserted itself, and he shrugged. "There is nothing to be done."

God, but he was weak, Giovanna thought. "Dear Caesare," she began, "I have no desire to see you cheated out of your birthright by some silly foreign slut. It is not right that the Parese lands and wealth pass to her English children. It is my feeling, despite the impression the earl is giving everyone, that the English girl has tricked him into marriage. She wants his wealth for herself and her children. I think, Caesare, that she is a scheming little bitch, intent on destroying all ties you now hold with the earl."

Caesare said slowly, "It is odd that he said nothing to me before he returned to England about bringing this girl back with him."

"That is because he did not know of her existence before he left. Do you not see, Caesare, she has tricked him. She knew she could not convince him to wed her unless she became pregnant with his child." She spread her hands in front of her. "I wonder if indeed the earl is the father of her child."

"My half-brother is not a fool."

"Mayhap not in this instance, but surely he has not treated you as he ought. That old fool, Montalto, still shares his confidence, while you—" She shrugged her white shoulders.

"Whilst I what?"

"I do not mean to imply that the earl does not hold you in affection. But has he ever allowed you to direct his business dealings?"

"You know very well that he has not. He treats me like
naught but an amusing, useless fribble."

"If he were alone again, I cannot but feel that you, his
half-brother, would gain in stature and trust in his eyes."

Caesare rolled away from her and rose to look down at
her. "What is it you are saying, Giovanna?"

"I am saying, my love, that you must not be cheated out
of what is rightfully yours."

Caesare looked deep into her doe-brown eyes, and raised
a surprised eyebrow at her audacity. Perhaps jealousy compelled her, but that did not, he discovered, overly distress
him. He thought a moment, and frowned at her. "Even if
what you say is true, what is to be done?"

"The earl must not wed the little strumpet." She gazed at
him beneath arched brows. "Do you not want her, Caesare,
perhaps just once? To keep the earl on a string, she must
employ quite tempting skills in his bed."

Caesare remembered the desire Cassie had stirred in his
loins. But when he spoke, his voice was harsh. "You expect
me to seduce the girl away from my half-brother? Hardly
likely."

"No, you could not seduce her, Caesare."

"I believe the Borgia's habits are long out of practice."

"But there are other ways, are there not? Other ways
that would never lead the earl to suspect his loyal half-
brother."

Caesare felt a thrill of excitement, despite himself, and
a tempering shaft of fear. "Yes," he said slowly, "there
are other ways. But it is dangerous, Giovanna, very
dangerous."

"But you are such a resourceful man, my love."

He looked deep into her eyes, then turned and pulled
on his discarded clothing.

"It must remain our secret, Giovanna," he said, once he
was fully dressed.

"Of course, *caro*. Our secret."

He leaned down and kissed her lightly on her soft mouth.

"Do not stay away from me too long, Caesare," she
called after him.

*   *   *

Cassie shaded her eyes with her hand as she walked up the stairs to an upper terrace of the garden and gazed toward Genoa and the sparkling blue Mediterranean. She felt strangely lethargic, as if she were somehow drugged, her thoughts strewn about her unpredictably. She supposed it was the severe bout of illness she had suffered that morning. In all her eighteen years, she had never really known illness—save, she remembered ruefully, for the time when she was seven years old and had stuffed herself with Christmas sweets.

She turned away from the spectacular view, knelt down, and pressed her nose against a full-blossomed red rose. The sweet fragrances that hung about the gardens like a perfumed mist would soon began to fade, as summer drew to a close. Most of all, she supposed, she would miss the vases of flowers that Rosina brought daily to her room. She straightened slowly, her eyes caught by Joseph, who was talking to Paolo in the lower garden. She loved to watch Joseph talk, for though his face rarely changed its placid expression, she could make out much of his conversation from his expressive gestures.

But this afternoon, she found no interest in him. Indeed, nothing seemed to touch her. She wondered if she was becoming vaporish, like that ridiculous Lady Cumberland who seemed to produce a child every year, all the while lounging indolently upon a daybed, her vinaigrette in hand.

Cassie turned away and began to walk briskly toward the vineyards. She drew up short at the sound of Joseph's deep breathing behind her. Her lips tightened in quick anger, and she whirled about to face him. "Damn you, Joseph, leave me alone."

Joseph, startled by her outburst, stopped some paces from her to catch his breath.

"Now, madonna," he said gently, "you must not excite yourself. You would not wish any harm to yourself or to the babe you carry."

His soothing words had just the opposite effect upon her, and she yelled at him, brokenly, feverishly. "Has the earl not done enough? Must he still set you upon me, to report to him my every action? Is he not yet satisfied with his victory? Do I not carry his accursed child? Damn you and damn him."

She picked up her skirts, turned on her heel, and made for the lake. Joseph stared after her, aghast at the near-hysterical pitch in her voice. He came to a quick decision and quickly retraced his steps to the villa.

Cassie heard his retreating footsteps and drew to a trembling halt. She wished she could wipe her mind clean of its terrible, jumbled thoughts, but she could not. The earl's victory had been complete, she could not deny it. She had succumbed to him in less than three months, she who had sworn over and over that she would never wed him, no matter what he did. It was an accursed child that she carried, a child conceived of passion and hatred. And she had been so weak that within days of learning of it, she had bowed to his wishes, given herself and her future over to him. She dashed her hand over her forehead, in a futile effort to control the vicious bitterness, to stem her burgeoning despair.

"Cassandra."

She whipped about to see the earl striding quickly toward her.

Something broke within her at the sight of him, and she lunged forward, away from him, toward the lake, her own high-pitched laughter sounding in her ears.

The earl heard that laugh and felt a cold knot of fear. For an agonizing moment, she was lost to his sight in the thick oleander trees. He tore through the trees, scarce aware that a low-lying branch rent the full sleeve of his shirt, gashing his arm. He saw her running full tilt toward the lake, her hair streaming loose down her back. Dear God, what could have happened?

"Cassandra!" he yelled at her again. For an instant, she froze, poised like a startled animal, before continuing her headlong flight.

She was but yards away from the water's edge when he grabbed her about the waist and hauled her back. Her arms were flailing wildly and she kicked at him, in a terror-stricken rage he did not understand. He quickly pinioned her arms to her side and jerked her tightly against him.

"Stop it, Cassandra. Leave go." He shook her. She stared up at him, mutely, her pupils black in her eyes.

She lashed out at him, beyond reason. "Damn you, let me go. I will not belong to you, do you hear? You will not bend me to your will, you and your accursed child. Don't you understand? There are no palm trees, no vineyards, no olive groves in England . . . there are no prison guards."

He grit his teeth, drew back his hand, and slapped her. Her head snapped back with the force of his blow, and he slapped her again. She staggered against his arm and would have sprawled to the ground had he not held her.

"There are no olive groves in England," she whispered, her voice broken.

For a moment he could feel the starkness of her fear like a living creature within her. She seemed as a child, violently torn from all that she knew, and she was carrying a child herself, his child. She was leaning against him, her forehead pressed against his chest, her arms hanging limply at her sides.

"No, Cassie," he said, stroking her hair, "there are no olive groves in England." He held her close, his cheek resting lightly against her hair, and softly rubbed her shoulders.

She was silent for many minutes. Finally, she straightened her head and gazed up at him, her eyes clear. "You have never before called me Cassie."

His fingers lightly touched her cheek as if he wished simply by touching her to clear the red splotches created by his own hand. "No, you are right. Just as there are no olive groves in England, I had believed there was not a Cassie in Italy, only a Cassandra."

He paused a moment, gazing out over the calm lake. When he finally spoke, Cassie could feel him struggling with himself, though his voice was calm, almost detached.

"Much has happened, and very quickly. If you would prefer to wait some months before we wed, it is your decision."

She pulled slowly away from him and he let her go. "Why do you still have Joseph guarding me?"

"He is no longer guarding you, *cara*. He is merely your companion, someone who cares about you and wishes to keep you from any harm. If his presence upsets you, then he will go."

She sighed and rubbed the palm of her hands against her still-burning cheeks. "No, I do not wish him to go."

"I am glad. If naught else, perhaps he will keep you from falling into the lake when you handle your sailboat clumsily."

His jest brought a slight smile to her lips and he allowed his muscles to relax. "And our wedding, Cassandra?"

She gazed up at him, a faint flush covering her cheeks. "I have behaved badly, I think." She faltered a moment, and then said straightly, "I do not want to be fat, and you know yourself, my lord, that nothing would change, even if we did wait."

He smiled, picturing her belly swollen with child. "No, nothing would change. That *accursed* child would continue to grow in happy ignorance inside you."

"He is not accursed." She hugged her arms protectively around her stomach. Bright color suddenly stained her cheeks, for he had used the word she had flung at him. "*That,* I did not mean."

"But the rest you did."

"Yes."

He smiled down at her quizically and offered her his arm. "If the babe is going to make his mother fly into rampages, and scare the wits out of his father, then I fancy I shall have to become stern with him, this very evening."

"I am certain, my lord, that the babe already believes his father to be a monstrous man, bent upon disrupting his peaceful existence."

"I shall take that as a compliment, my dear. Now, Cassandra, if you wish to go back to the villa, I shall let Marcello tell you the response of the Dutch shipping representative."

She forced interest into her eyes. "You know, my lord? Do not tease me. Come, what is the answer?"

He shook his dark head, delighting in the fact that she had regained her balance. "You must learn patience, madam, though I daresay that we shall, within a couple of years, recoup our losses."

She smiled and nodded her head. She lengthened her step to match his stride.

The earl toweled off his body and quickly donned the undergarments and breeches Scargill handed to him.

"I begin to believe it's back in Scotland I am," Scargill said, eyeing the rain-bloated clouds overhead and shivering in the unseasonably cool weather. "And ye, my lord, ye must still insist on yer exercise, even though the weather would make a Scotsman cover his kilts." He looked out over the lake, and fancied that the water was as cold as were his fingers. He shook his head. The earl, as was his custom, had dived from the narrow wooden dock and swum to the opposite shore and back again with long, powerful strokes, enjoying the invigorating water and, Scargill thought, the strength of his own well-muscled body.

"What are you muttering about, old man?" The earl had heard very little of what Scargill had said, his thoughts on his own sense of well-being after his arduous exercise, and on Cassandra. He was to be married in a week now, and although his friends had loudly and raucously bemoaned his demise as a bachelor, he had only laughed, enormously pleased with himself. After expending so much energy in the pursuit of the only woman he had long known would suit him, he could not imagine feeling any of the trepidation his friends seemed to expect.

Early that morning, he had ordered their breakfast brought to their bedchamber. Cassandra had dutifully consumed a slice of dried toast, blanched, and bounded out of bed, forgetting her dressing gown in her rush to reach the basin. When she returned to their bed, her body trembling with cold, she eyed the remains of the rare sirloin on his plate and said, "It is not fair that you stuff yourself and I am the one who becomes ill. And I would that you stop grinning at me like an officious bore."

But his grin only widened. Thank God he no longer had a girl who exploded in unreasoning hysterics on his hands. All was back to normal, and he was immensely pleased to have his sharp-tongued vixen back again.

"It's coming on to rain, my lord, and I don't like it one bit."

The earl turned his attention to the muttering Scargill as he shrugged into his waistcoat.

"What displeases you now?"

"The madonna riding out with Joseph on a day like this to have a picnic in the hills. She's but being stubborn, and you, my lord, do not rein her in."

"The fresh air will do her good. Joseph will see to it that they return if it begins to rain, do not fret yourself." He would have liked to accompany her himself, but *The Cassandra* had docked the previous afternoon and Mr. Donnetti expected him to discuss the trading he had done in Venice. He looked forward to inspecting the bolt of Venetian silk that he had ordered for Cassandra. It was calculated to bring out her woman's vanity, if, he thought wryly, she was possessed of any.

He did not bother with luncheon, but ordered Paolo to bring around his black stallion, Cicero, and left immediately for Genoa.

Sordello was not quite sure why he drew back into the thick bushes that lined the dusty road at the sight of the on-coming horsemen, but even from a distance he knew them to be strangers, and strangers he did not trust. He quickly jerked in his fishing pole and crouched down. He felt his heart plummet to his shoes as they drew up not far from his hiding place.

Their voices were low and muffled by their heavy greatcoats. He really had no wish to hear their conversation, merely to remain hidden from their sight, but he heard one of the men say quite clearly, "I know this is their direction. Giacomo saw the Corsican ride out with the English girl not more than an hour ago."

The man, who evidently was Giacomo, grunted in assent. "And *Il Signore* left the villa in the opposite direction."

The man who had first spoken, the leader, Sordello supposed, for he was a huge, burly man, with a loud voice, said even more loudly, "Then it's off we are, lads, if we are to be at Vannone's hut by nightfall."

Sordello heard one man curse at the light drizzle that had begun to fall. His voice was consumed by the galloping horses' hooves as they rode away. Sordello crawled quietly from his hiding place and watched the men ride up the snaking road that wound through the hills. He felt a quiver of fear. They were taking the same route as the madonna and Joseph had ridden earlier. His mind worked feverishly as he dusted off his trousers and clutched his fishing pole firmly to his side. He wasn't at all sure what the man's words meant, but the thought that they might hurt Joseph sent him hurtling over the high stone walls of the Villa Parese to search out Scargill.

He breathlessly repeated to the Scotsman what he could remember and watched fearfully as Scargill's ruddy face paled.

"Ye heard nothing more, lad?"

"No, signore. But they looked vicious and mean."

Scargill didn't hesitate. Even if the boy had totally misunderstood what the men were about, he could not afford to take the chance.

"Quickly, boy, tell Paolo and yer father to make themselves ready. I will fetch his lordship from Genoa."

Scargill never slackened his horse's pace, but he began to feel nagging doubts by the time he reached the harbor and *The Cassandra*. He was beginning to feel indeed the fool when he stepped into the captain's cabin. The earl and Mr. Donnetti were seated across from each other at the table. In the earl's hands was a bolt of singularly beautiful silk.

"My lord."

"Scargill! What the devil are you doing here?" He dropped the bolt of silk and rose to his feet.

"I think there may be trouble, my lord." He saw Mr. Donnetti's hand move to the slender stiletto at his belt.

"Very well, tell me what has happened." The earl's voice was controlled yet impatient, and it had the effect of making Scargill pour out Sordello's story with scarce a pause.

"That is all?"

"The boy said there were four of them and they were a vicious-looking lot." Scargill had done his duty, and waited for the earl to shrug and admonish him not to be an impressionable ass.

The earl turned to Mr. Donnetti. "Francesco, hire horses and bring two of your best men to the villa. I will assure that there is someone there to guide you further. Scargill, you said they mentioned Vannone's hut?"

"Aye, my lord, the boy was certain about the name. Ye know the place?"

"Yes, I believe I do. It's an abandoned shack, supposedly haunted by a blackguard, Vannone, long dead. Francesco, it lies about seven miles into the hills, west of the villa, just off the main road. Make haste, my friend."

The earl turned quickly and strode to his desk. Scargill saw him stare for a brief instant at one of the dueling pistols before he thrust them into his belt. It was the pistol the madonna had shot him with.

Cassie pulled herself forward from her comfortable position against a tree trunk and squinted heavenward. "Oh dear," she said, "I do believe the earl was right. I think a raindrop just fell on my nose."

"*Si*, and because you are headstrong, we are both in for a good soaking."

Cassie wrinkled her nose at him. "I suppose you will tell me now that you have not much enjoyed gorging yourself on the cold chicken and cheese. And the prospect is so beautiful. A little rain will not make us melt, Joseph."

Joseph rose unhurriedly to his feet and sniffed the air. "We will return now, madonna. If you will not take care of yourself, then I must."

"Very well." She stretched her stiff legs and shook out her velvet riding skirt. "It has grown somewhat chilly, I will grant you that."

Joseph's toes were feeling prickly with cold, but he curbed a sharp retort. Her perversity, he realized, was part of her charm, and like his master, he was not at all immune to it. He quickly packed up the basket and tossed Cassandra into her saddle.

"The feather in your hat will be a wilted mess by the time we return," he said, not without some satisfaction.

Cassie touched her fingers to the fast drooping feather and laughed. "If it will bring you pleasure, my friend, then I will pray for the clouds to flood us."

He tried to frown at her, but failed. She was indeed a minx, he thought. It surprised him greatly that after some twenty-five years of silence, he had found himself telling her about his young wife, Maria, and their short year together on Corsica. A lifetime ago, yet when he was with the madonna, the happy memories stirred themselves into life.

It began to rain in earnest, and Joseph motioned to Cassandra to quicken her mare's pace. He imagined the earl would have his head as it was, for returning her to the villa in sodden clothing. He corrected himself quickly, for the master was rarely unfair. It was Joseph's self-willed mistress who would receive a good trimming.

Joseph reined in his horse at a sharp bend in the rutted, now slippery road, and looked skyward. Already the afternoon was shadowed and gray, and the air had turned a muddy color.

His horse snorted and reared back in surprise, and Joseph's hands tightened on the reins. He looked down the winding road that crisscrossed in and out of the hills below them. Four horsemen, heavily cloaked, were riding purposefully up the road, several hundred yards below them. He felt growing alarm, for he recognized neither the horses nor the men. Suddenly, one of the men drew up, raised himself in the saddle, and scanned the hills above him. To Joseph's horror, the man pointed at him and yelled something to the others. He could hear the pounding hooves as the galloping horses strained forward toward them.

Cassie pulled her mare to a halt beside him. "What is it, Joseph?"

He turned in his saddle to face her and said in a low, hard voice, "Listen carefully, madonna, and do exactly as I tell you. There are four men coming and I know that they mean us no good." As he spoke, he pulled a pistol from his belt and carefully laid back the hammer.

"Dear God, whatever are you talking about?"

He waved away her question. "Do you know the direction of the villa if you leave the road?"

"I believe so, but—"

"I will halt the men here. You, madonna, will leave the road. You must go carefully, for the incline, though slight, is fast becoming a sea of mud. Ride through the trees yon for at least a mile before you return to the road. Then I want you to ride like the devil himself back to the villa. I will try to catch up with you."

"Surely you are mistaken. Joseph, I cannot leave you."

Joseph uttered a loud oath and for the first time since she had met him, she saw the fierce, set lines of the Barbary pirate on his face.

His fear communicated itself to her, and she shivered.

"Go, quickly." He drew back his hand and slapped her mare's rump hard with the butt of his pistol.

Cassie looked back at him. He was covering his pistol with his cloak to shield it from the rain, and studying the terrain around him with narrowed, calculating eyes. Cassie guided her mare off the road and down the incline. Brambles tore at her riding skirt and cloak, but she was scarce aware of them. The suddenness of what was happening made her fear somehow unreal, as if she had been thrust into a bizarre nightmare.

The trees were thick, but her Arabian-bred mare nimbly sought out the narrow passages between them, side-stepping dangerously thorned underbrush. Her mare pushed forward until they came upon a narrow, nearly overgrown footpath, Cassie click-clicked her into a canter, and at the same instant, her mare's ears flattened at the sound of a pistol shot, followed quickly by another. Their retorts merged into a single staccato echo off the hills.

"Joseph," Cassie croaked, and slewed her head back in the direction she had come.

She heard the loud crashing of horses through the thick underbrush and felt her mouth go dry. She whipped her mare forward, urging her into a gallop. Low-hanging tree branches tore at her riding hat, and her mare snorted angrily as thorny bushes ripped at her legs. The horses' hooves pounded behind her, through the thick forest, drawing closer. Suddenly, her mare burst through the trees.

She cried out in disbelief. On the road below her, a man

sat waiting on his horse, his face shrouded by a black mask. They had guessed what she would do. She eyed the distance between them, bowed her head close to her mare's neck, dug her heels into her tender sides, and whipped her into a mad gallop down the slope.

Giacomo watched the girl tearing toward him in some surprise. But he was experienced in his work. He grinned in anticipation, for she was bringing sport to what he had thought would be a dull post. He knew she would try to startle his horse out of her path, and he grasped his horse's reins more firmly. He whipped his horse into a gallop before she reached the road, and when Cassie's mare veered away at the last instant, he reached out and raked her off her horse's back. She clawed wildly against his arms, and he could not stop her mare, who was galloping erratically away from him down the hill road. He felt her nails rake at his neck, and with a bellow of fury, struck her jaw with his fist.

Brilliant flashes of white exploded in her head, and she slumped limply against him.

"Good work, Giacomo," Andrea said, as his mount gained the road. "You haven't killed her, have you?"

"No, but she's a feisty wench." He wrapped his hand roughly about a mass of golden hair that spilled loosely down her back. "She's a beauty, this one."

Andrea laughed heartily. "There'll be time enough for that once we get her to Vannone's hut." He whipped his horse about, and waved to Giacomo. They left her soaked, bedraggled riding hat lying trampled at the side of the road.

Cassie smelled wet, sweat-soaked wool. She gagged and tried to wrench herself away from the stench, but a strong hand pressed hard against her back.

"Make yourself easy, my girl," she heard a man say. "It won't be long now."

She opened her mouth to protest, but a sharp pain in her jaw held her silent. She discovered she was flung like a sack of grain face down over a saddle, her face pressed against the man's thigh. She tried once again to jerk herself free, and the man pulled viciously at her hair, until she cried out.

"Hold still," came a snarling command. She felt the man's

hand move downward from the small of her back, until he probed roughly at her buttocks through her thick cloak. She froze, every thought suspended, and swallowed convulsively, fear and bile rising in her throat. Dear God, where was Joseph? She remembered the two shots that had echoed off the hills, and closed her eyes tight against her mounting terror.

She fought against growing nausea and spasmodic pain that gnawed at her belly from the jolting horse's gallop. It had stopped raining and the gray afternoon shadows had lengthened before she heard the shout of a man and felt the horse beneath her come to a halt.

"Bring her in, I'll light the lamps." It was a man's loud voice.

Her fear made her wily, and she forced her stiff muscles to go limp when she was pulled from the saddle. She thought the man believed her to have fainted for he held her loosely with but one arm about her waist. Without warning, she twisted wildly in his grasp and smashed his face with her fist. He howled, and she was suddenly free, stumbling away from him, running blindly into the growing darkness.

She felt a tremendous weight strike her back, and she went hurtling to the ground, breathless. A man's heavy body covered her, grinding her into the earth. She heard a deep, throaty laugh close to her ear. "Giacomo is right, you are a feisty wench. More's the pleasure for us, my fine lady."

Cassie was jerked to her feet, her arms twisted behind her. She bit down on her lower lip to keep from crying out, to deny them the pleasure of hearing her pain. They dragged her up rotted wooden steps through the open door of a small cabin and shoved her inside. She staggered forward and sprawled to her knees.

"Madonna." Joseph's anguished voice restored her to reason, and she jerked her head toward him.

He stood in the far corner of the room, his arms held by two men. There was a wide red stain spreading down his shirt.

"My God, Joseph, you are hurt." She struggled to her feet, but the huge burly man flung her back to the floor.

"Leave her alone, you stinking pigs!" Cassie heard pain

beneath the fury in Joseph's shout. She had to help him—somehow.

She looked up at the huge man, whose hooded face made him all the more terrifying, for he seemed faceless. "Do you not realize who I am?" she said in a cold voice. "In case you do not, I am betrothed to Anthony Welles, the master of the Villa Parese. If it is money you want, you shall have it, but only if we are returned unharmed. I demand that you release us at once."

Andrea appeared thoughtful for a moment. He stroked his jaw and turned to the other men. "Well, my lads, what do you think of the lady's offer?"

"I'll tell you what I think of the little bitch." Cassie had no time to pull out of Giacomo's way, for he stood over her. His booted foot smashed against her ribs, and she doubled over, violent pain ripping her chest. She heard a ragged curse from Joseph, and then a strange, soft whimper. The whimper, she realized dimly, came from deep in her throat.

"That will teach you to fight me."

"Leave go, Giacomo. You don't want her unconscious, do you?"

"You'll not lay a hand on her, you filthy swine."

"Just see if we don't, my brave Corsican."

Cassie looked up through a haze of pain to see the huge man pulling off his cloak. Almost gently, he spread it on the rotting floor.

"Can we, Andrea?" she heard Giacomo say eagerly.

Andrea shrugged. "There was naught said. I was told to keep her here, the Corsican too, I guess, until he comes. If you've no taste for such a lovely morsel, then I'll take your turn as well."

A wild shout broke from Giacomo's mouth. "No, you'll not have her all to yourself." His voice was suddenly crafty. "We'll have the Corsican watch. He's probably lusted after her himself."

The two men holding the struggling Joseph broke into furious argument.

Cassie's heart froze within her. They were going to rape her. God, they were fighting over the order. She tried to get control of herself, to think of something, anything that would save her. A pistol. Perhaps she could get one of the men's pistols. Slowly, she pulled herself to her feet, but the pain in her chest was so great that she gasped aloud.

"Ah," Andrea said, "the little lady wants us to begin. Look at how she comes to us."

Frenzied, excited laughter met his words. He was on her in the next instant, tearing off her cloak, and ripping at her riding habit.

"No, damn you, no!" Cassie yelled. The pain in her chest faded from her consciousness and she fought him, clawing at his eyes through the black mask, kicking wildly at his legs.

"Hold the wildcat, Giacomo," Andrea shouted.

Andrea tore off her clothing, delighting, she thought wildly, in shredding every layer. She twisted frantically, even as Giacomo wrenched her arms behind her back.

Andrea stepped back, his dark eyes glistening, his large tongue running excitedly over his lips.

She stood naked, her body quivering with cold and fear, her hair hanging loosely down her back and over her breasts.

He reached out his hand and cupped her breast. A piercing scream broke from Cassie's mouth, and without thought, she leaned her head down and sank her teeth into the back of his hand.

He struck her, full in the face, and she fell back against Giacomo. Giacomo's hands moved urgently over her, down her belly, around her thighs. She could hear his breathing in her ear, heavy and rasping in his lust. Cassie jerked an arm free of him and thrust her elbow into his stomach.

She heard his bellow of rage and hoped that his blow would leave her senseless.

But it was Andrea who struck her. He drove his fist into her belly, and she fell to her knees, clutching her arms about herself. She was hurled upon the cloak, her arms yanked above her head and held there by Giacomo's knees. She felt his hands pulling her hair from her face and shoulders. His fingers closed over her breasts, tender from her pregnancy, hurting her badly.

"She does not like your gentle attention, Giacomo," Andrea said, laughing. "Let us see if she prefers this."

Cassie's eyes opened wide, despite herself. Andrea had dropped his breeches and bared himself. He was built like a bull, a brute, a raging animal.

She kicked wildly at his hairy belly as he grabbed at her legs. He grunted and thrust himself between her thighs.

Dimly, as if from a great distance, Cassie heard Joseph screaming curses.

"Lay the Corsican out, Giulio. I need both of you to hold her down."

"*Bastardo!*" Cassie screamed, and craned her neck forward to see Joseph slumping onto the floor. She was sobbing, screaming her own curses at them, English oaths that they did not understand.

Suddenly there were hands all over her body, rough fingers digging into her, pulling her legs apart. For an instant, the room was silent, save for the rasping breath of the men who held her. Then her body exploded into agony. Andrea drove into her, tearing her, his hands jerking her hips upward to engorge himself with her.

For the first time in her life, Cassie prayed for death, for blessed unconsciousness that would free her of this horror. But the pain continued, plummeting her mind into senselessness. She was scarce aware when the second man took his turn, for he could not tear her body more than had Andrea. Until Giulio. "Damn," she heard him curse, "the wench grows too slippery."

She was pulled onto her stomach. And she screamed, screamed until her voice was a hoarse groan in her throat.

"You rutting bastards."

It was a new voice, a man's voice, laden with fury.

She was rolled onto her back and the vicious probing hands left her.

"You did not say that we could not enjoy her," Andrea said, his voice sulky.

"Get out, all of you. What if someone comes, you fools, the lot of you mucking around with your breeches down. For God's sake, get out of here and keep watch."

For a moment, Cassie's mind detached itself from her torn body, and her eyes focused on the man. Like the others, he wore a black mask. But there was something different about him, other than the richness of his clothing, something that she couldn't quite grasp.

"Joseph," she whispered between swollen lips. It did not occur to her to beg mercy for herself. She knew with the hopelessness of certainty that there would be none.

"*Pazza fragitara nigli inferno,*" he said, his voice low and strangely slurred.

Caesare stared down at her and felt a spasm of revulsion at what his *bravi* had done to her. He had thought to take her himself, but now he wanted only to leave this place and forget her eyes staring up at him, wide with helpless terror, forget the sight of her naked body, bruised and bleeding. He turned abruptly on his heel and strode to the door. "Andrea!" he shouted. "Do as you like with them. Just be certain, if you value your life, that they are never found."

"No," she whispered after him, trying to pull herself up, but he was gone.

Andrea appeared in the open doorway. "No more need of these, lads," he said, and pulled off his mask.

Cassie stared up at his coarse-bearded face, his mouth slashed wide in a grin. "Let her see your handsome face, Giacomo," he said, again unfastening the buttons of his breeches.

Giacomo's thin face was drawn and sharp, his eyes a strange golden color, like those of a fox. He ran his tongue over his blackened front teeth. "Wait your turn, Andrea. She's mine now."

Giacomo was angry that they had beaten the fight out of her, for he had wanted to feel her heaving and struggling against him.

She moaned softly, helplessly, when he thrust himself into her, and he could feel her quivering with pain.

"Fight me, damn you." He slapped her breasts and belly with the flat of his hand.

But there was no fight left in her, only a vast emptiness shrouded in pain. Dimly, she remembered the man's words, their leader's words. "*Pazza fragitara nigli inferno.* May he rot in hell." She was to die now, as was Joseph. Somehow, the knowledge did not quite touch her. She raised vague eyes to Andrea, and saw him pulling down his breeches.

She cried out, deep in her throat, and fell into merciful blackness.

Andrea sat cross-legged on the filthy floor, eyeing his three comrades. "Well, what will you, lads? Kill them now or wait for the wench to come around again?"

"What a bloody waste to carve the wench," Giacomo said, rubbing his hand over the stubble of beard on his chin. "The Corsican though—" He pulled his knife lovingly from his belt.

Andrea nodded. "Gut the Corsican, Giulio."

Giulio rose to his feet and drew his stiletto free of its leather sheath. He was caressing its razor edge with the tip of his thumb when a shot shattered the silence of the room, and Giulio screamed, clutching his belly.

The earl hurled into the room, the force of his body tearing the cabin door from its rusted hinges.

"Out, men!" Andrea shouted, and kicked over the lighted lamp, plunging the cabin into darkness. The earl heard a booted foot shatter the back door of the hut. At the same instant, he fired his other pistol, and one of the men grunted in pain. He whirled about and rushed out of the hut, to see three men hurling themselves onto their horses.

He turned and dashed back into the hut, his pistols still clenched tightly in his hands. His jaw was grinding spasmodically in fear. He had had only a brief glimpse of Cassie, sprawled naked upon her back, unmoving.

He fell to his knees, his hands groping for the overturned lamp. Frantically, he pulled it upright and lit it with flint and steel from the tinderbox that lay next to it.

The earl strode across the creaking floor and dropped to his knees beside her. "Oh, Cassie, no," he whispered.

Her face was turned away from him. Her eyes were open, but she did not respond, locked so deeply into her own horror that she was scarce aware of his presence.

She felt a large hand, a man's hand, lightly stroke her cheek and shoulder. Her horror turned itself outward. "No, please—no," she whimpered, and tried to draw away.

"Cassandra, don't be afraid, there is nothing more to fear."

His fingers lightly stroked her face, smoothed back her tangled hair. Slowly, she turned her head to face him.

She saw her own pain mirrored in his eyes. "I did not think you would find us." It hurt so to speak. She ran her tongue over her swollen lips. "Joseph, please, you must help Joseph."

The earl saw movement from the corner of his eye and whipped about. Scargill stood in the open doorway, a pistol in his hand.

"My lord." He lowered the pistol slowly to his side as he took in the sight of Cassie, of Joseph lying slumped on his belly, and a second man lying in a pool of blood. "Paolo and Marco are outside," he said feverishly. "We couldn't keep up with yer stallion."

"I know, Scargill," the earl said firmly, seeing shock beginning to cloud Scargill's ruddy features. "Pay no attention to that scum. See to Joseph, quickly."

Scargill raised his head a few moments later, his eyes filled with impotent anger. "He's bad, my lord."

The earl closed his eyes to blot out his fury. His voice rang out in the silence of the small room, harshly cold. "Send Paolo back to fetch a surgeon to the villa. You and Sordello's father"—he could not seem to remember his head gardener's name—"take Joseph back. I will see to Cassandra. As to him"—he jerked his head toward the dead man—"we will fetch him later."

When the earl turned back to Cassie, her eyes were closed.

"Cassie!" he shouted at her. Her thick eyelashes fluttered open, and she looked at him, vaguely questioning.

"I must take you home now."

Gently, he slipped his hand beneath her back. She moaned at his touch. His hand froze when he saw a dark bruise over her ribs, beneath her breast. He carefully eased his hand away. Although there was a dank chill inside the cabin, he felt beads of perspiration form on his forehead.

"*Cara,* I am sorry, but I must hurt you." He thought of the relentless miles back down the dark, winding road to the villa, and his hands shook.

"I cannot hurt any more than I do now," she whispered.

She was wrong. Suddenly, the muscles in her belly drew taut as a bowstring, then contracted ferociously. She screamed, all vestige of control stripped from her. Her legs, as if from instinct, drew up, and her hands clutched wildly at her belly. She focused her eyes, deep pools of pain, dumbly upon the earl's set face.

"The babe," she whispered, and then she was lost to him. He felt the fierce power of the contractions as he gently probed her belly beneath her clawing fingers. Her screams burned into his mind, and he felt completely helpless. There was nothing he could do to help her, or the child.

Cassie was scarce aware that her body was being covered and that she was being carried. Dimly, she heard him speaking to her, but his words were meaningless sounds. She tried to bring up her legs, hoping to lessen the wrenching pain, but she could not. She struck at the arms that held her, clawing for her release. She became aware of a moaning, jagged scream, and understood vaguely that it came from her mouth. It was odd, she thought, dazed by a sudden absence of pain, that she had screamed so. She never screamed. She tasted blood and salty tears. Then she tasted nothing.

The earl felt a great shudder go through her body. Her head lolled against the crook of his arm, and he tightened his grip on her. He quickened his stallion's pace, thankful for the sliver of moon that shined weakly, lighting the road. His lips moved, and it shook him to discover that he was praying.

Chapter 18

The front gates of the Villa Parese were flung wide. Myriad candles lit the windows of the villa and splashed their light onto the courtyard. The earl flung Marco his stallion's reins and carefully dismounted, holding Cassie tightly against his chest.

"Joseph?" he said sharply.

"The surgeon has just arrived, my lord."

He saw Marrina standing at the foot of the staircase.

"Send me Rosina." He shifted Cassie in his arms, and realized the cloak in which he had wrapped her was soaked through, sticky and wet. He stared down at his hand and saw it was smeared with blood, Cassie's blood.

He shouted over his shoulder, "I must have hot water, and strips of linen," and took the stairs two at a time.

Bright scarlet blood covered her thighs. He pressed towels against her to stem the flow, and gently lifted her hips to place more towels beneath her. They were quickly speckled with vivid red. His hands trembled, and he forced himself to draw a deep, steadying breath.

"*La signorina* lost the child?"

"*Si,*" he said shortly, briefly turning to the white-faced Rosina. He waved his hand at the blood-sodden cloak on the floor. "Take it and burn it."

Rosina looked at the cloak and felt dizzying bile rise in her throat. She closed her eyes, blindly gathered up the soaked cloak, wrapped it in towels, and fled the bedchamber.

Cassie moaned, and his hands grew still. Her head turned slightly on the pillow, and she was again silent. He was not certain what was holding her from consciousness, her pain or her terror of what had happened to her.

The door opened and quietly closed. From the corner of his eye, he saw Rosina's black skirt swishing as she ran to the foot of the bed.

A deep, raging curse broke from his mouth. He had bathed off most of the blood and saw that her woman's flesh lay jagged and open. The filthy swine had ripped her. He thanked God she was still unconscious. "Fetch me a needle, Rosina, she must be stitched. And brandy," he added sharply. He needed it both to cleanse the needle, and for himself.

"I need your help, Rosina," he said once he had cleaned the needle and threaded it.

"Dammit, now. You must hold her legs."

But Rosina did not move. She saw her mistress's torn body, and the blood, and fainted quietly away, falling onto the floor in a noiseless heap.

The earl cursed and strode to the door. When he reached the landing, he bellowed, "Scargill!"

He returned to the bedchamber, stepped over Rosina's inert body, and peered anxiously into Cassie's face. "Please, Cassie," he said, "don't awaken now."

Scargill took in the situation at a glance. Weak-stomached wench, he thought, glancing cursorily at Rosina.

"What do you need me to do, my lord?"

"Those animals ripped her open. Quickly, Scargill, I would spare her this pain."

Scargill held her legs while the earl worked quickly and efficiently, until he had set four stitches. He laid the needle upon the night table and slowly straightened.

Scargill had himself sewn up many wounds, gaping tears from saber slashes, but none of them had left him so shaken. The madonna was so slight, her pink woman's flesh so soft and delicate. He closed his eyes but could not escape the image of faceless men ravishing her so brutally.

"Thank you, Scargill," the earl said quietly. He saw the murderous look in Scargill's eyes and said to him in a voice so low that Scargill could scarce make out his words, "I will find them, you may be assured of that. One of them is already dead, and I am fairly certain that I wounded another."

Scargill nodded numbly.

As the earl carefully placed strips of clean linen against her, he asked, "Will Joseph live?"

"The surgeon is digging the ball out of his chest. He is not a young man, my lord, and he also has a terrible gash on his head." Scargill paused a moment to regain control over his shaking voice. "If he regains consciousness, my lord, perhaps he can tell us who did this."

The earl straightened over Cassie. "I will be down to see him as soon as I can leave her safely. Send one of the men to fetch the dead man from Vannone's hut, Scargill. It's possible there may be something to identify him." He pointed to Rosina's motionless form. "Please remove her. Marrina can bring her back to her senses."

The earl washed the blood from his hands and sat down on the bed beside her. With infinite care, he traced the line of her jaw, and gently probed her head. Methodically, he pressed his hands over her body from her bruised breasts, still slightly swollen from her pregnancy, to the bruise over her ribs, larger and darker than it was at the hut.

Cassie opened her eyes unwillingly, and saw the earl bent over her belly, his large hands pressing her lightly. She waited for the tearing pain in her belly to consume her again, but it did not come. For an instant, she felt whole, until her mind communicated to her that there was still pain to be endured, throbbing pain between her thighs and a sharp pressure, like a vise, closing about her chest. She closed her eyes tightly and pressed her head down against the pillow to keep from crying out.

She felt his hand upon her cheek.

"Cassandra."

She drew a jagged breath against the pain and opened her eyes to him. For an instant, she was back in the hut, flung upon her back, and the men were digging their fingers into her, savaging her.

"Cassandra," his voice cut through the horror, and she fastened her eyes upon his face.

"Where am I?"

"You are at home, Cassie, safe with me. I know your pain is great, love. I will give you some laudanum."

Laudanum. Her mind held fast to the word. It would make her forget, hide her away from her body, from the pain. He lifted her gently, and she avidly gulped down the liquid.

She lay very quietly, waiting for oblivion. Slowly, the pain began to separate itself from her, as if it were outside her, someone else's pain. She stared at him above her before she slipped into sleep, curious at how his dark face could be set into almost impassive lines, but his eyes black with rage.

The earl wrapped wide strips of linen about her chest and covered her. He quickly bathed and changed his blood-stained clothes. He gazed down at her one last time, thankful that the laudanum would keep her in sleep for many hours, and pulled himself away.

When he entered the guest chamber where they had taken Joseph, the men around the bed did not for a moment notice his presence. The surgeon, Signore Bissone, a slight, balding little man, his shoulders bent by his sixty years, was wrapping thick white bandages about Joseph's chest.

"Well?"

Scargill turned quickly at the sound of his master's unnaturally harsh voice.

"He will live, my lord, he has told us so himself." A faint smile broke the tight lines about Scargill's mouth.

Signore Bissone slowly straightened and looked thoughtfully at the earl. "I have removed the ball from his chest, my lord, but I must be frank with you. The wound is deep, and I fear the fever. As for the blow on his head, that will not kill him." He shrugged. "It's a tough old man he is, my lord."

Joseph's eyelids flickered open as the earl approached him.

"I am glad you are such a resilient old bird, my friend," the earl said, and tightly gripped Joseph's hand. Joseph's gnarled fingers moved slightly within his grasp.

"The madonna?" Joseph's normally deep voice was breathless.

"That is all I hear from either of you. How is the other doing? She will recover, Joseph, I swear it."

"They hurt her so badly," Joseph mumbled, trying desperately to keep his wits focused. "I am sorry, my lord. I have failed you."

"Don't be a fool, you old pirate. You have very nearly sent your soul to heaven trying to save her."

Scargill said from beside the earl, "Joseph said there were four of them, my lord, masked to their eyes."

"*Si.* Though I could not see their animal faces, I know three of their names." Joseph felt the earl's fingers clutch at his hand. "Their leader, a huge man, was called Andrea. Giacomo and Giulio are slighter men, but as vicious as that bull, Andrea."

"I killed one of them," the earl said, "and wounded another. We shall soon know who they were."

Joseph smiled painfully. "The madonna could tell you nothing?"

"Not as yet, Joseph."

Signore Bissone interrupted them. " 'Tis rest he needs, my lord. Does the *signorina* need my attention?"

Before the earl could reply, Joseph said, "She fought them, my lord, fought them with all her strength and spirit." He added, not realizing that his words would tear at his master's heart, "They wanted me to watch, but even two of them weren't enough to hold her down. That is when Andrea ordered the blow on the head. Did they hurt her badly, my lord?"

"*Si.*" The earl's teeth were gritted, and his temples pounded with blood. He felt Scargill's hand shaking his sleeve. He forced his voice to calm. "You must rest now, Joseph, and regain your strength."

Signore Bissone finished his examination, wiped his hands, and turned to the earl. "You have much skill, my lord. I could not have set better stitches myself. As for the ribs, they are perhaps cracked, but not broken."

"Her miscarriage?"

"She is very young, my lord, and possessed of a healthy

body. You will have as many children as pleases you." He peered closely at the bruises on her belly and her pelvis, and shook his head. They lived in a violent time, and he had seen many women raped, but still the cruelty shook him.

"You will remain at the Villa Parese as my guest, *signore?*"

"*Si*, my lord. Both the *signorina* and Joseph will need my attention for some time to come. Allow me to write a note to my wife."

The bedchamber door suddenly burst open, and a panting Scargill flung into the room, his eyes bright with excitement.

Signore Bissone made haste to cover the young girl.

"It's Francesco, my lord. He and his men have caught one of them."

Signore Bissone felt a shiver of fear down his spine at the look on the earl's face. His mouth, grim until this moment, curved into an awful smile, and his dark eyes glittered.

"Do we know which of the swine he is?"

"Not as yet, my lord. But it cannot be that bull, Andrea. This one is slight of build, and he is wounded, in the thigh."

"Take him into the library," the earl said softly, "I shall join you presently."

The earl walked noiselessly through the open library doors. Scargill, Francesco, his two men, and their captive stood before him. He was dressed in dirty clothes, damp from the rain, his back to the earl.

The earl paused a moment, then said, "Giacomo?"

The man whirled about. His ill-shaven mouth gaped open, and his dark eyes held fear. He was perhaps thirty, but no more. Crusted blood flattened his breeches to his thigh.

"Welcome to the Villa Parese, Giacomo," the earl continued, his eyes resting placidly on the man's face.

"I don't know why your ruffians have dragged me here," Giacomo said, but his eyes were watchful.

Mr. Donnetti said sharply, "He fell off his horse, my lord, not far from Vannone's hut. And we found this." He drew a black mask from the pocket of his cloak.

"Ah. You were perhaps on your way to a masquerade ball, my friend?" He walked slowly to his desk, leaned against it, and folded his arms across his chest.

"*Si*, my lord," Giacomo said quickly. " 'Twas a party my sister gave last night. I still carried the mask."

"Sister, Giacomo? Do allow me to doubt your word, my friend. A creature such as yourself would have no sister. Indeed, I seriously wonder if you know who your parents are."

Giacomo sucked in his breath and backed away. The earl nodded to Francesco. His two men grabbed Giacomo, and he cried out as his arms were twisted roughly behind his back.

"Gently, do not hurt our guest. Can you not see that he has hurt his leg? Very careless of you, Giacomo. Do tell us what you were doing this afternoon and evening," the earl continued conversationally, "we are very curious."

"Nothing. I was riding to Genoa when these fiends grabbed me. As to my wound, I shot myself accidentally while cleaning my pistol."

"I see. Innocence shines from your eyes, Giacomo."

"He's a lying swine," Mr. Donnetti said. The earl frowned at him, and he held his tongue.

The earl picked up a gleaming stiletto from his desk top, and glided his fingers gracefully along its razor edge. Without warning, he stepped forward and slashed it twice cleanly through Giacomo's shirt from his neck to his waist.

Giacomo cried out, more in shock than in pain. He watched his shirt fall open and saw a long, bloody X carved on his chest.

"I have done nothing!" Giacomo stopped struggling, for he felt the muzzle of a pistol pointed in his back.

"Tell me, Giacomo," the earl asked thoughtfully, "how many of you did it require to hold her down?"

Giacomo licked his lips. He was afraid of this man, very afraid.

"How many?" the earl said again.

Giacomo stared at the stiletto, its tip red with his blood. "Three," he said. He could taste death. There was no hope for him.

"You mean that three of you held her down while the fourth raped her."

He nodded, mute.

"Who was the man I killed?"

"Giulio," he whispered.

"And Andrea, your leader, he was the one who tore her apart?"

Giacomo was suddenly confused. He shook his head, and words rushed from his mouth. "Tore her? Giulio must have done that. She was too slippery, so he took her from behind."

Oh my God, Scargill thought wildly, as his master's face went white. He would plunge the stiletto in the man's miserable heart. He held his breath, waiting for the blow to fall. But the earl's long fingers merely caressed the blade.

"Take off his clothes."

For a moment, Mr. Donnetti stared uncomprehendingly at his master.

"Now," the earl said more sharply. "I wish to see this marvelous specimen."

Giacomo struggled, but within moments he stood naked, his breeches in a dirty pile about his feet.

The earl looked him up and down, and Giacomo felt himself tremble.

"How very odd," the earl finally remarked. "You have blood on your member. Do you not think that strange, Francesco?"

"*Si,* my lord," Mr. Donnetti croaked, his eyes falling to Giacomo's limp penis.

"And the tattoo on your arm, Giacomo. A serpent twined about a sword. Your rotting friend in my stable has the same mark. Your career as a *bravi* has been successful?"

A hired assassin, Scargill thought, his wits jolted by the knowledge.

Giacomo did not answer.

"I will ask you only once to tell me who paid you and your three companions."

Giacomo was doomed, he knew it. He had been a *bravi* for five years and knew he would die horribly by another *bravi's* hand if he broke their unwritten code. And only Andrea knew the name of the man who had hired them. He licked his dry lips, and prepared himself. To die because he had fallen off his horse, faint from the wound in his thig It was a twist of fate that brought him no amusement.

"I do not know," he said. He forced himself to straighten and pull his shoulders back.

"The name of the fourth man?"

He shook his head.

"You are really quite stupid, Giacomo. My friend Khar El-Din does not mind stupid men, so long as they are no longer men."

The earl gazed down pointedly at Giacomo's penis.

"Perhaps the pirate would appreciate another eunuch for his harem. You would grow fat and lazy, Giacomo, but could feast your eyes for the rest of your days upon beautiful women. Of course your pleasure would have to be in contemplation, for there would be nothing between your legs. If you live, that is."

The stiletto flashed out and Giacomo screamed. A thin red line appeared across his belly, and blood slowly trickled from it.

"Prepare yourself, my friend. I don't want you to die. I want you to always remember your punishment for raping another man's woman."

The stiletto rose slowly. Giacomo's mind snapped. He screamed uncontrollably and tore himself free of the two men holding him. He clawed at the pistol Francesco held and bore it down to his chest.

A loud explosion tore through the room, its sound reverberating off the oak-paneled walls. There was a ghastly look of surprise on Giacomo's face, and he slumped backward, his chest torn open.

Scargill fell to his knees beside Giacomo. "He is dead, my lord."

The earl slowly laid the stiletto upon the desk and

straightened. He gazed impassively at the gaping wound and stepped over Giacomo's body.

"It is a pity," he said. He added over his shoulder as he walked from the room, "Do remove the scum. Even in death he offends me."

Chapter 19

Fingers were digging into her, rough fingers with jagged fingernails that tore her flesh. She screamed and struggled to free herself of their hold. She sobbed helplessly as her legs were wrenched apart.

"Cassie! Love, wake up."

The earl was shaking her, pulling her from the horror, but she couldn't seem to stop the wrenching sobs that tore from her throat. Her nightgown clung to her, damp with sweat, yet she trembled uncontrollably.

His strong arms closed around her, and she felt the warmth of his breath against her cheek. Cassie pressed her face into his shoulder, waiting for the terror to loose its grip on her.

"The nightmare again?" he asked gently. He held her close as she drew a shuddering breath.

"Yes."

The earl smoothed her tangled hair back from her forehead and eased her onto her back, careful of her bruised ribs. Her eyes were huge and dark in the dim light of dawn.

"It's over, Cassandra, and you are safe, I promise you." He balanced himself on his elbow and looked closely into her face. "Are you in pain?"

"Please make it stop," she whispered. "I cannot bear it. It is so real—"

He stroked her cheek. "I know. I cannot make it stop, Cassandra, but I think if you talk to me about it, it may help you to forget."

She gazed up at him uncertainly. His dark eyes were tender, but she looked away from him.

"Can you not tell me about it?"

She shook her head. The pain in her body was almost welcome to her, for it focused her mind on the present.

The earl did not press her. It had been two days since her rape, but the nightmare kept taking her back to it.

"Would you like some laudanum, *cara*?" At least, he thought, she allowed him to care for her body.

"No, I do not want to be drugged anymore."

He nodded, and lightly kissed her forehead.

"I don't want your pity." Oh God, she hated herself and him for her pain. She felt she could not tell him, for he would withdraw from her in disgust, just as she withdrew from herself.

"Pity you," he repeated, frowning down at her in surprise.

She covered her face with her hands. "I know that you must hate me, that I repulse you. Five men took their pleasure with me."

For an instant, his mind refused to work. *Five* men? No, there had been but four. Joseph had been certain of that. "Cassandra, you said five men, but there were only four."

She grew very quiet. She had not realized what she had said and even as she sought to remember clearly, her mind would not allow it. Only in her nightmare could she see them clearly.

"May he rot in hell," she said.

"Who?" he said, sitting up.

Cassie blinked and stared beyond the earl's shoulder. "It was the fifth man—their leader. Joseph was unconscious and I thought him dead. When I pleaded with the man to see to him, he said, 'May he rot in hell.' "

"So Joseph never saw this man?"

"No, he came later." Her mind was resisting her, pulling the man's image away from her. "He was different somehow—and he did not rape me. But it was he who told them to kill us."

"How was he different, *cara*?" the earl asked, forcing calm into his voice.

She shook her head helplessly, for he was locked away from her. "I do not know, I can't remember."

He smiled at her gently. "It does not matter, Cassandra."

"Joseph told me that you killed two of them, Giulio and Giacomo." She thought of Joseph, his face gray with pain. The earl had carried her to his bedchamber to see him, and had left her alone with him for a few minutes.

"What else did Joseph tell you?"

"That the men were assassins. Each of them had a tattoo on his arm—a serpent twined about a sword." She gazed up at him, her eyes wide with confusion. "Why would anyone want to kill us?"

"I don't know, Cassandra, but I promise you, I will find out." He allowed a slight smile. "It appears that Joseph was a fount of information."

"Will he live, my lord?"

"I don't know, Cassandra. He's not a young man, and his wound is grave."

She turned her face away on the pillow, for she felt tears close to the surface.

He stroked her hair. "Can you sleep now, *cara*?"

She felt raging bitterness suddenly break from within her. She drew a shattering breath and whispered, "The child. I lost the child."

He swallowed convulsively, and for a moment could not trust himself to speak. "Cassandra, listen to me. I am sorry about the child, but you are more important to me than anything or anyone. Please contrive to believe me and throw off this cloak of guilt you are wearing. You are alive and I love you. That is all that matters."

A lone tear fell from the corner of her eyes and streaked down her cheek. He gently flicked it away before it touched her lips. "At the very least you must begin to take me to task again, else I'm likely to become an overbearing tyrant."

She swallowed back her tears, and forced a smile. "You will always be a tyrant," she said, and turned her face to nestle against his hand.

Signore Bissone was tired the next afternoon when he joined the earl and Cassie in the earl's bedchamber, after completing his examination of Joseph.

He had had to leave the Villa Parese late the previous

evening to deliver Caterina Pisani of a small son, and the mother had hemorrhaged and died just before dawn. He spoke of it unwittingly as he sipped on a glass of wine.

"One wonders," Signore Bissone said, shaking his head, "why God in his infinite goodness would snuff out the life of a nineteen-year-old girl so cruelly."

"What of Joseph?" the earl asked, his voice harsh.

Signore Bissone apologized for his lapse before answering the earl. "My lord, were he a young healthy man, the fever would cause me less worry. I have, of course, drained the pus from the wound." He paused a moment, his tired eyes darting momentarily toward Cassie. She had refused to let him attend her once she had come to her senses. Her stubbornness had angered him, but now he was too weary even to care. He shrugged. "The Corsican has not had time to recover his strength from the wound. He is an old man, my lord."

"What are you saying?" Impatience was heavy in the earl's voice.

"I do not think he will survive."

"No, you cannot mean it." Cassie sat forward in bed, clutching at the cover, and shook her head back and forth. "I tell you he will get well. I will nurse him myself. Joseph has a great will, he will not allow himself to be felled by a fever when those men could not kill him."

She drew to a breathless halt. Signore Bissone was regarding her oddly.

"You are speaking in English, Cassandra."

"Oh," she said numbly.

"*La signorina* was saying that with proper care, Joseph could recover."

Signore Bissone carefully laid his crystal wine goblet on the table and bowed formally to the earl. "It is possible, my lord," he said stiffly. "I have instructed the woman, Marrina, to make up certain draughts. If he worsens, I will, of course, return as speedily as possible. Otherwise, I shall come to see him again this evening."

"This evening?"

Signore Bissone frowned at the young English girl. He wondered at her relationship with the earl, but supposed that he was allowing her license because of her condition. "There is nothing more that medical knowledge can offer, *signorina.*"

"An offer of nothing can hardly be described as knowledge, *signore.*"

The earl saw the offended tightening of the doctor's lips and said smoothly, "I know that you are doing all that is possible. My man, Scargill, also has experience with such fevers. I thank you, *signore,* for your help."

After the doctor had taken his leave, the earl turned to Cassie to remonstrate with her, but the sight of her stricken face stilled his tongue.

"Please take me to Joseph's room now, my lord."

"Very well, Cassandra." He wrapped her in a heavy blanket and gently lifted her into his arms.

Several hours later, when Joseph had finally fallen into a fitful sleep, the earl carried Cassie back to their bedchamber. "I do not wish you to exhaust yourself, little one. Now it is time for you to rest." He answered her unspoken question. "I will stay with him."

The earl looked at the clock on the opposite wall from Joseph's bed. It was four o'clock in the morning and Cassandra was finally asleep.

He stared down at Joseph, whose eyes were closed in a fitful sleep. His breathing was shallow and harsh, his cheeks sunken and flushed with fever. It struck the earl for the first time that Joseph truly looked like an old man. His cheeks were sunken and feverishly flushed. His fierce proud eyes were closed in his pain. The earl knew, even without Signore Bissone's opinion, that Joseph could not survive. He felt a tightness in his throat as he gazed down at Joseph's parchment skin. He took Joseph's limp hand into his and said softly to the sleeping man, "I do not want to lose you, old friend. We have shared many years together. Do you remember the time when Mr. Donnetti, drunk as a wheelbarrow, overheard a Spanish captain bragging about his invincibility and the cowardice of the Genoese? And you, brave fool that you were, managed to save him from five Spanish sailors, bent upon bashing his brains all over the tavern."

The earl was silent a moment, remembering how Mr. Donnetti, usually a silent, rigidly controlled man, had laughed and cursed all in the same breath when Joseph recounted trussing him up and dragging him back to *The Cassandra,* moored in the harbor of Cadiz.

"I remember." The earl jerked his head up, and looked into Joseph's shadowed eyes. He saw a spark of life and humor.

A rasping laugh broke from Joseph's throat. "Poor Francesco, he was so foxed he did not even realize the danger. For days after, he cursed me for a meddling ass."

"Francesco will be here tomorrow or the day after, Joseph. He is in Palermo." Joseph's fingers clutched about his hand.

"It is a pity that I will not see him again. You will remind him, will you not, that it was he who was the fool."

"I have a fancy that you will tell him yourself, my friend."

A deep crackling cough sounded from Joseph's chest. He was so weak that he lay choking, unable to draw his breath. The earl quickly raised him in his arms until the attack subsided.

"I do not want to lose you, Joseph. Cassandra is forever yelling at Signore Bissone about your great will." He buried his face in the old man's gray hair, unable to speak further.

Joseph sighed, and the earl eased him gently onto his back. "It is the madonna who has the great will, my lord. I have wanted for some time to let this rotting body find its final rest, but she will not allow it. I have tried to tell her that I am an old man, that I am content with what life has given me, but she scolds me, and refuses to listen to me." A travesty of a smile parted his lips.

"She loves you deeply, Joseph, as do I."

"She has never known the death of one who is close to her. Nay, do not tell me about her father. That one must have been a scoundrel, but of course she never said anything of the sort."

The earl saw that each word was a great effort for him. "You must rest now, Joseph. We will speak more after you have regained your strength."

"There is no more strength, my lord. I beg you not to blind yourself to my fate." He fell silent for several moments. When he spoke again, the earl saw determination shining through his dulled eyes. "I have tried to speak to her about what happened. You must heal her, my lord. She has a courageous spirit and pretends that her desire for revenge has erased her fear. But it is not true."

"I know."

"If Maria had had her spirit perhaps my life would have spun itself out in a different way. Do not let her go, my lord. She does not as yet realize it, but her freedom lies with you and of course within herself."

The earl nodded slowly. "Joseph," he began and stopped, for his throat constricted.

"I thank you for pleasuring the fair Zabetta. I would not have relished being a eunuch in Khar El-Din's harem. *Addio,* my lord."

"No!" The small word roared in the earl's mind, but it emerged from his lips as a whisper. He looked numbly down at Joseph's hand, now lying limply in his own.

Joseph's eyes were clear and sightless, free of pain. Very gently, the earl closed Joseph's eyes. He sat for many minutes gazing at him, words he wished he had spoken lying heavy in his mind.

Finally, he rose and pulled the cover over Joseph's face.

"Good-bye, old friend," he said, and snuffed out the lone candle. He walked into the garden, a quarter moon lighting his way, and sat down on a marble bench. It was dawn when he stood again and stretched. He looked up at his bedchamber, its long windows bathed in the gray light of dawn, and drew a deep breath.

"Cassandra." He shook her shoulder.

Her eyes flew open, and she stared up at him in the dim morning light, as if afraid to speak, as if she knew why he was awakening her.

"It is over, *cara.* Come with me now and say your good-byes."

"When?"

"About an hour ago. He died peacefully, Cassandra, his last words of you."

He helped her to rise and to put on her dressing gown. He had expected tears, but her face was closed and set.

He left her alone with Joseph. When she finally emerged from his room, there was no expression at all upon her face.

"You will help me go to Joseph's funeral, will you not?"

"Yes, Cassandra," he said, and carried her back to their bedchamber.

Cassie pulled her black velvet cloak more closely about her, but the damp chill still seemed to penetrate to her very bones. She leaned heavily on the earl's arm, for she felt wretchedly weak. We all look like black crows, she thought, staring about her. Even the priest. Mr. Donnetti and the entire crew of *The Cassandra* stood with heads bowed around Joseph's new grave. Caesare, present, she suspected, out of respect for his half-brother, for he had scarce known Joseph, shifted his weight first to one leg and then the other, some three feet from her. The earl stood beside her, his eyes straight ahead. Signore Montalto was sniffing with a cold, and looking miserable. There were other men she did not recognize. She listened to the droning words of the priest, but the Latin had no meaning to her. She felt stifled by the black veil over her face, and pulled it back over her bonnet, unaware that in the eyes of the priest, it was an act of disrespect. She had eaten little the past several days, and for a moment, as she gazed at the fresh earth piled atop Joseph's grave, the earth blurred and seemed to rise toward her. She gulped and took a step back. She felt the earl's hand upon her arm, and stared stonily ahead of her, wishing the pale-skinned priest would finish with his Latin. She had always thought that priests were ascetic men who had little liking for things of the flesh. Yet this one was fat as a flawn. She shook her head, chiding herself for unkind thoughts. She should be thinking of Joseph, but somehow, she simply could not relate the mound of earth covering the oak casket to the Joseph she had known.

Finally, the priest closed the vellum Bible and intoned a prayer. Cassie kept her eyes closed some moments after he had finished, and when she opened them, the black-garbed men were milling about, their voices soft. She was about to turn toward the earl, who was speaking quietly to the priest, when suddenly she heard softly spoken words, words that burned into her mind.

"Pazza fragitara nigli inferno." "May he rot in hell."

She looked wildly about her, but she saw only solemn faces, some familiar and some unknown to her. She tugged frantically on the earl's black sleeve, oblivious of the priest, who was regarding her with profound disapproval.

"He's here," she said. "I heard him—he's here." Her weakness and shock combined, and she felt the ground unsteady beneath her. For the first time in her life, she fainted.

The earl caught her up in his arms, and called to Mr. Donnetti. "Francesco, quickly."

"What has happened, my lord?"

Tersely, the earl told him Cassie's words. "Get your men together. Bring any man who is not known to them to the villa." But even as he gave the order, he knew it was hopeless. Many mourners had already left the graveyard.

"The shock was too much for her, Antonio?"

The earl looked at Caesare, who was peering with concern into Cassie's pale face.

"Perhaps. She heard one of the men who abducted her. If you will, Caesare, walk about and see if there is any man that looks suspicious to you. It would give me great pleasure to kill another one of the bastards on the day of Joseph's funeral."

Cassie felt a swaying motion beneath her when she awoke, and tried to pull her body upright.

"Hold still, *cara*." The earl's strong arms tightened about her. In the next moment, she was feeling inordinately foolish.

"Oh, it is the carriage."

"Yes. We shall soon be back to the villa." His soothing tone gave way to an amused one. "I had no idea that you were the kind of woman who succumbs to the vapors."

"I am hungry, and it is unkind of you to tease me."

The earl hugged her against his chest, and allowed himself to become serious. "What did the man say precisely, Cassandra?"

She shuddered. " 'May he rot in hell.' Almost the same words he said that night. I could not tell which of the men it was, and the words were so quietly spoken—with such pleasure."

"Then it was the fifth man you heard."

She nodded her head against his shoulder.

"Francesco and his men are scouring the area, Cassandra. I will question whomever they bring to me."

"I think even if you find him, he is too smart to give himself away."

"We will see."

They were silent for some moments. "You know," she said finally, "I do not think that Joseph would have particularly cared for that priest. He was terribly filled with his own importance, and so fat."

The earl's chest shook briefly with laughter.

"Yes," he said soberly, "you are quite right."

Chapter 20

Cassie peeled an orange and chewed thoughtfully on the succulent fruit. "It is odd, my lord," she said, "to be eating fresh fruit in autumn."

"I know," the earl said with a quick smile. "There are few fresh oranges in England in the fall. My name is Anthony, you know," he added.

"Yes, I know. It is just that you are more often a lord or lordship to me."

"Am I so remote then? It is not my intention to be."

She smiled and shook her head at him. "No, you are not in the least remote."

Indeed, she thought, in the past three weeks he had been unflaggingly kind and solicitous to her. He still teased her companionably, and berated her if he thought she was overtaxing herself, but he asked nothing of her save her company. He made it easy for her to be content simply to be with him, to allow him to care for her and keep the outside world at bay. He seemed to sense her desire not to confront anything for the present, what had happened to her or the future, but merely to exist and to mend in the comfort he provided for her.

The earl sat back in his chair, chewing on a roasted chestnut, and looked at her. They had spent the afternoon aboard her sailboat, and the trout they had enjoyed for dinner were Cassie's catch. It had brought a mischievous smile to her lips that he had caught but one small trout, a fish unworthy of the great earl's dinner, and she had teased him. Although she was still too thin, the outing had added color to her cheeks. And her eyes were sparkling at him more frequently, the haunted look they had worn slowly fading. Her nightmare had come to her but once in the last week, and although she had trembled violently in his arms, her fear had not held her long in its sway. He watched her savor a final slice of orange and sit back in her chair with a contented sigh.

"If you will wipe your hands, Cassandra," he said, "I will let you try your skill against mine in another pastime besides fishing."

She looked up, quirking an arched brow at him. She cleaned the sticky orange from her fingers as she spoke. "Another joust, my lord? Surely you have no desire to be brought low twice in one day."

"The lady grows cocky. We shall soon see if your luck is still with you."

"Luck, ha! Come, my lord, what have you in mind?"

He tossed his napkin on the table. "If you would join me upstairs, madam, you shall see." He helped her rise, careful of her still bruised ribs, and escorted her to their bedchamber.

A small fire he had had prepared burned in the grate, casting wispy shadows on the white stucco walls. The earl helped Cassie into a chair before the fire and handed her a soft wool shawl, already warmed by the flames.

"You make me feel like an old invalid, decrepit and useless."

"At least you are a warm old invalid," he said lightly. "Now, Cassandra, close your eyes, and promise me that you'll not look."

"I promise," she said, a sparkle of excitement in her voice.

He placed a long wooden box in her hands. Before she opened her eyes, she ran her fingers lightly over the intricate carving and gently caressed the cool marble inlay. He remembered her suddenly as a child, trembling with excitement as her small fingers tried to rip open a gift he had brought her from Turkey—tiny bronze bells strung together on a gold chain. He had laughingly told her to enjoy her present before demolishing it.

"Oh!"

He grinned at the stunned look on her face.

Cassie closed her fingers about an ivory knight and slowly drew it from its bed of purple velvet. "It is identical," she breathed. The cool feel of the ivory chess pieces brought a catch to her throat. "It is just like the chess set you gave me for my fourteenth birthday."

"Yes, the same craftsman made it for you. I wished to see if you ever managed to gain any skill in the game."

She remembered his long ago having patiently shown her the opening position and the lawful moves of the pieces. "It is most kind of you, my lord," she said finally.

"Anthony."

"Yes—Anthony."

His fingers touched hers for an instant as he took the knight from her and set it upon the chess board. "It has been a long time since I've had an opponent worthy of my attention. Let us see if you play chess as well as you catch trout."

She gave him a slow, wide smile. "Prepare yourself, my lord, to be destroyed."

She moved her white king's pawn forward two spaces, and he quickly moved the black pawn to face it. He glanced at her as the game progressed, pleased to see her lips pursed in concentration, and her eyes bright with burgeoning strategies. He was pleasantly surprised at her skill. He toyed briefly with the idea of letting her beat him, and dismissed it. She would guess, and he imagined that such a victory would bring her no pleasure.

"Beware my black bishop, Cassandra."

She frowned and saw that her queen, if not moved to safety, would be pinned to her king. She quickly interposed her queen's bishop and sat back with a satisfied smile. "And you, my lord, should beware my rook."

Several minutes later, the earl's fingers poised over his queen. He moved her slowly into position and raised his head. "Checkmate, my dear."

"Drat," Cassie said, frowning at her defeated king. "I do not suppose I can claim you had the greater luck?"

"You can, but it would only serve to make me feel all the more superior."

"Wretched man. Very well, I grant you this game." She

looked at him from beneath her lashes. "I choose to believe that you have bested me only because you have had so many more years of practice."

"You do not consider it likely that I am simply the more intelligent?"

The gleam of mischief in his dark eyes robbed his words of any insult, and she succumbed to a giggle. "Must you always have the last word, my lord? It is too bad of you." She drew up, her eyes drawn to his. His gaze was dark with tenderness, and she gulped.

"Another game, my lord?"

He obliged her.

Cassie eyed the swaying palm trees with disgust. "It is autumn," she muttered darkly. "You are supposed to lose all those ridiculous leaves."

The earl stood quietly on the balcony of their bedchamber and watched Cassie walking about the gardens. She had returned but minutes before from the Parese vineyards, her interest, he knew, not in the science of the grape, but rather in Liepolo, his master winemaker, and his gaggle of children. Particularly Alvise, a naughty three-year-old, whose pranks brought rosy color to her cheeks and a ready laugh to her lips. He silently blessed Liepolo for being the sire of such a large family.

The earl walked back downstairs to his library. He kicked the dying embers in the fireplace with the toe of his boot and stared thoughtfully at the orange sparks that flew upward into the flu. A month had passed since Cassie's rape and Joseph's death. A month, and he was still no closer to finding Andrea and the fourth man. Without them, it was unlikely that he would ever discover who had paid them.

At least Cassandra was physically healthy again. Since he had not approached her sexually, he could only guess that the bruises were gone from her body. He had had to buy her more nightgowns, for she cringed at the thought of his seeing her naked. She had allowed him but once to touch her, some ten day after her rape. Since she adamantly refused to allow Signore Bissone to examine her, it was the earl who had removed her stitches.

The day they were to be married was weeks past, and he had said nothing to her about it. He was content to wait.

He sat at his desk and opened an account ledger. He concentrated for some minutes on the columns of numbers, then flipped the ledger closed with a grunt of disgust at his wayward attention, rose and walked to the gardens. He wanted to be with Cassandra, to see her laugh, perhaps.

The earl raised his body from the copper bathtub and shook himself, somewhat in the manner of a wet mongrel. He wrapped a towel about his waist and strolled into the bedchamber, only to draw up short at the sound of Rosina gasping at him. Rosina stood behind Cassie with a brush in her hand, her face a vivid shade of red. Cassie sat comfortably in front of her dressing table, consuming an orange. "You may go to bed now, Rosina," Cassie said in an amused voice.

When he heard the bedchamber door close upon the maid, he walked forward to stand behind Cassie. She was covered in a thick blue velvet dressing gown. Beneath it, he knew, was a nightgown. "You know, *cara,* I have been thinking."

"It is a marvelous process, my lord, and I am most pleased that you have finally been granted the privilege."

He grinned, wrapped a thick tress of hair about his fingers, and pulled. She yelped and turned on him. "If you cannot use your wits, my lord, may I suggest—" She stopped in mid-sentence. The earl looked at her quizzically and saw that she was staring at him pointedly in the mirror. His knot was working itself loose and the towel had pulled open.

"You were speaking about wits, my lady?"

Cassie lowered her eyes, aware of a surge of feeling that left her cheeks a rosy red. She wasn't certain whether or not she wanted to ignore his nakedness. "You were saying, my lord, that you had been thinking," she said finally, trying to disregard him as he eased his body into an immodest pose into a leather chair near her.

"Well, actually, I have been waiting for you to tell me,

cara, that fall in Italy is simply not as it is in England. No clouds bloated with rain and no frigid winds."

She hunched her shoulder at him, resolutely keeping her unruly eyes upon her fingernails. "I am convinced that you have the fires lit only out of English habit."

"You are probably right," he said. In truth, he had wanted to ask her if she would enjoy a trip to Paris, perhaps in the spring, but all thought had fled upon her reaction to seeing him naked. He walked quickly to the great bed and climbed in between the covers, for his member was swelled with desire. The last thing he wanted was to frighten her.

He watched her finish brushing her hair, wondering what she was thinking. At last she rose, shrugged off her dressing gown and slipped into bed.

A single candle sent its spiraling flame toward the ceiling, bathing them in a soft glow of light. He gazed at her for many moments before moving toward her. Her eyes were closed and her golden hair spread out upon the pillow, framing her face.

"There is no reason for the nightgown, Cassandra," he said finally, gently stroking her halo of hair. "I believe we have both grown quite tired of it."

Cassie opened her eyes slowly and looked up at him, a mute question in her eyes. "I am not certain what you mean, my lord."

He balanced himself on one elbow and let his fingers lightly trace the contours of her face. "Perhaps we can reach a compromise about your nightgown."

"Compromise?" She felt the warmth of his breath on her face, and then the light touch of his mouth upon hers, undemanding. His fingers stroked her throat, and then closed over the ribbons on her nightgown. She grasped his fingers, staying his hand.

"Trust me not to hurt you, *cara.*"

She stared up at him, her eyes almost black in the dimlit room. Slowly, she pulled away her hand from his, and he pulled apart the ribbons.

Cassie sucked in her breath as he gently bared her breasts. She closed her eyes at the shiver of pleasure that

coursed through her when his mouth closed over her.
"Your compromise, my lord," she whispered.

"How can I discuss it with you, *cara,* if you will not look
at me?"

Her eyes flew open, wide with confusion, and he drew
back his hand from her breast, afraid that he was moving
too quickly with her. He forced lightness into his voice, and
tweaked the tip of her nose.

"My compromise, dear one, is that we give your nightgown a place of honor at the foot of the bed."

The thought of being held naked against him after so
many weeks was delicious, and she nodded mutely. She
wanted him to enfold her with his strength and tenderness,
to make her part of him. He laughingly folded her nightgown, and hurled it across the room. She lay naked beside
him and felt his hand again caressing her breast. "It has
been such a long time, *cara.*"

"I know."

He grinned, and moved his fingers slowly over her belly.
His expressive dark eyes became clouded, and she knew
what he must be thinking. Her belly would have been
rounded by now, if she had not lost the child. But she was
flat, her body empty. She remembered the terrible pain of
that night and shuddered involuntarily.

He felt her tremble and stayed his hand. "Are you
afraid, Cassandra?"

"A little. When I remember the hurt, I cannot seem to
help myself."

"I know, I feel the same way. Even though it has been
many weeks now, that night still comes to me and I am
terribly afraid."

"You, afraid?" She looked at him, surprised. "I have
never thought of you being afraid of anything."

"I would be a fool were I not. Is that what you think of
me, madam?"

"Oh no, 'tis just then when I think I know you, you say
something that I do not expect."

He smiled at her and felt the tension pass from her body.
He let his fingers lightly caress her belly again, and rained

gentle kisses on her nose, her chin, and her mouth. He pulled her tightly against him, savoring the feel of her.

"I have missed you much, *cara*."

"And I you, my lord." She slipped her arms about his back and pressed her cheek into the hollow of his throat. She felt him pressing against her belly and closed her hand around him.

When he could bear her touch no longer, he eased her on her back and grasped her buttocks urgently in his large hands.

The dim candlelight blurred his features, and his heavy, fast breathing sounded in her ears. She stared up at his large body poised over her, and felt his sex pushing against her.

He felt her tense and looked up at her face.

But it was not the earl who looked at her, it was Andrea. She struggled furiously against him, pounding her fists at his face and chest, scarce aware that she was screaming mindlessly. When she was free of his touch, when she felt nothing holding her, she was frenzied with freedom, and hurled herself from the bed.

"Cassandra!"

She drew up, panting at the sound of her name, her body tensed for flight, confused and uncertain. She saw a man coming toward her, but he stopped. Vacantly, she realized that he was holding out his hand to her.

"It is all right, *cara*," came a quiet, familiar voice. "There is nothing for you to fear."

"Stay away!"

The earl could feel her terror. "Would you care for a glass of wine, Cassandra?"

Wine? She looked at him wildly, but he turned and walked away from her.

He gazed at her from the corner of his eye as he uncorked the decanter and poured rich burgundy into a glass. She was standing perfectly still where he had left her, her hair streaming over her shoulders, her body outlined against the dark shadows.

He walked over to her, forcing nonchalance into his movements, and held out the glass.

"Your wine, Cassandra."

"Thank you."

If he had not been so concerned for her, he would have smiled. Even in her fear, she was every inch the English lady.

She sipped at the wine and silently handed the glass back to him. He took several slow steps, and set it upon a table.

"Are you not cold, *cara?*"

Cassie's wits had returned to her, and she was appalled at what she had done. She held out her hand, then dropped it back to her side.

"I am so sorry, Anthony. It was just that suddenly you were no longer you. You were—" She choked, unable to say his name.

"Andrea?"

She nodded dumbly.

"It makes no matter," he said. "Come back to bed, Cassandra."

He watched her retrieve her nightgown and slip it over her head. Her hands were shaking as they tied the ribbons about her throat.

When they lay in bed, Cassie rigidly on her own side, he said calmly, "You must tell me what this Andrea was like."

He felt her shudder. "It might help if you could bring yourself to talk about him, *cara.*"

"I cannot." She closed her eyes tightly against the onslaught of memories. "Please forgive me, Anthony."

"There is nothing to forgive, *cara.*" He held out his arms to her. He felt her uncertainty, the remnants of her fear. He said easily, hoping to occupy her mind, "I did not tell you, but some weeks ago, I hired what you might call an agent, a man named Daniele Barbaro, to help me find Andrea and the other man. We must catch them to discover the man who hired them. Daniele has now extended his search to Pisa."

He felt Cassie stiffen against him and wondered if he should not have simply kept his mouth shut. He was taken aback when she said in a flat, emotionless voice, "I would assist you, my lord, to find the other man and Andrea."

He was silent for some minutes. Her words troubled him,

yet he knew that she was at last willing to face what had happened to her. He said finally, "Yes, you can help us."

"Thank you, my lord," she said.

He lay awake staring up into the darkness for some time after he was certain Cassie was asleep.

Chapter 21

B ut Cassie did not accompany the earl when he rode to Genoa to meet with Daniele Barbaro. He left her sniffling with a cold, propped up in bed, a wadded handkerchief in one hand and a book in the other.

"Just do not bring back Signore Bissone," she called after him, "else I swear I'll sneeze all over him."

He met Daniele Barbaro in a small coffee house in the Piazza de Ferrari, a quarter that was a maze of narrow lanes and steps, and tall, crowded houses, whose every window-ledge overflowed with blossoming mimosa flowers and carnations.

"What news, Daniele?" he asked, regarding the younger man's heavily hooded eyes. As always, he was pleased with Daniele's appearance. Dressed in sober black, his narrow shoulders slightly hunched, he could easily pass for a Genoese man of business.

"I received word but yesterday from a friend, Ludovico Rialto. He believes that Andrea is playing off his vicious tricks in Corgorno."

Corgorno was no more than two days' ride from Genoa. "It would appear that the brute is something of a fool. When you find him, Daniele, send me word. Remember, you are not to kill him. Have you need of more men?"

"No, my lord."

The earl ordered them wine from a hovering waiter and waited until the man was out of earshot. "Before you take him, remember that he must have the same tattoo as his comrades—a serpent twined about a sword. I have discovered from Teodoro Cozzi, my man of business in Rome, that the tattoo was particular to a group of hired assassins who were active there some ten years ago. He tells me that he may be able to learn what became of them. If it turns out that the man in Corgorno is not Andrea, it is possible that we will be able to find him through Cozzi's efforts."

Daniele stroked his thick mustache, wiping off droplets of wine. "It is something," he said in his measured way. "I will keep you informed, my lord, in either case."

The earl had retraced his steps through the maze of narrow streets and was on the point of paying a boy for holding Cicero when a provocative woman's voice stopped him.

"Antonio, how delightful to see you."

He turned to see Giovanna, dressed in apricot velvet, gazing up at him, her dark eyes wonderfully wide, her soft lips parted in a beguiling smile. A maid stood near her, her arms weighed down with packages.

"Contessa." He bowed to her.

She offered him her hand, and he raised it to his lips and lightly kissed her fingers.

Giovanna laughed softly, and with a quick nod of her head, dismissed her maid. "I find myself quite fatigued, Antonio. Would you please escort me home?"

The earl looked after the retreating maid, his mouth tightening. He could hardly leave Giovanna unattended. "Very well," he said shortly, and proffered his arm.

"Signore Montalto tells me that you come to Genoa often, Antonio."

"Yes. I trust my business associate is well."

"He's an old man. Can an old man ever be well?" She shrugged and smiled up at him. "But what of you, Antonio? It has been months since I've seen you."

"As you've already been informed, Giovanna, I am often in Genoa. When I am not, I am at the Villa Parese."

She would have liked to question him further, but decided to bide her time until they reached her house. She stroked her fingers lightly on his sleeve and walked silently beside him.

"Would you care for a glass of wine?" she asked him the moment they stepped into the entrance hall.

"No, I thank you not, Giovanna." He bowed to her abruptly, and turned to leave. She stepped in his path, clutched her arms about him and buried her face against his chest. "*Dio,* I have missed you."

He clasped her arms and pulled her away from him. "I am certain, contessa," he said, "that there are many gentlemen vying presently for your considerable favors. But I have told you that I am no longer one of them."

"You cannot mean it. I know that you want me," she said, her eyes steady upon his face.

"It is, however, quite true."

"How dare you?" She was rigid with fury at his curt dismissal.

"You must learn to mind your manners, contessa, as well as your passions. Now, if you will excuse me." He turned on his heel and strode to the door.

"How can you go back to that little slut? When you take her, Antonio, do you ask her how it was she shared her favors with common *bravi?*"

"Leash your venom, Giovanna, else I might be tempted to forget that I do not strike women." He heard her panting behind him as he opened the door and let himself out.

"Damn you, my lord earl. You will pay for this."

The earl raised himself on his elbow and kissed Cassie lightly on her lips. Her eyes flew open and she stared up at him, her mind still blurred with sleep.

"Merry Christmas, *cara,*" he said.

She yawned and smiled up at him. "Merry Christmas to you, my lord." Her eyes darkened for an instant at the thought of Christmas in England, and she turned her head away. She did not wish to discomfit him, not today. She thought of their chess game the night before, and smiled. She had finally achieved a draw and had teased him mercilessly the entire evening.

"Oh dear," she said suddenly, and threw back the bedcovers. She quickly averted her face, for he was naked.

"Oh dear what?" he asked, rolling onto his back and pillowing his head on his arms.

"I cannot tell you, my lord Anthony. It is Christmas, you know." There was a distinct twinkle in her eyes as she whisked herself out of the bedchamber into the dressing room.

The morning passed swiftly. Cassie stood beside the earl as he dispensed gifts of money to his servants and colorfully wrapped packages to their children. After a light lunch, they rode in a closed carriage to Genoa to attend Christmas mass at the Church of the Annunciation in the Piazza della Nunziata. Cassie had never before attended a Catholic mass, and she found herself awed by the rich solemnity of the service. It did not matter that she did not understand the deep chanting voices, intoning Scriptures in Latin. She copied the earl's movements, kneeling when he did and mouthing the Latin responses he chanted. She thought it odd that everyone was dressed in severe black, particularly on such a joyous day as Christmas. During the priest's sermon, she gazed about the ancient stone church, lit with hundreds of candles that cast eerie shadows on the life-size statues of saints that lined the walls. She was reminded of an English Christmas service only when she saw the crèche, the manger surrounded with mounds of hay, with painted statues of Joseph and Mary leaning over the tiny Christ child. She felt as displaced as the figure seemed to her, and felt a wrenching tug of loneliness. I cannot continue in this way, she thought. I am locked away from myself, from what I know and must want. The earl's hand closed over hers in that instant. When the priest chanted the final prayer, she turned her hand in his and clasped his fingers to her palm.

She was thoughtful on their carriage ride back to the villa.

"What did you think of the Genoese Christmas mass, Cassandra?"

"It was beautiful," she said, breaking herself away from thoughts that did not seem to lead her anywhere. "I only wish that I could have understood what they said. But you know, it was so very different from—" She broke off, grinning self-consciously.

He patted her gloved hand. "One could tell that we are much together. I am able to finish your sentences for you."

As Cassie removed her heavy black veiled hat, the earl

called to her from the drawing room. "Come have a glass of mulled wine with me, Cassandra."

But it was not a glass of wine he handed to her, but a large box, wrapped in a bright red velvet ribbon. For a moment, she stood tongue-tied, staring at him and at the box.

"Merry Christmas, Cassandra."

She took the box from him and laid it atop an ivory inlaid table. She felt a tug of excitement, for she dearly loved presents. She carefully parted the layers of silver tissue paper and lifted out the most exquisite gown she had ever seen. It was dark blue silk, of such a texture that it seemed to ripple like gossamer through her fingers. The stomacher was woven with gold thread, as were the full sleeves that flared out from the elbows. The skirt was yard upon yard of billowing rich silk. She hugged the gown against her breast a moment, unable to meet the earl's eyes.

"It is incredibly beautiful," she said finally, shyly gazing up at him.

"It is Venetian silk. Mr. Donnetti brought it back on his last trip."

"May I try it on, my lord, now?"

"Certainly. I will await you here."

When she reappeared some thirty minutes later, he stared at her, his breath suspended. The dark blue matched the color of her eyes, the golden threads, her hair. She danced lightly toward him, paused, and performed a pirouette. As a final step, she curtsied deeply before him. The neckline plunged low, in the French style, and her white breasts blossomed above it in rounded splendor.

"It suits you," he said.

"Do you really believe so?"

"Most assuredly I do, *cara.*"

He was taken aback when she suddenly stepped toward him, rose on her tiptoes, and kissed him lightly on the mouth.

"I suppose it does feel more like Christmas now," she said, and backed away from him quickly, in embarrassment. "Eliott was forever giving me the most unromantic and practical kind—new fishing poles, the most scientifically proven baiting hooks and the like." The light momentarily left her face, and he knew her thoughts were upon her family, Edward Lyndhurst, and undoubtedly the giant fir tree set up in the drawing room of Hemphill Hall every Christmas. He felt a knot of frustration, but managed to force lightness into his voice. "Would you like to join me now for dinner? Caesare was unable to come, as he was already promised elsewhere."

"I would be delighted to, Anthony, but not just yet."

He looked at her, a black brow raised in inquiry. Tentatively, she pulled a small box from a pocket in her skirt and shyly thrust it forward. "Merry Christmas, my lord."

He felt the pleasure of surprise as he carefully unwrapped the square box. He opened it slowly, and stared a long moment at a gold ring. Carved in black jade in a circular setting was a small chess piece, a king.

"I hope you like it," she said uncertainly, as he was silent overlong.

"I shall treasure it, Cassandra," he said quietly, and slipped it upon his third finger.

She laughed nervously. "Since you beat me so regularly in chess, I thought your skill should be recognized. I designed it, and Scargill commissioned a goldsmith in Genoa."

"You are very talented, *cara*," he said. She looked up at him, and did not stiffen when he gently pulled her into his arms and touched his mouth to hers.

As the earl walked alone in the gardens, he admitted to himself that he was starting to plan Cassandra's return to his bed as carefully as he had planned her abduction from England. His body ached for her, and he could not help himself. He frowned, his thoughts momentarily at an impasse. He resisted the urge to simply inform Cassandra that enough time had passed, that she was now going to wed him and be done with it. She had come to trust him over the past months, and he knew that she needed the undemanding companionship he had offered her. But he knew too that their relationship could not continue in the gentle limbo he had created for her. During the past several weeks, he had found being in her company increasingly a trial to him, as his need for her grew harder to keep in bounds.

He looked up to see Liepolo, his master winemaker, approaching him. He forced a smile to his lips.

"All goes well with you, Liepolo?"

"*Si,* my lord. Marrina said that I might find you here. Forgive me, my lord, but I wanted to tell you that the grapevines you had shipped from France have arrived safely."

"Excellent, Liepolo." Although he did not care at the moment if the wretched grapes became wine or vinegar, he forced himself to comment appropriately on Liepolo's plans.

"Wine!"

"What, my lord?" Liepolo asked, eyeing his master uncertainly.

The earl grinned widely and thwacked Liepolo on his stooped shoulder. "Forgive me, Liepolo, but I must leave you now."

He turned and walked briskly away, leaving his winemaster staring after him.

The earl found Cassie seated in front of her dressing table, already gowned formally for dinner, brushing out her hair.

"Why do we not have our dinner here, Cassandra, on the balcony?"

She cocked her head at him and smiled. "If you like, my lord. Caesare has decided not to join us this evening?"

The earl omitted mention of the note he had hurriedly scrawled to his half-brother, postponing his visit. "He had to make other plans, unexpectedly, I understand."

Cassie lowered her hairbrush. "In that case, since we are not entertaining, I shall not bother myself with hair pins."

After Marrina served their dinner, the earl nodded his dismissal, and turned his attention to Cassie. He kept his conversation light and her glass filled with light fruity wine from the Parese vineyards. "Is not the full moon breathtaking, Cassandra?"

"Indeed it is, my lord," she said, tilting her head upward.

The night was clear and myriad clusters of stars shined brightly in the black sky.

"It reminds me of some of the evenings aboard *The Cassandra.*"

She gave him a censuring look. "The dinners are better here, I think," she said.

"I thought Arturo had a fine way with octopus," he said blandly as he filled her glass once again.

"Octopus?" She gulped and looked suspiciously at the scallops on her plate. "You are a wretched tease, my lord," she said, pursing her lips at him.

"Drink your wine, Cassandra, it will take the taste from your mouth."

When Marrina returned to clear the dishes from the table, Cassie was seated beside the earl on the settee, her cheeks flushed and her eyes bright. She was saying, laughter lurking in her voice, "Really, my lord, your reading of Shakespeare's sonnets leaves much to be desired. You must be more dramatic in your rendering."

"Be patient, madam, one must accustom oneself to the poet's high-flown phrases. More wine?"

She giggled and thrust out her empty glass. "I discover that I am liking your Parese wine more with each glass."

He allowed her one more glass before he laid down the red leather tooled volume and turned to her.

She saw a look in his dark eyes, one they had not held in a long time. When he lightly touched his fingers to her cheek, she realized vaguely that it was desire she saw.

"I think, my lord," she said slowly, "that you are trying to make me drunk."

"But you are already in your cups, Cassandra." He took the glass from her fingers and gazed at her ruefully. "Actually, *cara,* it was my intent to make you only sufficiently drunk so that I could seduce you."

She stared at him, her expression blank. "You want to make love to me?"

"Of course. Was not my selection of Shakespeare's most moving sonnets enough of a clue to you?"

She looked away from him and whispered vaguely, the

wine slurring her words. "It has been so long. And I am afraid."

"Afraid of me?"

She shook her head slowly. "More afraid of myself, I think, and what I would feel toward you, if we—"

"If we began to make love again?"

"Yes."

"What you want and what you feel toward me is not something to fear, *cara*. You do not still fear that you will see me again as Andrea, do you?"

"I do not believe so. But I am afraid that I will feel nothing, save disgust for myself."

"You did not tell me this before, Cassandra."

She shrugged helplessly, and gave him a crooked smile. "I was not drunk before."

He pulled her gently into his arms and held her. He felt her head loll against his shoulder, and cupped her chin in his hand, lifting her face to his. She closed her fingers over his, and to his delight, pressed her mouth against his.

He unfastened the row of tiny buttons over her bodice, and lightly brushed his palm over her breasts. She stiffened at his touch.

"Look at your breasts, *cara*."

Unwittingly, she lowered her head and stared dumbly at herself. Her breasts ached and felt swollen, as if he had been fondling them.

His voice continued caressing and soft, yet he remained motionless, his eyes holding hers. Her fingers clutched convulsively at her bodice, gathering it beneath her breasts.

"You want me, Cassandra. It is time you admitted that to yourself."

"I do not know what I want anymore," she said, and pressed her cheek against his chest.

He cupped her chin again and looked into her eyes, wide with uncertainty. "I will show you, *cara*."

He kissed her deeply, savoring the warmth of her mouth. He kept kissing her as he pulled her to her feet, leaving her only to ease her from her gown and undergarments. She was staring up at him, her eyes wide and questioning, but her body arched against him, as if with a will of its own. He molded her against him and breathed in the sweet fragrance of her hair.

He released her a moment, silently cursing the time it took him to strip off his own clothing.

When he stood naked before her, it was she who held out her arms to him, her body taut from the ache within her and the thought of how he would, soon, bring her to unbearable pleasure. His hand moved downward over her belly until his fingers found her.

"You are exquisite, Cassandra."

"So are you."

He leaned his dark head down and let his mouth caress her breast.

"I want you."

He clasped his hands beneath her hips and lifted her. "Wrap your legs about me."

She grasped his neck to steady herself and obeyed him, though she did not really understand what he was about.

He lifted her easily, and she felt his fingers gently stroking her, and then parting her. He thrust upward and she buried her face in the hollow of his throat, whimpering at the agony of sensation he was creating in her. His hands molded her hips tight against him as he thrust into her. She tightened her legs about his lean sides to heighten her pleasure, and sought out his mouth. But the difference in their sizes frustrated her, and without thinking, she reared back against his arms, upsetting his balance. He fell onto the bed with a roar of laughter, and she sprawled atop him.

"So my lady wishes to be more conventional, does she?"

He pulled her upright until she was straddling him, her hips upon his chest.

He caressed and kissed her until she was on the edge of her climax before he lifted her hips and eased her down upon him.

He could not contain his own moans when he felt the rippling convulsions grip her body, and he dug his fingers into her hips and pressed her downward, hard against him. He was deep inside her but the pain she felt was consumed by the waves of frenzied pleasure that ripped through her.

"Oh my," she whispered at last, and sprawled her length on top of him.

He laughed softly and squeezed her tightly against him.

Chapter 22

Cassie laughed and punched lightly at the earl's chest as he lifted her from the copper bathtub. He heard a tentative knock on the dressing room door, and quickly drew a large towel around her. "A moment, love," he said, shrugging into his dressing gown.

To Scargill, who was pacing restlessly to and fro in the bedchamber, he was less loving.

"I trust you have an excellent reason for this interruption," he said curtly, closing the door behind him.

"It's Daniele, my lord. He believes he has found that animal, Andrea."

"Where?"

"In Riva Trigoso. Daniele sent one of his men to fetch you."

"Damn, it is two days' hard riding," the earl said, rubbing his jaw. "Why does Daniele not simply bring him here?"

"His man says that Andrea is no longer alone and it will take some of your men to bring him back." Scargill saw his master gaze with a furrowed brow toward the dressing room, and drew himself up. "I will go, my lord, and bring that swine back myself."

"No, Scargill, it is my responsibility as well as my pleasure. How many men does Daniele feel we need?"

"If you go, my lord, not more than three others."

The earl cursed fluently under his breath. Mr. Donnetti and *The Cassandra* would not return from Alexandria for several days. As much as he did not wish to, he would have to take three of the men from the Villa Parese.

"You, Rapallo, and Girolamo will remain here, Scargill, and stay with Cassandra. We cannot afford to take any chances with her safety." He looked away toward the dressing room. "Have the men ready to leave within the hour."

Cassie became very quiet when the earl told her what had happened.

"I shall return—hopefully with Andrea—in five days, Cassandra, no more. I promise you."

"I will go with you, my lord."

He answered her brusquely. "No. I will not have you placed in such danger."

"Is it not my right?"

"If you wish it, you will come face to face with Andrea, but while he is free, I cannot allow myself to be distracted, and that is what would happen if you were with me. No, Cassandra, do not argue with me further."

She wanted to tell him that she wished to be with him only because she feared for his safety, but she realized he was quite capable of taking care of himself.

"You will be careful, my lord?" she said.

"You may be certain of it, Cassandra."

She watched him silently, Scargill beside her on the front steps, as he wheeled Cicero about to join the other men. She closed her eyes and listened to the pounding hoofbeats until they were lost from her hearing.

"Nay, madonna," Scargill said, "do not worry yourself. He will return safely—with that animal in tow—if Daniele has indeed found him."

She nodded, feeling at once dejected and abstracted, and walked back into the villa. She did not tell Scargill that all of her concern was not for the earl. She had spent the past several days in a pleasant haze, content to bask in their rediscovered passion, becoming once again at one with her own body and with his. They had not spoken of the future, as if by tacit agreement. She wondered what she would have said had he asked her to wed him when she lay in his arms, her body drugged with desire, her mind quieted by her need for him. She wandered silently through the villa, knowing that she must come to terms with herself. She thought about the future, of the days and nights that would inevitably flow from the present, and cursed herself for her weakness. Her anger at herself turned quickly to sadness, not only because he had left, but because his absence would force her to look within herself.

Though the sun was bright as it neared its zenith, a light breeze from the Mediterranean stirred the balmy air and made the ride to Genoa quite pleasant. Cassie rode her mare, flanked by Scargill and Girolamo, both heavily armed. They had set out before noon to enjoy a luncheon, Scargill told her, under the tall, gaunt façade of the Palazzo Ducale of Genoa's main square. It was Scargill's idea, one he hoped would cheer the madonna. She had never visited the Palazzo Ducale or the Sala del Gran Consiglio. Perhaps, just perhaps, he had decided, an optimistic smile lighting his eyes, she would enjoy wandering through the magnificent buildings.

They left their horses in the care of a youth whom Scargill knew, and climbed through the uphill maze of narrow streets to the Via San Lorenzo. The sights, smells, and noise of the city always seemed to fascinate Cassie, and today was no exception. In Genoa, though, Cassie soon told Scargill between heaving breaths, one never seemed to be able to simply walk. Scargill, whose own forehead was glistening with sweat, heartily agreed, and suggested they stop at a small sidewalk cafe. After downing a cool glass of lemonade, Scargill left Cassie with Girolamo and took himself off to the Palazzo Ducale, where he hoped to gain them entrance.

Girolamo, a short, wiry man of middle years, sat tugging on his left earlobe as his rheumy eyes studied every man within twenty feet of them. His gaze fell only briefly on the ladies, and only on those of tender years with wide smiles and sparkling dark eyes. He had sworn to the earl that the madonna would always be safe in his company, and he had no intention of violating that trust.

Cassie gave her attention to the soberly dressed gentlemen and ladies who walked past their table, many of their faces moist from exertion. Light women's chatter floated across the narrow lane above her head, from the crowded balconies of opposing houses.

"Buon giorno, *signorina,*" came a soft, melodious voice.

Cassie slewed her head about to see the Contessa Giusti standing above her. She remembered every venomous word that lady had spoken to her that long ago evening at the Villa Parese, but forced herself to nod coolly.

"It is fine weather, is it not, *signorina?*" Giovanna continued, undaunted. She felt a flush of excitement that the English girl was here at last, in Genoa, and not tucked away out of her reach at the Villa Parese.

"*Il tempo e cattivissimo,*" Cassie agreed. She watched the contessa's slender fingers lightly touch the exquisite lace that fell in gathered layers from her plunging bodice.

Giovanna airily dismissed her maid and gazed toward the frowning Girolamo. "Surely, *signorina,* you do not need this ferocious man to guard you from me."

Girolamo opened his mouth to protest, knowing well that no good could come from the madonna talking with the earl's former mistress, but Cassie stopped him. Short of being blatantly rude, she saw no way of turning away the contessa.

"Girolamo," she said, forcing lightness to her voice, "I fear that the lemonade is not quite to your liking. Across the street is a cafe that, I believe, might sell something a bit more invigorating."

"*Sí,* madonna," Girolamo said reluctantly. He searched the street for Scargill, and with one last harassed look at the smiling contessa, took himself off.

"Madonna," Giovanna mused aloud, as she sat herself gracefully in the seat vacated by Girolamo. "How terribly quaint. Did you choose the name yourself, *signorina?*"

"No," Cassie said shortly.

"You are not often in Genoa, *signorina.*"

"I find that there is a lot to occupy me at the Villa Parese."

"Ah. But the earl, I believe, now spends much of his time in Genoa, dealing with business affairs and other matters. It appears that the Villa Parese does not hold the attractions for him that it used to."

Cassie's fingers tightened about the slender glass at the contessa's words. She raised wary eyes to Giovanna's perfect oval face, but said nothing.

"His lordship gives you no explanation for his many absences?"

"I believe, *signora,* that you can speak more plainly."

"It is said, *signorina,* that the only ones to stir during *siesta* are mad dogs and Englishmen. Now I discover that the English also take little delight in the art of conversation, that they are, lamentably, overly blunt."

"Perhaps you will allow me to add, *signora,* that the English find no delight in petty, veiled insults. If that is your Italian notion of conversational art, then I must bow to your superb abilities."

Giovanna's eyes darkened dangerously. "How dare you, you little slut?"

Cassie forced herself to smile. "There, you see, my dear *contessa,* you are already learning English honesty. 'Slut,' though, is hardly a suitable epithet, I daresay. Mayhap you are thinking of your own propensities."

"At least, *signorina,* I was honorably married, whereas you—" Giovanna let her voice trail off.

"Whereas I what?" Though her stomach was beginning to churn, Cassie's voice was even. She made to rise, realizing that there was no reason in the world for her to remain to be insulted further.

Giovanna fanned her slender hands before her and allowed a wide smile to reveal her teeth.

"Are you so afraid to learn the truth, *signorina,* that you must run and hide yourself?"

"Very well, *signora.*" Cassie eased herself back into her chair. "If you know of a truth, I will gladly hear it."

Giovanna's voice was clear and taunting. "You will never be the Countess of Clare, you little English nobody. The earl is a discerning man, and he has come to his senses. It is I who will have that honor. I have shared his bed for some months now and soon I will share his name. He feels only pity for you now, my girl, pity and frustration because he cannot easily rid himself of you."

But Cassie had stopped listening. "He makes love to you?"

"But of course. I asked you before—just where do you think he spends his afternoons?"

"I don't believe you. You are wicked, unprincipled."

"Shall I describe the scar on his left shoulder? Although he has not as yet told me how he got it, it is quite recent." Giovanna smiled, delighted with herself.

Cassie felt suddenly numb. She jumped to her feet, tipping the table and sending her glass flying into Giovanna's lap. She picked up her skirts and fled downhill, back through the twisting maze of streets and alleyways.

From across the street, Girolamo slammed his mug of beer down on the table top, shot the contessa a venomous glance, and rushed after Cassie, Giovanna's high, tinkling laughter in his ears. He caught Cassie near the Palazzo Bianco, where the young boy held their horses.

"Madonna. You mustn't listen to that woman's spite."

Cassie raised a white face. Was Girolamo angry because he knew the earl's visits to Genoa were to Giovanna? She felt uncertainty, then empty rage.

She thrust out her hand. "I trust, Girolamo, that you have some money to pay the boy."

"But Scargill—"

"The money, if you please. I have no wish to remain in Genoa. Do you or do you not wish to return to the villa with me?"

Girolamo growled deep in his throat, gave the boy a few *scudi,* and tossed Cassie into her saddle.

Scargill's step was jaunty when he returned to the Via San Lorenzo. The smile on his face faded abruptly when he drew to a halt and realized that Cassie and Girolamo were nowhere to be seen.

"Oh, my God," he said aloud, his face turning suddenly ashen. He forced himself to calm. It could not be possible that the madonna could have come to any harm in the main square of the city.

He quickly drew aside the owner of the cafe and questioned him. Nothing untoward had happened. For some reason, then, the madonna had not wished to remain. Girolamo would, of course, have accompanied her back to the villa.

He raced back down the narrow streets. The boy stood

by Scargill's horse, a slight frown on his face. It seemed, the lad told him, that the girl and the man had seemed to be for a moment at odds, but then they had mounted their horses and ridden toward the western gate of the city.

During his ride back to the villa, Scargill found that as his fear for her safety diminished, his anger grew in equal proportion. When he saw Cassie's mare nibbling lazily upon the thick grass that bordered the graveled drive, the remaining grain of fear disappeared and his hands tightened angrily upon his horse's reins.

He found Cassie in the earl's bedchamber, standing by the open balcony, quite safe.

"Madonna, why ever did ye leave like that without telling me?"

Cassie turned slowly to face him. Her face was white with strain.

"Why, madonna?"

"Because I no longer had any wish to remain. You see, the Contessa Giusti was kind enough to speak to me, Scargill. She told me that she has been the earl's lover for several months now. She told me that all he feels for me now is pity."

Scargill stared at her, mouth agape.

Cassie whirled suddenly about and struck her fisted hand against the glass door. "How could he do such a thing? How could he serve me such a turn?"

Scargill's moment of stunned surprise was over. He stared at her, realizing that she was in a jealous rage, and smiled. If she did not care for the earl, she would now be demanding that he send her back to England.

"Ye must listen to me now, madonna. The contessa lied to ye, probably out of jealous spite. His lordship would never return to her bed, or any other lady's for that matter. It's only ye he cares about."

"You're but trying to protect him." Her voice faltered, for she had never known Scargill to lie. Perhaps, she thought, Scargill simply did not know.

It was as if he guessed her thoughts. "Nay, madonna, I have no need to protect him. He is an honorable man, not a loose philanderer. Think, madonna. Can ye really believe him guilty of such an act?"

Cassie ran a distracted hand through her hair. "Oh, I don't know. But he has been gone, hours at a time, to Genoa."

"Of course. He's spent much time with Daniele, as he has told ye. Lord, madonna, I thought ye'd come to know his lordship better than that."

Cassie drew a shuddering breath. She wanted to believe him. Slowly, she nodded. "Very well, Scargill. I suppose that I have been hasty, and possibly unfair."

"More than possibly," Scargill said, his eyes never wavering from her face.

"Oh, all right. You have dressed me down quite enough. I will consider all that you have said."

When Scargill left her, Cassie wandered out onto the balcony and gazed toward Genoa. It came as something of a shock to her to realize that she had been with him for nearly eight months now. She frowned and caught her breath. Ten months ago, she and Edward had been making plans for their life together. Try as she might, she could not seem to picture Edward's face clearly in her mind.

She looked down over the lush gardens, so very different from the gardens in England. Sounds of laughter and lilting Italian came to her ears, and it took her a moment to realize that it was not English she was hearing. It is I who have changed, she said softly to herself, and she knew a moment of panic. I have changed exactly as he said I would.

"Edward." Saying his name aloud brought nothing save vague memories that seemed to belong to another Cassie, a Cassie who was no longer she.

She wandered downstairs, stopping a moment to breathe in the sweet fragrance of a full vase of roses. Savoring the smell of them awakened her senses, and she knew that, even now, she ached for him. She pounded her fist savagely against the closed library door. It is lust you feel, she thundered to herself. How could you feel more toward a man who has done what he has to you?

She turned abstractedly at the sound of Marrina's voice. It was Signore Montalto, come to see the earl.

"Ah, 'tis a pity," he said after Cassie had informed him of the earl's absence.

She gazed at him, clearly distracted, her thoughts elsewhere.

He mumbled something about papers, and Cassie, in an effort to get him what he wanted and thus have him gone from the villa, motioned him to follow her to the earl's library. Together, they sorted through the ribbon-tied stacks of documents until Signore Montalto waved the paper he was searching for with a grunt of triumph.

"I have it, *signorina*. Please inform the earl that I shall return to discuss this matter with him."

But Cassie hadn't heard him. Toward the back of the drawer lay a neat stack of letters, letters that all carried the earl's name and direction, letters all written in the same spidery handwriting.

"Signorina?"

Cassie raised bewildered eyes to Signore Montalto's face.

"I have found the papers."

"Si signore," she said, forcing a smile. She wanted to scream at him to leave her alone, but instead, she schooled herself to escort him from the room and bid him a hurried good-bye.

Cassie quietly closed the library door and returned to the earl's large mahogany desk. She picked up the letters, four of them in all.

"It cannot be true," she said to the empty room. The spidery handwriting was as familiar to her as was her own messy scrawl. How many times Becky Petersham had chided her, had tried to train her fingers to form more economical, graceful letters.

With shaking hands, she pulled out a single page, dated not a month before. She read of Eliott and his growing regard for Eliza Pennworthy, an attachment that Becky believed would lead to marriage after Eliott's year of mourning. For an instant, she did not understand, until she realized that it was her death that Eliott was mourning.

She read hungrily for news of Edward, but found no mention of him until she opened the first letter, written some seven months before. "The viscount's grief," she read, "has given me many sleepless nights, though I know that we did only what was necessary. It is my understanding that he has already resumed his military career and is on his way at this very moment to join General Howe's staff in New York. I trust that he will come to no harm amid the rabble fighting against England. In any case, it is for the best. He was never meant to have my Cassandra."

Cassie scarcely comprehended the rest of the letter, filled with solicitous questions about her and her adjustment to her new life. Her eyes locked upon Becky's terse closing. "You will not forget your promise, Anthony. Once Cassie is your wife, you will return her to England. Your loving cousin, B. Petersham."

The letter floated unnoticed from her fingers to the floor. So many questions now had answers. Becky's blatant disapproval of Edward. And Becky's family, something of a mystery to Cassie and Eliott. The letters she received, foreign letters from someone whose name she had never mentioned. And Becky had even encouraged her to take her sailboat out one last time, the day before Cassie's wedding. She had known of the earl's intention, and between them, they had plotted her abduction.

Cassie forced her feet to move to a sofa on the far side of the library. She sank down into the soft velvet cushions and buried her face in her hands. Becky, the earl's cousin, came to live with her when she was but five years old. Becky, whom she had loved like a mother, the earl's agent. Cassie suddenly remembered something that had puzzled her, but so trivial that she had not thought of it again. When they were aboard *The Cassandra,* it had come as no surprise to him that she spoke Italian. She shivered. Had he even directed her education through Becky Petersham? What else that was part of her, which of her likes and dislikes, had he molded to his pleasure?

She looked out toward the blooming magnolia trees, the potted oleanders. Had he nurtured her, as would a gardener, raised her in the image that he himself had created for her? She felt silent tears sting her eyes. Her mother had died birthing her and he had wanted another Lady Constance. He had chosen her to take her mother's place.

She felt crushed with betrayal, made all the worse by her realization that he had succeeded in molding her according to his wishes. She had come to love him. She began to tremble with self-loathing. He had done just as he pleased, and she, without causing him too much concern, had responded to him. Had she not lost the child, she would at this moment be his wife, and likely quite content with her fate.

"I will not love you!"

She thought of the contessa, and her claim that the earl was her lover. She knew that she did not believe Giovanna. But somehow, it no longer mattered. She had changed, she knew it now, but at the same time the earl had not. He still would not let her go. He would still give her no choices. She rushed over to the large globe and spun it about until she found the North American continent. Edward was in the American colonies—New York. She quickly found the port city. He was on General Howe's staff. She did not imagine it would be difficult for her to find him. She straightened and looked grimly about the dark-paneled library. Everything about her was his. It was his library, his home, his country. Even she was his creation. She walked with a determined stride from the library, not looking back.

At first light the next morning, armed with all the money the earl kept in a strong box, and a sturdy portmanteau, Cassie stole quietly to the stable. She knew the men the earl had left to protect her were still abed, no thought in their heads that they needed to guard against her leaving the villa.

Her fingers froze suddenly on the saddle girth. She heard Paolo's shuffling footsteps. She clenched her jaw in determination and grabbed a haying fork. When Paolo walked into the stables, she struck him upon the head. He fell where he stood. She quickly bent down and felt for his pulse. "I am sorry, my friend," she said softly to his figure, "but you will have a great headache."

She dragged him into an empty stall, quickly finished saddling her mare, and walked her to the great gates of the Villa Parese. She did not look back when she reached the dusty road.

"There is a young woman demanding to see you, Captain."

Captain Jeremy Crowley raised his head from his breakfast and stared at his first mate, Mr. Thompson.

"Is this some kind of jest, sir?"

"No, sir. She is English, and a lady."

"What the devil is an English lady doing in Genoa, wanting to see me, for God's sake?" Captain Crowley knew his question was rhetorical. "Escort her to my cabin, Mr. Thompson, and keep the men from seeing her, if you can."

"Aye, captain."

Cassie did not need to be told to keep the hood of her cloak closely about her face. She had cursed herself more than once already for not having taken one of the earl's pistols, for a woman alone, no matter the time of day at the harbor, was bound to attract unwanted attention. When she had seen a Union Jack fluttering at the jackstaff of a large frigate, she had ignored the obscene taunts, most of them incomprehensible to her in any case, left her mare on the dock, and marched up the gangplank. Luckily for her, it was Mr. Thompson who had first approached her.

Mr. Thompson obligingly relieved her of her portmanteau and escorted her down the companionway to Captain Crowley's cabin. The frigate was more than twice the size of *The Cassandra,* and heavily armed. The narrow companionway was stuffy, and Cassie, whose heart was beginning to pound uncomfortably, breathed a sigh of relief when Mr. Thompson finally drew to a halt and opened a cabin door.

Cassie stepped into a smallish room lined with dark mahogany paneling that was covered with swords and muskets and wrinkled maps. The furniture was simple and unadorned, set about the cabin with stark precision. She sniffed in the heavy odor of pipe tobacco.

"Captain Jeremy Crowley, ma'am," Mr. Thompson said.

"You may leave us, Mr. Thompson."

Cassie stared at a tall bewigged gentleman of considerable girth, whose full dress naval uniform of blue and white, although clean, had known better days. He was possessed of a large nose, a recessed chin, and the coldest gray eyes she had ever seen. She gulped uncertainly under his equally sharp scrutiny.

"Please be seated, ma'am."

She nodded silently and seated herself on the edge of a black leather chair. Her eyes went toward the small table upon which sat the remains of a sizable breakfast, and she licked her lips.

"You would care, perhaps, for a cup of tea, ma'am?"

"Yes, sir," she said simply.

Captain Crowley said no more until she had sipped at the still-scalding tea.

"Mr. Thompson tells me you are an English lady."

Cassie heard the incredulity in his crisp voice and realized that it would be difficult at the very least to convince him to take her aboard.

"Yes, sir. I am the Viscountess Delford, Cassandra Lyndhurst by name."

The hood of Cassie's cloak fell back at that moment, and Captain Crowley found himself staring unabashedly at a beautiful young woman.

Cassie felt a dull flush creep over her cheeks, and her eyes flew toward the cabin door. She was suddenly afraid that she had placed herself in the hands of a scoundrel.

"You needn't be afraid of me, my lady," Captain Crowley said sharply, her look of panic not lost to him. He flipped up the blue tails of his coat and sat himself opposite her. "Now, my child, you will tell me how I may be of service to you."

He took on the look of a very stern grandfather, and Cassie eased her tense muscles. All the way to Genoa, she had rehearsed her story, one that sounded so outlandish that she hoped it would be taken as truth. Indeed, she had thought ruefully, there was quite a bit of truth to it.

"My husband, Captain Lyndhurst, is in the colonies, sir, in New York with General Howe. I was on an English ship bound for New York when we were seized for the masts and spars we carried. I was taken by a Genoese nobleman and brought here." Cassie saw Captain Crowley's gray eyes narrow in disbelief and hastened to add, "As you know, Captain, most masts that manage to reach English ships usually arrive in sections and must be bound together with iron. This means, of course, that they lack flexibility and many times snap in gale weather. The masts we carried were supposedly secret. They were of the finest seasoned oak from the Baltic. It is obvious to me that there was a traitor aboard, a man who had told the French of our cargo."

Cassie silently blessed all the books she had devoured, for Captain Crowley was nodding at her in assent. "You are a very knowledgeable young lady, viscountess. Indeed, that is why our frigate is here, in Genoa. It is difficult to make repairs on a rotted mast."

She heard the undisguised bitterness in his voice, but knowing nothing of the administrative weaknesses of the Royal Navy, she could do nothing more than nod wisely.

Captain Crowley pulled himself from his cogitations. "You said, my lady, that you were brought here by a Genoese nobleman."

Cassie felt a tightening in her throat at the mention of the earl and for a moment could not reply. It was perhaps just as well, for Captain Crowley saw the pain in her fine eyes and felt a tug of unprecedented emotion.

"Yes, sir. I have been here for several months now. At first I fought him, until it was borne upon me that such behavior would gain me naught. I became docile, subservient, and he was lulled into believing that I was content with my lot." She suddenly threw back her head and stared at the captain full face. "If you do not take me with you, Captain Crowley, he will find me, and I shall never again see my husband or England."

Although she did not plan it, Cassie suddenly burst into tears. She buried her face in her hands and her whole body shook with anguished sobs. That she herself was surprised by her tears was not apparent to Captain Crowley.

"My dear viscountess," he said awkwardly, leaning forward to pat her hand, "there is no need for you to distress yourself further. As an English gentleman, I must assist you. Shall I set my men upon this blackguard who has held you against your will?"

Cassie raised her tear-streaked face and gulped. "Please,

sir, I beg of you not to. The Genoese are peculiar, and he is a powerful man. I fear that such an action would be dangerous and could create an incident that could affect England itself. The Genoese are mighty bankers, you know."

Captain Crowley was beginning to view her as a very well-informed young lady. He nodded sagely. "You need not fear that a Genoese blackguard could lay England low, my lady. But I will do as you wish in the matter." He rose, dug his large hands into the pockets of his cream-colored breeches, and ruminated aloud. "I am bound for Boston on the morning tide. It is a long journey, and one that is not without danger."

"I am well aware of that, Captain."

"Aye, I suppose that you are."

"This Boston, Captain, is it near New York?"

"It is not too far distant, my lady. I see no reason why I cannot escort you myself to General Howe and your husband. If aught else, the Genoese are apt builders, and our repairs have been completed a week beforetimes." He stroked his receding chin thoughtfully while Cassie held her breath, fearful that he would change his mind.

To her profound relief, he was but concerned about her quarters. She most happily agreed to the dispossession of Mr. Thompson, adamantly refusing the Captain's cabin.

"You will, unfortunately, my lady, have to spend most of our journey below-deck. Some of his majesty's sailors are an unsavory lot and I want no unpleasant incidents on my ship." He pointed to a neat pile of dusty tomes set on a low shelf. "My library is, of course, at your disposal."

He beamed at her, the coldness gone from his gray eyes. "If you will excuse me, my lady, I will see that Mr. Thompson settles you in."

"Thank you, Captain."

After Captain Crowley had left her, Cassie rose slowly from her chair and walked to the port windows.

Mr. Thompson found her there, staring toward the verdant hills behind the city.

Chapter 23

The Union Jack lay limp against the flagstaff, undisturbed by the ruffling cool breeze from the bay that
rippled through the fortified encampment at the Battery. It
was another pleasantly warm March day in New York. His
majesty's sailors called out to each other cheerfully as they
cleaned their guns and polished their boots, over the noise
of scores of black men, naked to the waist, unloading cargo
from the merchant ships onto the docks. Their muscles glistened with sweat as they heaved, in a steady rhythm, bales
of woolen cloth, crates of candles, every variety of liquor,
Bibles, navigators' instruments, horsewhips, and tooth-
brushes, over the docks to waiting horse-drawn carts,
bound for Broadway.

Trade was brisk. For the British army and the loyalists,
New York was an oasis where food was cheap and plentiful
and the markets overflowed with merchandise that catered
to the British taste in comfort. Even throughout the winter
months, when snow covered the frozen ground and howling
winds whistled through the city, dinners, balls, and plays
were not uncommon diversions to while away the frigid
evenings. With the coming of early spring, the colonial loyalists threw themselves into a frenzied succession of social
gatherings, seemingly intent on proving that, despite the
rebellion, New York could still be a place of extravagant
gaiety.

Edward learned forward and patted his gray mare's
glossy neck. She had no particular liking for the noisy harbor, preferring, he knew, the quiet of the countryside or
the order of the March. She was skittish and tensed for

action, reminded, Edward supposed, of the tumult of battle by the boisterous human activity of the thriving dock.

He laid his hand on his left thigh and rubbed it. The saber wound he had suffered in one of the many skirmishes with the rebels on Staten Island still ached. He stroked Delila's neck once again in gratitude. Had it not been for her rearing up to protect him, the wild-eyed rebel's saber would have slashed through his belly.

He turned her away from the Battery to his destination, Number 1 Broadway, General Howe's residence. A message from the general had interrupted him just as he had finished the review of his troops at City Hall. He shook his head in frustration at the prospect of speaking to Howe. The general's calmly announced plan to open communication lines with Burgoyne marching from Canada by removing south to Chesapeake had left Edward and many of his fellow officers stunned. Edward knew that General Howe and General Burgoyne held each other in mutual dislike, but it seemed fantastic to Edward that such petty rivalry could cloud Howe's military judgment. To leave Burgoyne in the lurch would be of incalculable assistance to the rebel forces. It was a ridiculous plan that Edward still hoped to forestall. Time, at least, was on his side, for it was unlikely that Howe would move before summer.

The Kennedy House at 1 Broadway was a stately two-story Georgian mansion set back from the busy street and overhung by giant elm trees. Edward's summons here rather than at General Howe's headquarters north of the city at Beekman House likely meant that the general was readying for the encounters the spring would bring and wanted to be closer to his troops. Edward grinned ruefully as he handed Delila's reins to a young private and walked up the wide front steps. It was not so much that he would have liked to join Howe's expedition southward, it was rather that the assignment would have freed him of the person of Sir Henry Clinton, who was to take over Howe's command as lieutenant-general. General Clinton, in Edward's opinion, was more unfit even than General Howe. A more haughty, churlish, and stupid man Edward had yet to meet. General Howe, at least, was well-liked by the Tories in New York for his fairness in his dealings with them, particularly after the fire of the previous September, and was a credit to his rank at social gatherings. Even General Clinton's aide, Major Andre, himself a brilliant ornament in New York society, agreed with Edward on this point. But they were both helpless in the face of General Howe's unlikely decision.

"The General is expecting you, sir."

"Thank you, Dobbs." The fresh-faced young lieutenant newly arrived from Dorset was, like Edward, assigned to remain in New York and endure the command of General Clinton. As he walked past Dobbs, he wondered about the excited undercurrent he had heard in his voice. Perhaps General Howe had changed his mind. He walked faster, ignoring the twinge of protest from his thigh.

A young private scurried to open the door to the General's sitting room. Edward nodded at him, smiling. He was scarce more than a boy out of short coats, and yet, he was proving to be eager and not unintelligent. When General Clinton finally assumed command, he would see to the boy's eagerness, poor lad.

Edward squinted while his eyes adjusted to the bright sunlit room. The long curtains were opened wide to the morning sun, which was enough to warm the room pleasantly.

"Good morning, sir." Edward saluted General Howe smartly. "I received your message."

General Howe rose from his chair and Edward saw that the man whose mercurial humors left many of his officers quaking in their boots appeared jovial today. Indeed, a deep smile promptly indented his heavily jowled cheeks.

"I have a surprise for you, my boy." Again that beaming smile.

"You have changed your campaign plans, sir?"

General Howe's smile disappeared. "That discussion, Captain, is closed. Accustom yourself, sir, to remaining in New York. You and Major Andre will have the important assignment of keeping General Clinton within the ropes, so to speak, when we finally have a change in command. No," he continued, his good humor restored, "I asked you here

for a very different reason. Captain Crowley, allow me to
introduce you to Captain Lord Delford, one of my finest
officers."

Edward turned to see a man emerge from the far corner
of the large sitting room. He was of the general's age, and
heavyset like him, but dressed in a naval officer's ornate
blue and white uniform.

Somewhat surprised, Edward extended his hand. "My
pleasure, Captain Crowley." He turned again to General
Howe, his brows raised in question.

"Captain Crowley has just arrived from Boston, early
this morning, on his majesty's frigate, *The York.*"

Edward sensed that he was being studied closely, and
he stiffened.

"You are Viscount Delford?"

Captain Crowley's deep voice was oddly assessing. Edward's gaze was locked by the man's cold gray eyes.

"I have that honor, sir."

What the devil is this about, he wondered, shifting his
weight to his sound leg.

"I believe, my lord," Captain Crowley said, his gaze
flickering briefly toward General Howe, "that you will indeed be pleased at the surprise General Howe spoke
about."

"Surprise, sir?"

"Aye, my lord. And I have personally escorted her
from Genoa."

Edward thought the world, or the captain, had taken a
faulty turn.

A door opened at the far end of the sitting room.

"Your wife, my lord, returned to you safe and sound."

"My *what?*"

Edward's question hung unanswered. "No," he whispered, his face draining of color. She was an apparition,
some cruel jest played upon him by his mind. She stood
very quietly, watching him. Edward took in her long thick
golden hair, her exquisitely slender figure, and her deep
blue eyes upon him, holding gentle affection.

"Cassie?" He was shaking his head even as he uttered
her name.

"Yes, Edward, it is I."

"But you are dead; it cannot be." He groped for the chair beside him. "My God—Cassie?"

General Howe and Captain Crowley ceased to exist for him. Edward took a stumbling step toward her, his eyes locked upon her, as if to prevent her image from vanishing. Numbly, he stretched out his hand.

Cassie gazed mutely at Edward. He looked striking and elegant in his scarlet and cream uniform, his brown hair powdered as white as the cravat around his throat. His deeply tanned face looked older than she remembered, and his bright hazel eyes were incredulous. When he reached out his hand to her, her throat closed on a mighty sob. She dashed toward him and flung herself into his arms.

"Edward, my dear Edward."

"Cassie, oh my God, I thought I had lost you." He whispered her name again and again, and clutched her tightly against his chest. He pushed her away from him and stroked her hair and her cheeks, still repeating her name.

Vaguely, Cassie heard Captain Crowley's deep, pinched voice. "Well, General, it would appear that I have executed my most pleasant mission in this wretched rebellion. As to the viscount's taking good care of my cargo, my mind is now at ease."

Cassie gently freed herself from Edward's arms.

"I must leave you now, viscountess. Although our voyage had its interesting moments, I am pleased to have delivered you sound as a roast to your husband."

Edward showed no surprise at the captain speaking of him as Cassie's husband. Indeed, it scarcely penetrated his mind. He clasped Captain Crowley's large hand and pumped it.

"My deepest thanks, Captain. There is no way I can repay you, except to assure you that we are both profoundly grateful."

"And I too, Captain," General Howe said. "I am certain, my boy, that we can rub along without your presence for say a week."

Edward nodded, so clearly befuddled that General Howe guffawed.

Captain Crowley's cold gray eyes rested upon Cassie for some moments, and softened.

"Good-bye, Captain, and thank you."

"Take care, viscountess, and strive not to get yourself lost again from your husband. I am not always to be found in odd parts of the world, you know."

"I shall, Captain." Cassie stood on her tiptoes and kissed the Captain's cheek. "Do give my thanks again to Mr. Thompson. Both of you were exceedingly kind to me."

Captain Crowley, as if embarrassed by her show of affection, merely nodded, saluted smartly to General Howe, and took his leave. There was suddenly silence, broken only by the sound of his retreating footsteps, amazingly crisp and controlled despite his great weight. Edward was gripping Cassie's hand tightly, so tightly that she winced.

"I trust your lodgings are suitable for your lady wife, my boy?"

"Indeed they are, sir."

"Then off with you both. I trust you will find sufficient to occupy your time." He paused a moment, and when he spoke again, his voice was strangely sad, for he knew that Edward would now not long remain in New York. "At least you have gained from this wretched rebellion, Edward. When all is said and done, the rebels may have their way. I will look forward to seeing both you and your lovely wife in England some day, I hope not too long distant."

"Yes, sir," Edward said only. Unlike General Howe, he had not yet realized that the strife in these colonies would soon be an ocean away from him.

"Off with you now, my boy, I have much to do. Goodbye, my lady. Keep that husband of yours away from Staten Island. I don't want him stuck again with a rebel sword."

Cassie bent her knee in a slight curtsy and allowed Edward to lead her from the room. She could feel the tension in his hand as he escorted her through the outer rooms to the entrance hall.

"So this is your wife, Edward."

"It seems that I was the last to know, damn you, John. Cassie, this is Major Andre, aide to General Clinton."

"A great honor, my lady." Major Andre lifted Cassie's

hand and lightly kissed her wrist. She regarded the slightly built officer, and knew him immediately to be a charmer with the ladies. His pale blue eyes held warmth and interest, and his genuine smile was a pleasure to behold.

"Thank you, Major Andre."

"Now, Edward, don't get on your high-ropes. Old Howe himself said you weren't to be told." He added in a pensive tone, "I hope this doesn't mean I won't be seeing much of you anymore, old man."

"Of course you will." A faint smile turned up the corners of Edward's mouth. "Well, perhaps not in the next few days."

"Aye, that's as it should be. Perhaps I will let the captain find me a wife on his next voyage. I'd say that he did a superb job for you." He gazed at Cassie with undisguised approval. What a lovely girl she was, her ample woman's charms ill-disguised by the light yellow muslin gown. And that glorious hair. It had amazed him to learn that Edward had been married, but then, Edward wasn't much of a lover of society. Perhaps believing such a woman to be dead was reason enough for his aloofness. He wondered if Edward's beautiful viscountess would change her husband's hermetic habits.

Edward, who knew Major Andre's thinking well, since he usually spoke his assessments of women aloud, pulled Cassie gently to him. "I am certain you have much to do, John."

"Yes, I believe that I do." Major Andre turned to Cassie. "Welcome to New York, my lady. I do not believe that society will allow Edward to keep you to himself. *Adieu,* Edward, for a couple of days!" Major Andre gave Edward a jaunty salute and turned away.

"My portmanteau, Edward."

He looked at her blankly.

"It contains all that I own and I cannot leave it."

"Oh, of course," he said, and picked it up.

Cassie shaded her eyes with her hand when they emerged into the bright sunlight. "How very changeable the weather is here, Edward."

"Is it not in Genoa?"

She stared up at him, an unpleasant knot growing in her throat.

"Captain Crowley said he had brought you from Genoa," he said gently. He touched his fingertips to her cheek. "I do not wish to cause you discomfort, Cass. We can talk when we reach my lodgings."

She nodded, without speaking.

He pulled up suddenly and frowned. "I have only my mare, Delila. If you are tired, Cass, you may ride."

"No, Edward, I am not the least tired. Are your lodgings far from here?"

"Not very far. I live in an inn, The King George, on William Street. 'Tis not more than half a mile."

She watched him silently as he fastened her portmanteau to his mare's saddle. He led them onto Broadway, which seemed to her to be teeming with scarlet-coated soldiers, many of them fully equipped with gear and weapons. And ladies. So many ladies, most of them elegantly dressed. Yet they seemed overly open with the soldiers.

"For the most part they are prostitutes, Cassie," Edward said, reading her thoughts. "Where there are soldiers and sailors, there are always women gladly willing to part them from their guineas." Edward paused a moment, running his hand along his jaw. It was ridiculous to chatter like this. *She has returned from the dead to me and here I am prosing about prostitutes and soldiers.*

"Cass."

He spoke her name so softly that she was uncertain whether she had imagined it. She turned and looked up at him.

"I cannot believe that you are here." He suddenly dropped Delila's reins. He gave a shout of joy, closed his hands about her waist and lifted her high off the ground.

As Edward set her back down upon her feet, the feel of his mouth against hers was still vivid in her mind, and her color was high. She tried to relieve her embarrassment and her uncertainty with inconsequential chatter. Edward smiled down at her, his once painful memories of her rapid-fire way of asking questions, of saying whatever popped into her mind, becoming again, quite naturally, amused tolerance.

He answered her questions in a normal tone of voice, as if they had never been apart. "They are Scots, to the man, of the 42nd Highlanders. They are known as the Black Watch and mightily feared by the rebels."

Cassie stared at their checkered bonnets and their bare, knobby knees. "This is very exciting, Edward. I have never before actually seen their battle dress."

"That group to the right are Hessian grenadiers. You can always recognize them by their blue coats and the high brass-fronted caps. It is said that their mustaches are as black as they are because they use the same colored wax paste as on their boots. Like the 42nd Highlanders, they are effective, disciplined fighters, but they are barbarians."

"Barbarians, Edward?"

"Yes. The stories of their atrocities, recent in fact, from New Jersey, make my blood curdle. Unfortunately, even here in New York, they are many times like unleashed dogs. One of the bastards even tried to force himself on Jen—" He immediately broke off, cursing himself for his loose tongue.

Cassie quirked an eyebrow at him. "Jen, Edward? Who is she?"

He shrugged. "Jennifer Lacy. She and her father are loyalists and friends of mine."

"You must tell me about her sometime," Cassie said.

Edward gazed down at Cassie's proud, classical profile. He could not converse with her even about the most mundane, trivial matters as if nothing had ever occurred. Important things, painful things, kept cropping up, willy nilly. Dear God, he thought, I don't even know what happened to her.

It was as if Cassie had become as uncomfortable as he. "There is much to tell you, Edward."

"Yes, I know." He drew in his breath and kept walking.

But she did not intend to tell him that this vast, uncivilized land made her feel she had been transported to the very ends of the earth. She glanced up at him and smiled. She had known Edward all her life, trusted him implicitly and loved him. Yet she felt afraid and terribly uncertain, at a moment when her happiness should have been complete. It would have been complete, she told herself angrily, if it had not been for *him.*

"We will soon be at my lodgings."

She marveled at his dispassionate tone, as if she were a soldier in his command about to provide him with a report. Yet she knew that it was just his way. She had expected him to try to protect her from his own sense of shock and confusion.

She felt nervous, and said aloud her first inconsequential thought. "Everything looks so new, so unfinished."

"Yes. Shortly after we took New York from the rebels and their General Washington, there was a huge fire. It is likely that the rebels started it. Unfortunately, the rabble had stolen all the church bells so there was no way to raise the alarm. The fire began in a sailors' brothel, down near the Battery, at Whitehall Slip. It spread rapidly, for there was little water and practically no equipment to fight it with."

"You were here in the fire?"

"I was, but there was little to be done. A good third of the city burned. Even the beautiful Trinity Church was gutted." He paused a moment and waved his hand. "This is a fortunate section of New York. All is finally rebuilt here, thank God. The New Yorkers are sturdy folk, and the rebuilding continues. I fancy that the Great Fire of London in the last century was no more devastating than was this one."

"I did not worry much for your safety, Edward. And yet you were here, during the fire and during all the fighting."

To her surprise, Edward laughed grimly. "That I was. It has been a winning display of military strategy on both sides. Had General Howe but given the order during the battle for New York, we could have cut the main body of General Washington's army to shreds. But he did not act. He is always one to ponder, to mull over every alternative, pertinent or not, to stroke his fat chin and do nothing. This *rebellion* is being conducted by amateurs, Cass, but I begin to believe there are a greater number of fools in the English command than in the American ranks." Edward drew to a stop, thankful that he could at last stop blabbering at her.

"This is where I live, Cassie. Not Delford Manor or Hemphill Hall, I'm afraid, but still sufficiently comfortable."

The King George Inn on William Street had no graceful elm trees to gentle its gaunt lines. Like many of the buildings they had passed, the King George was spanking new, yet it looked as raw and as unfinished as the bare ground on which it stood. Winter had prevented even the grass from growing back. There was no foliage to soften its stark façade, no flowers. *Flowers. For God's sake, Cassie, that is another world, only a bad memory. I never wanted it, never wanted him.*

"Are you all right, Cass?"

Cassie raised dazed eyes to his face. "Yes, Edward, quite all right. I am tired, that is all." *I must forget him, else I'll never know peace.* But she knew, had known for some time, that she would never be able to push him from her thoughts.

Cassie gingerly picked up the skirts of her muslin gown and walked up the unpainted steps of the inn. Edward gave over Delila's reins to the stableboy and joined her, bearing her portmanteau.

"Ah, Captain Lord Delford. I had not expected you until this evening."

Cassie attended to a short, monstrously fat man with a face like a full moon and small eyes of sparkling light brown. He wore a huge white apron around his considerable waist, an apron that looked well used. His strange, twangy accent brought a smile to her lips. Did all the colonials talk like this?

"I would like you to meet my wife, Mr. Beatty. She arrived just this morning to join me."

The light brown eyes narrowed upon her face for a moment. A dimpled smile appeared.

Mr. Beatty had not known the captain to have a wife, but then again, he thought it just like a very proper English gentleman to speak little of his personal life.

"I regret, sir, that I have no other accommodations to offer you and your lady wife."

"I know there is not an inch of extra space in the city, Mr. Beatty. Please bring her ladyship's portmanteau upstairs. And tea, Mr. Beatty."

I do not like tea. Why does Edward not remember?

"Yes, sir. Right away."

Cassie had been in an inn but once or twice in her life. She climbed the solid oak staircase, uncarpeted and unadorned. The odor of raw wood, ale, and sweat reached her nose. Like New York itself, it was both intriguing and discomfiting. *Everything seems so unfinished, even the people.*

"I have a small sitting room and bedroom. It is a corner room with a pleasant view of the river."

"Your valet? Grumman?"

"Batman," Edward corrected her absently. My God, he thought, as he opened the door, I am taking her to my room as my wife. He felt his loins tighten and drew back at the intense shock of desire he felt.

"Yes, your batman."

"Grumman occupies a small room on the third floor. Do you wish a maid, Cassie?"

Cassie remembered the two and some odd months she had spent aboard *The York,* fending for herself, and smiled. "No, it is not necessary. If there is someone to care for my gowns, 'twill be sufficient."

She stepped into the sitting room and smiled again. No, it was not like Delford Manor or Hemphill Hall—or like the Villa Parese. Clean dimity curtains covered the windows, and several small rugs were scattered about on the wooden floor. The furniture, what there was of it, was plain to the point of starkness, constructed, she thought, with utility in mind. Still, it was a bright, well kept, airy room, fitting for a soldier. After so many days cooped up on *The York,* she was pleased with its spaciousness.

"It is quite satisfactory, Edward."

A young boy, hardly older than fourteen, appeared in the open doorway, Cassie's portmanteau tucked under his arm.

"The lady's luggage, sir."

Edward seemed oblivious of the fact that the boy's wide brown eyes, of the same shade as Mr. Beatty's, were looking at him with open worship.

"Thank you, Will. You may put it in my—the bedroom."

"My Ma's bringing your tea, sir, and on her best silver."

Mrs. Beatty turned out to be as reed thin as her husband was rotund. She stared with unabashed curiosity at Cassie, and, at the natural patrician nod she received from the young lady, she quickly set the silver tray upon the small circular oak table and dropped into a low, quite awkward curtsy. That Cassie appeared to pay no particular attention to her served only to make her seem all the more the great lady.

When they were finally alone, Edward unbuckled his saber and laid it upon the table beside the tea tray.

For the first time, Cassie noticed his slightly limping gait and remembered General Howe's mention of a saber thrust. "Is your leg badly injured, Edward?"

She seated herself in a none too comfortable chair, sipping the despised tea.

"No. My men and I were on Staten Island—it's off the southern tip of Manhattan Island—and came across a pack of rebels. One of them managed to strike me in the thigh. It's nearly healed now."

"You must be more careful, Edward."

Cassie received a wry smile. "I am a soldier, Cass."

He stood over her for some minutes, seemingly searching for something to say.

"Eliott and I searched for you for over a week."

He told me that you would. "Thank you, Edward."

He began to pace up and down in front of her.

"Tell me now, for God's sake, what happened to you?"

Cassie set her tea cup next to Edward's saber and clasped her hands tightly in her lap. "I am sorry that I had to pose as your wife, but I did not believe that Captain Crowley would take me aboard otherwise."

"It matters not."

His voice was impatient, and she looked away from him. Of course it did not matter what she said, for as a gentleman, honor would dictate his actions, and she did not doubt that she would quite soon become his wife, at his insistence. Unless—

"I am no longer a virgin, Edward."

She saw his lips tighten, but he quickly recovered. "It has been a long time, Cassie. That you are alive is all that is important." But his hands remained clenched at his sides. She closed her eyes briefly, knowing that he would never tell her how important her baldly delivered fact was to him. His honor would forbid it, and his regard for her feelings.

"Please sit down," she said finally. "The story is a long one."

He obliged her.

"The afternoon before our wedding, I went out fishing, with Becky's approval and encouragement."

"What the devil does Becky Petersham have to say to anything?"

"You will know, shortly. Do you recall the beautiful yacht you and I saw from the promontory the day before?" He nodded. "It appeared again. It drew quite close, and I saw it was named *The Cassandra*. In short, Edward, the sailors threw ropes about the mast of my sailboat. The owner and captain of *The Cassandra* was the Earl of Clare. He abducted me."

"Anthony Welles?" Edward pictured the earl, a virile and dashing nobleman, and felt a wrenching tightness in his belly. "But why?"

"He told me he intended to make me his wife. He had planned on my spending a season in London and was going to court me there. Your return to England ruined his plans. Rather than let us marry, he abducted me and crashed my sailboat into the rocks, knowing that everyone would believe me drowned."

For a long moment, Edward was too stunned to speak. "I don't understand, Cass. Anthony Welles has known you since you were a child. I am not aware that you ever offered him any encouragement."

"No, of course I did not. He loved my mother, Edward, before I was born. Perhaps he is still drawn to her, through me." Even as she spoke the words, she did not believe them.

"That filthy bastard." Edward smote his thigh with his fisted hand and winced. "He—he forced you?"

"Yes. I told him that he was insane and that I would never wed him. But he would not listen." She saw the pulse in Edward's temple pounding furiously. "I am sorry, Edward, to distress you, but you must know the truth."

"Of course I must, Cass. He took you to Genoa?"

"I tried to escape him once, near Gibraltar, but I could not." There was no point in telling him of the pirate, Khar El-Din, and her shooting of the earl. "As you know, Lord Welles's mother was Italian. He took me to his villa, just west of Genoa. That is where I have been until two months ago." Nor would she ever tell him of her miscarriage. What a miserably brief tale it was, like a person stripped down to a skeleton.

"How did you escape him?"

I escaped him because he did not believe that I wanted to. "He left the city and I was able to slip away. If *The York* and Captain Crowley had not been in the harbor, it is likely I would have been caught."

Edward was suddenly struck by a coincidence. "You speak Italian, Cass."

"Aye, Edward. And that is due, as you know, to Becky Petersham. I had always wondered at her disapproval of you. She is related to him, Edward. In her eyes, I was intended for the earl and none other."

Edward's thoughts returned to that afternoon on the beach two days before they were to be married. Cassie would have given her virginity to him then, had it not been for Becky Petersham's interference. "She appeared distraught at your supposed death. It was a sham, all a sham."

"She corresponded with the earl. Quite by chance I found her letters. That is how I knew where you were."

"Eliott still believes you dead?"

"Yes. I have written to him, but the letter will not arrive in England for two months."

"Did you tell him what had happened to you?"

Cassie thought of the phrases she had penned to her brother, reassuring phrases that expressed little of her feelings, of her uncertainty with herself. She had written less to him than she had told Edward. "A little. I told him I was coming here, to you, and that I was well. I did not mention Becky's part in all of it. That must wait until I return."

Edward nodded, but Cassie sensed he was not really attending her words. He turned suddenly, his voice harsh with anger.

"How could that bastard have forced you to live with him all this time?"

"Because he always believed that I would change." At least he hadn't asked her if the earl had forced himself upon her all those months. She did not know if she could lie to him.

Edward's hand foolishly went to his side, but his saber was on the table and the earl was in Genoa. He looked again at Cassie's face and saw a lone tear streaking down her cheek.

He felt stricken with remorse at his own fury. She needed him as she never had before in their lives. He clasped her arms and drew her to her feet. "Oh, God, Cass, please do not cry." He nuzzled his cheek against hers and stroked his hands down her back. "It is all right now, my love. I will help you to forget, I promise you. All of it will pass like a bad dream, you will see."

She sobbed quietly, her tension easing at his gentleness. But she knew it would not pass like a dream.

He spoke quietly, sensing her pain. "I will make it up to you, Cass. We will wed and return together to England. Believe me, I have no wish to remain here now." He thought of Jenny and felt a shock of guilt that made him go numb. "Oh, God," he whispered. He gazed down at the beautiful girl he had cherished most of his life. She had miraculously been returned to him. "All can be as it was, Cass," he said.

"Yes," she said slowly, sniffing back the tears, "all must be as it was." Cassie pulled away from him, fighting to get hold of herself. She gave him a tentative, watery smile. "And now, Edward, you must tell me of yourself. I have thought about you much, you know, and what you were doing and feeling."

His eyes darkened in remembered grief. "I could not stay after I believed you dead. I received a letter from the ministry in London, asking me if I would consider resuming my command. It did not matter to me that I was to join General Howe here in the colonies." He paused, remembering bloody battles against men ill-trained and poorly armed, but desperate to win. He had been a formidable enemy, for he had not cared whether he was felled by a rebel bullet. His men had followed him without question, not knowing that he gave not a damn for his own life. He was lucky to be alive. But he would not tell Cassie of that, just as he would not tell her about Jennifer Lacy.

"I have received letters from Eliott, not with any regularity, of course, but enough to know he is well."

"I read in one of Becky Petersham's letters to the earl that Eliott is planning to marry Eliza Pennworthy."

Edward smiled faintly. "Eliott has written nothing about that." He was silent for a moment. Suddenly, anguished memories wrenched words from his lips. "God, Cassie, you cannot imagine what it was like, the days searching for you, the nights, alone, cursing the wretched sea. And there was nothing, simply nothing I could do." He caught himself, and turned away from her, to stride angrily about the room. "I swear that I will kill him for you, Cass. He does not deserve to live, after all that he has done."

"It is likely, Edward, that we will never again see the Earl of Clare. If he does, sometime in the future, return to England, you must promise me that you'll not do anything rash." She lowered her eyes from his face, unwilling to let him see her despair at the thought that she might never again see the earl. She remembered the Contessa Giusti and her hands curled into fists in her lap.

"I can well take care of myself, Cass," Edward said. "And you as well, now."

Edward, her protector, her knight throughout her growing up years. She smiled, reminded of the many little things that bound them together.

"How did you spend your time when you were not getting yourself wounded on this Staten Island?"

He shrugged and she saw a cynical light enter his eyes. "I did naught of anything, really. Insignificant encounters with the rebels. And there were, of course, balls and dinners held by the New York Tories." He paused a moment, the image of Jenny stark in his mind. He looked away from her. "Time passed, Cass, as it always does."

Edward's recital of his long months without her seemed as brief and stark to her as her own recital. She wondered, staring at his straight, lean figure, if he had omitted as much as had she.

Chapter 24

Cassie took a last bite of Mrs. Beatty's apple pie and sat back in her chair with a satisfied sigh. The landlady had appeared at their door an hour before, napkin-covered dishes weighing down her thin arms. It was thoughtful of her to have guessed that they preferred to be alone in their room their first evening together, and not come downstairs to the inn parlor. Actually, Cassie thought, if Mrs. Beatty had not obligingly brought them their dinner, they likely would have forgotten it.

She gazed at Edward over her coffee cup. He had grown ill at ease during their dinner, and she easily guessed the reason. Night had fallen and they were alone but a few feet away from his darkened bedchamber, as man and wife.

It was fortunate that their lives had been so closely intertwined, for it had allowed them to fall easily into pleasant reminiscing. During the afternoon, they had allowed themselves to blot out the months they had been apart. Edward had reminded her of the time he had knocked down Edmond Danvers for calling Cassie naught but a bothersome little girl who had more tangles in her hair than a sparrow's nest. Her unrestrained laughter still sounded in her ears. But now it was evening, and they could no longer pretend to be carefree children.

During the last few weeks aboard *The York,* Cassie had argued with herself for hours at a time about how she would approach this moment with Edward. She knew that consideration for her feelings was as natural to him as was his sense of honor. And given what she had told him about the past months, she did not doubt that he was in a quandary about the prospect of lovemaking with her. It was her belief that he loved her deeply that eased her mind. And because he loved her, she wanted to give him all of her that she could. He was her lifelong friend, the man she was to have married, the man she now would marry. "I should very much like a bath, Edward."

He blinked at her. "A bath? Certainly, Cass. I shall see to it now." There was relief in his voice as he rose stiffly from his chair and strode with alacrity toward the door.

He returned some fifteen minutes later, followed by the boy, Will, each of them carrying steaming buckets of hot water.

"There is a hipbath in the bedroom," he said, not meeting her eyes.

She would have smiled at his obvious discomfiture were she not herself so nervous about their first night together. She rose and trailed after him. The bedchamber was a small, square room, its furnishings, like those in the sitting room, built for utility. She saw Edward looking toward the bed.

She walked to the hipbath. "I would imagine that you are far too large to fit in it, Edward."

"It is quite adequate," he said, stiffly. "I will leave you now, Cass. If you have need of anything, please call."

"Thank you. I shall be fine."

Edward saw Will out the door and sat himself down in his favorite chair, a high-backed mahogany affair with solid unfinished arms. He leaned his head back and closed his eyes. Each time he tried to think about what the incredible events of the day meant to him in a controlled, reasoned light, he was stopped by a quickening in his loins. Cassie was in his bedchamber, now likely naked, and in his bathtub.

He frowned down at his enthusiastic member straining tightly against his cream breeches, then eyed the blunt-edged, thinly cushioned settee in front of him. He supposed it would be his bed until they were married. It would have to be a very private ceremony, since Cassie was already known as his wife. He reviewed the request he would make to the only Anglican parson he knew, and shook his head.

The florid-faced Mr. Danvers would never keep a still tongue in his mouth.

Fury, pure and undiluted, took control of him at the thought of the Earl of Clare, dampening his passion. "You bloody bastard," he said aloud. He would have killed the man without a qualm for having ravished any English gentlewoman. But it was Cassie he had forced himself upon, had repeatedly taken against her will during the long months Edward had thought her dead.

Edward rose and slowly removed his coat and boots. He and Cassie had talked throughout the day of everything that did not touch the months they had been apart. He smiled, remembering her unaffected ready laughter. But he realized he still knew very little of what her life had actually been like during the past months. She had spoken not at all of the earl, and Edward, not wishing to cause her pain, had not pressed her.

"Edward."

He turned at the sound of his softly spoken name. Cassie stood in the open doorway of the bedchamber, dressed in a light muslin wrapper. He caught his breath at the sight of her. She was as exquisitely beautiful as the near-perfect vision of her he had nourished in his mind during the lonely nights of autumn and winter. He restrained his impulse to crush her in his arms.

"You enjoyed your bath, Cass?"

She smiled at the painful calm in his voice. To his discomfiture, his body leaped in response.

"The water is still warm, Edward. Would you like me to scrub your back?"

"Cassie, for God's sake."

Under his horrified gaze, she lowered her face and began to sob into her hands.

His stocking feet made no sound on the oak floor. He gently pulled her against him, though her hands still covered her face. "Please don't cry, my love." He nuzzled his cheek against her silky hair, savoring its sweet sandalwood scent. He felt her stiff and unyielding against him and set about to soothe her, and himself, with low, soft words of reassurance.

"No one will ever hurt you again, Cass. I swear it to you.
You are safe now, and this time I shall protect you."

Cassie lowered her hands and mutely raised her face.
There was no one to protect her from now. *You cannot
protect me from myself, Edward.*

"You even cry beautifully," he said as he touched a fingertip to her cheek and gently brushed away her tears.

"I am sorry, Edward. It is not my habit to be a weeping
woman." Her hands stole up his arms and her fingers
locked about his neck. "Please stay with me tonight."

He looked down into her clear blue eyes and knew himself to be lost. "If you are certain it is what you want,
Cassie."

It must be what I want.

"Yes."

"Then we shall be ahead of the parson by a few days."
He scooped her up into his arms and laid her gently in the
center of his bed. Cassie sank deep down into the trough
she created in the soft featherdown mattress.

She laughed. "Oh dear, I fear that we shall be sleeping
like two cards in a deck."

Edward gave her only a slight answering grin. He was
pulling off his clothes with a speed that would have surprised his batman, Grumman.

Cassie watched him. He was of slighter build than the
earl, his body wiry and taut from his years of campaigning.
She turned her eyes away from his erect organ. Instead of
desire, she felt a surge of panic. For an instant, he was a
stranger to her, frightening and unknown. She drew a deep
steadying breath. *Don't be a fool, Cassie. Your life is as it
was supposed to have been. You are with Edward. It is he
who will be your husband.* She fastened her eyes upon his
face and held out her arms to him.

"Let me help you off with that wrapper, Cass."

She closed her eyes tightly for a moment, and jerked
open the sash. She felt Edward's hands pulling the soft
material from her body. She heard his sharp intake of
breath.

"God, you are so beautiful."

"You have already seen me unclothed. Do you not remember, Edward?"

"Yes," he said slowly, easing himself down beside her. "But I tried to forget, Cass." Had he continued to think of her as he had those long months ago, he thought, he would have gone mad. He looked at her breasts and swallowed convulsively. Just the thought of the Earl of Clare touching her, forcing her, made his belly cramp.

He looked down at her, his eyes wintry. He felt her fingers tentatively touch his shoulders, and slowly, he lowered his mouth to hers.

Although she was not a virgin, he knew he should treat her as gently as he had that long ago afternoon in the cave. He pressed his mouth softly against hers, until he felt her part her lips to him. As his hands stroked over her, he thought of the man who had taken her innocence, the man who had caressed her body as he was now doing. Although he did not wish it, he thought again of the months of pain, the nights of empty bitterness, at the cruelty of fate. He felt consumed again by the wrenching loneliness. She had left him, had made life itself seem meaningless to him. He thrust his tongue into her mouth, and rolled on top of her, feeling the soft giving of her beneath him.

Cassie froze, numbed with confusion. Whenever she had thought of this moment with Edward, she had remembered only his tenderness, his gentleness. She felt her body tense in protest. You love me, she wanted to tell him. Why are you doing this to me? He released her mouth and his lips closed over her breast. She heard his breathing, ragged and deep, and knew that he wanted her, wanted her so badly that what she felt no longer mattered to him. She prayed silently to feel something, but an instant of desire. She tangled her fingers in his curling chestnut hair, and forced her hands to stroke down his back.

"Oh God, Cass." He reared over her and pushed her thighs apart. She felt herself stiffen as his member touched her. But I am not ready for you, she wanted to yell at him. She swallowed a cry in her throat as he thrust into her unwilling flesh.

Cassie moaned softly, for his every movement hurt her.

But her muted cry broke Edward's control. He drove into her wildly until his body tensed uncontrollably above her. He felt as if he were breaking apart, each convulsive spasm pulling him farther out of himself, away from all reason. Jagged groans tore from his mouth. Suddenly there was a great easing within him and he fell forward, resting his cheek next to her face on the pillow.

His release erased the violent emotion that had consumed him. He felt Cassie lying motionless beneath him.

"I am sorry, Edward."

He raised his head at her soft, sad words and saw tears swimming in her eyes. He drew a deep breath. Damn. He felt the perfect bounder. After all that had happened to her, he had done little else than force her himself. But she had accepted him, she had stroked him and wrapped her legs about his hips to open herself more fully to receive him. The earl's darkly handsome face rose in his mind's eye and Edward saw him rearing over her, parting her thighs, burying himself in her woman's body. He shook himself, blotting the image from his mind.

"It is I who am sorry, Cassie. Next time it will be better, you will see."

But I don't want there to be a next time.

"It will be, Edward," she whispered. He pulled himself out of her and stretched his full length beside her.

He tried to think of comforting words to say, but somehow the violent emotion he had felt and his guilt at what he had done emptied his mind. Both of them needed time. He said only, "It's been a long day, Cass. You need sleep now."

She settled her cheek against his shoulder. Sleep eluded her for some time, even after Edward's breathing evened. What was wrong with her? Though she did not wish to, she remembered how passion leaped in her when the earl but touched her. And once, long ago, she had desired Edward. What had changed? Perhaps Edward was right. Perhaps it was her own tension, perhaps it was his newness to her, and hers to him. But her body tensed in protest at her thoughts. She sighed and forced all thought from her mind.

*   *   *

Cassie stared down at the fluffy scrambled eggs and felt her stomach tighten.

"Will there be anything else you require, my lady?"

"No, Mrs. Beatty. The breakfast is fine, thank you."

"I'll send Will up later for the dishes, my lady."

Cassie nodded and watched Mrs. Beatty dip her a credible curtsy.

"Captain Lord Delford sounds mighty happy that you've joined him."

"It would seem so." The sound of Edward's whistling came loudly through the closed bedchamber door.

After Mrs. Beatty had left, Cassie pushed away the heaping plate of food and sipped at her coffee. She knew that she must tell him now. She would have told him last night, but somehow the words simply would not say themselves. So much had happened and so much was new to both of them. She cursed herself for a coward.

If she thought that Edward would not notice her lack of appetite, she was mistaken.

"If I am to give you a tour of New York, Cass, you must eat something."

"I have boundless energy, Edward, you know that. It is just that I am not particularly hungry this morning."

"I don't want a skinny wife, Cass."

She felt herself flush under his warm scrutiny.

Edward was very careful where he guided Cassie. There were areas of New York that were unsavory, others that reeked of human misery, no less than parts of London. The day was cooler than Edward had expected, and there was a light breeze blowing from the bay past the upper end of Broad Street.

"What an odd jumble of buildings."

"Yes, a mixture of old and new. The fire was strangely fickle. See the gabled house there on your left? It was built in 1698 by a Dutchman and is now occupied by James Bryson and Moses Smith. The spire to the left of the old Federal Hall is St. Paul's Chapel, on Broadway. We'll walk down Wall Street, and I'll show you what's left of Trinity

Church. Unfortunately, the wooden spire burned in the fire and collapsed into the interior."

They reached the foot of Broadway and Edward directed her to Bowling Green. "And there, Cass, was where a statue of George III used to stand. The rebels pulled it down and melted it for bullets and guns."

"But everyone seems sympathetic to England, Edward. Where are all the rebels?"

"The rebels are in the minority. Here in New York, they were a vocal, vicious bunch. Before General Howe took New York, a group that called themselves the Liberty Boys were responsible for much destruction, particularly of Tory homes and businesses. Many families loyal to England fled New York, and returned when we took the city. This rebellion is nothing more than a series of ragtag skirmishes scattered about this huge land." Edward shrugged. "What will come of this is anybody's guess."

Cassie looked thoughtful for a moment. "As you said, Edward, this is a vast land. How can England, thousands of miles away, hope to control its destiny?"

"You are beginning to sound like Jen—, like Tory friends of mine." He looked awkwardly away.

"Sometimes I think," Cassie continued, gazing at him intently, "that everyone should simply leave everyone else alone. War seems such a waste."

"True. But if what you suggested should happen, what would become of all the loyalists? I assure you that their fate would not be enviable."

"There never seems to be a simple solution to anything, does there?"

"No, there does not." Like Cassie, Edward was thinking about his own life. No, there was never a simple solution to anything.

"There is a young lady who appears to know you, Edward."

Edward pulled himself from his thoughts and looked up. Jenny stood not fifteen feet from them, holding herself so rigidly that she seemed carved in stone.

"Jenny," he called, trying to instill calm into his voice.

"Miss Lacy. Come, Cass, I would like you to meet a friend of mine."

Jenny wanted nothing but to turn on her heels and walk away. But she could not. She stood in miserable silence as Edward, and the undeniably beautiful girl at his side, walked toward her. The young woman could not be one of Madam Harper's delectable girls, solely for the use of the officers. She was undeniably a lady. She felt a sickening lurch in the pit of her stomach. Suddenly, Jenny knew. The elegant girl with her glossy golden hair was Cassandra. A hopeless *no* sounded in her mind, for she knew she was Edward's lost fiancée, supposedly drowned, here, in New York, returned to him.

Jenny drew herself up, calling upon her deep steely pride. To her amazement, her tongue moved in her mouth and she heard herself say quite calmly, "Good morning, Captain Lord Delford."

"Jenny—Miss Lacy, I would like you to meet Cassandra Brougham. Cass, Miss Lacy."

Cassie nodded pleasantly toward the young woman, wondering silently at the sudden tension in Edward's voice. "A pleasure, Miss Lacy."

Even her voice is beautiful, Jenny thought, and she forced herself to say something acceptable. "You have just arrived?"

"Yes, yesterday. Edward is showing me your city."

Jenny suddenly felt that she would retch. The cobblestone pavement seemed to rise, and she weaved where she stood.

"Jenny, are you all right?"

Again, there was a strain in Edward's voice. Cassie looked more closely at the young woman. She was magnificently tall, and carried herself gracefully, her figure full and deep-bosomed. Thick masses of auburn hair were piled atop her head, and soft ringlets framed a face of classic features. Her wide green eyes were fastened upon Edward's face.

"Yes, I am fine. It is the death smell; with the breeze from the south, it makes me faint."

Edward reached his hand toward her, then dropped it

helplessly again to his side. He held himself rigid. "Can we see you home, Jenny?"

Cassie felt as though she had just stepped into a scene in a play fraught with unspoken passion, a scene in which she was an unwitting player.

"No, thank you, Edward. I assure you that I am quite all right now. Miss Brougham." She nodded briskly, picked up her green velvet skirt, and hurried across the street, her head held high.

"Who is Miss Lacy, Edward?" Cassie inquired, careful to keep her voice indifferent.

Edward replied with taut lightness, "As I told you, Jenny and her father, Benjamin Lacy, are good friends of mine. Her father is a writer and partner of Ambrose Searle who publishes the *New York Mercury,* a staunch Tory newspaper. Jenny did not look well," he added, almost as an afterthought.

"Perhaps you should insist upon seeing her home, Edward. Perhaps you should speak with her."

He was silent for many moments. "No, she will be fine," he said firmly.

Cassie was not blind or deaf. Jennifer Lacy was clearly in love with Edward. She saw the rigid set of his shoulders, and forebore to question him further. Since she had not told him everything, it would be unfair of her to demand more of him.

She asked easily, to relieve him of any embarrassment, "What is the smell she spoke about?"

"It is the stench from the prisons. All over New York, prisoners of war are kept in appalling conditions—in churches and windowless sugarhouses that are stifling in summer and frigid in winter. I have been told that many of them lie dead for days with their comrades before they are removed."

"But that is horrible!"

"The rebel prisoners kept aboard the British prison ship, *Jersey,* docked in Wallabout Bay, are no better off. They are locked below-deck in conditions that would kill rats, much less men." He sighed.

"Is there nothing you can do, Edward?"

"No. Since the fire, there are not sufficient buildings to hold all the prisoners of war. They must be confined someplace; were they released, they would only return to the rebel army to fight us again one day. It is only their plight that angers me. Men, regardless of which side they fight on, are still men and not animals. General Howe will not discuss the matter."

Cassie sniffed the air as they continued their walk. If there was a smell, her nose did not, today, detect it. Her thoughts kept returning to Miss Lacy. There had been such pain in the girl's vivid green eyes.

When they had returned to the inn, Edward took Cassie's hand for a moment and squeezed it. "I must seek out a parson, Cass. Please do not walk out alone. I would fear for your safety."

"Edward, I must speak to you."

Because he was abstracted, he did not hear the desperation in her voice. "When I return. I will not be long, Cassie." He planted a chaste kiss on her cheek and left her.

She looked after his retreating figure helplessly. Tonight, then, she would have to tell him. If he changed his mind, he could always tell the parson that it had been a mistake.

Edward returned bearing the tale of having found a Mr. John Morrison, a hook-nosed Presbyterian parson, who, as best Edward could determine, was as discreet as they could wish.

"He will wed us whenever you wish, Cass. I think you will like him despite his monstrous nose. I gave him few details, but I fancy that he is musing about all sorts of marvelous possibilities."

Whenever I wish. "Soon, I suppose, Edward."

"There is a ship sailing for England next week. Unfortunately, I do not think I can be relieved of my responsibilities so quickly. I will speak with General Howe tomorrow. Perhaps next month we can return. Would you like to write to Eliott? At least he can be informed that we are to be married. I fancy your homecoming will be as impressive as any prepared for the king." He paused a moment, eyeing her closely. "You must decide what is to be done about Becky Petersham. I cannot imagine that you would want her there when we return."

"You are right, Edward. I do not think I could bear to see her again."

He said abruptly, "Was the earl cruel to you, Cassie?"

A knot formed in her throat, and for several moments she was unable to speak. "No, Edward, he was not."

His eyes encouraged her to continue, but she turned away. She knew that Edward wanted her to tell all that had happened to her, but he was far too much the gentleman to press her. *And I am far too much the coward.*

They ate dinner downstairs in the small private dining room, their host, Mr. Beatty, in constant attendance. Cassie imagined, after consuming a hearty meal of roast lamb, boiled potatoes, crisp green beans, and a thick rice pudding, that Mrs. Beatty had spent her entire day in the inn's kitchen.

"That was a delicious meal, Mr. Beatty," she said as their host made haste to fill her wine glass. He seemed disinclined to leave, and at a wink from Edward, Cassie said, "Won't you please join us, Mr. Beatty?"

"Don't mind if I do, milady," he said, and pulled out a chair at their table. Cassie blinked, surprised that an innkeeper would want to share his guests' company. But Edward seemed amused.

"I tell you, my lord," Mr. Beatty said, sitting back in the high-backed chair and swirling the wine about in his glass, "this fellow, Paine, continues to have tremendous influence over the Americans. Did you know that damned pamphlet of his—begging your pardon, milady—has sold thousands of copies?"

It seemed to Cassie that she had stepped into the middle of a conversation whose subject was, unfortunately, as alien to her as this raw, unpainted city. She fastened a fascinated eye upon Mr. Beatty.

"Yes, sir," Edward replied easily, "only last week, as I recall, you were not damning it."

"I gave you a copy of *Common Sense,* my lord. I trust you have read it as you promised you would."

"I have read part of it, sir. It is hardly common, I believe. As to the sense of it, Paine has perfected, I grant you, the grandiose style."

" 'O! receive the fugitive, and prepare in time an asylum for mankind!' " Mr. Beatty rubbed his plump hands together. "It has a ring to it. Unlike our squalid little island of Britain, this land does hold endless opportunity for men of every nation."

"I would hardly term England squalid," Cassie said, her patriotism ruffled.

"Nor would I, sir," Edward said. "But you are right to say that life here is very different, so unstructured. It seems to me that England's hand simply cannot encompass so many beliefs from so many nations."

"At least New York is now safe once again in English hands," Cassie said.

"Yes," Mr. Beatty continued, "New York is once again safe, thanks to men like yourself, my lord, and your General Howe."

"General Howe has upon occasion spoken of Paine," Edward said, turning his eyes from Cassie back to Mr. Beatty. "It is his opinion, of course, that Paine's firebrand words will lead the rebels only more quickly toward their destruction."

Mr. Beatty said, "Aye, that's true enough. 'Ye that dare oppose not only the tyranny but the tyrant, stand forth!' Yes, quite a way with words the man has."

As Cassie sat blinking at such an appreciation of eloquence from an innkeeper, Mr. Beatty rose from his chair and patted Edward's arm. "I'll leave you be now, my lord. I fancy you and your lady wife have much to talk about."

"Yes, sir, I believe that we do," Edward said, looking toward Cassie. Mr. Beatty bowed deeply to Cassie. He stopped at the door, his sausage fingers upon the knob. "Do you know that before he started writing, Tom Paine did not seem to be able to do anything but fail? The damned fellow—begging your pardon, milady—bungled being a sailor, a grocer, a tobacconist, and a tax collector. His wife even cut him loose." Sudden humor lit Mr. Beatty's round face, and he shook his head. "You'll not believe it, but he could not even make a living as a corsetmaker!— begging your pardon, milady."

Cassie clapped her hand over her mouth, but still her laughter bubbled out.

"Do not poke fun at the locals, Cass," Edward said, his voice mock-reproving. "You'll discover that every New Yorker holds staunch views, though it seems to me that Mr. Beatty has of late begun to show a rebel chink in his Tory armor."

"But a corsetmaker, Edward."

Cassie's smile lasted until they reached Edward's rooms. She knew that finally she must tell him. As she could think of no smooth preamble, she said only, "Could we please talk a moment, Edward?"

"Of course." She looked suddenly pale to him. "Sit down," he said gently, and propelled her to the settee. "What is it, Cass?"

"There is something I must tell you. I fear that I have been a coward, for I could not bring myself to tell you before. But I must tell you now."

He gazed at her intently, not speaking.

She looked at him desperately. "Edward, I am going to have a child."

"*What?*"

"I am pregnant."

"No, you cannot mean it." Unconsciously, his eyes flitted over her body.

It was impossible for her not to see how truly appalled he was. She lowered her face, unable to bear the shocked, glazed look in his eyes.

"It is the earl's child."

She flinched at the harsh flatness in his voice.

"Yes," she whispered.

Edward leaped to his feet, his chair scraping loudly on the bare floor. "That bloody bastard. Oh my God, Cassie. Are you certain?"

She nodded, mutely. How stupid she was ever to have thought that Edward would react differently, but she had nurtured the memory of how the earl had behaved when she had told him that first night they were together that she was pregnant with Edward's child.

"I will fetch a doctor. Perhaps you are mistaken."

"No, I am not mistaken. I am sorry, Edward, but there is naught I can do about it."

His son, his heir, to be a bastard. The earl's seed. Murderous, confused thoughts mired his mind. "God, no," he croaked, unable for the moment to look at her. When he did, he saw that she was deathly pale, her lips drawn in a tight line, her shoulders squared.

"I will do what you wish, Edward."

"Damn him for a scoundrel."

Cassie turned her face away from the fury in his voice.

Edward forced himself to calm. It was not Cassie's fault. God, he could not blame her. He managed to make his voice clear and taut. "We shall be wed Friday, and leave for England as soon as I can be relieved."

"Very well, Edward." The words fell like ashes from her mouth. The earl would never even know that she would bear his child.

"No one must ever know, Edward."

"No," he said, slowly shaking his head. He took a jerking step toward her and awkwardly patted her shoulder. "It will be all right, Cass." He straightened. "I would like to be alone for a while. I must have some time to myself, to think. You must rest now. I will return soon."

"Yes," she said, "soon." She watched him leave, his bearing so taut with control that she wanted to weep for him.

Cassie lay wide-eyed in the dark bedchamber when she heard Edward's footsteps in the sitting room. She could feel him hesitate before he walked into the room. At least, she thought, there were no more secrets between them. She felt a tightening within her. At least no more secrets they could share with each other.

"Cassie, are you awake?"

"Yes, Edward."

He sat down beside her and tenderly pulled her against his chest, and rocked her in his arms.

"Forgive me for leaving you, but I—"

She laid a fingertip against his lips. "Do not torture yourself, Edward." Or me, she added silently. "Have you decided what it is you wish to do?"

"I told you my decision before I left, Cassie. I want you to become my wife."

She felt tears well up in her eyes, and she buried her face against his shoulder. "I have been so miserably unhappy, knowing what I was keeping from you. Please forgive me for being such a coward."

"It was I who was the coward for leaving you alone."

"Oh no, do not say that. God, I should probably have never come to you."

His hand stroked through her soft hair. "Hush, Cassie. I will not let you reproach yourself anymore."

He felt her soft breasts heaving against him, and leaned down to close his mouth over hers. He sensed a desperation in her as she closed her arms about his back and returned his kiss urgently. It occurred to him that he did not know when her child was to be born. He felt her need for him, and knew that such questions must wait.

"Would you make love with me, Cassie?" He drew back so that he could see her face in the dim light.

He felt a shudder of relief go through her. "Yes, Edward, I should like that very much."

Edward was gentle with her, and quite thorough in his attempts to arouse her. As his mouth closed over her and his hands drew her hips upward, she felt his tenderness, and allowed herself to be comforted. His entry did not hurt her, for his tongue had made her moist. She accepted him into her and clasped her hands tightly about his back, urging him to his climax.

"We have aught but time, Cass," he said gently afterward. "I will make you forget all that happened to you."

But he wondered, even as Cassie nestled against his shoulder to sleep. He knew the Earl of Clare by reputation, though his personal meetings with him had been few in recent years. He was a man who had women of all stations eager to enter his bed. It made no sense to Edward that, if the earl wished to marry her, he would repeatedly hurt her, that he should fail to arouse passion in her. He began to wonder what she felt toward the Earl of Clare, and the nagging doubts that had gnawed at him when he had walked alone on the street returned to haunt him. He tightened his hold about her, certain only that Cassie was with him now and that she would become his wife.

Chapter 25

Cassie brushed her freshly washed hair vigorously, until it rippled, free of tangles, heavy and damp down her back. She would have liked to open the curtained windows to let it dry more quickly, but the March air had turned chill once again. She dressed slowly, gazing toward the clock atop the small dressing table as she fastened the hooks on her bodice. It was nearly noon, and Edward had been gone since ten o'clock. She had managed to talk him out of fetching a doctor when she had awakened early in the morning, ill once again. She wanted no doctor about her in any case, but she knew also that it would be more than peculiar for Edward's wife to have been with her husband less than a week and be more than two months pregnant. Edward had grimaced when she pointed this out to him, and finally agreed. He had finally left her, still abed, with a tray of dry toast for her breakfast on her lap, to see General Howe about arrangements for their return home to England.

She walked into the sitting room and forced herself to nibble at the cold baked chicken and fresh bread Mrs. Beatty had sent up for her lunch. The babe in her womb seemed to take no exception to the chicken wing, and Cassie was wiping her fingers when Edward walked into the room, lightly slapping his arms from the cold.

"Damn," he said, "you're right about the changeable weather here, Cass. I wouldn't be surprised if it were even to snow."

He leaned down and lightly kissed her uptilted cheek. "Your hair smells good. I apologize for the primitive conditions. With all that hair to wash, and only the hipbath to wash it in, it must have taken you hours."

"Not quite hours," she said, smiling up at him.

He unfastened his sword and laid it on the table.

"Lunch, Edward? I saved you a chicken wing and a leg."

"Your generosity is overwhelming," he said, grinning, and seated himself across from her.

"What did General Howe say?"

"Who?"

She cocked her head at him and repeated her question.

"Oh, General Howe." He paused a moment and she saw him look fixedly at the chicken leg in his hand. "Actually, I wasn't able to see him. Perhaps later."

"You seem distracted, sir. May I ask just how you have spent the last two hours?"

To Cassie's surprise, he seemed to stiffen at her joking inquiry. "Naught of anything, really," he said finally. "There were people I had to see. I am still a soldier, Cass."

"I did not intend an inquisition, Edward," she said, sipping at her coffee.

"Of course you did not. Are you feeling all right, Cass?"

"Indeed, I am the picture of good health." She giggled suddenly and pressed her napkin over her lips.

He arched an inquiring brow.

"I was just thinking about your mother. I think she would be more inclined to approve of me if I displayed enough sensibility to lounge the hours away with a vinaigrette in my hand."

He smiled faintly. "Illness is one of her few joys, I fear. She thinks me a most undutiful son for giving the army much more attention than her. I understand from her letters that my agent, Mr. Prudeck, has shown himself to be a boorish oaf who refuses to show proper deference for her fragile nerves. I must remember to give the fellow a raise in his salary."

Cassie thought about meeting Lady Delford with her belly swelled with child. It was on the tip of her tongue to inquire whether Edward had yet written to his fond parent when she noticed that he was staring beyond her at nothing in particular. Instead, she asked, "What plans have you for the afternoon, Edward?"

"The afternoon?" He pressed the napkin against his lips. "I must leave you again, Cass, but not for long. Major Andre and I are meeting with some other officers, and General Howe, about the spring offensives."

"Perhaps when you return we could go riding. I should like that very much."

"But you are pregnant."

He was clearly aghast at such a suggestion, and Cassie hastened to reassure him. "I am not sick, Edward, merely indisposed some mornings. I promise not to beg you for a race."

He rose and fastened on his sword before he answered her, a frown drawing his brows together. "We shall see. It will probably rain, you know."

Cassie sighed, knowing a put-off when she heard it.

"Edward?"

"Yes, Cass?"

She rose from her chair and walked over to him. "I—that is, if you would rather that we did not wed—"

He interrupted her harshly. "Of course I wish us to wed. No more silliness from you now, my girl." He patted her cheek gently. "Rest while I am gone."

"Yes, I shall."

Cassie looked about the small sitting room after Edward had left, feeling almost as closed in as she had on *The York*. Rain pattered against the windows, and all fond thoughts of riding were dashed.

She picked up a pamphlet that lay on the table. It was the infamous *Common Sense* that Mr. Beatty had raved about, and she shook her head, bemused. She thought the high-flown phrases rather ridiculous. She raised her eyes at the sound of a light tap on the door.

She rose slowly to her feet, wondering if it was Mrs. Beatty, come to take the luncheon dishes away.

"Come in."

Cassie was surprised to see Jennifer Lacy, the young woman she and Edward met the day before.

"May I speak to you, Miss Brougham?"

"Certainly, Miss Lacy, do come in."

"You remember my name."

"Yes, it is a talent of mine."

Cassie motioned Miss Lacy to a chair and seated herself opposite upon the settee.

"You are feeling better today, Miss Lacy?"

For an instant, Jenny stared at her, not comprehending. How quickly she had forgotten her lie.

"Yes, of course."

The look was not lost upon Cassie. "Would you care for tea, or perhaps coffee?"

"No, thank you." Jenny lowered her eyes to her lap where her fingers were fretting at her reticule. "I waited until I saw Edward leave," she said finally, raising her vivid green eyes to Cassie's face.

"May I inquire why, Miss Lacy?"

Jenny grit her teeth, aware that Cassandra was regarding her closely, one elegant arched brow raised in inquiry.

"Because I wanted to speak with you without Edward being present. I hope you will not think me impertinent, but in truth, it is my intention, I suppose."

Cassie blinked and smiled uncertainly at Miss Lacy's candor. "You may be as impertinent as you like, Miss Lacy. Whether I answer you though is another matter."

"I had imagined that you were beautiful when Edward finally told me about you."

Cassie stiffened.

"Do not blame Edward. If you would know the truth, I rather forced it out of him. He was ill, from the wound in his thigh, and spoke of you in his delirium. When I asked him who Cassandra was, he told me that you were his fiancée. I asked him if you had done him a great wrong. His response was that you had died. I hope you will forgive me, Miss Brougham, but I must admit to giving your memory little sympathy."

"This is straight talk indeed, Miss Lacy."

Jenny said simply, "I must speak what I feel, for I am fighting for my happiness as well as Edward's." She paused a moment, an elusive smile indenting the corners of her mouth. "I had rather hoped that you would be a bitch.

Then I should not feel so guilty about coming here like this."

Cassie was feeling rather overwhelmed, and she could not help herself. She burst out laughing. "I do hope that I am not, though the earl—" She bit her lip and looked away from Jenny's questioning eyes.

"I have told no one that you and Edward are not wed."

"Thank you. I fear it would embarrass Edward were you to do so. You see, I was forced to come here as Lady Delford, and Edward, obligingly, has maintained the deception." Cassie saw that Jenny's eyes were fastened on the open bedchamber door, and on the rumpled bed beyond it. Her vivid eyes dimmed.

Jenny recovered and spoke, for the silence was growing long between them. "You are fortunate, Miss Brougham. Edward is an excellent lover." She saw a flush rise in Cassie's cheeks, and hastened to add, "Please forgive me for causing you embarrassment. I cannot seem to swallow words that want to be said."

Cassie said slowly, "It is a fault that I share with you. Does Edward take you to task?"

"He does now, but didn't, not at first. You see, he held himself quite aloof from people when he first arrived, so much so that he was thought to be a rather cold, cynical man without much sensibility. But I saw he was troubled, though I did not understand the reason. He grieved for you, and would not allow anyone to be close to him. I met him one evening when he rescued me from the loutish attentions of a German captain. Any man who was capable of such anger could not be without feeling. I began to love him that night, Miss Brougham. It frightened me, for I had never before met a man who touched me as he did. And it only grew stronger as the weeks passed. I finally admitted to myself that there was nothing I could do to stem it, that indeed, I was bound to him."

"And you are here to fight for him."

"Yes."

Cassie was forced to admire the courage that brought Jenny to see her. It was something that she would do. She bowed her head, remembering her pitifully brief encounter in Genoa with the Contessa Giusti. She had been a coward then. She had run, leaving the contessa laughing in triumph behind her. And now she was facing another rival, for another man. What a lunatic thought it was.

"Does Edward love you, Miss Lacy?"

"Yes, he does." She paused a moment, her green eyes clear and straight on Cassie's face. "Perhaps you wondered where Edward was this morning. I am certain that he did not tell you, but I must. He was with me. Indeed, I was waiting for him, knowing that he would come, knowing what he would say to me. He was so formal, like the old Edward. It was as if he had practiced the words he would say to me. He asked my forgiveness, but I could not give it to him. Perhaps I am not a very kind person, but I asked him to tell me that he did not love me. He could not say it, Miss Brougham."

Cassie stared at her, stunned. Edward's distraction over luncheon—it made sense now.

"Edward is such a bloody gentleman."

"Yes," Cassie said, "he is."

"The first time he told me he loved me was after I seduced him."

Cassie thought of that long ago afternoon in the cave. Like Jenny, she had been the seductress.

"Please do not think me an immoral woman, Miss Brougham. But I wanted him so badly. He was ill and staying at my father's house. Such a proper gentleman he was." A smile lit up Jenny's face. "Do you know that I drugged his wine? Even with opium lulling his mind, he protested. When I finally told him that I would give my virginity to a Hessian if he did not take me, he grinned in that special way of his, and then gave me such pleasure that I regretted not seducing him months before." Jenny drew to a sudden halt. "I hope that I have not shocked you, it is just that—"

"You needn't explain, Miss Lacy, I quite understand." She thought of the pleasure she had known with the earl, and lowered her face so that Jenny would not see her eyes.

Jenny suddenly rose and paced about the room. She whirled about, misery filling her voice. "I want what is best for Edward. Dammit, you left him."

"Through no fault of my own," Cassie said quietly. "It is a very long and quite arduous story, Miss Lacy, and I would never think to bore you with it."

What an elegant setdown, Jenny thought, and not delivered unkindly. She had tried to nurture fancies of Cassandra as a proud, willful girl, in the final summation a disagreeable witch. She had not been certain which would hurt more—to be right or wrong.

"What a wretched coil," Jenny said. "Edward's wretched honor forces him back to you. He has no choice."

Choice. The earl had never given her a choice. Could Jenny be right? Would Edward marry her because there was naught else for him to do? She was on the point of asking Jenny why the devil she believed that Edward's honor was his only motive for wishing to marry her. But she drew up short. Neither of them had spoken of love. She because she could not. Could Edward not? She tried to picture a future with Edward, but there was only the earl's dark face in her mind. And the earl's child in her womb.

Cassie said finally, "You wish me to give him up then. Go home to England." She paused a moment. "You have known Edward for only months, Miss Lacy. I have known Edward all my life. We grew up together. The day before we were to be wed, I was kidnaped. Have you any idea what that was like, Miss Lacy?"

Jenny stared at her numbly.

"Kidnaped by a man I had known since I was a child, a man who wanted me because—" She could not repeat the story about her mother she had told Edward. She knew the earl loved her for herself. At least he had, before she had escaped him.

"What happened?"

"So very much." The words were wrenched out of her, leaving her naked to herself. Cassie was trembling. She said brokenly, her hands covering her face, "Oh God, what is to be done? I was such a coward, such a blind fool. Are there never choices? Must we always follow stupid, meaningless dictums without regard to our feelings?"

"I wish that you were a bitch," Jenny said. "It is I who

am the bitch, selfish and thoughtless. It is just that I want Edward so very much."

"You are very different from Edward."

"Perhaps. Edward is gentle and very kind. But there is a streak of iron strength in him. I will never love another man as I love him."

And I will never love another man as I love the earl.

Cassie rose slowly. "Edward will be back shortly, Miss Lacy. You must give me time to think."

"It is all that I ask."

"Good-bye, Miss Lacy." Cassie took a white shapely hand into hers.

"Oh, incidentally," Cassie said, halting Jenny in the open doorway, "do you particularly like to sail?"

Jenny looked taken aback. "Sail? No, not particularly. If you would know the truth, I have always preferred being the passenger, and not the one doing the work."

"That is good," Cassie said, a smile lighting her eyes.

Cassie wondered, as she wandered back into the sitting room, what Eliott would say when his sister arrived on his doorstep, unwed and her belly large with child.

Chapter 26

Although the yellow dimity curtains were drawn tight across the windows, the bedchamber was still uncomfortably cool as the early afternoon sun tried to break through the overcast.

Cassie lay on her side, her knees drawn up to her belly, clad only in her light muslin shift. The small luncheon she had managed to eat had not settled well, and now she felt drained and weak in the aftermath of having been ill. She moved her hand over her still flat belly, wondering if her violent retching could in any way harm the small babe in her womb. She remembered the many mornings the previous fall when she had returned to bed, pale and trembling, and the earl had gathered her in his arms and stroked her gently until her stomach had righted itself. Although she did not wish it, tears welled up in Cassie's eyes and a soft, broken sob broke from her throat. She had never felt so alone and uncertain in her life. And she was still so far from her home. Over and over again, she thought about what she felt, about what she wondered if she had known even before Jennifer Lacy's unexpected visit. She would not marry Edward, no matter her unborn child.

She thought of the man she loved, now a world away from her. It had been she who had allowed unreasoning anger and willful pride to destroy the bond that had grown between them. Even last fall when she had agreed to wed him, there would have been love between them. She knew, with helpless fury at herself, that she would have come to return the love he felt for her. If only he had allowed her freedom, allowed her to make her own choices. If only he had told her about Becky Petersham.

Cassie was locked so deeply into herself that she did not hear the outward door open and close. She felt a light hand upon her shoulder.

"Cass."

She tried to sniff back her tears. She turned over on her back and gazed up at Edward. She remembered vividly how she had loved his face, had memorized its every plane and contour. A wan smile touched her lips, and she sniffed yet again.

"Are you all right?"

"Yes, 'twas just a bout of nausea. Mrs. Beatty's luncheon was not to the child's liking." She saw his hazel eyes flit quickly to her belly, and he made his face impassive. She wished she had remained silent.

"You are looking dashing, sir," she said, hoping to set his thoughts in another direction. "Did you see General Howe?"

"Aye, I saw him, and also General Clinton—with John Andre's help."

"Ah yes, Major Andre. A man, I think, who dearly loves the ladies."

"Indeed," Edward said stiffly. "Would you like your dressing gown, Cassie?"

How often had she shocked or displeased him, she wondered. "Yes, thank you, Edward." She swung her legs over the side of the bed and rose slowly, for she had begun to feel dizzy of late if she suddenly jumped up. She met Edward's eyes and felt herself flush with embarrassment. Her swollen breasts strained against the soft muslin shift, and the material had slipped up, revealing her legs. She lowered her eyes as he handed her the dressing gown.

Edward's eyes fell on her hair, tumbled sensually, full and loose, over her slender shoulders and down her back. He turned away from her, cursing the burgeoning ache in his loins. She had been violently ill and even now looked pale and listless.

"Would you care for tea, Cass?"

"I do not like tea, Edward. I have never liked tea."

There was bitterness in her voice, and he turned back to her in surprise.

Cassie felt instantly contrite and splayed her hands apologetically in front of her. "Forgive me for my wretched tongue. I would not have you think me a raging termagant." She rose slowly, shaking her dressing gown over her ankles.

He smiled at her gently. "You are not a termagant, Cass. It was stupid of me to have forgotten."

Edward followed her awkwardly to the sitting room and watched her seat herself carefully upon the settee. He unfastened his sword. "General Howe was not particularly obliging, Cass. Indeed, I fear there is little chance of his releasing me before summer."

Cassie drew in her breath, thinking of the ship sailing for England the following week. She watched him nervously as he set his sword precisely upon the table.

"I see," she said.

"And also," Edward continued, sitting himself opposite her, "General Clinton ordered me, and you, of course, to a ball Friday evening. He is a boorish, stubborn man, but listens to John Andre. Thus the ball. He hopes, I suppose, to impress the Tories with his generosity and graciousness. It will serve him well, for a little time, at least. I hope you will not mind attending."

"As Lady Delford?"

"You forget that by Friday you will be Lady Delford."

God help me, she thought, and said quietly, "I have given the matter much thought, Edward."

"What matter? I just told you of the blasted ball."

"The matter of my future and yours. No, please do not interrupt me, for I must say this. I made a terrible mistake in believing that your sentiments, as well as mine, could remain unchanged for so many months. Both of us are not what we were, Edward. And I see now that even if we had not been parted, we are not really suited to each other."

"What nonsense is this, Cassie?"

She winced at the cold impatience in his voice. She knew it as the tone of an English gentleman when honor and duty were at stake.

"I am giving us back choices, Edward. I have decided

that I cannot wed you. I will leave next week for England.
I am going home."

He sat forward, and clasped his lean hands tightly together between his thighs. "I am willing to grant you lapses
of reason, Cassie, because of your condition. But if you
seriously believe I would ever allow you to journey alone
back to Hemphill Hall, unprotected and carrying a bastard
child, you sorely mistake my character. If I were to allow
such a thing, I would expect Eliott to put a bullet through
my gullet."

She smiled at him sadly. "You cannot always lead your
life bound to such unrestrained honor, Edward."

"Do you forget that if that black-hearted devil had not
abducted you we would have wed?"

"But then, Edward, you fancied that you loved me. And
the earl, in his own right, believed it too."

"How can you defend that bastard? By God, Cassie, I
begin to think your wits are gone awry. Is it not enough
that you carry the man's child?"

They were arguing senselessly, hurtfully. Cassie wished
she could somehow weave her thoughts so that Edward
would understand. "We are tearing at each other, Edward,
and to no purpose. If I pose you one question, will you
reply honestly?"

He hesitated, and his hazel eyes narrowed in frustration.
"If you insist upon this ridiculous game, Cassie, very well."

"How do you feel about being a father to another
man's child?"

"Since I have no choice in the matter, I will learn to
accept it. It is your child, as well as his."

She said very quietly, "You would probably begin to hate
me for it and the child."

"So now you will accuse me of cruelty." He rose abruptly
and paced away from her. He turned suddenly, his face
hard. "I would that you keep your woman's vacillating
emotions to yourself. We will do what is right, and that's
an end to it."

"That is probably one good reason why we would never
suit, Edward. I refuse to be dictated to. I assure you that
you would pull your hair out—or mine—at my stubborn-

ness. As to my woman's emotions, I would ask that you examine your own feelings—without that cold rock of duty weighing down your heart." She knew by the sudden dazed look in his eyes that he was at last thinking of Jenny.

"You were granted the opportunity to see me as I really am, Edward. The idealized girl you lost need exist no more. Perhaps some day soon you will thank me, Edward, for I have rid you of a ghost." *And myself as well.*

He paced again in front of her, the muscles of his lean jaw clenching and unclenching. Finally he turned to her, his face rigidly set.

"I think, Cassandra—"

Don't call me that, only he used my full name.

"—that you have closed your heart to men after the vile treatment you received at the earl's hands. The nights we have spent together have been a trial for you. I am not stupid or insensitive to your feelings, you know. I will give you all the time you need. I will make no physical demands on you, unless you wish it."

She stared at him, knowing the effort it had cost him to once again push Jenny from his mind. He would give up anything, even his life, for his sacred honor.

At her continued silence, he said sharply, "Dammit, Cassie, you need not fear me. I am no ravisher of women. If you will but recall, it was you who invited me to your bed."

"I do not fear you, Edward, and you are quite correct, of course. I wanted you to make love to me because I believed you wanted me, that you still loved me. It was a way, a stupid way, I know, to try to bind us together again."

"What do you mean you believed that I *still* loved you?"

There, it was said. She drew a resolute breath. "You were ever a bad liar, Edward. I know that you are not in love with me, and you will not deny it if you still feel anything for me at all."

His face paled.

"It is this wretched country," he said at last, his voice low and taut. "Once we are in England again, everything will right itself. I have known you all your life, Cassie, and have always held you dear. Can you imagine that would ever change?"

"No, I believe that you would always be kind toward me. But you are being a statesman, Edward, and are trying to avoid confronting a truth that makes you feel the dishonorable man."

"This passes all bounds, Cass. For God's sake, do you count respect, likeness in taste and background, as naught? What if there is no longer a *grand passion* between us? I assure you that neither of us will die of misery." He ran his fingers through his carefully powdered hair and grunted in disgust at the white flecks on his hand. He felt stabbing anger at her, even though the words *grand passion* had stuck in his throat as he uttered them. Damn her. She had returned from the grave to reclaim him and now, when he insisted upon doing precisely as he had assumed she wished, she was ranting ridiculous nonsense to him about his not loving her. Jenny's image, her velvety green eyes dazed with passion, took hold of his mind. "Damn all women to the devil."

He reached for his sword and buckled it on. "I am going out, Cassie. Perhaps by the time I have returned, you will have come to your senses."

"Edward, I have come to my senses." She rose to face him. "I am sailing next week for England. I know you cannot accept my reasons, but my mind is made up. I hope you can forgive me, Edward."

He seemed suspended for a moment by the finality in her voice. He turned on his heel without answering her, and walked from the room.

"You'll be the most beautiful lady at the general's ball," Mrs. Beatty said, her thin voice enthusiastic as she gently tugged two thick curls over Cassie's bare shoulder. " 'Tis wise that you do not cover your hair with that nasty powder. It's all the rage, I know, but such a mess it makes. At least it's not raining anymore. March is a saucy month. Not like July. Now that's the time to shut all the shutters to stay cool."

Cassie smiled absently at Mrs. Beatty's speech, content to let her cluck on as she worked, as was her habit.

Mrs. Beatty helped Cassie step into a pale blue silk gown,

the only one she had brought from Genoa at all suitable for a formal gathering. "Och, it's tight across your bosom, m'lady and that part of you can't be sucked in."

Cassie stared at herself in the long, narrow mirror. Her breasts blossomed above the tiny row of white lace that gathered above the plunging bodice. She tried to tug it upward, but the stiff stomacher held the gown rigidly in place. She sighed. At least her waistline did not yet tell a tale.

Mrs. Beatty chuckled knowingly. "Captain Lord Delford will have to slap the gentlemen's hands, m'lady. They'll be like bees to the honey pot." As Cassy gazed up, appalled by this thought, Mrs. Beatty hastened to add, "Just a manner of speaking, m'lady. Do not fret yourself." She stopped her monologue to a halt and drew her sandy brows together. "The captain told Mr. Beatty that you would be leaving for England next week. It's sad that you must be parted so soon."

Cassie was careful that her eyes did not meet Mrs. Beatty's. "It is likely that the captain will return to England in the summer. General Howe has requested that he stay on in New York for the present." Actually, Cassie wasn't at all certain what plans Edward had made, if, indeed, he had yet made any. Since their conversation three days ago, Edward had tried to remonstrate with her, but Cassie had remained steadfast. It seemed to her that, finally, Edward was occasionally allowing himself to be relieved. When she had teasingly pointed out how lucky he was to have such a narrow escape from a shrewish woman, his tight reserve loosened, and for a brief moment, he smiled crookedly. But he was worried for her, thinking, she knew, about what her life would be like when she returned to England and to Hemphill Hall. Because he was troubled, she forced laughter into her voice when she was with him. He spent all his time with her, save at night. Whilst they were eating luncheon at a barge restaurant docked off Brooklyn Heights, she unwisely broached the subject of how Edward was going to court Jenny when much of New York believed him to be married.

"I believe, Cass," he said coolly, "that that will be *my*

problem. I will muddle through it, as I always do." She sensed that he had given it thought. She was quite confident that Jenny, if not Edward, would contrive something suitable.

Cassie turned at the sound of Major John Andre's laughing voice in the sitting room. Even when he was enjoying a good joke, his voice sounded husky, as if in case a lady were within hearing. Mrs. Beatty draped a white shawl over Cassie's shoulders and shuffled to the bedchamber door to open it.

"Now you enjoy yourself, m'lady. I was telling Mr. Beatty just the other day that you were looking a trifle peaked, but you certainly don't tonight."

"Thank you, Mrs. Beatty, for your assistance." She smiled toward the sitting room. "With two such amusing gentlemen, I am certain to enjoy myself."

Major Andre whistled softly under his breath. "Good God, Edward, it's a close eye you'll have to keep upon your lady this evening. You are a vision to a starved man, Lady Delford."

"She is passable, I suppose," Edward said as he took her hand.

"Thank you, Major Andre, Edward. I hope I have not keep you gentlemen waiting overlong."

"Not at all, Lady Delford." Major Andre glanced curiously toward Edward. If Cassie were his wife, he thought, he would not let her out of his sight or his bed, much less let her leave for England alone. His gaze lingered on her thick golden hair, and his fingers fairly itched to touch it.

Cassie supposed that Major Andre was accompanying them because there was no available carriage to carry them from the King George Inn to Kennedy House. At night, a lady escorted even by one gentleman was not sufficiently safe in many parts of the city.

This March night was cool, and the sky was clear. There was a light breeze from the river, and Cassie was reminded briefly of Genoa. But there were no fragrant flowers, no silvery moon casting its soft glow over the Mediterranean. She closed her eyes an instant, chiding herself, and turned her attention to the gentlemen.

The walk to Kennedy House was pleasant, for Major Andre was an amusing conversationalist. Cassie found herself laughing more than once at his droll comments, many of the more sarcastic ones about General Clinton.

"The general likes to fancy that he is riding in the Quorn," he said, his voice full of irony. "This morning, he insisted upon tearing down the middle of Broadway, pretending he was in the midst of the hunt. Had I the time, I would have trapped a wretched fox and placed him in the general's path. That would have shaken the old fool, I imagine. The New Yorkers were rather taken aback by his antics, I assure you."

Cassie laughed. "I look forward to meeting your commander, Major Andre."

"To you, Lady Delford, he will appear to be all that is gracious. I only hope that he will have the good sense not to ogle you too openly and that you will have the good fortune not to have to dance with him. He is really as clumsy as he is boring."

Although the evening was young, the long, rectangular ballroom set at the back of Kennedy House was already thronged with scarlet-coated officers, ladies far more sumptuously gowned than Cassie, and New York gentlemen, their elaborately clad figures and powdered heads in hearty competition with the English officers. An orchestra of be-wigged musicians was upon a dais at the far end of the room. Though there were few ornaments or decorations in the huge room, it was not difficult for Cassie to imagine herself, for a moment at least, back in England. Cassie gave over her shawl to a black maid, for all the windows were closed, and the press of people made the room quite warm.

With Edward at her side, she made her curtsy to General Howe. She smiled to herself when Edward introduced her to General Clinton, remembering Major Andre's words. He was not all that was gracious. Indeed, his ogling, Cassie thought, forcing a prim smile to her lips, was more in the nature of a tentative leer. She wished she had not discarded her shawl, for the general's eyes kept flitting to her bosom.

"Edward tells me you are leaving us next week, Lady Delford."

"It is true, sir. I must return to England." Although Cassie was not overly tall for a woman, General Clinton was overly short for a man, and her eyes met his bulbous nose.

General Clinton gave Edward a commiserating look. His pale eyes were set rather wide, and it was difficult to know specifically to whom he was speaking unless he looked at one directly. "The summer, Edward, the summer. We need you here now to drive those rebels into the wilderness." He heaved a sigh that strained the buttons of his scarlet waistcoat. "We must all of us make sacrifices. The time will pass quickly, you will see. I ask to reserve your permission now for your lovely wife's hand in a dance before she is besieged. Your servant, my lady," he added, and bowed brightly, not to her face, but to her bosom.

"General Clinton makes me feel naked," Cassie whispered behind her hand to Edward.

"You should hear what Jen—"

"I think you can begin finishing her name now, Edward. What does Jenny have to say about him?"

"That he's a lecherous old fool she would very much like to kick soundly in his shins."

Cassie said, "A most suitable amusement, I think." She was silent for a moment. "Will Jenny be here this evening, Edward?"

"Yes. She is a favorite with both generals. You can be assured that she will be discreet."

Cassie saw that Edward was ill at ease with such conversation, and hastened to say, "Kennedy House did not succumb to the fire, I gather."

"No, the fire was fickle, as I told you."

Cassie looked up to see an older woman bearing down upon them, a monstrously huge wig upon her head.

"That is Mrs. Winston, Cass," Edward murmured. "She much admires English officers. It is all I can do to remain polite to her. Her husband is quite influential."

Cassie said polite how-do-you-dos, marveling as she did so at the expanse of bosom the lady was displaying. Mrs. Winston accorded Cassie only cursory attention before turning to Edward. "Well, my dear sir, the musicians have a fine way with the minuet, do you not agree?"

"Most assuredly, ma'am," Edward returned in his most noncommittal tone. "I was just on the point of asking—"

"How marvelous, sir. I should be delighted to stand up with you."

Edward shot Cassie a harassed look before he was borne away, Mrs. Winston's beringed fingers clutching possessively at his sleeve.

Cassie was suddenly alone, a startled expression on her face.

"Something disturbs you, Lady Delford?"

Cassie turned to see Major Andre at her elbow. She grinned. "Your Mrs. Winston is a most overpowering person."

"Believe me, Lady Delford, most of the officers are in Edward's debt. That she has a *tendre* for your esteemed husband has made them all breathe a sigh of relief."

For an instant, Cassie wished that Major Andre knew the truth. She felt uncomfortable being called Lady Delford.

She said, her eyes narrowed briefly on a woman who was laughing overloud, "If I did not know better, I would believe that we were in England."

"Do not judge our local Tories too harshly. They deserve to enjoy their little displays of luxury and gaiety, for who knows what the future will bring?"

"You are right, of course, Major Andre. It is a fault of mine, I fear, to judge too quickly."

"A woman of your beauty can be allowed almost any fault, my lady." Major Andre looked around the room, then turned back to her, amusement in his eyes. "Only my rank as aide to General Clinton keeps the gentlemen at bay. Shall I leave you to your fate as Edward has done?"

"I would just as soon that you did not, Major Andre."

"Ah, there is Montresor, my counterpart to our famed commander. He's a dull fellow, Lady Delford, but an accomplished dancer."

"You are generous in your praise, Major."

He smiled at the irony in her voice. "You did not give me time to finish. Montresor is also one of the most brilliant strategists I have yet to meet. General Clinton heartily despises him for it."

While Major Andre was fetching her a glass of punch, whose ingredients he laughingly refused to name, Cassie caught Jenny's eye and nodded toward her. She looked radiant with her auburn hair piled high atop her head, in a gown of forest green velvet cut low over her deep-bosomed figure. Her laughter lilted in Cassie's ears. Jenny would be a sore trial to Edward's dignity, Cassie thought, but no more than she herself had been.

"Well, Lady Delford, what do you think of the pleasures offered by New York?"

"Very impressive, General Clinton. Everyone has been kind."

"Even the ladies?" He laughed suggestively.

"Even the ladies," she said. Cassie was careful to mind her toes when she danced the minuet with General Clinton, for he was every bit as clumsy as Major Andre had warned.

She had no time to search out Edward when the dance was done. General Howe laid his hand on her arm as soon as General Clinton finally released her. "There is a gentleman who desires to dance with you. My lord, allow me to present you to one of the fairest ladies to grace New York."

Cassie would have preferred to sit down for a moment and catch her breath. But good manners dictated otherwise. Because she had accustomed herself to General Clinton's unprepossessing height, she found herself staring at an exquisite waistcoat of pale blue silk embroidered with intricate gold thread when she turned.

"*Lady Delford* and I are old friends, sir."

"Well, I will leave you two young people alone to renew your acquaintance," General Howe said, and turned away.

"No," Cassie whispered, "it cannot be." She raised her widened eyes to meet his mocking dark ones. "No," she whispered again, her voice faint. She stumbled backward, and the earl cupped his hand under her elbow.

"You are looking well, Cassandra."

She ran her tongue over dry lips. "I—I don't understand."

"You don't understand why you are looking well? I have wondered the same thing myself." A mocking smile mirrored his tone. "I fear that the blues of our respective dress do not quite match. Still, we make a striking couple."

He offered her his arm. "The music has begun, my dear."

She looked numbly down at the fine lace that spilled over his dark hands. He wore the ring she had given him for Christmas on his third finger. She laid her hand tentatively upon his proffered arm.

They took their places in the long line of ladies and gentlemen. It was fortunate that Cassie knew the steps so well, for her mind seemed frozen, her thoughts suspended. He had come after her, halfway across the world. The thought that he still wanted her careened through her mind, over and over. She was scarce aware when he grasped her arm and deftly removed her from the row of dancers.

"I would not wish you to faint, *my lady*. Only think of the scene it would create and the eyebrows that would be raised."

"I would not faint," she said.

Within a few moments, he had led her to the outer entrance hall. She looked up at him in question.

"It is my opinion that you need a breath of fresh evening air." She nodded, for she could think of nothing else to do. They walked past brightly uniformed soldiers to the front veranda.

They were alone on the wide portico. The earl turned to face her, and grasped her shoulders. His voice was meditative. "When I left, Cassandra, I vowed to myself that if I found you safe and well I would forgo my anger. To my chagrin, however, I have discovered that I want nothing more than to thrash you soundly."

Conciliating words, words of love, died on her lips. "Since I am no longer your captive, my lord, I need not fear your threats. Since we are talking about anger, perhaps you can tell me why you lied to me. Damn you, you lied to me."

He leaned back against a white-painted pillar, his arms

crossed negligently across his chest. "Lied to you, Cassandra? I have done many things, but lying to you was not one of them."

"Then, my lord, how do you explain your so interesting relation, Becky Petersham, a woman who has lived with the Broughams for more than ten years?"

"Ah yes, Becky Petersham. I assume that you read all her letters, *cara*. If you did, then you will know she is a distant cousin. I placed you in her care because she herself wished a post as a governess in England, and your father did not concern himself with you. You could quite easily have grown up to be a little savage, if I had not intervened. As to my lying to you—" He shrugged. "I suppose that I did deceive you by what I did not say. I would have told you, eventually, after we had wed." He paused a moment and brushed a fleck of dust from his coat sleeve. "I regret that I had to use Becky to secure your presence that afternoon, but it was unavoidable."

Cassie sucked in her breath, furious at his calm dismissal of what he had done. "Your charade was despicable, my lord. And as to Becky Petersham, I shall strangle her if it is ever my misfortune to lay eyes upon her again." Even as she spoke, she realized that she would see Becky as soon as she returned to Hemphill Hall. She shook that thought from her mind. "I am relieved, my lord, to learn that you can so easily excuse your own perfidy. You are beyond ruthless, and I won't have it." She paused, seeing that he was looking down at her, a smile upon his lips.

"It seems when it comes to you, Cassandra, that I have more than once behaved strangely."

"How did you find me?"

"Your anger at finding the letters dulled your thinking, love. I have decided that you must have wished me to come after you, for you were not at all careful in how you replaced the evidence. I suppose, when all is said and done, that I must be grateful to Captain Crowley for being in port. I trust that he took good care of you on the crossing."

She felt suddenly like a mouse being toyed with by an omniscient cat. "How did you know of Captain Crowley?"

The instant she asked the question, she knew she could have answered it herself.

As if he guessed her thoughts, he chuckled. "Really, *cara,* would you not expect me to be aware of every important ship docked in the harbor? I assume the story you concocted for the poor captain wrung his withers."

He was speaking to her as if to a stupid twit, and in retaliation, she pulled her damaged pride about her like a cloak. "I told Captain Crowley that I was Lady Delford and that I had been captured by an Italian nobleman. I begged him to take me to New York, to my husband."

His amused expression fled at the word, and anger filled his dark eyes. Cassie had the distinct feeling that he would like very much to shake her until her teeth rattled. Strangely, she found herself not at all frightened or distressed by the prospect.

The earl, with no little effort, regained the tight control he had on himself. The lazy animal grace reappeared in his stance, and he said, "For the past two days, Scargill has kept watch over you, Cassandra. He has watched you chat gaily with Edward Lyndhurst, even stroll through this wretched city on Major Andre's uniformed arm. Scargill was filled with remorse, you know. You see, it never occurred to him that you would bolt. He, like I, assumed that you no longer wished to leave. You succeeded in making fools out of both of us. As for the bull, Andrea, I failed even there. Daniele was wounded and Andrea long gone by the time I arrived in Riva Trigoso."

"Damn you, my lord, you want me to writhe in guilt for escaping from a man who abducted me in the first place? I find your wounded pride about it ridiculous." She lowered her head, away from the pained tenderness in his eyes. "I am sorry that you did not catch Andrea."

"Why did you do it, Cassandra?"

She looked up at him tentatively, trembling now at the hollow sadness in his voice. "I felt that you had betrayed me, that you had lied to me, and I was naught but what you had wished to create. I felt I had to leave, and fate in the person of Captain Crowley made it possible."

"That is not what I meant."

She faltered, her eyes narrowed in confusion.

"I believed, fool that I am, that you had come to care for me. Yet you rushed into Edward Lyndhurst's arms and wed him the moment you arrived in this miserable city." His voice became harsh. "Are you pleased with your choice, *Lady Delford?* Do you moan with passion in his arms? Have you rendered the poor fellow ecstatic, or is he beginning to see that you are not the gentle, malleable girl he had believed you to be?"

She shook her head stupidly at him. "You are quite wrong, my lord."

"Wrong about what, Cassandra?"

She took a stumbling step toward him.

"You touch her, you miserable bastard, and I will dispatch your soul to hell where you stand!"

Cassie froze at Edward's shout. She turned numbly to see his hand poised on his saber, his eyes fastened with cold hatred upon the earl.

"Edward, you are wrong. Please—"

"Silence, Cassie." Edward turned and offered a contemptuous bow to the earl. "Well, Lord Clare, what an unexpected surprise. Your lordship's pride is such that you could not allow your captive mistress to escape you?"

Jenny's frantic voice cut through the air. "Edward, you must stop—he will kill you."

The earl turned his dark gaze toward Jenny, and a black brow winged upward.

He offered her a negligent bow before straightening to his full height. "I have come to reclaim what is mine, Lyndhurst. You have had your time with her, and you will have no more. I suggest that you choose to divorce her."

"I offer you no choice, my lord earl. By tomorrow afternoon, the birds will be feasting upon your black heart."

Cassie's mind planted itself once again in her body. She waved a warning hand toward Jenny, who looked as though she would grab Edward's sword and run the earl through herself. "Both of you will cease this nonsense right now. For your information, my lord earl, I am not Lady Delford."

"Damn you, Cassie, keep a still tongue in your head."

A surprised smile lit up the earl's dark eyes. "Still another lie, Cassandra?"

"It matters not." Edward stepped between them. "It is a question of honor, my lord. Do you wish me to strike you, or will you, as a gentleman, accept my challenge?"

"As you wish, Lyndhurst," the earl said.

"You will not do it, Edward," Jenny said. Suddenly, she weaved where she stood and crumpled into a faint.

"Will you see to the lady, or shall I, Lyndhurst?"

Edward gritted his teeth at the earl's tone, but he had no choice but to drop to his knees and gather Jenny into his arms. When he rose, he said sharply to Cassie, "You will come with me. I trust that he has given you sufficient disgust of him."

"Oh, hush, Edward. See to Jenny. I assure you that I can find my way home without your assistance."

Edward turned stiffly on his heel and carried Jenny past several staring soldiers into the house.

Cassie turned at the sound of the earl's softly mocking voice. "Well, *cara,* it would seem that another has gained the viscount's affections. A touching scene, and, I might add, the lady is quite beautiful. Poor Cassandra—did your lost love refuse to wed you? Has he shattered all your romantic young girl's illusions? It would appear that I have arrived barely in time to save your shredded virtue. Tell me, *cara,* how has it felt to bed with a man who does not love you?"

It was unlike him to be so cruel, but there was so much truth in what he said that she could not forgive him. He had made her feel like a harlot. "You wonder, my lord, how it feels to bed with a man?" she said slowly. "Since it is my first such experience, I vow that I enjoyed it much. When I return to England, I do not despair of finding other such men to please me. They will, after all, be entirely English, and not half-breeds, bloated with masculine conceit."

There was such blazing fury in his eyes that her body tensed. And there was something else, something that made her feel hollow with despair.

"I bid you good night, Cassandra," he said dispassionately. "After I have satisfied Lyndhurst's honor, I shall come to fetch you."

"No," she shouted at him, but he did not look back. She stared after him until he was swallowed by the darkness. Cassie sank down upon the front steps and closed her eyes against hated tears. She felt gentle fingers upon her shoulder and looked up to see Scargill kneeling beside her.

He shook his head sadly. "You wounded him deeply, madonna, and he was too angry to see through your lie."

"He deserved it, all of it." Her voice broke. "Oh God, Scargill, what am I to do now?"

"I do not know, madonna, would that I did." He rose and stared down at her a moment in silence. "Now it is a matter of pride." He pulled on the shock of red hair over his forehead and left her.

Chapter 27

Gray streaks of dawn lighted the bedchamber when Cassie heard a soft knock on the outer door. She heard Grumman's soft voice and Edward's subdued response. She waited only a few seconds after the door closed before she swiftly threw back the bedcovers, straightened her gown, and pulled on her cloak.

She tiptoed down the creaking oak stairs, relieved that there was as yet no one about. She quietly pulled up the latch on the front door of the inn and peered out into the courtyard. She quickly drew back inside at the sight of Major Andre astride his bay stallion waiting for Edward to mount Delila. Cassie waited until they disappeared from view along the road, then slipped out the front door and ran to the stable, her skirts pulled up in her hands. She pulled several coins from her pocket and pressed them into Will's sleepy hand. She stepped back, tapping her foot impatiently while he bridled the mare she had selected the previous evening.

She stayed him when he leaned over to heave up the saddle. "Nay, Will, do not bother. There is not time. You are certain that they are going to the Commons?"

"Yes, milady. Major Andre spoke clearly. And besides, it is there that all the gentlemen fight their duels."

Cassie felt a wrenching tightening in her stomach at his matter-of-fact tone. She raised her foot for Will to toss her up upon the mare's wide back. "I pray I will not be gone too long. And thank you, Will."

Cassie flicked the reins, and her mare broke unwillingly into a trot through the courtyard and onto the road. She shivered in the chill early morning air and thrust her free hand into the pocket of her cloak. She clenched her teeth against a bout of morning sickness that raised bile in her throat.

Curious eyes followed her progress through the near-empty streets, but she paid them no heed. The sky was overcast and Cassie found herself praying for a violent downpour, anything that would put a stop to this madness.

"It is a matter of pride." Scargill's quiet words floated through her mind. She had lost hers during the long hours of the night as she lay huddled in her bed.

She guided her mare onto the Commons, a stretch of barren ground surrounded by naked-branched trees. She saw them at the far end of the Commons; Scargill and Major Andre standing together, the earl and Edward apart, stripping off their overcoats. She heard the whinnying of their horses, tethered to scraggly bushes. She sucked in her breath at the sight of a silver rapier cutting through the air. Edward was testing the flexibility of his blade. The earl stood quietly, his fingers caressing the razor edge of his sword.

She slipped off her mare's back. She ran quickly toward them, her footsteps noiseless in the dew-soaked grass. She froze in her tracks at Major Andre's cold command, *"En garde!"*

The earl and Edward, both stripped to their frilled white shirts and tight, dark, knitted breeches, circled toward each other, slashing their rapiers in front of them. She ran forward, her cloak billowing out behind her, as the sound of clashing steel rang in the heavy air.

"Lady Delford." Major Andre's shocked, reproving voice rose above the raging foils, and she felt his hand grab her arm.

"Let me go, you fool. I am not Lady Delford, and this madness must be stopped."

"Madonna, it is too late."

Cassie turned stricken eyes to Scargill. "You said it was a matter of pride. Dammit, I cannot let this happen. Let me go, Major, else I shall do something very unladylike to you."

"But—" Major Andre sputtered, taken aback by her unexpected ferociousness. He dropped his hand.

Cassie knew that both the earl and Edward were aware of her presence, but neither of them paid her any heed. She heard a growl from Edward as he lunged forward, his foil a blur as it whistled toward the earl. The earl deflected his blade and drew him into a wild flurry.

Cassie jerked the small pistol from her cloak pocket and dashed forward. She was close enough to see beads of perspiration upon Edward's brow, and hear his rasping breathing. He was defending himself with poise and swiftness, but the earl was easily the more powerful, and his body moved with deadly grace, the foil an easy extension of his arm.

"Stop it, both of you."

"Leave, Cassandra," the earl shouted, his eyes flitting toward her for a brief instant, "else I promise to thrash you."

Slowly, Cassie raised the pistol and pressed it against her temple. "If you do not cease your madness this instant, I swear I will pull the trigger."

"Cassie." Edward stared at her, drawing in his foil. The earl turned slowly toward her, and dropped his rapier to the ground.

"Put that pistol down, Cassandra," he said. She could hear fear in his voice.

Cassie tightened her grip on the butt. "I mean it, my lord. Damn both of you. Edward, leave go. Forget your wretched honor. I love him, do you hear? I could not bear it if you harmed him. And you, my lord, do you wish to destroy our lives by being the cause of Edward's death?"

Her eyes were pleading on Edward's face, and he looked at her uncertainly.

The earl strode toward her. She lowered the pistol from her temple, and aimed it at his chest. "I shot you once, my lord," she said in a voice of deadly calm. "Do not doubt that I would do it again."

He stopped abruptly, his eyes boring into hers. "Cease this nonsense, Cassandra. You interfere where you do not belong."

"Do not belong?" she shrieked at him. "Are both of you

so lost to reason? I swear to you that I will put a bullet through you if you do not promise me you will stop."

She thought she had won, for Edward nodded his head at her. As she looked at him, her hand was suddenly borne violently downward. A sharp explosion rent the silence, and the bullet tore into the cold ground.

The earl grasped her shoulders and shook her.

Cassie stared stupidly down at the useless pistol dangling from her fingers. She raised her face to his and whispered brokenly, "Please, no, my lord. Please do not do this. I lied to you last night. It is you I love, you must believe me."

He pulled the pistol from her fingers and tossed it aside. "So you will do anything to protect your lover," he said coldly. "Even though he does not want you, you plead for his life."

"No. You must listen to me, Anthony. Please, listen to me."

"Are you ready to continue, my lord?" Edward asked, his face a set mask.

"Certainly, Lyndhurst. Scargill, take her away from here."

Just as Scargill's hand closed over her arm, the sky rumbled with grating loud thunder and rain burst through the thick gray clouds.

"En garde!" Major Andre's command rang out once again.

"Major, you cannot allow this. We must stop them." Cassie felt impotent tears sting her eyes and wet her cheeks, mixing with the raindrops.

"Honor must be satisfied," he said sharply. He stared straight ahead at the earl and Edward, refusing to meet her eyes.

Through the heavy veil of rain, Cassie watched the earl and Edward, their clothes plastered to their bodies, their movements tentative on the slippery ground. Suddenly Edward slipped on a muddy clot of earth, and he clutched frantically at the empty air to regain his balance.

"Damn, the earl could have had him," Major Andre said.

Cassie drew in an appalled breath. The earl had held

back. God, what was he trying to do? Did he seek to kill himself?

Cassie suddenly went limp against Scargill's arm, and her head lolled back against his chest. "Dear God," she heard him cry. "Help me, sir, she's fainted."

The instant he released his hold upon her to lift her into his arms, Cassie whirled about and drove her heel against his shin. Scargill gasped more in surprise than in pain and stumbled backward.

"Madonna, don't!"

Cassie rushed toward the earl and Edward, jerking off her sodden cloak as she ran. Their figures were indistinct through the thick haze of rain, and even the loud clashing of steel against steel was muted in the downpour.

The earl saw her rushing toward them and quickly drew back from Edward. In the next instant, she threw her cloak between them, and flung herself against the earl.

Edward did not see her until the moment she covered the earl's body with her own. His foil caught in the sodden cloak, but his momentum carried his thrust forward. The tip of his blade sliced through the cloak and sank with sickening ease into her shoulder.

He jerked the foil free and gazed, horrified, at the bright red blood covering the tip.

Cassie felt nothing, save a sharp prick high on her shoulder, near her left arm.

"Please," she cried, her face buried against the earl's wet shirt, "no more." She clasped her arms tightly around his neck and sobbed softly against his chest. "Please, if there must be more fighting, let me be the one. I cannot lose you. I would rather die than lose you."

She felt the warmth of his breath against her forehead. "You are forever a surprise, Cassandra," he whispered, as his hands ripped through the bloodied material of her gown. He drew a relieved breath. The foil thrust was not deep.

"Please take me home, Anthony."

"That will be in large measure up to Edward Lyndhurst, *cara.* Well, Captain? Has your thirst for honor been slaked?"

"Cassie, you are hurt," Edward said, "My God, what have I done?"

Cassie turned slightly in the earl's arms. "It is nothing, Edward. All that matters is that you and he are safe. Please tell me, Edward, that you no longer wish his blood."

"Dammit, Cassie, think of what he has done to you. How can you want such a man?"

"I do not know, Edward, but the fact remains that I do. It is true, you know I would not lie to you."

Edward blinked the rain from his eyes. He stared blankly as the earl lifted Cassie into his arms.

"I believe, Lyndhurst," the earl said quietly, "that the die has been cast. I, for one, certainly have no wish to be impaled on your foil."

Slowly, Edward nodded. "Your shoulder, Cass," he said, staring at the red stain that was spreading over her gown.

"If you wish, Lyndhurst, you can accompany me back to *The Cassandra*. I will take care of her there."

"But you cannot. It's I who must—"

"She has made her choice. Enough, let us leave this place before we all succumb to an inflammation of the lungs in this blasted rain."

Cassie raised her head from the earl's shoulder. "Thank you, Edward. You need have no more fears for me. I am going home." She was smiling.

"It's but a scratch, *cara*. I will give you two days before I lay you over my knee." The earl straightened and pulled the bedcover higher on her back.

"Do you wish some laudanum, my lord?" Scargill asked as he handed the earl the basilicum powder.

"Nay, if she suffers any pain it will serve her right. I have had enough of your dramatic antics, Cassandra, to last me a lifetime."

"He is cruel, Scargill, but I shall make him pay, never fear."

Her grin became a wince as he gently bound the wound with a light bandage. He pulled her damp mass of hair away from her body and tucked the covers more tightly around her.

"We will give her a glass of wine for her breakfast, Scargill."

"Yes, my lord, right away." Scargill sprinkled a goodly amount of laudanum into the red wine.

As the earl helped her onto her back and puffed the pillows behind her head, she eyed the wine warily. "I really don't wish any, my lord."

"Nonsense, it will put you in a better frame of mind, and, I trust, calm your shrew's tongue."

"Oh, very well," she said, and downed the wine. "I do wish that you would give me a nightgown."

Before the earl answered her, he turned to Scargill, who sported a beaming smile. "Thank you, Scargill. I believe I can well handle our patient now. Go remove those wet clothes. I want none of us to become ill."

"Now about that nightgown, Cassandra," the earl said after Scargill had let himself out of the cabin. The smile disappeared as he gazed down at her white face. "For God's sake, what is the matter?"

"It is the wine," she gasped, and looked wildly about for a basin. "Please, my lord, I am going to be ill."

He got her the basin with not an instant to spare. When at last she lay against the pillows, pale and blown, he said gently, "Lie still, love. This time we will try some water, no wine."

After she had sipped at the water, she became aware that he was looking at her oddly. She thought of the child in her womb, but decided that now was not the time to tell him of her pregnancy. She stared up at him, and set her jaw.

"Should you not remove your wet clothes, my lord?"

His odd, assessing expression gave way to a grin. "Only if you will promise to spare my male modesty."

"I assure you that anything you do will leave me unmoved."

Indeed, her words were true, she thought. She started to feel very drowsy and the pain in her shoulder seemed to be easing. She heard his boots drop to the floor, but she was no longer paying attention.

* * *

The earl laid down the hairbrush and surveyed his handi-work. "You are presentable now, Cassandra."

"What is the time?"

"Late afternoon, near four o'clock. You slept a long time, little one."

She sighed and pulled the dressing gown more closely over her breasts, a dressing gown that he had put on her whilst she had slept.

"Are you hungry?"

Cassie consulted her stomach and discovered that she was ravenous. "Is Arturo aboard? I think I could eat three horses."

A light knock came upon the cabin door.

"Enter."

Scargill's smiling face appeared in the open doorway. "The viscount and a young lady are here, my lord."

"Well, Cassandra?" The earl's gaze was questioning.

"Yes, Anthony. I believe proper good-byes are in order."

Edward stepped awkwardly into the cabin, a radiant Jenny at his side.

"My lord," he said stiffly, bowing to the earl. "I would like you to meet Jennifer Lacy. Jenny, Anthony Welles, Earl of Clare."

The earl took in Jenny's flushed cheeks, and her rich auburn hair tumbled artfully about her shoulders. He was aware that she was eyeing him closely. He raised her gloved hand to his lips and lightly kissed her palm. "A pleasure, Miss Lacy. I trust you are fully recovered?"

"I am not certain, my lord," Jenny said, "to which recovery you are referring. There have been several of late."

The earl grinned down at her. "Actually, I was thinking of your most recent timely swoon, ma'am."

"It was, was it not?" Jenny agreed smoothly.

Edward, whose eyes were upon Cassie, turned to Jenny, frowning comprehension dawning. "Jenny. You little wretch. Are you telling me that your fainting was an act?"

"Well, yes, Edward," she admitted. "But enough of that." She smiled toward Cassie. "I only wish that I had had the courage to put a stop to your dueling. But what one lady doesn't manage, another does. Well done, Miss Brougham."

"Thank you, Miss Lacy."

"Well, Lyndhurst," the earl said smoothly, "it would appear that our destinies have been determined by two chits, barely into petticoats."

A faint smile replaced Edward's appalled expression. "I think, Jenny, that you are deserving of whatever fate I choose for you."

Jenny lowered her eyes to hide their lurking laughter. Her voice was demure. "So long as I do not have to faint anymore, Edward, for effect, you know, I shall be content."

"You are a minx, Miss Lacy," the earl said, as Edward turned stiffly to Cassie.

"You are all right, Cass?"

"Of course, Edward. His lordship has put me back together again. It is but a scratch. Do not worry yourself over it."

"Let her suffer a bit, Lyndhurst," the earl said. "After all her machinations, she deserves to pay the piper. I trust you will join us for a glass of wine."

"Wine glasses filled with rich bordeaux," Jenny said. "All's well that ends well?"

"The taming of the shrew," the earl said.

"Do make that shrews, my lord," Edward said, looking at Jenny.

"Let them have their little joke, Jenny. Gentlemen adore so to swagger about, believing themselves lords of all they survey."

Jenny held back her giggle, aware that Edward was not at his ease, particularly in the earl's presence. She raised her eyes some moments later to the earl, and said ingenuously, "You have a lovely boat, my lord."

Cassie nearly choked on her wine, but the earl merely nodded graciously. "I and my boat thank you, ma'am. Perhaps you would like a tour whilst Lyndhurst talks to my patient?"

"Yes, Jenny," Edward said. "I will meet you shortly, above-deck."

Jenny walked to the bed and took Cassie's hand. "All is as you wish it to be, I can see that plainly."

"I will never wish for anything more. Perhaps I shall see you in England."

"Oh yes, I am certain of it. Good-bye, Miss Brougham."

"Good-bye, Miss Lacy."

The earl offered Jenny his arm and led her from the cabin. Cassie heard her say to the earl, "I do not know much about sailing boats, my lord. Perhaps you will enlighten me."

Edward gazed down at Cassie, his expression intent. "You are certain that this is what you want, Cass?"

"Oh yes, Edward." She took his hand and squeezed it tightly. "Our lives have been fraught with adventure. Enough I think to make me want to grow old in one place. Or perhaps two places," she added, smiling to herself.

"Will you return to England, Cass?"

"We have not had time to discuss our plans. Poor Eliott will be in for something of a shock."

Edward shook his head. "He'll believe that we've all lost our minds." He paused a moment, and smoothed a strand of hair from her forehead. "Does his lordship know yet of his child?"

"No, and I would ask that you not tell him, Edward. It is up to me, you know."

"How long have you loved him, Cass?"

"I cannot remember the beginning of it, yet I am quite secure in my feelings for him."

"Despite all that he did to you?"

"Yes."

"What you did this morning was outlandish."

"Perhaps, but I believe that you would have done the same, had you been me. There was everything to lose, you see."

"I will never understand you, Cass."

"You will forgive me everything, Edward?"

"There is nothing to forgive you for," he said quickly. "The earl, though, is another matter." He leaned down and kissed her. "Good-bye, Cass. Perhaps our children will be playmates some day."

"And mine will lead yours into wicked adventures."

He stared at her a moment, bemused. "That," he said, straightening over her, "remains to be seen." He looked toward the open cabin door, hearing Jenny's bright laughter.

"Good-bye, Cass."

"Until England, Edward."

Chapter 28

Cassie heaved a sigh of contentment, wiped her fingers on her napkin, and sat back in her chair. She quickly leaned forward again when she felt the wooden back press against her shoulder.

"So you like Arturo's way of preparing oysters?"

"Cleaning my plate from one end to the other should convince him of my approval."

"They are fresh from the bay. Although Arturo is quite outspoken in his disdain of New York, he does admit that the variety of fish is remarkable."

Cassie sipped at her wine, suspecting that the earl had laced it with laudanum. She gazed about the cabin, her body lulled by the wine and the gentle rocking of the yacht.

"How odd," she said aloud, "that one's perspective can shift so dramatically. This cabin is exquisite. I did not remember it this way."

"Both the captain and his cabin are pleased at your new perspective, Cassandra. How does your shoulder feel?"

"I fear, my lord, that you must be disappointed. I am strong as a horse, you know, and the wound is trifling. But you must keep your word—you must wait a full two days before you thrash me."

"If I do not have to treat you as an invalid, *cara,* then I fancy I shall discover equally pleasurable pursuits to fill my time until I can, in good conscience, bare your bottom."

She felt a quiver of pleasure and a rosy flush rose to her cheeks. She looked down at his strong hands as he deftly peeled an orange.

"I have not had an orange in a long time," she said.

He handed her a section and sat back in his chair, watching her nibble delicately.

"When do we leave New York?"

He was silent for some moments, gazing at her intently.

"Is there orange juice on my chin?"

"No. You asked me this morning, Cassandra, to take you home. I must ask you if you meant what you said."

"Given the circumstances, my lord, I can hardly believe you would doubt me."

Again, he fell silent. Cassie felt suddenly uncertain. "You no longer wish to wed me?"

"I have never before offered you the choice, Cassandra. Now I find that I must. Would you, you adorable girl, you most exquisite creature in all of England—and the colonies—do me the great honor of becoming my wife?"

Cassie pursed her lips, stifling laughter at his flowery delivery. It was odd, she thought, but she preferred him to be overbearing. He was easier to deal with that way.

She said matter-of-factly, "If you do not wed me, I shall have to gullet you and throw your miserable body in the bay."

"In that case, to save my wretched hide, I shall fetch a discreet parson on the morrow. Is that soon enough for you?"

"I suppose that it must be," she said. "But be warned, my lord. I will have you leg-shackled by tomorrow noon, else you will be the worse for it."

It suddenly occurred to her that all her clothing was still at Edward's lodgings. "Oh dear," she wailed, "I have nothing to wear. This dressing gown would hardly be appropriate."

He rose slowly and walked over to the armoire. He flung open the doors. "I think, my dear, that all you need is right here."

"I don't think you ever doubted my answer for an instant." She made to rise, to go to him, but found to her chagrin that she weaved where she stood.

"Drunk again," he said, shaking his head. "I believe the best place for you, my love, is in bed." He yawned prodigiously. "Do you mind if I join you? It has been a long, quite fatiguing day."

"But we are not yet married, my lord."

"True."

"And my shoulder is paining me terribly."

"I shall be very careful of it."

He laughed, a deep, satisfied laugh and scooped her up into his arms. She clung to him when he set her upon the bed.

"Madam, you cannot seduce me unless you allow me to remove these damned clothes."

She lay back, watching him peel off his clothing. When he stood naked in front of her, she pulled her dressing gown more closely about her and sat up. Words came from her mouth in a torrent. "It is my fault—all of it is my fault. I sold myself, just as would a harlot. I let him take me though I hated it and hated myself. I had nothing to give to him for you had already taken everything—my love, my passion. How can you forgive me? How can you say nothing when you know what I did?"

"Are you now quite through?"

"I am afraid that I have nothing to give you, don't you understand? I am afraid that I can no longer feel passion after what I did."

"I have never heard a more comprehensive recital of recriminations. Remind me, when you are an old woman, and I a doddering old man, to provide us both with the amusing tale of Cassandra's fall from grace. I might even tell our grandchildren if ever your termagant's tongue pushes me too far."

"But you must hate me, you must."

He grabbed her arms and pulled her forward on top of him. "If I yell and rave at you will it make you feel better? Or, perhaps I should beat you senseless. Would that assuage your ridiculous guilt? I do apologize for refusing to wallow with you in this spate of self-hatred. Actually, what you have done required a good deal of courage and determination. And, more importantly, my love, Edward Lyndhurst is no longer in your heart."

She stared at him, opened her mouth, and closed it again. He laughed and gently flicked her chin.

"Now, Cassandra, what is it to be? Lovemaking with your future husband, or sleep?"

"You are strangling me with your nobility."

"Oh no, I am your devil, do you not remember? I assure you, there is not a noble bone in my body. You have not answered my question, *cara*." He stroked his hands gently down her back.

"You swear that you are not noble, that you are being honest with me?"

"I swear it."

"But what if I no longer feel passion?" She felt his fingers stroking her hips.

"Your body does not seem to be aware that you are a passionless woman. And your eyes, *cara,* are becoming vague and smoky. Surely, that is not because of disinterest."

There was still a faint protest in her mind, but when she opened her mouth, only a breathless sigh emerged.

"Your dressing gown, Cassandra."

His voice made her urgent, and she tugged frantically at the sash at her waist.

"Hold still, little one."

The dressing gown parted under his deft fingers, and he slipped her arms gently out of the full sleeves. He pressed her upon her back and lay beside her, his eyes on her body.

"You are too thin," he said, still not touching her, "save for your breasts." He leaned over her and kissed her. Her breasts were swollen and tender, but the touch of his mouth made her arch her back upward.

And then he was on top of her, and she felt the familiar hardness of him, the raw masculine strength of him. He crushed her breasts against his chest, and she felt his black hair pressing against her.

She felt a surge of joy as he forced her lips to part. He pushed against her belly, and her hands urgently kneaded his back as she parted her thighs. But he would not allow it.

He brought her to release before he entered her. To his besotted surprise, when he thrust deep inside her, she quiv-

ered anew with passion. She cried out his name, clutching
him feverishly to her, and he closed his mouth over hers,
willingly losing himself in her.

Belatedly, he was reminded of her shoulder and gently
eased himself off her. He smoothed back the tousled hair
from her forehead and solemnly kissed her nose.

"If you show any more passion, my love, I will be a
dead man."

She smiled vaguely, replete, and in the next moment, she
was fast asleep, her face against his shoulder.

Their wedding was conducted aboard *The Cassandra,* in
the captain's cabin. Mr. Donnetti and Scargill supported
the couple under the suspicious eye of a Father Donovan,
lamentably Catholic.

After waving Father Donovan off the yacht, his step
jaunty from the excellent champagne provided by the Earl
of Clare, *The Cassandra,* sails billowing and men swarming
nimbly over the rigging, prepared to sail out of the harbor
of New York.

"Where are we bound, my lord?" Cassie turned to face
her husband, her back against the bronze railing.

Anthony wrapped his fingers about strands of her hair
that whipped across her face in the crisp afternoon breeze.
For some moments, he simply looked down at her, savoring
her closeness, secure in the belief that she had finally accepted him.

"I have been given to understand, wife, that England is
lovely in the spring."

Her eyes glistened with pleasure, for she had expected
him to say Genoa. She laughed. "I do hope that we do not
beat my letter to England. To be faced with a supposedly
dead sister would be no mean shock to Eliott. And of
course, there is Becky to be considered."

The earl dropped his hands to her shoulders. "Becky
loves you, *cara,* as would a mother. Surely you can find
forgiveness for her, just as you have for me." He added
with masculine arrogance that he knew would gain her attention, "You must admit that everything worked out just
as I planned. Becky but followed my instructions."

"Conceited man," she said, no heat in her voice. "I suppose since I am so very happy that I can afford to be generous." She turned abruptly, her eyes alight with her joy, and flung her arms about his shoulders. She hugged him tightly to her. "It is so marvelous to be able to show you how I feel, with no more pretense, no more reservations."

"And how do you feel, Cassandra?" He held her lightly in his arms, imagining that Scargill and Mr. Donnetti were in all likelihood staring at them, self-satisfied grins on their faces. He wanted her to tell him now that she loved him. She raised her face, her blue eyes shining with mischief.

"I feel, my lord, that if I stand close to you much longer, you will become an embarrassment to your men."

"And just what, madam, do you propose doing about my masculine predicament?" The humor in his voice matched her own. He had long ago learned the value of patience with her.

"I suppose," she said, "that I shall simply have to ask you down to my cabin."

"*Your* cabin?"

"I trust you will be just, my lord. Since you have finally convinced me to wed you, is it not fair that you bestow upon me at least half of your worldly possessions?" She added, her eyes all wicked, "I am sure that my half of the cabin is the part that holds the bed."

"I shall think about it, madam." He drew her arm through his. Once below-deck, he said, "If you please me enough, perhaps I shall be generous."

"Then I shall feign a mighty passion."

When they were in the cabin, he grinned at her and turned to grate the key in the lock. "No interruptions, madam."

When he turned back to her, he felt a surge of desire twist in his groin. Cassie was standing in the middle of the cabin, busily stripping off her clothes. He stood watching her, her face slightly flushed, in seeming concentration on the long row of buttons down the front of her gown. He walked to the table and poured two glasses of wine, still watching her from the corner of his eye. She wriggled out of her gown and, without pausing, pulled the lace straps of her chemise off her shoulders. At last, aware of his eyes upon her, she raised her face and looked at him squarely. The chemise rested only a moment about her hips before it fell softly atop her gown. "I want you now, husband."

He grinned at her and set down the wine glasses. "Could it be, my love, that we are here for more than to solve my own predicament?"

"Yes, if you would know the truth."

His eyes danced. "May I always have a ready remedy, my lady."

"And I for you, my lord."

When the earl was naked, he grasped her hand, and they eased each other onto the bed. They caressed each other leisurely, each savoring the other's touch, the feel of each other's flesh. Cassie wanted desperately to give, give in the same measure as he had given to her. She wriggled out of his arms to run her lips over his chest and downward over the taut muscles of his belly. She laid her face against his thigh and lightly touched him, caressing his swelled member, and breathed in the male scent of him.

He sensed the freedom she felt, freedom to show him her love as he had always shown her. He felt stretched like a bowstring, his sex aching to be taken into her mouth. He lightly stroked her hair. And waited. He felt her pressing her breasts against him, and the pulsing of her heartbeat.

When her lips softly touched him, and finally covered him, he thought his body would betray him. He tried to pull away from her, but she would not release him. She thought she would die of pleasure when he moaned.

When he could bear it no more, he cupped her face in his hands, and pulled her toward him. She gazed up at him, her eyes asking him what he wished.

He groaned and pulled her astride him. And then he was driving inside her, his hands caressing her until she was beyond herself, lost in the sensation of him. She felt him exploding within her as he groaned into her mouth. She wanted that moment to be timeless.

"I love you," she said, stroking the black hair from his forehead.

"And I you," he said. He thought about his long voyage, halfway across the bloody world to find her, the long empty nights on the endless ocean, with nothing but his rage and his nagging fear. "I alternately beat you, ravished you, and pleaded with you. Then I would imagine you dead and that angered me even more, for you would have escaped my wrath and all the venom I was storing up."

She was silent for some moments, until her mind gave meaning to what he had said. "At least you did not hate yourself. You see, I could not imagine that you would come after me. I thought I had lost you."

His arms tightened almost painfully about her. "Do you know that I planned our meeting at Kennedy House, that I had even rehearsed my speeches to you, for I believed that I had lost you, that you had willingly wed Edward Lyndhurst."

She nuzzled her chin into the hollow of his throat. She thought of the small babe in her womb, but she would not tell him tonight. This was their wedding night, a night for them alone. Tomorrow, perhaps, she would tell him. She raised her face, and kissed him lightly on the mouth. "And do you know what I felt when I first saw you?"

"The devil had come to claim you again."

"Nay, nothing so dramatic. If you would know the truth, I thought you dazzling, devastatingly handsome. But your anger made you unfamiliar, somehow alien to me. I think I would have gladly accepted oblivion at that moment."

"Your pride is as great as mine, *cara,* and you gave me measure for measure." He grinned at her suddenly, and his hands loosed from about her back and dropped downward to her hips. "You have complained not one whit about your shoulder. Perhaps you should have your promised thrashing today."

"The pain is great, my lord, it is simply that I am a stoic. You promised me two days. I shall hold you to it."

He eyed her silently for a moment, and grinned. "I do not believe it."

"Believe what, my lord?"

"That you are still awake, my love. Have I given you so little pleasure that our lovemaking no longer serves as a sleeping drought?"

"I would never be so inconsiderate to my husband," she said, "only to my lover."

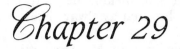

Chapter 29

She talked with boundless energy, of everything. There were no more private, secret places in her mind from which she kept him. Except for the child.

Her only bout of morning sickness happened when she was alone. She was creeping quietly along the companionway after washing out the basin herself when Scargill appeared.

He looked at her pale face, and the basin, and shook his head. "Ye must tell him, lass."

He held out his hand, and she silently handed him the basin.

"Ye're being foolish, ye know, 'twould give him great joy."

She sighed. "I know. At least I think I do. You and Joseph, both of you always knew what was in my mind." She felt her mouth tremble; she gulped and straightened her shoulders. She still felt weak from being ill, and it was making her behave foolishly.

"I can't imagine, lassie, how ye could ever believe otherwise. Joseph would have told ye the same thing. Go lie down now until ye recover yer energy. Ye've so much. The men would likely blame the captain if they saw ye so woebegone and limp.

"His lordship will be here at any moment, lass. He is never long apart from ye." He nodded encouragement and left her, carrying the basin under his arm.

Cassie waited for the earl, watching the white-topped waves and the sails billowed by the stiff March breeze. She tired of waiting for him, and shaded her eyes against the

bright morning sun, making her way nimbly toward Mr.
Donnetti, who hovered as always like a lean hungry hawk
over the wheel.

"Where is his lordship, Mr. Donnetti?"

Her tone was diffident, for she did not know Francesco
as well as Scargill.

Mr. Donnetti smiled down at her in what looked to be
an assessing way, but it was merely the habitual set of his
mouth, and the measured droop of his eyelids.

"The captain is settling a minor dispute."

"What dispute? He told me nothing of it. What has happened, Mr. Donnetti?"

"Nothing to cause any particular concern, madonna." His
voice was almost indifferent. These were halcyon days for
his master and mistress, and he wished now that he had
kept his mouth shut.

But Cassie was not to be put off. "I repeat, Mr. Donnetti,
what is the dispute?"

He shrugged and hunched more closely over the giant
wheel. "One of the men, madonna, a new man, in fact,
hired on just before we left Genoa. Capable enough, I suppose, and until last night, quiet to the point of being surly
toward the other men. Unfortunately, he got his hands on
a bottle of gin. Turned nasty he did and drew a knife on
Arturo of all people. Claimed Arturo was feeding the crew
swill fit only for pigs." Mr. Donnetti shrugged again, philosophically. "I disarmed him, of course, but the captain had
to be told."

"What is the captain doing?"

"Twelve lashes. I'd throw the swine overboard myself."

Cassie turned inadvertently toward the mainmast.

"Below-deck, madonna," Francesco said, following her
eyes. "The captain would not want you to witness the
flogging."

She gulped, remembering the sting of the earl's belt upon
her own back.

"What is the man's name, Mr. Donnetti?"

"Luigi. I would not have hired him on save for the fact
that the fellow came highly recommended from another

trading captain. He does his work well enough, I suppose, and leaves the other men be, as a rule."

When Cassie asked the earl about the incident at luncheon, he, like Mr. Donnetti, merely shrugged. "It was all quite unnecessary. The fellow should not drink spirits. He will recover soon enough, I would imagine."

"You flogged him yourself?"

"Yes." He shook his head, swirling his wine thoughtfully about in its glass. "Odd fellow. Whimpered like a coward but refused to take off his shirt. Left him with a bloody rag on his back."

"However did Luigi get the drink?"

"From Arturo, if you will believe that. The fellow was mucking about in the galley and discovered Arturo's stash."

Cassie grinned. "I wonder now if Arturo put some of that vile stuff in my Yorkshire pudding."

"If it would make you eat more, I shouldn't dislike it." His eyes traveled assessingly from her face to her breasts, thrust upward over the lace of her bodice. "Perhaps you are adding some pounds, my love."

Cassie lowered her eyes to her glass of wine. It was true that her gowns had grown a trifle snug.

The earl tossed down the remainder of his wine and pushed back his chair. He sat back, and made himself at ease, crossing his arms over his chest and stretching his long legs with negligent grace. "It occurs to me, *cara,* that I did not keep my promise."

"Promise, my lord?" She raised her eyes and saw a wide mocking grin on his face.

"I will examine your shoulder most thoroughly, though, before I proceed."

"I shall toss my wine in your smug face if you do not cease speaking nonsense." She raised her glass, as if readying to hurl it.

"Like that first night, Cassandra?" he asked, his voice thick with memory.

"Aye," she said slowly, recalling now, vividly, the furious, terrified girl who had naught but foolish bravado.

"I prefer to remember our second night together."

"I am certain you would, my lord. Will you now tell me how your precious Contessa Giusti—and *she* doubtless needed little encouragement—reveled in your marvelous masculine talents?"

"I do not think you would enjoy the telling."

He walked to where she sat, and with a firm, careful motion, pulled down the gown from her shoulder and gently lifted the small bandage covering it. The wound was healing nicely. "Do you have any pain?"

"No, as you said, it was but a scratch."

He let his hand travel slowly to her breasts. "Then it is time you paid the piper, madam. My promise. Do you not remember?"

She did remember and her eyes widened. "You would not, would you?"

She saw the caressing laughter in his dark eyes, and smiled impishly. "If ruthlessness is a part of your character, my lord, I suppose it would be unfair of me to break your spirit completely."

Because she wanted to, he let her undress him. By the time he was naked, Cassie was red in the face from exertion. Because she was still on her knees in front of him, her inquisitive eyes had not far to travel to take in all of his body, and her face remained flushed for a different reason. "If I could look like you, my lord, I daresay I would not mind at all being a man."

He passed a caressing finger over her cheek. "I thank the lord that he saw fit to leave you just as you are."

"You are tempting, my lord."

He suddenly pulled her to her feet. "Now off with those damned clothes, *cara.* I'll not be driven to distraction, only to have to call a halt to bring you to your natural state."

After he stripped her, he lifted her into his arms and carried her swiftly to the bed.

Before she knew what he was about, he sat down and flipped her face down over his thighs. He pressed his hand against the small of her back when she tried to rear up.

"I am a man of my word, *cara,*" he said.

"I do not want you to beat me, I want you to make love to me."

Her voice was a wail of protest, and he chuckled. She ceased her struggles when his palm stroked over her buttocks. When he turned her over to kiss her, she whispered, "I think love and lust go together quite nicely." And when at last they lay replete, she said, "I thought perhaps that you were asleep."

"In the middle of the afternoon? I beg you, madam, to grant me some stamina."

He slipped away from her and she drew herself up on her side. "There is something I would tell you."

He quirked a black brow, and raised his hand to smooth her hair from her face.

"I would never have married Edward, regardless."

"I know," he said only. He sat up and pressed her upon her back, propping his head on his hand.

"You do not understand." Somehow she could not make her eyes meet his. His fingers gently cupped her breast, his eyes still thoughtful upon her face.

He was not making it easy for her, she thought. The words still seemed stuck at odd angles in her throat. She heard a soft whimper, and realized with a confounded start that it had come from her own mouth.

His fingers stopped their light caressing.

"I am so sorry," she whispered, her voice liquid with tears.

"I cannot imagine why."

"I am being a fool."

He merely smiled, and kissed her lightly, and waited.

"Oh damn you. I am pregnant."

He remained silent. His hand moved from her breast to her belly, and remained there.

"I know, Cassandra."

Her mouth dropped open, and she stared at him, utterly undone. "I do not understand. How—?"

"When I brought you here, after the duel, you became ill from the wine I gave you."

"But everyone is occasionally ill."

He looked faintly amused. "Yes, that is true. But you forget that I know your body very well. Your breasts, *cara*. Your pregnancy has made them swelled, heavy."

She felt very much the fool. "Then why, my lord, did you not say something?"

"Because, my little simpleton, it was for you to tell me. Now that you know babes do not come from cabbage patches, I thought it only fitting that you be the bearer of the news this time."

She gazed up at him in silence, and when she finally spoke, her voice was uncertain. "And did you not doubt me? Believe me conniving, dishonest? Believe that I wanted to return to you only because of the child?"

"Only until last night."

"And why last night? It makes no sense. Last night was no different from any of our preceding nights together."

He looked taken aback. "I do believe you are right. Last night was no different. Perhaps," he continued, his hand caressing her belly, "it was not last night, but the night before."

"You are making sport of me, my lord. This is a very serious matter."

"Indeed you are quite right, Cassandra. If my calculations are correct, our babe will be born in mid-October, and I will have a fat wife after the Season and during the autumn round of visits that many of my friends make to Clare Castle." He drew a resigned breath. "I suppose I shall simply have to invite Eliott, and the wife he will doubtless have by that time, since you will be far too bulky to travel to Hemphill Hall."

"I had planned to return to England, you know—alone."

"Then I must be grateful for the speed of my yacht. Another two months searching you out would have rendered me more a black-souled fiend than I was in New York."

"No more secrets." She heaved a contented breath and snuggled against his side. She sprawled a thigh over his belly and relaxed her arm over his chest. "No," he said. "No more, ever."

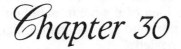

Chapter 30

The full-bellied sails slapped loudly against the rigging when the wind suddenly shifted.

"Ease off, madonna."

Cassie nodded and pulled the heavy wheel toward starboard, a surge of joy sweeping through her as the yacht yawed in response.

"Our daughter will love the sea," she said, licking the salt spray from her lips.

"Or your son."

She looked over her shoulder to see a rare smile upon Mr. Donnetti's lean, weathered face.

"All of them, sons and daughters," she said firmly, her eyes on the endless horizon. "What will you do when we reach England?"

"*The Cassandra* never molders at her moorings. During the summer months, we will sail to the West Indies, then return to Genoa until the spring. The captain is much more the Genoese man of business and banker than your English aristocrat. When he is in England, he hires couriers whose only task is to carry his instructions to Genoa, Paris, and Amsterdam to his trade and banking houses. He is a man of considerable vision and energy."

Cassie blinked at such a long speech from the normally laconic Mr. Donnetti and wondered if he was worried that the earl's wife would try to discourage such unaristocratic behavior. She gazed up at his stolid countenance and said softly, "I am young, Mr. Donnetti, but not a fool." At least not usually, she amended to herself. "I learned something of his lordship's business dealings in Genoa. I hope that I may prove not altogether worthless to his lordship." She said no more, knowing that Mr. Donnetti was no doubt appalled at the idea of a woman dabbling in men's affairs.

She glanced port and saw the man, Luigi, looping a rope. "His back has healed?"

"Aye, but he's as surly as ever. Good riddance to that one, once we reach England."

Cassie was to think of his words a day later when she left the cabin to join the earl on the quarterdeck. Luigi seemed to appear out of the shadows, his dark eyes fastened on her.

"*Sí?*" she said, reverting easily to Italian.

He merely gazed at her insolently, and said nothing.

"What do you want? *Che cosa Le abbisogna?*"

There were suddenly footsteps, and he said only, "*Voglia scusarmi, signora,*" and disappeared down the companionway.

"What is it, madonna?"

"I am glad that you came, Scargill. That man, Luigi, he makes me uncomfortable."

"That lout was down here?"

"Yes. Doubtless he was lost."

Scargill snorted. "The captain will hear about this."

Cassie was feeling particularly foolish and laid her hand on his sleeve. "Please do not trouble his lordship with such nonsense. He simply took me by surprise, that is all." As Scargill still appeared uncertain, she turned the topic to Scotland, knowing that he would be spending some months with relatives near Glasgow once they were settled at Clare Castle.

"Aye, 'tis near Loch Lomond my brother lives. A lovely area, lass, wild and steeped in lore." His brogue deepened as he grew more expansive. "Ye'd love the land, lass, save that now poverty makes bellies growl, and wrings hope from the heart. I'll not be heartily welcomed, ye know, since my loyalties are to a Sassenach—an Englishman—lass. I tell them of his Ligurian blood. It makes him more acceptable."

"Damnation. But one week from England and the sea must vent her spleen."

Cassie looked at the bloated black clouds gathering to the east and shivered. "Have we until evening, my lord?"

"Perhaps, with any luck. It will not be pleasant, Cassandra. Another storm in the Atlantic is a mischief I would just as soon do without."

But as the wind grew stronger, whipping tendrils of hair across her face, Cassie felt excitement bubble within her. She shouted over the wind and the flapping sails. "I will don my breeches and hold the helm steady with you."

"The devil you will." He grabbed her arms and wheeled her about to face him. "You will go below-deck to the cabin and stay there."

"No," she shouted back at him. "I want to stay with you."

He released her abruptly and strode to the wheel. She frowned at his back, wondering what he was saying to Mr. Donnetti. A white tear of lightning rent the sky and she jumped, then smiled. She would not be treated like some simpering little miss and locked away, unable to share the thrill of the storm.

She felt oddly deflated when he returned to her, a wide smile on his face. "Come with me, love."

She eyed him suspiciously. "To get my breeches?"

"If you like."

"Very well," she said finally, "but do let's hurry. The sky is nearly dark. The storm will break within the hour."

She raced ahead of him, pulling her skirt above her ankles. When she reached the cabin she walked swiftly to the armoire and jerked it open. "Where are they? Did you bring them or must you fetch another pair for me?"

He stood with his back against the closed cabin door. "There are no breeches."

"Then you will fetch a pair for me."

"No, *cara.* You will stay right here until the storm has blown itself out."

"You tricked me!"

"Yes, that is true, but you gave me no choice. You will stay in the cabin and there's an end to it."

"I told you, my lord," she said, holding her temper, "that

I will do precisely what I like. I will not allow you to treat me like a child."

"Then, madam, you will stop acting like one." The yacht suddenly lurched to starboard, and Cassie grabbed the edge of the dresser to keep her balance. He was at her side in an instant, steadying her. "And what if you were on deck and that happened? I will not allow you to take such risks."

The yacht lurched heavily again. He clutched his hands tightly about her arms. "I have not the luxury of time to argue with you, Cassandra. You will obey me in this, else I'll tie you down. Dammit, think about my child."

Furious words died in her throat. The babe. In her excitement, she had forgotten its existence in her womb. Her shoulders hunched forward. "Very well," she said, not looking up at him.

"You promise?"

"Yes, I promise."

His fingers lightly caressed her cheek. "There will be another storm." He released her and strode to the door.

"You will be careful?"

He gave her a crooked grin. "I know that you do not consider me as good a sailor as yourself, but I shall contrive, rest assured."

Cassie stared at the closed door for a minute, then let out a sigh of resignation. He would have to be in the right. She hugged her arms about her thickening stomach and walked to the table.

"Since there will be no dinner tonight," she said to herself, "I might as well enjoy the wine." She poured a glass, gulped half of it down, and choked on a hiccup. The glass slipped from her fingers and shattered to the floor, splashing red wine down the front of her gown.

"Clumsy oaf." She continued her bickering with herself as she tugged impatiently at the buttons on her gown. By the time she was wrapped in her dressing gown, the storm was upon them.

She could feel the billowing, angry waves slapping against the yacht, hear them flooding over the deck over the sound of the lashing rain. She made her way to the square stern windows, clutching at the back of a chair at the edge of the earl's mahogany desk to steady herself. She could see nothing through the thick gray veil of rain. She shivered and drew her dressing gown more closely. Distantly, over the tumult, she could hear men shouting, their voices muted by the raging wind.

"If it were not for you, my small babe," she said softly, patting her belly, "I would be in the midst of it, feeling the rain slap my face, leaning against the howling wind."

She pictured the earl battling at the helm to hold the yacht steady, his black hair plastered against his forehead, and she ticked off the orders he would be giving in her mind.

"It is simply not fair." She poured herself another glass of wine, only to see the rich red liquid slosh over the sides as the yacht heeled sharply to port. With a muttered oath, she carefully poured the wine back into the decanter.

The cabin was bathed in eerie gray light, and she lit a lone candle in the brass holder that was firmly fastened atop the earl's desk. She waited impatiently for the growing spiral of flame to light up the dark corners of the cabin.

She made her way slowly to the bed, careful to step over the fragments of broken glass from her first glass of wine. She considered cleaning it up, but she was afraid she would cut herself on the shards of glass with the yacht heaving as wildly as it was.

Cassie stretched out on the bed, pulling the thick blue velvet spread over her, and stared up at the ceiling, trying to will herself to sleep.

She was drowsing lightly, her head lolling on the pillow, when she heard a sound near her bed. She sat up and swung her legs over the side to look about. The cabin was bathed in the soft dim light of the candle she had lit, now nearly gutted. She fastened her eyes on the door and watched as the knob slowly turned. Her body tensed, for the earl would enter without a pause, swinging the door widely open. Perhaps, she thought, shaking her head at herself, it was Scargill with her dinner, moving quietly for fear of disturbing her.

But it was not Scargill.

The door opened only wide enough to allow a slender man to slither through. It was Luigi. He looked at her, and their eyes met for a breathless moment.

Cassie stumbled to her feet and yelled at him, "How dare you come in here! What do you want?" The man frowned, and she switched quickly to Italian. *"Che cosa Le abbisogna?"*

She looked at him closely. He was not above medium height, his complexion a deep olive, and his eyes opaquely black in the dim light. His sailor's clothes were sodden, and his long black hair hung in wet strands about his bristled face.

"Che cosa Le abbisogna?" She closed her fisted hand over the front of her dressing gown.

"Ah, *signora,* do you not know what I want? Do you not recognize me?" His coal-black eyes swept over her body.

"No." Her mind refused to work. "Get out, or it is more than a flogging you will get."

He closed the door gently behind him and leaned against it, his thin mouth relaxing into a wide smile. His piercing eyes still stripped her naked. "It is time for retribution, *signora.* Your esteemed husband, you see, brutally slaughtered two of my comrades, and is out for more blood. Ah, now you know me, do you not?"

Cassie mouthed her words, her voice barely above a whisper. "The fourth man—the last of the *bravi.* The one whose name we did not know."

He swept her a contemptuous bow.

She dully recited their names. "Giulio, Giacomo, Andrea—and Luigi."

He slapped his thigh and laughed, a wet strand of hair swinging across his cheek.

"Such an impression we made upon your great ladyship. So you remembered having men between your legs, *signora.*" His voice turned from mocking insolence to grim fury. *"Sì,* two of my friends dead now. Dead because of you and your bastard of a husband."

The yacht lurched into a deep trough of a wave, and Cassie was thrown backward. She grabbed at the bedpost to keep her balance. She was panting, drawing hoarse breaths. The storm was raging mercilessly overhead. No one would hear her scream. No one would help her.

"There were five of you, not four. But you, I fancy, are too cowardly to reveal his name." She thought dispassionately that he would kill her now, and yet she was taunting him. She saw that his fingers lay against the silver handle of a stiletto in his belt.

Luigi shrugged elaborately. "I have had many weeks to plan your deaths, *signora,* yours and your precious husband's. The storm has served me well. First you, and then that arrogant bastard."

"If you will kill me, then why not tell me the name of the man who hired you?" How calm she sounded, as if she was asking for a morning cup of coffee. But her mind was racing, sharpened by a knife of fear that lay cold and hard against her heart.

"You, my fine English lady, do not know what it means to be a *bravi.* Not even in death will you know who has paid to send your soul to the devil."

"But why, Luigi? Why am I to be killed?"

"It is none of your affair, *signora.* Enough talk." His voice was calm again, almost detached.

"Then you really do not know, do you, Luigi? Your employer did not see fit to tell you—a miserable peasant, a paid murdering animal."

He growled, deep in his throat, and Cassie drew back from him, pressing her side against the bedpost.

"Damn you, you bitch! Shut up! My comrades said nothing—nothing, do you hear? They protected me and him. I shan't complain, for he will make me rich, while you and your husband, *signora,* float in the sea until the fish tear the flesh from your bones."

Luigi straightened from his slouched position against the cabin door. His black eyes swept again over her. "I will not enjoy sticking my stiletto between your ribs, for you are but a woman. It is the blood from your husband's throat that will make this miserable voyage worth my while."

Anthony. He would be easy prey, all his attention fastened on the storm, on *The Cassandra.* He would not even know why he would die. A great fury welled up inside her, and she was not aware for a moment that he was walking slowly toward her, his eyes dark with lust.

"I really did not enjoy your body that first time, my lady. Andrea had spoiled you. There was so much blood, so much sticky seed smeared on your thighs. But it will be different now. You will know a man before you die."

He was unfastening the buttons on his breeches, not even bothering to pull them down.

He had nearly reached her while she screamed, and he laughed savagely, spurting flecks of saliva into her face.

"You are already hot for me. Give me pleasure, *signora,* and I will make your death easy."

I am only a woman, she thought frantically, and he fears naught from me. The thought seared deep into her. Her only hope was her woman's weakness, her woman's helplessness. Her eyes fastened upon the fragments of glass on the floor, near the table.

His hands were reaching for her, and she could smell his lust, could see his bulging sex, freed from his breeches. She fell toward him, and when his arms closed about her, she drew up her knee and kicked his naked groin with all her strength.

He bellowed with rage and pain, and grasped his belly.

"You damned bitch! You miserable little whore! God, how you will die!" He lunged at her, though his body was bent in his pain.

Cassie slammed her fist in his face and tried to struggle past him, but he hurtled her to the floor, throwing her upon her back. Sharp white lights exploded in her head. She bucked her body wildly against him, until she saw his fist poised to strike her. With a desperate strength, she lurched sideways, throwing her arm above her head. His blow caught her cheek, but it made no impression in her fear. And now he was the one yelling, cursing her, pummeling her, ripping at her dressing gown.

She felt a tremendous sense of elation. Her fingers closed over a jagged triangle of glass, and with cold dispassion, she watched her arm swing forward, the raw glass a spear held tightly against her palm. As he reared up, his hands jerking at her thighs, she saw nothing but his distorted face, felt nothing save that fierce triumph. The jagged glass sliced easily down his cheek, from his eye to his jaw.

He rocked backward, screaming with pain, his hands covering his face. She jerked the stiletto from his belt, pushed away from him and scrambled to her feet. She was at the cabin door, twisting at the knob, before he could stagger to his feet. The yacht careened wildly and both of them teetered, grasping at anything to keep their balance.

Cassie rushed down the dim companionway, her body reeling with the heeling yacht. She saw the stairs that led to the deck and felt a sob of defeat rise in her mouth. The hatch was securely battened down. It would take precious time to wield the iron fastenings. She heard him cursing behind her, heard his booted feet drawing nearer, and she stumbled up the wooden steps, moaning aloud when they caught in the hem of her dressing gown. She thrust the stiletto between her clenched teeth and jerked frantically at the heavy handles. She could hear his agonized breathing before the handles gave way.

She shoved upward with all her remaining strength. The heavy wooden panels flew outward and she was blinded by a torrential blanket of rain. She saw bloated mountains of water crashing over the deck, with force enough to wash her overboard. She jerked herself to her feet and threw herself forward on her stomach on the swirling deck. And then she couldn't move. His hand clutched her dressing gown, pulling her backward. She kicked wildly at his arm, but he held fast. He was facing death now. He could not let her escape.

She tried to wrench her arms free of the sleeves, but the force of the wind and the water pounded at her. She felt his fingers digging into the back of her legs as he pulled himself through the hatch, using her body as an anchor.

She felt herself strangling on her own fear. The sharp edge of the stiletto cut the corner of her mouth. She had forgotten the stiletto.

She grasped it in her hand, savoring the feel of it, and rolled over onto her back. He was above her, his disfigured face inhuman, like a creature from the blackest pit of hell.

The wind whipped the rain across the gash, and blood welled out, splattering her face and breasts.

There was only hatred in his eyes. He made a gurgling sound, and his hands, curved like claws, flew to her throat. As he fell forward, she locked her fists between her breasts, the point of the stiletto upward. She felt it tear through the flesh of his neck.

For an endless instant, he stiffened above her, his dark eyes filled with surprise. Blood spurted from his mouth and throat, and her scream momentarily pierced the howling wind. She pushed at him, and his inert body rolled sideways over the slippery deck. A wave broke over the railing and dragged him further away from her. His foot caught on a coil of rope as he was pulled back, and he flipped like a stuffed doll onto his back.

She screamed again and closed her eyes against the sight of him, bloodied and limp, the silver handle of the dagger gleaming brightly as it rose upward from his pinioned neck.

Her cries were swallowed by the raging wind and rain until Dilson, agilely making his way aft, slewed his head about at the thin wailing sound. He scrambled down, clutching at the open hatch doors to keep his balance, and peered into Cassie's rain-blurred face.

He sucked in his breath in consternation. Her dressing gown was ripped open and her body shone white, save for rivulets of red that streaked over her face and breasts. He tore off his canvas cloak and covered her.

"Dilson, fetch the captain."

Her voice was a low whisper, dulled with shock. He saw Luigi. "Oh my gawd." He flew toward the quarterdeck, yelling even before the captain could possibly hear him.

The earl whirled about at his shouts. He passed the helm to Mr. Donnetti and stared at the white-faced Dilson.

"My God, man," he shouted over the wind, "what the devil has happened?"

"The madonna," Dilson croaked. "Quickly, captain, quickly!"

He froze for an instant, and then lunged after Dilson.

Dilson yelled back at him. "She killed him, captain. Stuck a dagger in his throat."

"What the hell are you saying, man?"

Dilson pointed to Cassie, who lay stretched naked upon her back, the canvas cloak blown off her body, her legs dangling into the open hatch. There were rivulets of blood streaking over her white skin. He fell to his knees and gathered her into his arms.

"Cassandra!"

Cassie pulled her mind from Luigi's ghastly face and forced her eyes open.

"He is dead—really dead?"

He felt bewildered until Dilson shook his sleeve and pointed.

The sight of Luigi, the stiletto embedded into his throat like a stake, froze that moment into his mind. His face was ripped open, the jagged flesh laid back.

"He's dead, Cassandra."

He gathered her awkwardly into his arms, pulling her sodden dressing gown about her, and hauled her down the wooden steps.

"Dilson," he shouted over his shoulder. "Don't let him wash overboard. Bring him below-deck."

The cabin was in total darkness. He felt his way to the bed, laid her down, and turned to light the candles. He saw the broken fragments of glass, one of them covered with blood, and splotches of blood on the carpet.

Her face was turned away from him and she was shivering violently. He swallowed his questions, stripped off the wet dressing gown, and toweled her body dry. The streaks of blood came off on the towel, and his eyes traveled every inch of her. There was a cut in the palm of her hand. He could see nothing else.

"He was the fourth man—the other *bravi.*"

He did not allow himself to answer until he had tucked her beneath a mound of covers. Gently, he gathered her thick wet hair and spread it away from her face onto the pillow.

He realized that he himself was sodden and was drenching the bed, but he was loathe to pull away from her. He cupped her face in his hands. "Are you hurt, *cara?*"

"No," she said, her voice calm, too calm for his ears.

"He thought that since I am a woman that I could do nothing. He was going to kill us, my lord, both of us."

"He told you that he was one of the assassins?"

Cassie couldn't seem to stop her violent shivering. She was cold, so cold. She nodded in his hands.

"Cassandra, the babe. Is the babe all right?"

The babe. She tried to fasten her mind on her body, on her belly. She felt nothing, only the sickening rippling of the stiletto as it sank into Luigi's throat.

"I couldn't let him kill you." She clutched his shoulders with frantic hands. "He would have killed you."

The earl whipped his head up as the yacht shuddered from the force of the storm, the timber creaking in pained protest. He drew her into the circle of his arms and rocked her gently. "It is all right, Cassie. It is over now." He kept talking to her, trying to calm her, to soothe the terror from her mind.

"I am all right, my lord," she said finally, knowing that he must leave her. If he did not see to the yacht, they might all die. "Please, you must go now. I have nothing more to fear."

He eased her down and tucked the covers tightly about her. "Sleep now, Cassandra. I will be back when I can."

She nodded and forced her eyes shut until he closed the door.

She felt curiously light and supple, all her energy focused on hoisting the mainsail of her sloop. But somehow she didn't seem to have the strength, and the flapping canvas slapped at her face. There was a man's voice, deep and censuring, complaining that she hadn't the wit to figure out the simplest of problems. How could she be trusted with her own boat if she was such a stupid child. I am not stupid, she yelled, unable to see the man's face. It is too heavy! I am not stupid!

Cassie reared up. "I am not stupid, Father."

She blinked at the bright light and the dream slowly ebbed from her mind. She gazed about the cabin, bathed in brilliant sunlight. The yacht was rocking gently in the waves. The storm had blown itself out. She turned slowly and saw the earl stretched upon his back beside her. He was snoring. It was a marvelous sound.

She slipped quietly out of bed, rose and stretched. She looked down at her slightly rounded belly, and lightly patted herself. "Both of us have survived this time," she whispered.

She was ravenously hungry, but she bided her time, for she did not wish to disturb the earl's sleep. She bathed, dressed, and brushed out her tangled hair, pulling it back from her face with a velvet ribbon. She was on the point of going to fetch her breakfast when Scargill quietly opened the door and peered warily into the cabin.

He said nothing, merely looked at her with worried eyes.

"I am quite all right, Scargill," she said, "and so, I fancy, is his lordship." She turned at the absence of any sound from the bed and saw him stretching gracefully, the covers barely covering his belly.

"Ye're ready for your lunch, I trust," Scargill said cheerfully.

"Lunch?"

"Aye, madonna. Ye slept the clock around. And ye, my lord, ye'll join yer brave wife?"

"That I will," the earl said. He bounded out of bed and stretched prodigiously.

"And how is my brave wife?" He pulled her into his arms and nuzzled his chin against the top of her head.

Scargill was clucking good-naturedly behind him, the earl's dressing gown already in his hands.

As Cassie ate, trying not to wolf down her food, she was aware of the earl's eyes upon her, narrowed in concern.

"For heaven's sake, my lord," she said, "I have no intention of collapsing into hysterics."

His answering smile did not reach his dark eyes. "You were quite right, you know, *cara,* he was the fourth man. The serpent wrapped about the sword—it was on his left arm." The earl shook his head and softly cursed. "If only I had had his shirt stripped off before I flogged him. We would have known then, and none of this would have happened. Can you talk about it, Cassandra? Tell me what happened?"

How strange, she thought, she could think about the previous night quite calmly. She faltered only when she told him of the stiletto, clutched in her fisted hands. She shuddered, memory vivid.

"Remind me, *cara*," he said at last, "never to get into a violent argument with you."

A cleansing smile lighted her face. "You have nothing to fear, my lord, for you, I am persuaded, hold me and all my abilities in healthy respect." She paused a moment, frowning. "I goaded him, you know, taunted him, trying to make him tell me who had paid him to kill us. But he would tell me nothing. Not even a clue, my lord, save it was a man. He said the man would make him rich."

The earl stroked his unshaven jaw. "The mystery remains, then. I did not tell you, Cassandra, but before I left Genoa, I arranged to pay a sizable reward for the name and removal of Luigi's employer. That is one reason I decided we should go to England. I wanted you in no danger until I discovered him. It never occurred to me that we would carry one of the assassins with us."

"Do you think we shall ever know?"

"Given the number of enthusiastic villains who will try to fatten their purses, I am willing to wager that we shall."

Cassie took one of his large hands into hers. "At least we are safe now, my lord."

"Sometimes, my love, I am doubtful that I deserve you." At the gleam in her eyes, he added in a lazy drawl, "But then I think of you floundering and utterly impotent at arranging your own affairs and my heart is warmed."

She laughed, deep and warm, and he held her against his heart.

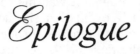

Epilogue

The earl smoothed a single curl of Cassie's hair back from her forehead. Looking at her in sleep, it was impossible to tell that she had just given birth. But their child, a beautiful boy, lay curled peacefully in a small cradle next to Becky Petersham's bed.

Exhaustion beckoned him to bed, but he was too elated to give in to sleep just yet. He touched his lips to her cheek and strode soundlessly across the thick carpet to the narrow curtained windows. He eased back the heavy burgundy velvet curtains and peered out at the south lawn and the home wood beyond. A half moon muted the vivid October colors of the trees, their leaves heavy with dampness after a brief rainstorm. He dropped the curtain, wondering idly if Dr. Milpas, a man of excellent repute with a string of successful births to his name, was at last resting in comfort after an afternoon spent sitting in sodden clothes in a mud-filled ditch, cursing his broken leg.

The earl looked back at the large Tudor bed, its stolidly English oak frame and thick burgundy hangings so unlike the delicate furnishings of his bedchamber in the Villa Parese. He grinned at the thought, for it was Cassie's. She appeared lost in the featherdown depths of the bed, a fluffy cover pulled to her chin. "Little fool," he said softly to her under his breath. He should have guessed she would not go through her labor as would other ladies. He saw Eliott in his mind's eye, his face perfectly white, clutching his wine glass and whispering, "Oh my God."

Trust Cassie to say not a word about it during the Harvest Day festivities. She had sat beneath the red and white striped canvas canopy on the wide, sloping east lawn, not wanting anyone to know, not wanting to spoil anyone's enjoyment of the yearly event that she herself had planned. She greeted each of his tenants throughout the morning, taking no part in the dancing to be sure, and presided beside him at the mid-afternoon dinner, more quiet than usual, he realized now. But he had not remarked upon the occasional tensing about her mouth, or her absence of appetite, his attention distracted by his duties as master of Clare Castle.

There had been so much gaiety, such high spirits, particularly on the part of Eliott and his bride of five months, Eliza, that no one noticed Cassandra's forced smiles. He had not guessed that anything was amiss until Becky motioned to Cassie at the close of the long meal to rise and stand beside him under the billowing canopy. He had looked at her with a questioning smile on his lips when she did not immediately rise to join him. But she averted her face.

"Cassandra." His sharp voice stilled the boisterous talk about the table. He saw a lone tear streak down her cheek.

"I am sorry, my lord," she said, "the babe will not wait longer."

"Oh my God," Eliott said.

Cassie wailed in frustration, "But our people are still here."

"How long have you been in labor?"

"You needn't shout at me, my lord," she said.

"Well?"

"Since early this morning."

"You stubborn little wretch."

"Really, Anthony," Eliott said.

But Cassie laughed.

Becky Petersham was on her feet, tottering a bit perhaps, her voice high and commanding. "Eliott, send a footman for Dr. Milpas. Eliza, help me assist Cassie to bed."

The earl held up a restraining hand. "No, Becky, since my foolish wife has not had the good sense to say anything, she will have to bear with my attentions."

He held out his hand to her, but she could not move at that moment, for a contraction ripped at her belly.

"I cannot," she panted.

"At least you are not so fat that I can no longer carry you," he said, and lifted her into his arms.

She gasped, and clutched her arms tightly about his neck, for the contraction still gripped her.

"What a Harvest Day you have chosen to give me, *cara*. Steady, love, I'll have you more comfortable in a moment."

"I don't think you can," she said.

She was gritting her teeth together to keep herself from crying out when the earl was informed of the carriage accident an hour later.

Becky Petersham wrung her hands in soundless agitation. "What are we going to do?"

"Fetch me Scargill, Becky."

"What?" she fairly shrieked at him. "Even you should not be in here and now you want another man. Oh, my poor Cassie."

"She is young and quite healthy, Becky," he said calmly. "I have a fancy to deliver our babe, and Cassandra, I think, would prefer it in any case."

His confident words sounded hollow in his mind not long thereafter. Cassie's hands clawed at his with each contraction, as she struggled to keep hold of herself.

"Why will not the babe come?" he bellowed at last.

Cassie looked up at his face, and there was suddenly fear in her eyes. "Am I to be like my mother?"

"Don't be a fool, Cassandra," he said. "You are nothing like your mother."

Pain glazed her eyes, and she turned her face away, her fingers dropping listlessly from his hand.

"Cassandra! Dammit, you will not give up! Look at me!"

"I am sorry, my lord."

"I do not want you to be sorry, I want you to show some spirit! Dammit, Cassandra, give me my child!"

He ripped the light cover off her. "Now, push down! All your strength, Cassandra, else I shall beat you. Again!"

He splayed his hands over her swollen belly and pressed down.

She screamed, a high wailing cry that rent the silence of the bedchamber.

"The babe is coming!" Scargill shouted.

The earl's hands gently closed about the small infant's head, covered with a mass of curling black hair. "Again, Cassandra. Push!"

He caught his son with a shout of triumph, and laughed aloud when the small mouth opened on a fierce angry wail.

The earl walked over to the black-mouthed fireplace. He kicked the red embers with the toe of his boot and watched the scarlet flames dance upward. He smiled again at the indignant look on his small son's puckered face. The tension was beginning to pass from his body. He breathed deeply and let himself relax, admitting fatigue into his mind.

He stretched and bent down to retrieve his waistcoat, tossed heedlessly onto the carpet. He felt the small square of paper folded in the pocket, and slowly drew it out.

There must be a beginning and an ending to everything, he thought, and unfolded the sheet. The letter was dated in late August and written in flowing script, undoubtedly by a learned servant.

It should not surprise you, Antonio, that it is I who am to part you from your English guineas. It required only my word to the proper people that I wished to have the brave Andrea at my side. The stupid lout scarce tried my ingenuity, my friend, either before or after he had the pleasure of meeting me. Indeed, he was on his knees begging me for his miserable life, a little joke that my men enjoyed. He has taken his rest in hell.

As to his employer, Antonio, he tried very hard to convince me it was your half-brother, Bellini. A pity that greed should break the bonds of blood. I have always been a simple man, my friend, and your instructions were clear. It was quite a shock to Signore Bellini and his charming contessa to be trussed up like chickens and brought to my palace of delights. He died well, if it is any consolation. As for the contessa, I find her a savory morsel, though she offers me little sport. My fair Zabetta wishes you luck with your mad countess.

Addio, my lord earl,
Khar El-Din

The earl read the letter once again, and looked over at Cassie. He wadded the paper slowly into a tight ball and tossed it atop the glowing embers. He watched as the smoke engulfed it and it burst into brief orange flame, then collapsed onto itself as blackened ashes.

He turned at a soft sigh that came from the bed, and quickly strode over and sat beside Cassie. He smiled into her unclouded blue eyes and traced his finger down the straight line of her nose.

"I had thought, love, that you would sleep until the new year."

"Our son, my lord, he is perfect?"

"Since, at the moment, he strongly resembles his father, I daresay he is as close to perfection as possible."

Her answering smile was weak. "I feel so very empty."

He saw her hand slowly move under the covers and lightly touch her flat belly.

"I trust so unless you plan to give our son a twin brother or sister."

"Thank you, Anthony."

He cocked a black eyebrow at her. "You, my lady, did all the work. I merely yelled at you a couple of times."

"I remember another man's voice. That wretched doctor was not here, was he?"

"Nay, it was Scargill. That wretched doctor suffered a broken leg from a carriage accident."

She looked quite pleased.

"I'll think you a witch, Cassandra, if you don't wipe that self-satisfied look from your face."

She drew a deep breath and he saw that she was remaining awake with difficulty.

"I used to think you the devil himself, my lord. If I am a witch, then we are well suited, I think."

"Very well suited," he said, and kissed her with infinite tenderness.